# Chapter One

Emily lay in bed with Jake spooning against her. As the first rays of daylight slowly lit the room, she was wide awake. But he slept on, his strong arms around her and his deep breathing stroking her back in long warm whispers. She felt like leaping up and greeting the day, but couldn't bear to break the spell. Instead she lay there with a warm glow in her belly, thinking that she could quite possibly be the luckiest girl in the world.

She had a kind, gentle man who loved her and whom she loved in return, and she was so grateful to Simone for bringing about their reunion. The trip to Melbourne had changed everything. She was so glad she'd been there for Jake when he'd needed her. If only the circumstances had been different.

Death had been such a theme in her life recently – her gran's passing, John's fatal accident, and now the incident on Jake's work site – hopefully that was all behind her. She'd been through so much and survived, and she now knew she could get through anything else that came her way, especially with Jake by her side.

After all the financial stress, she no longer had to search for a job – at least for a while. Thanks to her inheritance from John and the annual lease payments from Barbara and David on the land, and the income from the sheep, she was fine for the time being – and for life if she was careful.

Emily still felt a little guilty about how it had all come about, but at least she had the blessing of John's parents. She just hoped the Wattle Creek locals would be as understanding. A townie, a woman, inheriting a decent slice of prime land and everything with it was one thing, but how would they feel when they heard she'd moved a new man in just days after John's funeral?

*Speaking of which.* She felt him stirring behind her.

'Good morning sleepyhead,' Jake said, kissing the back of her neck. She rolled over to face him, kissed him deeply in reply, and wrapped her arms around him.

'Hmm,' she groaned as he pulled her towards him.


Later they lay entwined, just like they had last night before going to sleep. Emily could feel her breathing matching Jake's, their chests rising and falling together.

'God, you smell good,' he said breathily.

'I was just thinking the same thing,' she said, smiling at him. 'How are you feeling? Did you sleep okay?'

After the flights from Melbourne, the long drive from Whyalla, and then David and Barbara staying on for dinner, they had both been exhausted. They had spent the next two days taking it easy, going on gentle strolls, and making a huge fuss of Grace, who Emily had missed terribly whilst she'd been away. The little border collie was such an important part of her life – they'd been through so much together in such a short amount of time.

'I slept okay. But I'm still pretty tired. I can't seem to shake it.'

Emily knew how debilitating grief could be.

★

'I've got to go into town to run some errands. Do you want to come along?' Emily asked.

After lingering over a big breakfast, they were standing side by side doing the dishes – her hands in pink rubber gloves beneath a thick layer of suds, his tea-towel-covered hand stuffed into a mug.

'If you don't mind, I'd rather stay here. If that's okay?'

Once upon a time she'd have been hurt. 'Of course it's okay, Jake. We've both lived alone long enough to not need another person to entertain us all the time. Although don't get me wrong, I do enjoy your company,' Emily added, starting to get a bit flustered. Isn't that what love was? Wanting to be with someone all the time?

Jake let out a sigh. 'It's not that I don't want to spend time with you. I do. But I'm just not used to having someone else around all the time.'

Emily nodded.

'You've probably only just got used to living alone. And I wouldn't mind betting you've quite enjoyed being independent,' he said, looking at her sympathetically. 'So, can we make a pact? Can we agree that it's okay to spend time apart without getting all paranoid about why? That it's not a sign there's something wrong between us?'

'I guess,' Emily said, not quite convinced. *Where is this coming from? Maybe he's had a clingy girlfriend before.*

'I don't mean to sound pushy, but I once had a girlfriend who came to stay and insisted on spending every second of every day together. It drove me nuts.'

*Bingo!*

'Sorry. The only peace I got was in the loo,' he said with a gentle smile.

'It's fine, Jake, we all need our space,' she said.

'So it's a pact?'

'As long as we also agree that if one of us has a problem – big or small – we discuss it,' Emily said. 'I don't want to end up where we were last time.'

'Okay,' Jake said.

'And while we're on ground rules...' Emily continued.

'Uh-oh, here we go,' Jake said, smiling at her.

Emily flicked a handful of suds at his chest.

'I'm being serious,' she said. 'I want you to feel at home; come and go as you please. But it would be helpful to know what meals you will and won't be here for.'

'Now you're making me sound like a boarder.' He went behind her, wrapped his arms around her waist, and nuzzled at her neck. 'I mean it when I say I love you. I'm serious about us, about this working out, even though it's so new. I only meant I want to be free to head off for a walk on my own if I want to. I might not even want to.'

'I love you too. And I mean it when I say I want you to feel at home – what's mine is yours. Honestly, you should feel free to use the car, internet, phone; whatever you need.'

They finished the last few dishes and then sat at the table to write up a shopping list. Jake gave her some money towards expenses, which she very reluctantly accepted, and she handed him the spare key to the sliding glass door.

'Right, last chance to change your mind,' Emily said, collecting her handbag and keys from the bench. 'Sure you don't want to visit the thriving metropolis?'

'I'll pass, thanks,' Jake said, getting up and going over to her. 'I *am* looking forward to getting to know the area, but I don't think I'm ready to become the talk of the town just yet. I know what small towns can be like. I might just go for a stroll. Maybe take a few shots. I'm planning on being here for a while, so there's no rush – for anything.' He gave her a peck on the lips. 'Have fun.'

'You too. Gracie, you look after Jake for me while I'm gone,' she said, bending down to ruffle the border collie's ears.

Jake was standing at the glass door when she backed out of the shed and drove off. She returned his wave and the kisses he blew her.

Before driving to town, Emily drove a short way up the road to run a quick errand. David had put the sheep on the stubble in the paddock over from the cottage ruins, where she and Jake could keep an eye on them. She'd promised to check the trough each day. Under their lease agreement, David was taking care of them in exchange for a profit share, but there was no point in him driving down just to check that a trough had water in it.

After satisfying herself that all looked well with the trough and the sheep, she did a U-turn and headed off to Wattle Creek.

Emily collected her mail and paid a couple of bills at the post office, and visited the newsagent to get *The Advertiser* for Jake. Being Thursday, Wattle Creek was swarming with people – well, as busy as a district of two thousand people could get. Tuesdays and Thursdays were the main shopping days, thanks to the delivery of fresh fruit and veg. Emily had to go around the block twice to find a park halfway between the bank and the supermarket where she could just pull in – she was no good at reverse parallel parking.

As she walked the aisles, every second person stopped her to enquire if it was true that Donald and Trevor's cousin, Tara Wickham, had turfed her out of the house she had an arrangement with them to buy. 'And is it true that you've moved back to the farm?'

'Yes,' Emily said. There was no point in being evasive. When asked how John's parents, Thora and Gerald, were doing, she replied, 'As well as can be expected,' whilst kicking herself for her forgetfulness. She'd been in touch with Gerald by phone about

John's estate, but hadn't seen them since the funeral. And they'd been so good to her the day she'd gone out and told them the truth about her and John. She vowed to keep in touch.

At least without Jake beside her she didn't have to deal with, 'Ah, so who is this? And where are you from? And how long will you be visiting with us?' Locals – particularly the elderly – could be very nosy around newcomers. And then there would be the raised eyebrows, along with, 'So you're staying at the farm with Emily, are you?'

She could see how Jake moving in mere days after John had been laid to rest could be seen as inappropriate. It was hardly surprising that tongues were wagging. It had been fine while Jake could be seen as just a friend of her cousin Liz…

But love doesn't work to a timetable.

*If only Jake had happened about a year into the future*, she thought, as she stowed the three green eco bags of groceries in the boot. Then it would all be aboveboard. She let out a deep sigh as she shut the lid. But he hadn't, Barbara would say; he was meant to be there now. The universe had all this stuff sorted out and everything happened when and how it was supposed to.

Maybe so, but it still didn't make it any easier to deal with the gossip.

Emily had sometimes fantasised about leaving Wattle Creek. But where would she go? The truth was, she couldn't see herself living anywhere else. And having already moved house twice in a matter of weeks, she was keen to stay put.

Perhaps Jake would want to spend time in Melbourne down the track and gradually she'd be able to tear herself away. Could she consider living there, if that's what he wanted?

God, who was she kidding? Other than seeing him and meeting his sister Simone, she hadn't enjoyed her trip to the big city at all. Dealing with all that traffic and so many people in such close proximity, practically running everywhere, was overwhelming. No, thank you very much. And the low cost of living was a major redeeming feature of life in the country.

Just before Emily left town she remembered to pop into the bank. She wanted to consult the spinning displays for term deposit and other investment brochures, but was also hoping to see Nathan Lucas, a friend who had recently moved to Wattle Creek from Adelaide to become the Assistant Manager.

A few weeks ago – a lifetime ago it seemed – Nathan had wanted Emily to rent him a room in the house she'd bought from the Bakers; correction, *nearly bought*. While she'd desperately needed the extra money, she'd turned him down. She'd needed more time on her own. Then she'd been evicted. Thankfully they had remained friends.

Thinking of Nathan made her realise with a bit of a shock that she didn't have many people she considered friends. She knew plenty of people to wave to in the street, say g'day to and chat about the weather. But there were very few she trusted enough to confide in – only really her dad, David and Barbara, and now Jake. But surely it hadn't always been like this. What happened?

Prior to getting married, when she'd worked in the insurance office, Emily had had lots of friends, and had always felt a part of a community. But she'd become withdrawn whilst being with John. They'd had a few dinner parties in the first few months together, but then stopped – they hadn't been much fun; she'd done all the work in the kitchen and John had just got drunk and belligerent. And their friends had never reciprocated. Or perhaps John had never passed on the invitations.

Emily paused by the wall of the bank and pretended to study her shopping list. But what she was really doing was wondering how she'd come to have so few close friends. She was easy to get along with. Wasn't she?

She'd had plenty of girlfriends in high school and during her twenties. But one by one they had moved away to the city in search of work and men. She'd just moved to the next small town over. And then she'd married John and he'd become her world.

Stepping inside the bank, she spotted Nathan in his glass-walled office, tapping away at his computer keyboard. When he looked up and saw her, he grinned and waved her over.

'Come in,' he said, pecking her on the cheek. 'Sit down, take a load off,' he added and slumped back into his chair.

'How are you settling in?' Emily asked. 'Have you found somewhere to live yet?'

'Yep. One of the girls from the other bank, Sarah Poole, has a spare room. *They* provide housing for the Assistant Manager. I'm clearly with the wrong bank.'

'Isn't it a conflict of interest, or something?'

'You mean sleeping with the enemy?' He winked. 'No idea. I'll just have to spend more time with my non-bank friends – like you. So, how're things?'

'Great. Speaking of housemates, remember I told you about my friend Jake, in Melbourne, who came for Christmas? Well, he's staying again. Hopefully for a few months.' *Hopefully forever.*

'Ooh, do I detect romance?'

'You do, indeed,' Emily said, blushing slightly.

'Well, I hope you checked his horoscope before letting him move in.'

'And I hope you've checked your compatibility with Sarah,' she said with a laugh.

'I have, actually. And you might scoff. But take it from me, you can save yourself a lot of heartache if you ask the question up front. As a Capricorn, you need a Taurus or a Virgo. But your love-life is your business. I've said my piece. Just being a friend and looking out for you.'

'Thanks Nathan. I appreciate it,' she said, wondering about Jake's birthday. He knew that hers was New Year's Eve, because he'd sent the lovely plans for the Bakers' house to Barbara and David's that night. But when was his?

'So, did you just drop in to say hi, or was there something of a banking nature I can help you with?'

'Well, I did want to say hi. But I've been thinking I should look at some investment options.'

'How are you going with settling the estate?'

'Okay, I think. It seems to be just a matter of putting information together and applying for probate – I've mainly let the lawyers deal with it. John's dad was kind enough to send them a list of assets, which saved me a lot of palaver. Hopefully in two months it'll all be rubber stamped.'

'That's good. I've heard these things can be a nightmare.'

'Well, it helped that John was recently bought out of the family company and had plenty of cash on hand for me to pay the outstanding bills.'

'Phew for that.'

'Yes. There was also an insurance policy. The payout from that should come soonish. And then there will be the proceeds from the estate to think about. I want to be sensible, do the right thing for my long-term future.'

'Right, then, let's see what we've got to offer.'

Nathan ran through some of the bank's choices – the interest rates, potential returns and costs involved, but said if she was talking about investing large amounts she should probably think about seeing one of their visiting financial planners at some point. By the time he finished, Emily's head was swimming.

'Hey, do you and Jake want to go and do some wineries or have lunch sometime? Sarah's quite new in town too, and we need to make some friends.'

'I'd love to.' *I should give Jake a proper welcome, too.* Maybe over the weekend they could all splurge on lunch with Barbara and David.

Emily hadn't visited any of the cellar doors that had popped up on the far side of the district in the past few years. Her deceased husband hadn't been one for romantic Sunday drives. Farming, football, beer, and sex were the extent of John's interests. But she was really looking forward to playing tourist with Jake.

'God, this is just like high school all over again, isn't it?' Nathan said.

'Ha ha. I'll see what suits Jake and let you know.'

And then Emily was on her way back out of town, thinking again about what a whirlwind the past few months had been.

When she'd driven away from the farmhouse that day with Grace curled up on the passenger's side floor of the car she'd thought – hoped – it would be the last time she would ever drive this particular dirt road. And now look where she was. Life certainly was full of surprises.

Lost in her thoughts, Emily was suddenly jolted by two hard clunks as first the front tyre and then the rear one hit a large pothole – one she usually managed to avoid.

She slowed. The car seemed to be okay, so she continued on. But one thing was for sure; when the insurance payment came through for John's written-off ute, she would definitely replace it. Now that she owned a farm, she really needed something all-terrain. But what sort? And should she keep the car as well, or was running two vehicles too extravagant?

She was glad she had Jake to discuss these sorts of things with. Proud as she was of her newfound independence, there certainly were benefits to having a man around.

# Chapter Two

'Hi honey, I'm home!' Emily called, smiling to herself. *What a cliché! I sound like a character from a soap opera.* She dumped the four heavy bags of groceries onto the lino floor of the kitchen, then rolled the stiffness out of her neck and shook the circulation back into her fingers.

'Jake?' She shut the sliding glass door she'd shouldered open moments before. *He mustn't be far away to have left the door unlocked*, she thought.

Emily quickly unpacked the groceries, all the while listening for movement. If Jake was inside he would almost certainly have come to help carry everything in; he was that sort of guy. And Grace would normally have bounded up to greet her. She wandered through the house, but found no trace of either.

By the time she finished she was starting to get concerned. She checked her watch; almost two p.m. She went to the bedroom to change into her farm clothes, thinking she'd look for them outside. Maybe Jake and Grace were exploring and hadn't heard her return.

Entering the room, she said hello to Granny Rose via the big jar of buttons on the tallboy. The old Bushells coffee jar had been her gran's last gift to her, and together with its precious contents, it meant more to her than anything. Emily wrapped her hands around the cold glass and put her chin on the rough, slightly rusty, faded red lid.

Again she found herself wondering if Gran had remembered the rough diamonds in there amongst the buttons. The frustrating thing was that she'd never know. But she would have treasured it anyway, even if it weren't for the diamonds.

Being a sentimental romantic, Emily loved the button jar for the symbolism it held. Trust Gran to hide her wedding gift from the Indian prince in there. Was it before or after that – because of the precious stones – that she'd decided never to take any buttons out?

Over the years Emily had seen many added – usually when Gran was cutting up worn-out clothes for rags – and had never understood why Gran would drag her off to the shop to buy new buttons whenever she needed one. One of her favourite things to do as a child – well, actually, even now – was to rotate the tightly closed jar and listen to the hiss, whoosh and rattle the different buttons and other objects made against themselves and the glass.

She couldn't believe that in all that time she'd never spotted one of the seven diamonds lurking about in there. Or perhaps she had and had dismissed them as one of the other strange things Gran had added over the years: old coins, buckles, hair clips, the odd seashell. It wasn't like diamonds in the rough were anything that would catch your attention.

But what a beautiful, sentimental gift. Emily thought about the prince's letter – the evidence that the family story had been no myth.

When Jake had first discovered the diamonds, she had immediately wanted to phone her mother up and gloat, 'See, Gran was telling the truth.' But that would have opened one big old jack-in-the-box – and there was no way Jack could be stuffed back in again. She had since decided to keep them a secret. If they found out, Enid and Aunt Peggy would no doubt argue they belonged to them as heirs, and then they'd cash them in for sure.

Emily was grateful every day for whatever had caused Gran to thrust the button jar into her arms on that last visit, rather than see it end up amongst all the things they'd had to sort through after her death. Back then she wouldn't have had the courage to defend her choice of keeping such an obviously sentimental – and apparently worthless – item. She was now much more able to stand up for herself. 'Oh Gran,' she whispered. 'I wish you were here to meet Jake. You'd love him.'

As she absently glanced out of her bedroom window, she looked past the ugly steel skeleton of the half-built hayshed to the pile of rubble behind it. Once it had been her beloved cottage – before John had taken a front-end loader to it.

Something caught her eye – Jake's red shirt. It stood out like a beacon against the pile of pale limestone around him. He was sitting amidst the ruins of the cottage, leaning against the base of what had once been the stone chimney to the original outdoor kitchen. Grace was lying at his feet.

Emily hugged the button jar again, put it back down on the tallboy, and got changed.

As she made her way over to the pile of rubble, she wondered if she would feel less sad about it if she had it removed. Would she eventually forget what had been there and who had been responsible for its demise?

'Hey there you two,' Emily called as she approached. Jake looked like he might be snoozing, and she didn't want to startle him. He and Grace were mostly in the shade, but their legs were stretched out in the sun. Grace raised her head and slapped her tail a couple of times before lying back down and becoming still again.

'Hello,' Jake said, smiling up at her. 'How was the thriving metropolis and cesspit of gossip?'

'Thriving,' Emily said, smiling back. 'You look like you've found a good spot.'

'Sure have. Care to sit?' He patted the smooth patch of earth beside him.

'Don't mind if I do,' she said, sitting down. Grace immediately got up, stepped over Jake's outstretched legs, and flopped down with her head in her mistress's lap.

'Hello girl,' Emily said, giving Grace's ears a rub as the dog stared up at her adoringly. 'I thought you'd traded me in for Jake.'

'Not a chance. She was just being polite to the new guy, weren't you, girl?' Jake said, reaching over and patting the dog's belly. As he leant back again he paused to kiss Emily. Her heart surged.

'So, what did you guys get up to while I was out?'

Jake checked his watch. 'I've actually been sitting here the whole time you've been gone,' he said, frowning.

'Really?' She looked at him closely. 'Are you okay?'

'I'm fine.'

'Are you sure? If you've been sitting here all this time without realising...'

'Really, I'm fine. Just feeling a bit washed out.'

'You'd tell me if there was something wrong, wouldn't you?' She watched as he plucked at the dried grass. 'Jake, I'm worried about you. Is it about Shane?' Emily's heart began to race a little.

Jake shook his head, but kept his gaze down.

'There's a psychologist in town, Jacqueline Havelock, if you think she might be able to help. Or there's Doctor Squire. Though, it can take a while to get in – one of the pitfalls of country life...' She shut her mouth abruptly, aware she was babbling. She was scared. What was going on with him?

Jake looked up and fixed his gaze on her. He looked worse than a bit washed out. There were beads of sweat on his forehead. As he brought his hands into his lap, she saw that they were shaking.

'It's not a big deal. I didn't want to worry you. I *don't* want to worry you.'

'Now you are worrying me.' She tried to sound light-hearted, but failed.

He grasped her hands and took a deep breath.

'Last week, before you came to Melbourne, I saw my GP.'

'Okay. That's good. And?'

Emily didn't like prying, but poor communication had been a problem for her in the past. It had almost lost her Jake and her two best friends, Barbara and David, and she was determined not to repeat her mistakes. She bit her lip in an effort to wait out his excruciating silence.

'I'm fine. Well, I *will* be fine, in time. I need to take it easy for a bit. Lots of rest. My GP thinks I have adrenal fatigue, but we'll know more when she gets my test results back.'

'Is it like chronic fatigue syndrome?'

'Quite different, as far as I can tell. With chronic fatigue, you're always exhausted and just want to sleep. With me, I'm often fuzzy and weary, but not in the way I want to actually sleep. I'm quite tired in the mornings, but I seem to often get a second wind in the afternoons and evenings.'

*I've noticed that — in Melbourne and the other night with Barbara and David.*

'A lot of the time I feel jittery. It's like a fight-or-flight response — surging adrenaline — but for no reason. And you can't stop it.'

'You poor thing, it sounds awful. Did something happen — other than Shane's death — or is it because you're too stressed? Until I saw you in Melbourne, you always seemed so okay with everything.'

'I'm always busy with work, and I've usually got a lot on my mind. I guess I just accepted that. But Shane's death seems to have triggered something, tipped me over the edge.'

Emily felt terrible that their tiff might have contributed to his stress as well. 'So, did something happen, something specific, that saw you go and see your GP?'

'On Thursday morning – I think it was Thursday, anyway, last week is all a bit of a blur – I was watching the news on TV. Suddenly the noise seemed miles away and I couldn't make out the specific voices. It was like everything was distorted, out of focus. And then I couldn't get up. I felt glued to the couch. My heart started racing. I was sweating. And when I thought about what I was meant to be doing, I couldn't remember. I couldn't think. It was terrifying. I didn't know what was happening to me – if I was having some sort of seizure or stroke. Eventually things became clear again, like coming out of a fog. I'd probably only been like that for minutes – maybe half an hour – but it felt like I'd lost a whole day. I didn't know what else to do, so I phoned the clinic. I was really freaked out. Thankfully they could fit me in that morning.'

'God, you poor thing.'

'I guess it's being based in a city and dealing with so many stressed people, but my GP picked it straight away. She thinks the test results are just a formality. It'll be good to know for sure, but it won't really change anything. Regardless, she wants me to take three to six months off.'

'Can you afford to take that much time off?'

'I don't see I have a choice. If it happens again, there's a chance I could find myself totally catatonic, like a complete shutdown, and not be able to move. Imagine if it happened when I was driving.'

'That's a scary thought.'

'So, I'm looking at Shane's death as a big wake-up call. If there's one thing good that can come out of that, I'll take it. What's the point of working so hard if it's just going to kill you? I've got some good people working for me. And Sim's got someone in mind as project manager. I'm not too concerned about the business. And I'm fine for money, thanks to a good insurance policy. I have to focus on getting better, at this stage just take each day as it comes. It's all about playing it by ear and listening to my body, really.'

'So, Simone knows everything?'

'Yes.'

Sometimes Emily wished she had a sibling to confide in. 'And there really isn't any specific treatment?'

'Just lots of vitamins and long walks in the country. Watching my stress levels and concentrating on getting myself healthy through diet and exercise. I've cut way down on caffeine too. I was drinking coffee right through the day. I had no idea how many cups I was having – I always had one on the go in the office.'

'Actually, I had noticed you weren't drinking so much coffee. And I did wonder about all the vitamins you've been taking.'

'Yes, I practically rattle in the mornings now.'

'You know you can always talk to me about things. If this is going to work, I don't want there to be secrets between us.'

'Thanks for understanding,' Jake said, pulling her to him and kissing her.

'Of course. I love you,' she said, snuggling into him. 'I'll take good care of you.'

'I love you too.' After a short cuddle, they sat back and spent a few moments looking about in silent contemplation. Jake was the first to speak. 'It's such a shame about the cottage, because there really is something quite magical about this place. It's got good energy, or something.'

'I felt that the first time I came over here,' Emily replied, picking up a small stone from beside her. 'I thought it was the building, but perhaps it's the trees and nearby creek.'

'Well, I can certainly see why they chose here for their home,' Jake said.

In front of them, the dry creek bed twisted its way through the paddock. 'The stream would have run most of the year before they dammed it way back up in the hills in the nineteen fifties. Why does progress have to be so brutal on the environment?' Emily said wistfully, running a hand through Grace's soft fur.

'It doesn't have to be. The old and new can coexist. I've made a business out of blending them. It just takes some thought and sometimes a bit more effort.'

'I bet it isn't easy convincing people to keep the old when the new is so often cheaper.'

'The people who approach me tend to know and like my work, and be serious about having me involved. There's not a lot of convincing to be done. I guess I've been lucky that there are enough people out there who still have a conscience and also appreciate traditional aesthetics. Speaking of aesthetics, what are you going to do with that?' Jake said, nodding towards the half-built hayshed a little way off.

'David said he could use the extra storage, so I wouldn't mind it moved down to the end of the other sheds. I don't know why John didn't put it there to start with,' she said, shaking her head.

'I had a quick look on my way past,' Jake continued. 'It's just bolted together like a giant meccano project. Shouldn't be hard to deconstruct.'

'Yeah, that's what I thought,' Emily said, rolling her eyes. 'But I've learnt my lesson about trying to do it on my own.' She was still embarrassed about not knowing how to start the tractor and then getting stuck up the ladder, but was starting to see the funny side of the incident. 'Thank goodness Barbara and David came along when they did. I might have been stuck up there forever.'

'I think between the two of us we might be able to manage it,' Jake said, patting her knee. 'But perhaps it would be more sensible to get David involved. He'd know more about this sort of thing than me. I'll ask him.'

'I would so love not to have to look at it from the bedroom window each morning. And all this rubble,' she added. 'What do you think I should do about it? John said he was going to just push it into the creek.'

'I've been sitting here wondering the same thing myself.'

'And?'

'I reckon we sort out that monstrosity and then tackle this. One thing at a time. What do you say?'

'Fair enough. Now, would you like something to eat? I know it's late, but I got some fresh rolls and ham from the bakery.'

'Sounds perfect,' he said, getting up and then holding out a hand to help her up.

They walked back to the house with their arms around each other and Grace bounding ahead of them.

'Hey Jake?'

'Yeah?'

'When's your birthday? Since you know mine, it's only fair.'

'April twenty-third. I'm coming up to thirty-six.'

'Okay. Great.'

'I'm a Taurus, which I understand is highly compatible with Capricorn – you,' he added with a cheeky grin.

*Yes, yes, YES!* 'Oh, really? Cool,' Emily said, impressed at how nonchalant she'd managed to sound. 'I don't know much about astrology,' she added with a shrug, and put a little skip into her step.

# Time
# Will Tell

Also by Fiona McCallum

*Paycheque*
*Nowhere Else*
*Wattle Creek*

*The Button Jar Series:*
*Saving Grace*

# Time Will Tell

## Fiona McCallum

First Published 2014
Second Australian Paperback Edition 2014
ISBN 978 174356904 7

TIME WILL TELL
© 2014 by Fiona McCallum
Australian Copyright 2014
New Zealand Copyright 2014

This is a work of fiction. Names, characters, places, and incidents are either the product of the author's imagination or are used fictitiously, and any resemblance to actual persons, living or dead, business establishments, events, or locales is entirely coincidental.

Published by
Harlequin Mira
An imprint of Harlequin Enterprises (Australia) Pty Ltd.
Level 19, 201 Elizabeth Street
SYDNEY NSW 2000
AUSTRALIA

® and TM are trademarks of Harlequin Enterprises Limited or its corporate affiliates. Trademarks indicated with ® are registered in Australia, New Zealand and in other countries.

Printed and bound in Australia by McPherson's Printing Group

*In loving memory of my aunt, Anne de Wit,*
*who was also a very dear and special friend.*

## *Acknowledgements*

Many thanks to editor Lachlan Jobbins for bringing the best out in my writing and to Sue Brockhoff, Cristina Lee, Michelle Laforest and everyone at Harlequin Australia for continuing to believe in me, make my dreams come true, and turn my pages into beautiful books.

Thanks also to Jane and Emma at Morey Media for spreading the word and to the media outlets, bloggers, librarians, booksellers and readers for your support. It means so much to hear of people enjoying my books.

Thank you to members of the Gemmological Association of Australia SA Division Inc. for help with research and for very generously showing me some diamonds in the rough. Fascinating! Any errors of fact are my own or down to me taking creative liberties.

Finally, a huge thank you to my oldest and dearest friends Carole and Ken Wetherby, Mel Sabeeney and Arlene Somerville for being the best friends a person could ever hope to have.

# Chapter One

Emily Oliphant and her best friend Barbara stood on the verandah, staring out into the still country evening. Birds rustled in the trees, settling themselves for the night, and a multitude of insects chattered and sang in the summer air.

'What a gorgeous evening. And what a really lovely spot, Em,' Barbara said with a sigh.

'It is, isn't it?' Emily reached down to pat her border collie pup, Grace, who was at attention by her feet. 'I could stay here forever.'

They were out the front of Emily's house – the house that would be hers if she accepted the Baker brothers' proposal. She thought of all she'd been through in the last two months – leaving her husband, meeting Barbara, saving Grace. And now, finally, settling into a home of her own. Could she find the courage to do this too?

'Seriously Em, you can do this – the house, everything. Don't let fear stop you. And don't worry about your mother.'

Emily nodded. Her friend was right; being offered the house was one hell of a Christmas present. And not too shabby as a thirty-second birthday gift either. Forget what Enid had to say about it. *This is my life.*

'Well, I'd really better go before they send out a search party,' Barbara said, kissing Emily on the cheek.

'I'm so glad you stopped in.' The two friends hugged, neither wanting to be the first to let go. As always, Barbara had turned up at just the right time.

Finally they broke apart, and Barbara made her way down the steps and over to her car. 'See you Saturday,' she called.

'Don't forget the tinsel,' Emily called back sardonically.

'No fear there. And the champagne; we're going to celebrate.' She got in the car with a wave of her hand.

Emily watched until Barbara's tail-lights were out of sight. She smiled wryly. Her mother would indeed have a fit when she found out she was buying the run-down old place.

Thankfully it didn't matter what Enid thought. It was to be Emily's home and no one else's.

As she stared out into the last fading light of the warm summer day, her head began swimming with possibilities, risks, and calculations. The chance to buy the house really was a huge opportunity, if a little daunting – well, very daunting. But it was meant to be, wasn't it? A home of her own.

A home that was as much Grace's as hers, she thought, looking down at the small black and white dog beside her. Grace was a typical border collie except for the missing white ring around her neck. Emily still found it hard to believe it was only six weeks since the day she had picked her up as a tiny puppy – it felt like Grace had always been a part of her life. And Barbara; they'd become firm best friends almost instantly. She was so blessed to have met her. Along with Grace, Barbara had been her saviour; her rock, her voice of reason.

She bent down and ruffled Grace's ears. The puppy looked up at her with love and adoration. Emily smiled. That look would melt anyone's heart. Well, except her estranged husband's.

At the thought of John Stratten, her face clouded. Thankfully the bully was now out of her life. He'd completely ripped her off in the financial settlement, but at least he was gone.

'Come on Gracie, let's go inside.'

They made their way down the hall, Grace's claws clicking on the bare floorboards punctuating Emily's thoughts.

*Why didn't I leave him sooner?*

Her mother had told her that once she had made her bed she had to lie in it. If only she had ignored her. It was the twenty-first century for Christ's sake, not the nineteen-fifties! *How could I have been so damned gullible?*

But of course Emily knew. It had nothing to do with gullibility and everything to do with that old chestnut that shaped your life growing up in a small country town: what will people say? What could possibly make a woman like her give up a marriage to one of the wealthiest farmers in the district?

She cast her mind back to the afternoon she had finally decided to leave him. John's threat to shoot Grace had been the last straw. A shiver ran the length of Emily's spine. At least she had saved her from the brute.

Forty thousand dollars?! It wasn't fair. Perhaps if she'd known she was going to be offered the old house to buy she might have fought for more in the settlement.

Emily sighed. At the time she'd just wanted to get it over with, to get on with her life and never have anything to do with him again. She had hoped that feeling would last; that when twelve months had elapsed it would just be a matter of the divorce papers being signed and rubber-stamped.

She paused in the hallway and looked around her. The old place had so much potential. She'd love to turn it into something worthy of *Home Beautiful*. But her meagre funds would barely cover updating the kitchen – even the most basic design.

The Baker brothers were only asking for ten thousand up front and then ten thousand per year for twenty years – and the costs associated with subdividing, however much that would be. It was a bloody good deal in anyone's book, but still felt precarious to Emily in her current situation.

She had approximately forty-seven thousand dollars in savings, but no job, and nothing on the horizon thanks to the Global Financial Crisis and a couple of years of drought since.

But she was going to stay positive. 'Fake it till you make it,' Barbara had said not so long ago. She had to have faith that it would all work out. Really, what else did she have?

She could see now that Barbara had really been gently telling her to stop feeling sorry for herself and get her act together. It was something Emily's gran might have said if she'd been born fifty years later than she had. As it was, Granny Rose would have been more likely to say something gentler, like: 'Put on a happy face, dear. No one likes a sourpuss.'

With that thought Emily hoicked up her shoulders and carried on into the kitchen.

She filled the kettle and waited for it to boil. She really had to start believing that good things could happen. Like her cousin Elizabeth turning up with a friend who just happened to be an architect and a qualified builder; what were the odds of that?

Jake would be able to give her a good idea of how much the house would cost to fully renovate. He'd certainly indicated it was worth looking into. And he wasn't just humouring her or being polite. He was genuine – the gift and proceeds from the jam he had sent were proof of that. It was such a pity that he lived so far away in Melbourne.

She looked across at the old Bushells coffee jar on the kitchen table. It was an almost identical match for the original jar from the nineteen-thirties. Even the tone of the faded red tin screw-top lid was the same.

The night before she died, Granny Rose had given Emily her button jar. The thought of how serious Gran had been — her insistence that she take good care of it — still brought a sad smile to Emily two months on. The Alzheimer's had made her wise old gran say the strangest things.

The jar was precious to Emily too. It had been since she'd first seen it as a four year old. She'd always loved the bright colours and the rattle it made when gently shaken. She'd especially loved the weird tradition that buttons were constantly put in on top, but none ever removed, nor the contents ever tipped out and rifled through. Since Gran's death, she had felt a sense of comfort whenever she held it.

And she felt dreadful that in just a few months it had got broken. She still had no idea how the jar had fallen from the bench to the floor in the middle of the night. It would remain one of life's mysteries.

Emily forced thoughts of Gran aside — she was getting too melancholy thinking about her — and wondered if she should phone Jake again. She'd rung him earlier to thank him, but had got his voicemail. She could try again later.

*No, that would be weird and stalkerish. You've already left one message*, she told herself. *But I'm really grateful to him.* The replacement jar was such a thoughtful gift.

*Fiona McCallum*

The roaring kettle distracted her and she set about preparing a mug of Milo.

At the kitchen table sipping her drink, she looked around the large space and wondered who else she could ask for advice about the purchase. Her dad would be her first port of call – he'd already helped her repaint the inside of the house and sand the floorboards – but he wasn't in the actual building game, so he wouldn't know about how much things would cost.

Suddenly Emily yawned. It was only eight o'clock, but it had been a big day; with the funeral for Barbara's father-in-law and the Bakers' visit afterwards. She was weary, but her brain was still spinning a little too fast and her thoughts were too disconnected. She needed some down time to let it all seep in.

She would have loved to soak in the tub for a while, but still didn't like the idea of lying naked and vulnerable in the bathroom outside on the back verandah.

As she brushed her teeth and waited for Grace to have her last pee for the night, Emily found herself daydreaming of a plush ensuite, right off her bedroom, with plenty of heating for the cold winter months. When the time came, and funds permitted. That would be a long way off, she thought pessimistically as she followed Grace inside and closed the kitchen door behind them.

She said goodnight to Grace, who was settled on her bed in the corner of the kitchen, and made her way slowly and heavily down the hall to her bedroom, turning off the lights as she went.

She changed into her summer pyjamas and climbed into bed. She ignored the small wad of paper from the Bakers that contained the conditions of the purchase – she was way too tired to study it again – and picked up her book. But she couldn't focus on that either.

Was she about to open a can of worms by trying to buy the old place? It sure would be easier just to stay renting and trying to find a job. But wouldn't she then be letting herself down; not fulfilling her full potential?

Perhaps she didn't have any unfulfilled potential. Her mother had certainly never seen her as more than wife material. And John had never let her help out on the farm. That had been her dream; for them to stand shoulder to shoulder and run the place together, as a true partnership. But he hadn't even let her do the books.

*Oh for God's sake, stop feeling sorry for yourself, Emily! When haven't you been prepared to work hard for something?*

Barbara was right; she could do this. She had been
brave enough to finally leave John, and she'd be
brave enough to do this too. Somehow she'd make it
happen. On her own.

One of Gran's sayings came to her now: 'Nothing
come by quickly is ever as satisfying as that which
has been waited for or toiled over.'

She was right. Yes, bit by bit, slow and steady
wins the race, and all that.

Emily banished the quotes from her head and
picked up Donald and Trevor Baker's handwritten
offer. Her whole body began to tingle with excitement. She reread it carefully and was making notes
and listing questions to ask – of whom she wasn't yet
sure – when her mobile chirped into action beside
her. Her heart rate doubled as she saw Jake's name
lit up on the screen. *Oh!* She took a deep breath and
pressed the button to answer.

'Hi Jake,' she said cheerily.

'Hi Em.'

'I got your parcel this afternoon. Thanks so much.
It does seem rather a lot of money for just some jars
of homemade jam.'

'Well, it's very good jam.'

'Thanks. And thank you so much for the jar – I
can't believe you found one the same.'

'I hope it's the right one. The antique dealer seemed to think there weren't many variations.'

'It's perfect. Thank you again.'

'My absolute pleasure. Now I would love to chat, but I don't have long. I actually called to ask you a favour.'

'Oh. Okay.'

'I'm in Whyalla – working on a project with a friend of a friend. Bit of a long story. I was wondering if I could come and stay for the weekend. You did say you don't do anything special for Christmas, right? I'm sorry about the short notice.'

'Of course you can stay – I'd love to have you!' As soon as the words left her mouth, Emily blushed. She was glad he couldn't see her embarrassment at her poor choice of words.

'It's just I have to be here again next week – we're working right through while most businesses are shut – but I'd rather not spend the Christmas weekend here on my own. I hate to impose, but this project has come together in a bit of a rush,' he added, sounding a little breathless.

'Jake, really, you wouldn't be imposing. I'm just having Mum and Dad and Barbara and David here for lunch Christmas day, and you're very welcome to join us. It's just casual. And absolutely no presents are being exchanged,' she added.

Emily had always hated the awkwardness of being given a gift and not having one to offer in return. It had almost become a phobia. When she had invited Barbara, she had put the 'no gifts' rule on the table and had been relieved when Barbara had agreed, albeit reluctantly.

'Okay. Well, perhaps I can have a bit more of a look at that house of yours if you like – to earn my keep,' Jake offered.

'Your timing would be perfect actually; there's been a bit of a development on that front.'

'Oh?'

'Yes, the old brothers who own it have offered to sell it to me.'

'Wow, that's great.'

'It's a bit of a long story, but I really would appreciate your opinion on the structural aspects of the house, and any other advice you can offer.'

'It would be my pleasure.'

'So when should I expect you – and do you have someone with you or are you on your own?' She hoped it was the latter.

'No, it's just me. And Saturday – Christmas day – if that's okay? Say mid-morning?'

'No problem at all.'

'And I'm really sorry to have to cut this short, but I'm being collected for dinner and my hosts have just arrived.'

'Okay. See you Saturday then. Drive safely.'

'Thanks very much, Em, I look forward to it. See ya.'

'Me too,' Emily said quietly, but she suspected the call had already been disconnected.

Her heart rate subsided to a thud of nervous excitement. Wow, Jake wanted to visit – alone; without Elizabeth! And for Christmas, no less! She couldn't wait to see him. This would make the day a bit special.

Emily was no longer tired, and in fact couldn't imagine how she'd get to sleep at all now. She mentally ran through her list for Christmas; what she still had to do, what ingredients she had on hand and what she had left to buy.

When the reminder of the expense seeped in, she picked up her book. She'd found reading fiction the best antidote to the pressures that regularly threatened to overwhelm her.

Especially the thought that she wouldn't be in this mess if she'd listened to her mother and continued to lie in the bed she'd made – her marriage to John Stratten.

For a moment she wondered what her husband was doing for Christmas. Had John arranged to see his parents, or would he be spending the Christmas weekend alone on the farm? She cut off the thought before letting herself feel any sympathy for him — he deserved everything he got.

# Chapter Two

Emily woke up Christmas morning feeling ener-
gised and full of purpose. She leapt out of bed and
went down to the kitchen.

'Merry Christmas Gracie,' she said to the dog,
who was looking at her and flapping her tail.

She put water in the kettle and stared out the
window while she waited for it to boil. It was a
lovely cool morning and the forecast was for a perfect
twenty-eight degrees with a slight easterly breeze.
After her coffee she would take a walk up the gully.
Then she'd start getting the roast organised.

With coffee in hand, she sat at the table and went
through her to do list, making sure she hadn't missed
anything. Jake would be arriving in a few hours.

Everything was ready: the house and bathroom
were clean, and the spare room was made up and felt
inviting. She'd bought the groceries the day before

and there was plenty to make do with in the freezer: a leg of lamb and some chops; mince; some chicken pieces. Enough for the weekend.

Suddenly she wondered if Jake would rather eat at the pub. She really didn't want to waste her precious financial resources by eating out. She'd already blown next week's budget on Christmas lunch.

No, she'd prepare for meals at home – sandwiches for when he arrived, roast lamb and all the trimmings for Christmas lunch, and leftovers and perhaps spaghetti bolognaise for tomorrow. She'd worry about beyond that later.

Pausing for a moment, she noticed the creased pages outlining Trevor and Donald's proposal at the end of the table. She'd been carrying it from kitchen to bedroom and back for the last two days.

The Bakers' offer was very generous. Emily knew she'd be a fool not to do her best to take them up on it, providing the house was worth renovating.

So the question was really whether it was a sound proposition. She was glad her father would be here to discuss it with Jake, but she really didn't want Enid's negativity dragging everything down.

Enid had described the place as 'disgusting' and a 'knockdown job'. She had no idea why her mother was so opposed to her living there.

Emily's shoulders slumped slightly. It wasn't as though she could ask Jake and Barbara and David to not mention the house business – something was bound to slip out. She'd spend the whole day being a nervous wreck. Not to mention that Jake would think her weird and pathetic for hiding something like this from her mother.

Emily practically snorted. *Just grow up. It does not matter what your mother thinks. It has nothing to do with her.*

She got up to make another cup of coffee, and had just sat back down again when her phone started vibrating on the table in front of her. Speak of the devils, she thought at seeing her parents' home number on the display.

'Hello, Emily speaking.'

'Hi Em, it's Dad. Merry Christmas!'

'Hi Dad. Yeah, merry Christmas,' she said, relaxing signific-antly. 'How are you?'

'Good thanks, but your mum's not feeling so well and won't be joining us. She's woken up with one of her "heads".'

'Oh, is she okay?' Emily asked automatically. Enid's 'heads' usually meant her parents had had a fight and her mother was staying at home to sulk and prove a point of some sort. Strangely, she only ever had one when there was a social engagement they were attending.

'Fine. You know how it is – just needs a quiet day at home.'

Emily thought it had more to do with having people asking after her in her absence and then phoning later to check she was okay than punishing Des. Emily could just picture him now rolling his eyes.

'So I just wanted to check if there's anything you need brought out before I leave,' he added brightly.

'Actually, could I borrow a ladder?'

'Okay. Of course. That wasn't quite what I had in mind,' he said with a little chuckle. 'Nothing's happened, has it? You haven't lost the roof or anything?'

'No, the roof is fine as far as I know. But something has happened – the Bakers have offered to sell me the house and about twenty acres around it. At a very good price and on a *very* generous purchase plan. I'll tell you all about it later.'

'Oh. Okay. That's brilliant news. When did this happen?'

'They dropped by the other day after Doug Burton's funeral. Somehow I don't think Mum will see it as cause for celebration.'

'Hmm, no, probably not,' he said thoughtfully. 'So why the ladder?'

'Well, Jake is staying – you remember, Elizabeth's friend you met the other week – and I want him to have a good look at it.'

'Good idea. He seemed a very nice chap. I'm sure he'll steer you right. I wouldn't mind hearing what he thinks of the old place.'

'Great. And as you're always saying, two heads are better than one.'

'Exactly. Your mother was talking to your aunt Peggy last night. She didn't mention Elizabeth was coming back over this way so soon.'

'She isn't. Jake rang on Thursday from Whyalla – he's doing some work there – and wanted to spend the weekend down here. All very last minute. Didn't want to go back to Melbourne. Good timing for me, though.'

'Indeed. So what are Donald and Trevor asking for the house?'

'It's not that clean-cut – I'll show you their proposal.'

'I didn't think they'd ever sell. Wonder what changed their minds.'

'Apparently they want to take an overseas trip and need some extra cash.'

'I'm sufficiently intrigued. Okay, I'd better get going. I'll go and put the ladder in before I forget. So nothing needed from the corner shop?'

'No, that's it, thanks very much. I'll see you in a few hours.'

'Very good. See you soon.'

'Bye.'

Emily consulted her list again. Almost everything was ticked off. Suddenly the mobile phone began to vibrate again. She picked it up.

'Hi Barbara. Merry Christmas.'

'And a merry Christmas to you too. How's things?'

'Great. And you?'

'Good now all the rellies that were here for the funeral have left. I am *so* looking forward to a low-key day and not having to cook or entertain.'

'We're going to have ourselves a great day!'

'You're sounding especially gleeful this morning.'

'Am I?'

'You are. Come on, spill. What's going on?'

'Well, Mum's not coming – got a headache or something...'

'So I take it from your happy disposition that you're not cancelling Christmas lunch to go off and spoon-feed her chicken soup?'

'Er, no,' Emily said with a laugh. 'I know it's terrible, but I'm actually relieved she's not going to be here.'

'Oh well, you can't help how you feel. And I do know how tense Enid makes you, especially when you're trying to cook.'

'Hmm. It's not just that.'

'Oh?'

'No, Jake Lonigan's coming for lunch. He's actually going to stay for the weekend.'

'Ooh, the lovely Jake. Goodie! With or without Elizabeth?'

'Without. But don't you go getting any ideas. He's in Whyalla for a while and wants to escape for the weekend – no doubt for more photography. It's purely platonic.'

'How do you know?'

'He rang the other night.'

'No, silly, how do you know it's purely platonic? Especially now there's no Elizabeth in tow.'

Emily found herself wondering at her assumption and realised she had nothing to base it on.

'Come on Barb, we both know I do not need a relationship at the moment. I thought you agreed with me on that.'

'I know – just teasing. But, you know, that's when they happen – when it's the last thing you're looking for.'

'So I've heard. But I've got too much else to deal with right now.'

'Brilliant timing on Jake's part, though. He'll be able to give you some advice on the house.'

'That's what I'm counting on – an objective opinion.'

'Oh well, it might be good to keep it businesslike, then.'

'Hmm.'

'What about Nathan Lucas?'

'What about him?'

'I thought he was nice. Well, the little I saw when I met him at David's dad's funeral.'

'He's nice enough.'

Nathan, an assistant bank manager, was the son of some family friends, and was fresh from his own marriage breakup. His mother and Enid had recently – and none-too-subtly – tried to match-make them. Emily found him friendly enough, and they'd got along well. But she wasn't prepared to think anything of him beyond that.

'Is he still single?'

'Jesus, Barbara, you're sounding like my bloody mother!'

'Sorry, just curious. So are you going to ask his advice – from a financial perspective?'

Emily had wondered if it was worth discussing with Nathan. He had, after all, offered to give her any financial advice she needed. But what could he say? It wasn't like she could afford a loan.

'No. I thought about it and decided there isn't any point. Like you said, it's a good deal. I need a lawyer more than a banker. He'd probably want to lend me money I can't afford to pay back.'

'I think the GFC put a stop to that, Em.'

'I know, but you know what I mean. Anyway, for all I know, he's probably back in Adelaide by now. So why are you calling, anyway?'

'Oh, just to check there wasn't anything extra that you needed.'

'Why does everyone assume I've forgotten something? I've just had my father asking the same question.'

'No need to get prickly. I was just checking.'

'I know. Sorry. I'm a bit stressed.'

'About Jake coming to stay?'

'Yes and no. Actually, about telling my mother about the offer to buy the house.'

'Well, you don't have to worry about that now that she's not coming. You just relax and enjoy the fine company,' she added with a chuckle.

'I've been so on edge I hadn't quite processed that I've got a reprieve on that one. You're right. I'll worry about telling her another day. Thanks Barbara, you're a darling.'

'I know. So if there isn't anything you need, I'll get cracking.'

'Thanks. And sorry about being snippy.'

'Already forgotten.'

Emily hung up, smiling. She was just so lucky to have Barbara in her life.

She went through her mental checklist yet again and concluded that everything was definitely ready for Jake's arrival, as it had been the time before, and the time before that.

There was nothing more to do, but if she had another coffee she'd be squelching when she walked – not to mention looking like a rabbit caught in the headlights from all the caffeine. She got up, called Grace to her, and left the kitchen.

She and Grace took their usual route up the gully, past the orchard to the disused well. But as she started to come back down, she took a moment to pause and study the house and its surrounds, trying to work out where the boundary of the proposed twenty acres would be if she went ahead with the subdivision.

*If* she went ahead? She frowned. The only 'if' was around finance.

It was a damn good deal — a no-brainer as Barbara and then David had pointed out. They'd even offered to loan her some money if she needed it. And they were soon to be quite flush thanks to David's father's recent death. It was very good of them to offer, but of course Emily could never accept money from her friends.

The actual cost wasn't really the problem — she could manage the first year's payment and then had time to gather the next. The problem lay in what happened after that. The house would need extensive renovation. Most of it could probably be done over time, but some things like the roof needed replacing as soon as possible. That would be costly.

One decent hail storm and she'd be well and truly stuffed. There were pinholes in the roof that let the sun shine through onto the verandah — who knew how bad the main roof sheets were? She stared down at the rusty iron and asked no one in particular to hold it all together.

And what if two months down the track the electricity shat itself and the whole place needed to be re-wired?

She'd have to find some way to make money in the absence of a job, which seemed to be as rare as hen's teeth at the moment. She was pretty sure selling jam at a Melbourne market wouldn't cut it, no matter how good the jam and how swanky the market. Anyway, the main fruiting season was almost over. She'd have to wait until April for the figs to be ripe. She could do orange marmalade, but oranges wouldn't be ripe for ages yet either. There had to be some other way.

She told herself it wasn't just about proving her mother wrong; it was about proving herself right — that she'd made the right decision leaving John, and that she could be successful in her own right, without the tag of 'John Stratten's wife' hanging around her neck. She didn't want the label of 'wife' at all. Possibly forever.

Emily sighed. If only she were more of a risk-taker. Plenty of people would just jump in and worry about all the boring details later. But Emily wasn't like that, and she doubted she ever would be. Of course she'd signed John's financial settlement without any thought, but that was different. She took a deep breath.

Maybe Jake would have some ideas – he seemed pretty grounded and cautious. Emily found it odd that she was okay with the thought of discussing her poor financial situation with him, a relative stranger.

She didn't think she'd ever have such a conversation even with her cousin Liz, and they'd known each other for ever. But Liz tended to be a bit critical and blunt, and had hurt Emily quite badly a few times. And if Liz discussed it with Aunty Peggy, *she'd* tell Enid, and then there'd be a whole conference of people telling her what and what not to do.

Emily took another deep breath and marched on. Grace ran on ahead with her nose to the ground, following the scents of the early-morning rabbits, foxes, and wild cats.

Instead of following the creek bed straight back down to the house, she turned towards the outbuildings that were to be included in the subdivision.

What would she do with a smelly old shearing shed, she wondered, peering through a window so grimy it was almost a mirror. Nothing for a long, long time, she concluded. There was no point going inside and beginning to dream of what it could be turned into.

Next to the shearing shed was a smaller shed with a set of double wooden doors, their grain wide and grey in colour – signs of paint long gone. The door opened stiffly but easily enough, its hinges issuing a deep metallic protesting groan. A raised slab of concrete with large rusting bolts standing up out of it sat on a dirt floor stained dark by many years of oil and fuel spills.

The old generator room, Emily surmised, from the days before the main power line crossed the paddock from the main road to the house. Now it seemed to be a storage room for empty chemical drums.

The toxic smells filled Emily's nostrils and she puckered up her nose in distaste. The first thing she'd do if she bought – *when* she bought – the place would be to get rid of them via the Council's farm chemical drum disposal program.

Though she couldn't really complain. It was a small job compared to other farms she'd been to where rusting car bodies and junk of every sort was mixed with scrub, hidden behind sheds, and left for the next generation to deal with. Trevor and Donald Baker were quite tidy compared to many around.

Emily's stomach growled, reminding her she was yet to eat breakfast. She'd been too busy and too nervous earlier. She headed down the gentle slope to the back of the house and around to the side door into the kitchen.

She made herself two pieces of toast with butter and vegemite and sat side-on to the glass-panelled door that led out onto the verandah.

Strips of green and red light cut across the table in front of her. She nibbled her toast, taking small mouse-like bites to kill time. Occasionally she glanced at Grace – who was snoozing on her mat in the corner – and wished she too could so easily shift between being totally excited and totally relaxed.

Emily was suddenly startled by a hefty three-barrelled knock on the front door, so loud that the echo bounced around in the emptiness of the hall. Grace leapt to attention and sat with her head cocked, waiting.

Who could it be? It was too early for Jake – well, unless he'd left Whyalla really early, which he could have, she supposed.

She got up, her heart pounding with the anticipation of seeing him again.

'Coming!' she called, and made her way quickly down the hall.

# Chapter Three

With a shaking hand, Emily opened the door and was surprised to find Nathan Lucas on her doorstep. His face lit up with a big grin.

'Hi. Merry Christmas. Thought I'd pop by to see your new digs.'

*On Christmas friggin' morning?!*

Emily was momentarily speechless. She frowned slightly, then her upbringing kicked in.

'Oh, Nathan. Hello. Right, well, it's not very exciting I'm afraid. But it's home,' she said with a shrug.

She felt rooted to the spot. The polite thing to do would be to invite him in, but knowing her luck, Jake would then turn up. And how would *that* look?

*Um, like you're having coffee with a friend.*

'I'm sorry, I shouldn't have just turned up unannounced – you're probably really busy,' Nathan said, starting to shift his feet and look about awkwardly.

'Not at all, come on in,' Emily said, finally shaking off her hesitation. She stepped aside to let him in. 'I do actually have a friend coming a little later – to stay for the weekend – and Mum and Dad and some friends are coming for lunch…' *Well, Mum isn't, but… Shit, should I invite Nathan for lunch too? No, surely he's having it with his parents.*

'Well, aren't we the social butterfly,' Nathan teased as he pecked her on the cheek and stepped past her into the dark hall.

She didn't know what to make of his tone, but found herself bristling in response. 'It's not normally like this, believe me.'

'Wow, lovely wide hall,' he said, gazing about.

'Yes, it's what they call a cricket pitch hall, though I haven't measured it.'

'Great colour – you've just repainted haven't you?'

'Yes. But the colour wasn't my choice. It was leftover from a friend – Barbara, who you met at the funeral. I do like it, but I probably would have gone more marigold than cream. I may as well give you the grand tour, since everything's pretty much on the way to the kitchen at the back.'

'It's gorgeous. And these floorboards are beautiful.'

As she showed him through the house, the initial tension left Emily and she felt prouder with every bit of praise Nathan heaped on her. She offered him a coffee and they sat at the kitchen table.

'I can't believe you and Des did all this yourself,' he said. 'I'm not a bit handy with tools – I wouldn't have known where to start.'

'Actually, Nathan,' Emily said, after they'd been sipping their drinks for a few moments, 'there's something I've been wondering about. Maybe you can help me. Do you have any idea how much it costs to subdivide a property?'

'Not off the top of my head, but I could find out easily enough – this place you mean?'

Emily was suddenly unsure if she should be discussing it with him. Would it jinx things? Would he tell anyone? Could she really trust him?

'Oh, just dreaming really,' she said, blushing slightly, and peering down into her two-thirds full mug.

'Come on Em, you can't just leave it at that. Honestly, I'm the vault of discretion if you want someone to bounce ideas off. You'd have my absolute confidence. Trust me, I'm a banker,' he said with a grin, before taking a long slug of coffee.

She took another sip while getting her thoughts in order. 'All right – if you promise to keep this to yourself. Because it might not happen anyway.'

'Scout's honour,' he said, saluting.

'Well, my landlords have offered to sell me the house and surrounding land if I pay to have it surveyed and subdivided...'

'Can you afford to buy? The place must be worth a couple of hundred thousand.'

'They're both on the pension, which they have to be careful not to jeopardise. So they're offering the most amazingly generous terms.'

'If it sounds too good to be true, Emily, chances are... Sorry, I don't mean to sound negative – it's the cautious banker in me. Sorry. Go on.'

'The place looks quite tidy, but there's a lot of work to be done – it was empty for years, so it's not worth nearly what it once would have been. Anyway, they only want twenty annual payments of ten thousand – five to each of the brothers. No interest.'

'Wow, well that really is a good deal then, and probably too good to pass up if you've got the first payment and can afford the subdividing costs. Maintenance might be your biggest problem. But I don't suppose you'd be living here if the main structure was a total disaster.'

'Yes, Dad had a pretty good look before I moved in and said it wasn't bad, but the roof will need replacing fairly soon. So I'll have to factor in the cost of that. I've told them I'm definitely interested but that I've got to do some sums.'

'Do you think you'll want a loan? You'd need a twenty percent deposit to avoid mortgage insurance, which is pretty hefty.'

'No point – I don't have a job, so I wouldn't be able to pay anything back.'

'Hmm, I wouldn't be much use to you then,' he said, thoughtfully.

'I wasn't expecting you to be,' Emily said, beginning to wonder why he had come here.

'No offence, but I thought you said you got a really rough deal – financially – from the ex. How are you planning to pay for all this?'

She felt a little taken aback. *You turned up out of the blue on Christmas morning; I didn't invite you to come out and discuss my finances!* She wanted to say these things aloud, but didn't.

She stared down into her mug, wondering if she'd done the right thing telling him she was unemployed. Thanks to her mother's prolonged conditioning, unemployment was much the same as having 'loser' tattooed on her forehead.

'So how did you find me, anyway?' She asked as the thought suddenly struck her.

'Your mum gave me directions the other day. Bumped into her in the street.'

'Oh God, I'll never hear the end of it. "That nice young Nathan, blah, blah, blah." No offence.'

'None taken. Anyway, I've already had plenty of subtle-as-a-sledgehammer hints from my own mother,' he said, rolling his eyes.

'So that's why you're here – because Mummy sent you. This was to shut her up, right?'

'No, I'm here because I wanted to see where you live. And I needed to get out of the house for a while. It's like a couple of tinsel and fairy light factories threw up in there.'

They both chuckled.

'Seriously, I like you, Em, but that doesn't mean I want to seduce you or anything,' Nathan added.

'Good. At least we're clear on that,' Emily said.

'It's not that I don't find you attractive, but I really do think we'd drive each other nuts.'

'Because we're astrologically incompatible, right?'

'Exactly,' Nathan said, clearly missing her sarcastic tone. 'Matching a Capricorn with a Cancer would be astrological hell. So why waste the time, energy and emotion and end up hating each other when we can just be friends and save all the palaver. You should be looking for a Taurus or a Virgo.'

'If only our parents agreed,' Emily said sardonically.

She'd almost forgotten all about their discussion of star signs the night they had met again at Emily's parents' house.

When they'd walked to the corner shop to get the cream Enid had forgotten – clearly another ruse in the matchmaking plan, because Enid Oliphant never forgot anything – he'd asked for her star sign and then straight out said they weren't compatible. Just like that.

Emily still couldn't believe anyone took star signs so seriously, especially someone like Nathan, who seemed the epitome of conservative.

She'd always dismissed astrology as ridiculous. There was no way all the people in the world could be classified into twelve categories. But now she found herself wondering for the briefest of moments what Jake Lonigan's star sign was.

'Now, back to your house-buying venture. My advice would be to get a good lawyer who's had plenty of experience in the area of subdivisions. I did meet a guy at a networking function a while ago. I might still have his card back in Adelaide. I'll have a look when I get back there next week. Can I borrow that pad?' he asked, indicating past Emily.

She slid it across the table to him.

'So I'll try and hunt out the guy's details and find out what I can,' he said, writing on the pad. 'Anything else I can do, do you think?'

'I don't want to put you to any trouble.'

'It's no trouble, honestly. Anyway, I'm most grateful for your company for an hour or so. Anything to get me away from my parents – you've no idea...'

'Oh I think I do. Why you'd want to move back out here I wouldn't know,' Emily said, shaking her head.

At the same time it dawned on her that she could just as easily move away herself. But then where would she find somewhere to rent for just one hundred dollars a week? And the thought of not having Barbara a few minutes' drive away made her feel almost queasy.

'It will probably mean lots of travelling back to the city for weekends until the novelty wears off,' he said, shrugging.

'You sound like you've got it all planned.'

'Oh, didn't I tell you? I got the job. I start in the new year.'

'Congratulations! We should have been drinking champagne!'

'It's a bit early for that.'

'True. But, wow, you're really going to be living here in Wattle Creek?' Emily was interested to know why he'd actually chosen to live in this tin pot country town after the excitement of city life. 'Your career must be *really* important to you.'

'I guess so,' he said with a shrug. 'I don't really think about it like that. I'm actually looking forward to life being a little quieter – the opportunity to save more with less to spend money on. It seemed the best, most obvious next step, too.'

'Fair enough. At least you have a career and know what you want. I don't have a clue.'

'You will when you're meant to,' Nathan said, sagely.

'Thanks. Very profound,' Emily replied with a groan.

'Who knows, I might only be doing this because of Dad's influence. Maybe it's not really what the universe had planned for me at all. Who knows?'

'But you enjoy it, don't you?'

'Most of the time, yeah. I guess I'm lucky there.'

'Another cuppa?' Emily asked, getting up. 'I couldn't fit another one in but I'm happy to make you one.'

'No thanks, but I'll stay a little longer, only if I'm not holding you up.'

'No, not at all.' And Emily meant it. She was genuinely enjoying his company, and liked the idea that he'd be around more.

'In that case, how 'bout you give me a quick tour of this kingdom you're going to own.'

'Well okay, come on.'

They were standing under the fruit trees up the gully, with a good bird's-eye view of the house. Now that she was actually showing someone where the proposed boundary would be – give or take – it was becoming more real. Nathan showed genuine enthusiasm as he looked over the twenty or so acres surrounding the house.

No longer did Emily have the feeling she might jinx it. She would make this happen if it meant living on baked beans on toast for the next twenty years. Later, after she had run it by her dad, she'd phone the Baker brothers, wish them a merry Christmas and tell them she accepted their offer.

'It's great that the house is smack bang in the middle,' Nathan said.

'Yeah, it's good, isn't it?'

'But if they ever sell the rest, how will you get in from the main road? The driveway's part of the main farm isn't it?'

'Yes and no. It's an easement, so no matter what happens, I'll always have access.'

'Ah, well, that's good. I had visions of you having to have your supplies choppered in,' he said, grinning.

'Ha ha, very funny.'

'I hate to say it, but the roof really does look a little the worse for wear from here.'

'I know. That'll probably be my first big expense. I'm hoping I'll know soon how much a new roof will cost me – round about. My friend who is coming to stay used to be a builder.'

'Well he, or she, will be a handy person to know, taking on a project like this.'

'He,' Emily confirmed, unsure why she felt the need to.

'It's a pretty big house for you to be living in all alone,' he said thoughtfully. 'You could rent out a couple of rooms and make a bit of money if you wanted to.'

'Who, other than me, would put up with a bathroom being outside and pay for the privilege?'

'Desperate people – like me…'

Emily stared at him and felt the realisation dawn on her. Nathan was looking elsewhere and didn't notice her expression.

*So that's why you're really here.*

She'd been played. She'd fallen for his act of being friendly and wanting some company, and pretending to be interested in the house. But all along he was looking for somewhere to stay. Irritation started to bubble.

'You know, there are absolutely no houses to rent in town. Plenty for sale, but I'm not ready to make that sort of commitment.'

'I thought the bank had houses for their managers.'

'Unfortunately, not for the *assistant.*'

'There's no way you'd want to live here though,' Emily said, staring at him.

'Why not?'

'It's a dump, for a start!' *And what would people say?* she wanted to add, but stopped herself in time – doing so would sound just like her mother.

'Em, if you're not interested in having a boarder, you only have to say,' he said, putting a hand on her arm.

Emily stared at his hand while going through the pros and cons. A bit of cash, some company; versus losing her solitude, the gossipmongers' assumptions.

*The money.* She so badly needed money.

'You don't need to decide right away, but please Em, at least think about it. Seriously. My only other option at this point is living with my parents and I'd rather camp in a paddock than do that. As much as I love them, I just don't want to move back in with them at my age. But there will be no hard feelings if you decide you want to be alone.'

'Okay, I'll think about it. I can't promise anything though. How much rent do you think would be fair?'

'There's an allowance of one hundred and fifty a week on top of my salary, so you can have that.'

*Wow, that's great*, Emily thought.

'That's way too much!' she said.

'We could say it includes utilities then.'

'Hmm.'

'Well, I'll leave you to ponder it.' Nathan suddenly glanced down at his watch. 'I'd better get back!'

They headed back down the hill and Emily walked him to his car, a sporty-looking sedan.

'Thanks for the hospitality. I think the house is great.'

'Thanks for saying so, and for dropping by,' she said, despite still feeling a bit irked.

'Well, have a merry Christmas,' he said.

'And you too.'

She allowed him to peck her on the cheek, and then stood watching as he drove off.

# Chapter Four

Emily prepared slivers of fresh garlic and tiny sprigs of rosemary and then poked them into the slits she'd made in the lamb. She did all this on autopilot while the pros and cons of Nathan's proposal ran through her head. She kept coming back to the same point – she needed the money.

As she washed her hands and dried them on the hand towel from the bench, she decided that she was being ridiculous. The ball was in her court. She didn't have to make a decision right now. And he'd said there would be no hard feelings if she declined. So why was she feeling so pressured?

No, she said to herself after taking a deep breath, she had to take the time to really think it through. No point making a quick decision and then living to regret it. No point deciding a couple of weeks in that she really didn't want company and making

Nathan move again just after he'd become settled. Or worse, not having the guts to tell him, and then living in silent angst and retreating to be alone at every opportunity.

Not unlike her marriage, really.

She suddenly realised all the parallels were there; a decision made for the wrong reasons, before all angles were considered and because of feeling pressured – by herself, yes, but also by her mother. The spoken and unspoken, the subtle and not so subtle.

All the references to so and so's lovely wedding, the news that such and such's daughter had just blessed them with their third grandchild and weren't they lucky? The barely disguised comments about her age. In Wattle Creek, any woman not married by twenty-three was considered 'on the shelf', and would be for life. Still unmarried at twenty-eight was a definite cause for panic. And panic was what Enid had done, right up until Emily and John had said their vows. You could almost hear her exhaling in relief at the words, 'And you may kiss your bride.'

A close second to getting your daughter married off was the particular match you'd managed. If it was a good one, mother would take the credit. If not, at least the girl was married.

In Emily's case, Enid had been particularly chuffed: 'And from such a good family; the Strattens are so community- and church-minded for such a wealthy family – you don't often get that these days.' The unspoken part being, 'Now we're a part of their world.' But of course the Oliphants weren't and never would be. Emily knew that, but it wasn't worth bursting her mother's bubble.

Emily had been as eager to marry 'up' as her mother – she'd been well and truly indoctrinated. But when she got into the fold she saw first-hand the truth of those well-worn phrases about the wealthy being wealthy because they were tight-fisted.

It was one of the things she'd liked about John – he was determined not to be like his parents and instead chose to splash his cash around.

But it had taken ages for her to see it for what it really was – boasting on a very superficial level. Rounds of beer at the pub, new mag wheels for his car, the odd trip to the city to get away – not to take her shopping or lavish her with jewellery or gifts, but to lose wads of cash on the chocolate wheel at the casino. *Of all the games available*, Emily had thought at the time, shaking her head while obediently standing beside him and waiting for him to get bored or run out of money.

Enid would never have believed her if Emily had told her; she was so smug about getting her daughter married into the wealthiest family in the district she wouldn't have heard a bad word against any of them. And for a long time Emily hadn't wanted to fully admit to herself what a huge mistake she'd made. What would have been the point? Marriage was for life; you had to take the good with the bad.

As she wiped the bench, Emily wondered for the umpteenth time if she'd ever truly been in love with John – John the man – or if it was what he'd been made out to be – mainly by her mother – that she'd been in love with. Could she really have been that shallow?

In the beginning John had been fun, had made her laugh, and had been kind and caring. She remembered their shared glances of admiration, their hopes for the future as he'd shown her his vast holding of land and his thousands of prime wool-growing merino sheep.

There had definitely been love at the beginning. The feeling that you would do anything for the man you stood beside while watching the sun setting over the groaning windmill up on the hill.

Pity the feeling wasn't returned for much longer than it took to place a ring on her finger and get her settled at the sink. Was she such a fool to have believed in the traditional marriage vows, to have believed in him?

*So it seemed*, she thought with a scowl.

Emily looked across at Grace and wondered if the dog had any memory of the day John had shot at her. She hoped not. John thought she'd overreacted – was no doubt dumbfounded that she'd left him because he'd taken pot shots at her dog.

Just because Grace had been in the same paddock as the sheep. Probably nowhere near them, just snuffling around the fence for fox and rabbit scents and fossicking for old bones.

'Next time it won't be so lucky,' he'd said. 'It needed a fright. If I'd meant to kill it, I would have.'

Emily still hadn't told her mother the real reason for leaving him.

At that moment Grace, as if reading her thoughts, looked directly up at Emily, stretched, yawned, turned herself around, and settled back down on her mat. Emily smiled. No matter what she went through, no matter how hard things got financially, it had been worth it to keep Grace safe.

She got the vegetables out of the fridge and set about preparing them for roasting. It took her less than twenty minutes. She then looked around the kitchen.

There was nothing left to do – even the finishing touches had had finishing touches. She'd even put a vase of bottlebrush flowers in Jake's bedroom after deliberating over whether it looked too try-hard or feminine or just plain ridiculous – finally deciding it was a nice welcoming country touch.

*Ah*, she thought. *I'll put Gran's buttons into the jar he sent.* If Jake saw it empty, he might think she hadn't really appreciated his gesture, which she had – very, very much.

It was a lot more than John had ever done without prompting. God, she wished she could erase him from her mind. Would she ever feel detached and unemotional about him?

'Time heals all wounds,' Gran would have said. *I bloody well hope she's right*, Emily thought, retrieving the dark-blue ice-cream container of buttons from the pantry.

She laid out a clean hand towel flat on the bench and tipped the multi-coloured, multi-shaped buttons and other assorted bits and pieces onto it. After the jar had mysteriously fallen, Emily had accidently cut herself while picking up the buttons off the floor. There were probably more bits of broken glass she hadn't found, but if she picked through them carefully by hand, she'd get any remaining pieces out.

Emily began picking up each button one by one, and putting them into the jar. She decided it might be fun to capture one type and colour of button at a time and remove all examples from the pile before moving onto another. She started with the plain round khaki plastic ones with two holes that had once been on all her grandad's work trousers and shirts. There were heaps of them, but the pile didn't seem to have diminished at all when she moved onto a similar style in navy blue.

While rummaging through the buttons, she took great care to check for shards of glass, many of which she found nestled in the weave of the terry towelling. Those that were big enough she took out, the rest she had to leave, picking the buttons out carefully with thumb and forefinger. Occasionally the tiny specks of glass sparkled like glitter in the morning sun.

After focusing on plain red buttons for a while, she paused, closing her hand around those she had already collected. She stood up taller, lifted her head and stretched her neck, aware it had begun to get cramped from stooping.

At that moment she heard a deep, male voice at the front door.

'Hello, anyone home?'

*He's here.*

'Coming!' Emily called, leaping up and practically skipping down the hall.

Grace trotted along behind, her thick black and white tail waving high above her back.

Emily opened the heavy front door to find Jake Lonigan standing there.

She'd previously thought him handsome in a warm, friendly sense, but now she decided he was handsome, full stop. His hazelnut-brown eyes seemed deeper and his lashes longer. She felt her knees go weak when he smiled broadly at her – a smile that captured his eyes and crinkled the corners around them.

'Welcome back!' she cried, and was surprised to find herself enveloping him in a hug, and not feeling at all awkward about it.

'Thanks. Great to be back,' he said into her hair. 'Hi Gracie,' he said, pulling away and bending down to give the grinning dog a pat. 'Oh, merry Christmas – I almost forgot.'

'Yeah, easily done. We're not exactly looking very festive around here. But thanks, and a merry Christmas to you too. Come on in, I've given you the same room as last time,' Emily said, grabbing the extended handle of his wheelie case and dragging it over the stoop. 'Though you're more than welcome to have the other one if you'd prefer, I wasn't sure, I should have checked...' Emily suddenly shut her mouth. She was rambling. *Well, I want him to be comfortable, what's wrong with that?* she asked herself indignantly, willing the colour of her cheeks to return to normal.

It was odd to be alone with Jake – without Elizabeth as buffer – and her nerves turned Emily into a ridiculous, overly effusive hostess; pointing out the towel, which was very obviously hanging over the back of a chair. She had indicated the wardrobe and chest of drawers before stopping herself.

'Brilliant, thanks,' Jake said, clicking shut the handle of the case he now stood behind.

'I'll leave you to freshen up then,' she said, and turned to leave, feeling like banging her head against the wall on her way out. She was sounding exactly like her mother.

'I'm putting the kettle on if you'd like a cuppa,' she called from the hall.

'Coffee would be great, thanks,' Jake called back.

Emily had boiled the kettle twice and resumed sorting the buttons when he finally came in, giving her a fright by appearing silently beside her.

'Sorry, didn't mean to scare you,' he said.

'No worries, I was just in deep concentration.'

'Huh. That's how I'd do it, too – each colour at a time,' he said, looking approvingly at the jar with its layers of colour and the handful of red buttons in Emily's palm.

'Just killing time, really,' she said, tipping them into the jar.

'I see you meant it when you said you're not really into Christmas,' he said, grinning at her.

'Sure did. Not a piece of tinsel nor coloured light in sight,' Emily said proudly. 'Though that will change when Barbara arrives. She's insisted we at least be a little Christmassy. Other than popping some crackers and reading some really bad jokes, I'm hoping it's going to be a very laid-back day. There'll be just us, David and Barbara, and my father. Mum can't make it, she's not feeling well,' she added, trying not to sound too pleased. The kettle whistled and she moved over to it. 'White with one, right?'

'Yes, thanks. Mind if I do some?' Jake said, indicating the buttons.

'Not at all.'

Emily stole a couple of quick glances at Jake, who was now engrossed in picking buttons out of the pile. She smiled. She decided she liked having him in her house. Especially without Elizabeth.

She asked herself whether she would like it so much if Nathan was here as well. The dynamic would be completely different.

Jake was only here for the weekend, and it wasn't as though there was anything romantic between them – it might be fun to hang out with both men together.

Maybe. What about having someone else here all the time?

She'd have the place to herself during the day when Nathan was at work. But she couldn't just come and go as she wished when he was home – like on weekends – could she?

She'd be forever feeling the need to explain what she was up to and invite him to join in. How could she balance her obligations to a housemate with her need for independence?

Like her mother, who had never been content with her own company, Emily had hated being left alone at the farmhouse.

But during the first weeks of their friendship, Barbara had tactfully enquired if perhaps she just *thought* she was lonely because Enid had her programmed to think that. Just because she was alone, didn't necessarily mean she was lonely. People could feel the same sense of despair when others were in close proximity. The realisation that Barbara was absolutely right had come as quite a shock.

Looking back, Emily could see that some of the loneliest days and nights of her life had been while married to John; not only when he'd gone away on camping trips with mates, but more often when he was just over in the shed, right across the table from her, or sitting watching television in silence.

She thought about Nathan again and pursed her lips. No, as much as she'd love the extra money, she could see it would be a backwards step. She needed the space to truly find herself – as naff as that sounded – and she was sure Barbara would agree.

Nathan would be disappointed, but she could only hope he'd meant it when he said there'd be no hard feelings. She'd better tell him soon so he could make other arrangements.

Meanwhile she had Jake to entertain and Christmas lunch to cook. She poured the steaming water into their mugs, and was just adding milk when he spoke, startling her.

'What the hell?!'

'What's wrong? Oh God, you didn't cut yourself, did you?'

'No, but have you seen this?!' he asked.

Emily looked over at him, frowning. Jake was holding up a smoky blue-grey stone about the size of the nail on her index finger.

'Oh, yeah, Elizabeth noticed that the other week when you guys were here – weird, huh?'

'Do you have any idea what this is?!'

Emily shrugged. 'Just a pretty little pebble; Gran was accumulating all sorts of stuff near the end.'

'It's an uncut diamond.'

# Chapter Five

'Don't be ridiculous,' Emily said with a laugh, moving towards him. Something tugged at her memory, but she was unable to secure whatever it was, and returned her focus to the tiny object in Jake's hand.

He held it out to her.

Emily closed her fingers around it and pulled both hands to her chest in an exaggerated theatrical gesture.

'What? You mean I'm rich?!' she said, doing her best Scarlett O'Hara impression. She then held it up for a closer look.

It was a strange-looking little stone, a deep grey-blue colour, sort of clear, but not quite, and with a slightly milky sheen. Up close, she saw that it was oddly shaped – long in the middle and pointy at each end.

'Seriously, Jake, you shouldn't get a girl's hopes up like that. It isn't fair,' she said, pouting, before handing it back to him.

'I'm telling you, Em, it's an uncut diamond!'

'How would you know anyway, you're a...'

'An architect? Actually, I'll have you know I'm a man of many talents,' he said, grinning at her. 'I did an introductory course on gemmology a few years back. And I would put money on that being an uncut diamond. See, the shape – a tetrahedron – it's how they're formed. It looks silky and smoky, but not really opaque,' he said, sounding more and more excited. 'There's no other gem quite like it.'

Emily had never seen a loose diamond before, let alone one in its uncut state. 'Looks like quartz or opal to me, or scratched glass, or something.' She frowned slightly.

'Well it's not, trust me. Bloody hell, this could be worth a fortune! How did it get here? Where did it come from?'

Emily rolled the small object slowly around between two fingers. Something in the back of her mind was fighting to be remembered, but it was still too small to grasp.

'It does feel sort of silky,' she said thoughtfully, as she tried to focus her mind. 'They come out of the ground in this shape?'

'Pretty much – in different sizes of course.'

'It's actually pretty big, isn't it?'

'And, being such an unusual blue-grey colour, I wouldn't mind betting it's really quite rare. Probably worth a fortune.'

Emily suddenly felt as if the blood had drained right out of her body. Feeling quite unstable on her feet, she dragged the nearest chair away from the table and sat down. Oh God! The letter she'd found among Granny Rose's things.

Jake continued to inspect the object, turning it over and over, around and around. She watched, stunned, struggling to form thoughts or words.

'Wonder if it was mined in India or South Africa,' he muttered.

'India,' Emily said. 'Golconda, India. They're from India.' She had no idea why she was sounding so calm; she felt anything but. Jake was staring at her wide-eyed.

'They're!? *They're* from India? Emily, how many are there?'

'There were originally seven of them – but that was back in the forties.'

'Seven! Jesus Christ, Em! You knew about them?'

Emily nodded. 'Yes and no. There was always a family myth that Gran had chosen Grandpa over an Indian prince. But there was never any more detail than that. After she died I was going through her recipes and found a letter. It was from an Indian prince, and it said he was giving her "seven of Golconda's finest" as a wedding gift. When I Googled Golconda, I found out diamond mining was big in the 1940s, so guessed that was what she'd been given.'

She remembered how excited she'd been as she'd waited for the pages to load, and the overwhelming urge she'd felt to rush off on a romantic crusade to India to find this man her grandmother had known. When the page revealed he had died five years before, she had been quickly brought back down to earth. That was the end of it. Or so she'd thought.

'I figured the diamonds must have been lost or sold, or even sent back. I can't imagine Grandpa being too thrilled with another man giving his wife a gift like that. Even Mum pooh-poohed the idea. So I just thought it was an unsolvable mystery. Wow! My head is spinning.'

'I'm not surprised. You know, if there are six more just like this, your money worries are over, my friend,' he said, starting to earnestly pick through the pile of buttons.

Emily knew she should be getting out the letter to show him, but she couldn't make herself move. And then the lightness she was feeling was suddenly replaced by a realisation that if she proceeded, everything would change, and not necessarily for the better.

If the diamonds mentioned in the letter were real, then technic-ally they'd belong to her mother and aunt — they were Gran's next of kin. Neither Enid nor Peggy were sentimental or romantic; they'd cash them in at the first opportunity. Emily would never see any of the proceeds.

On the other hand, if she did keep them a secret and somehow sold them herself, she'd never be able to use the money without serious probing from her mother.

And if some of the diamonds had survived unsold this long, then perhaps that's how they should remain. She owed it to Gran to keep her secret, didn't she? After all, Gran had asked her to take good care of the button jar when handing it over.

Emily's heart was beating so slowly she thought it might stop.

'Come on, Em, you could be rich; give me a hand here, will you?'

Emily remained where she was.

Jake looked up from the towel. 'Are you okay? You look like you've seen a ghost. Don't you want to find them?'

'Honestly, I'm not sure I do,' she said, shaking her head.

Jake stopped what he was doing, collected the cups Emily had prepared for them and joined her at the table.

'I'm sorry; I've come in like a bull in a china shop. They're your diamonds to find or not. No pressure.' He smiled kindly at her. 'Though, I can keep a secret if you need me to. Scout's honour,' he added.

Emily didn't know what to say.

'Seriously, if you don't want to take it any further, that's up to you,' he said, taking a long sip from his mug. 'But you've got to admit, it's pretty bloody exciting,' he added, grinning mischiev-ously. 'And here I thought I was coming to the country for a nice quiet weekend away.'

Emily rolled her eyes in mock consternation. She sipped her tea silently while trying to put her thoughts in order.

'So where's the letter?' he asked after a few moments of silence. 'Sorry,' he said, holding up a hand briefly in apology before returning to his coffee.

'You said no pressure.' But she was smiling gently. Of course she'd show it to him.

'I know what I said, but this is bloody excruciating.' He started squirming in his chair. 'You do still have it, don't you?'

'What, you think I'd throw it out?!'

'I don't know. I wouldn't put it past Elizabeth.'

'I'm the one who's held onto a jar full of old buttons just because they were my Gran's, remember?'

'All right, all right, I get it; you're soppy and sentimental. Are you going to show me this damned letter or not?!'

Emily went to the pantry cupboard and got down the large cardboard shoe box in which she now stored Gran's pile of old recipes tied up with her trademark grey string. Back at the table she took off the lid, untied the bundle, and began carefully taking out each fragile and stained piece of paper and well-thumbed book, turning them over to keep them in the same order. After she'd read it the first time, she'd put the letter back in exactly the same place, between the recipes where she'd found it. She liked the idea that it might have been there for over sixty years, filed between Mother's Irish Stew and Quince Jam the whole time.

Emily finally found the folded blue sheet of paper she was looking for.

The letter looked so out of place it was hard to believe it could have been missed for all those years. But then again, there were lots of other odd pieces of paper with recipes from various friends and family members.

Now Emily thought about it, Gran had always been extremely protective of her recipes – but not the *recipes* as such, just the ori-ginals. If you wanted one of her recipes, she was more than happy to share it, but she would find it, write it out herself, and then hand over the copy – no one was ever allowed to rifle through her papers willy-nilly. Emily thought she knew why.

She unfolded the letter and handed it to Jake, then sipped her now lukewarm tea and watched his face light up as he read.

*October 18th 1947*

*Dear Miss Rose,*

*It really was the greatest pleasure to again make your acquaintance in London this last year.*

*Your uncle tells me you are betrothed to a grazier and soon to be married and then make your new life in the interior of the wide brown land that is Australia. He tells me the place is a small village called Woop Woop, but the twinkle in his eye, not unlike your own, and the fact*

*I could not find the name on any map, suggests he may have been doing what you taught me Australians are very apt to do; that is, 'pulling my leg'. You are indeed an intriguing people with a peculiar language. But I digress.*

*Please accept my gift for your nuptials of seven (a sacred number in my land and faith, and I believe your own) of Golconda's finest — left rough for you to have cut and set as you desire. They are, I think, almost the exact shade of your unusual and enchanting eyes.*

*You and your husband would be extended the most gracious welcome should you ever find yourselves in my, what would you say, 'neck of the woods'? (See, I have managed to retain some of what you taught me in our short time together!)*

*I wish you all the very best of health and happiness for the future.*

*With the kindest regards,*
*Prince Ali*

After a few minutes Jake carefully put the note aside.

'Wow, Em, that's beautiful,' he said, gazing at her. 'You've got the same coloured eyes as she had, haven't you? I didn't really notice before, but they're quite like the diamonds too. And very lovely.'

'Thanks.' She felt uncomfortable under his close scrutiny. 'Yes, mine are almost exactly the same as Gran's, except I think hers were a darker blue,' she said. Her eyes were the only physical attribute Emily had ever really liked about herself. Otherwise she was quite plain, from her boring mouse-brown hair – these days in a bob – to her average height, weight, and breast size.

The silence stretched into awkward territory.

Jake was looking at Emily, but she was still thinking about Gran. And thinking about Gran was making her feel sad and emotional. With a jolt she realised this was her first Christmas without her. *Don't you dare cry!* She needed to change the subject, not that that was really possible. She swallowed hard before speaking.

'So how did you come to do a gemmology course, anyway?'

Jake seemed to snap back to the present. 'A couple of years back I was looking into obscure ways to meet women and went and did a weekend course – figured I may as well learn something while I was at it.'

'And did you, meet the woman of your dreams, that is?'

'God no! It was the weirdest group of people I've ever come across in one place at one time. There was something odd – unnervingly odd – about all of them. Except me of course. I was the only normal one there. But it was interesting.'

'Well I'm glad you went.' *And didn't meet the woman of your dreams*, Emily mentally added, then wanted to kick herself. *Where did that come from?* A relationship really was the last thing she needed right now.

'So what do you want to do? I'm dying to know if they are all still here.'

'Hmm, me too, sort of. For all I know, she sold them off one by one when she needed to – she and Grandpa went through some pretty tough times on the farm,' Emily said.

'Selling them would have been next to impossible up until around ten years ago. De Beers had a monopoly; uncut diamonds wouldn't have been able to be bought or sold. Unless of course your dear old gran had some black market connections.'

'Who knows? I didn't know she had diamonds rattling around in her button jar all this time. Anyway, if they *are* there, they belong to Mum and Auntie Peggy – they're the next of kin.'

'Not necessarily – it's your button jar, given to you by your gran herself...'

'But...'

'She knew the diamond or diamonds were in there, remember, and she gave them to you *before* she died. For that reason they'd never be considered part of her estate, if it came to the crunch.'

'Hmm.'

'You probably should put them somewhere a bit safer, though.'

'Like where?'

'I don't know. A bank vault?'

Emily thought for a moment. 'No; if there are any more, they've been here this long and they belong with the buttons — it's what Gran would want.'

'I'm not sure that's wise. But fair enough; it's your decision. So, do you want to keep looking for the other diamonds or not?'

'I can't decide. Of course I'm dying to know, but it could change everything. While I don't know, things can stay much the same.'

'Nothing ever stays the same for long, you know. Anyway, it's fate. If I wasn't here, you wouldn't have found them today and we wouldn't be having this conversation.'

'So it's meant to be — I'm meant to look for them, you reckon?'

'Yes I do. If you weren't meant to, none of this would have happened.'

'That's what Barbara would say.'

'Well, from the little I've seen, she's a very smart woman.'

'All right, I'm convinced. But I think we should carry on with how we were doing it and see if they turn up.'

'Good plan.'

They got up and went back to the bench where the buttons were waiting.

# Chapter Six

'Yoo-hoo, anyone home!?'

'Oh, that'll be Dad,' Emily said to Jake, still standing beside her at the bench. 'I'll put these away.'

He stepped aside as she picked up the towel, folded it over the remaining buttons and put it back into the ice-cream container. After placing the three uncut diamonds they had found on top, she put the container back in the pantry along with the half-full jar. As she did, she marvelled at how calm she was about it all.

*Could I really be sitting on a fortune?* Emily wondered as she went down the hall to let her father in. *Imagine being able to fully renovate in one fell swoop!*

'Coming,' Emily called to buy some time to compose herself. *What a morning!*

Just before she got to the door, she turned to Jake. 'This is going to sound strange, but can you please not mention the diamonds to anyone yet? Not even Dad?'

'Sure. And it's not strange at all.'

Emily wasn't sure why she wanted to keep them a secret, but she felt better knowing that she could always change her mind later. She took a deep breath and opened the door.

'Hi Dad,' she said, giving her father a big hug. 'Merry Christmas, again.'

'Hi Jake, lovely to see you again.'

'Likewise, Des. Merry Christmas,' Jake said, stepping around Emily onto the verandah to shake his hand.

'For you,' Des said, holding out a bottle of wine.

'Thank you.'

'So, Jake, I hear you're doing some work in Whyalla – that's a long way from home, isn't it?'

Emily cast her mind back to the ice-cream container in the kitchen and the possibilities within.

They were still standing on the verandah – Emily deep in her own thoughts and Jake and Des in conversation – when David and Barbara arrived a few minutes later.

Cries of 'Merry Christmas!' rang out as they emerged from the car. Barbara was in her often worn attire of sandals, beige tailored pants and a neatly pressed but untucked short-sleeved shirt in emerald green. Being lean but robust, she always seemed to have a no-nonsense, efficient air about her. As usual, David was well-dressed; today in navy pants and a white long-sleeved shirt with a self-stripe and brocade design. For a moment Emily was struck by how much like a younger version of Des he was — except for his fine head of thick brown hair compared to her father's wiry grey.

Once they had greeted each other, they all banded together to bring in what seemed an extraordinary number of bags and an esky from David and Barbara's white dual cab ute.

'Makes my wine look a little paltry,' Des said, accepting a carry bag from Barbara.

Barbara laughed. 'Don't worry, Des, it's nothing exciting — just some crackers and tinsel for us to drape about.'

'I was hoping you'd forgotten,' Emily said, rolling her eyes.

'Never!' Barbara said, making an exaggerated show of kissing her on the cheek. 'Time for you to get into the Christmas spirit, missy.'

'Sounds like we're in for quite an afternoon.' Des laughed.

'You better believe it!'

The small group made its way inside.

'Something smells good,' Barbara said, as they entered the kitchen. 'Anything I can help with?'

'Nope, everything is under control,' Emily said. 'I've decided to keep it all simple. You can make the place look festive if you like.'

'Good plan.' Barbara gave her arm a pat. 'Why don't you help since you're so organised?'

Emily raised an eyebrow, but reluctantly gave in. 'Right, Jake and David can be in charge of drinks and Dad, you can take a seat.'

'Sounds good to me,' Des said, beaming, as he settled onto one of the wooden kitchen chairs.

As Barbara and Emily set to work draping tinsel over everything that could be draped over, Emily found herself beginning to like the idea of Christmas.

They finished by constructing a simple but very lovely centrepiece out of crackers, strings of beads, bright shiny glass baubles and other assorted Christmas decorations. It was quite an impressive transformation, especially considering they'd only taken a few minutes.

Before long they were all seated at the huge wooden kitchen table with drinks in front of them. They toasted merry Christmas and clinked glasses.

Then Emily got up to put the vegetables on whilst urging Barbara to remain seated.

'So, Jake, what brings you over our way again?' David asked.

'I've been consulting on a project for a friend of an old friend from uni who's the planning officer for the City of Whyalla. I suppose you've heard about the Civic Centre renovation they're doing – spending an absolute fortune on it.'

'Yes, I think I saw something on the news the other week,' David said, nodding.

'Well they want to keep the old buildings, add more space and tie it all together – blend the old and the new. Right up my alley. I'm designing it, drawing up the plans, and then continuing to consult on the project. It'll be something quite special when it's finished. Probably take a bit over six months to complete. So I might be needing to escape to the country for quite a while yet.'

'So you're moving to Whyalla for six months?!'

Emily was aghast. Next to the sort of life she imagined he led in Melbourne, it seemed unbelievable that he'd choose to spend so much time in a place like Whyalla.

She'd always found Whyalla a bit grimy and drab. After all, the steelworks was its lifeblood. If Emily wanted to shop at one of the larger stores only available in a city, she preferred to drive down to Port Lincoln instead. The ocean views were much more prominent there, and the whole place had a cleaner, calmer feel to it.

'Oh come now, it won't be that bad, surely?'

Emily responded with raised eyebrows. She exchanged a look with Barbara, who winked.

'I'm teasing. No, I won't be staying for the whole six months; I'll be travelling back and forth a bit. I'm only consulting – not managing the whole project.'

Emily felt the slightest ache of disappointment seep into her heart.

The next few hours passed with loud chatter punctuated by clinking of cutlery, people moaning about eating too much, and then consuming yet more food and drink. Emily's meal was a hit and everyone was effusive with their praise.

'You have no idea how good it's been to do absolutely nothing today after all the work around the funeral and having people to stay,' Barbara declared when the tea and coffee and chocolates Jake had brought had been consumed and the table cleared.

'I'm sorry, have you lost someone recently?' Jake said, concern in his voice.

'Sorry, I forgot to tell you,' Emily said.

'David's dear old dad,' Barbara explained.

'Oh, I'm so sorry. And right before Christmas too,' Jake said. 'Golly, that's tough.'

'Thanks mate,' David said. 'But honestly, it's a bit of a blessing. He was heartbroken after losing Mum last year. They were married for forty-eight years.'

They fell silent.

'Actually I'm exhausted,' Barbara said after a minute or so. 'Would you mind terribly if we went home, darling?' she asked, laying a hand on David's arm. 'Sorry to be a piker, Em, but I think it's all finally catching up with me.'

'Not at all. You rest up for our barbeque tomorrow,' Emily replied.

'Can I help do the dishes before I go?' Barbara said.

'No way, they can wait.'

'I'll do them later,' Jake chimed in.

'Don't worry about the decorations either – I'll return them another day.'

They all got up and made their way out of the kitchen and down the hall.

'Are you okay?' Emily asked, putting an arm around Barbara when they got outside and onto the verandah. Looking at her friend, she realised for the first time just how exhausted she looked.

'Yeah, it's probably nothing a decent sleep and an empty house won't fix. I'm sure I'll be fine for tomorrow. Sorry to skip out on you like this.'

'Oh don't be ridiculous! You've got nothing to apologise for. Thanks for coming,' Emily said, hugging her. 'And it's really no problem if you do decide you don't feel up to heading out tomorrow.'

'I'm sure I'll be fine. Thank you for a lovely Christmas day,' Barbara said.

'Yes, thanks, Em,' David said, giving Emily a quick hug. 'See you tomorrow, eleven o'clock at the mailboxes. Right?'

'Perfect,' Emily said.

'And bring your camera, Jake. I've got a good spot in mind for your photography.'

'Great, thanks mate,' Jake said.

'Hopefully you'll get a nice day; I think they're forecasting rain,' Des said, and Emily wondered if she shouldn't have mentioned their plans in front of him. She hadn't invited her parents. But her father didn't seem at all perturbed.

Enid would have been very annoyed not to have been included, and would have sulked until Emily relented and invited her, which was what Emily used to do. These days she was getting better at ignoring the cold shoulder.

Why shouldn't she have her own friends and do things with them? Why did she have to always invite her mother or be made to feel guilty about it if she didn't? It was all very childish; behaviour more reminiscent of a school playground. She couldn't believe she'd put up with it for so long – pretty much her whole adult life until leaving John.

Barbara was right when she'd said that in leaving John she'd been essentially standing up to her mother as well. Emily could see that now; and she did feel stronger, and freer, for doing it. *Two birds with one stone*, she thought. She just had to stay strong.

Des and Jake exchanged handshakes with David and pecked Barbara on the cheek, and then Emily, Jake, and Des waved them off from the high verandah before heading back inside.

'I'd probably better get going too,' Des said, hovering in the hall.

It looked to Emily like he didn't want to go, but was concerned about outstaying his welcome.

'You can't go yet. You haven't given me the ladder,' she said, remembering her request from that morning. No one had mentioned the topic of her buying the house over lunch. She supposed everyone thought it was her place to bring it up.

'I'll just get it now,' Des said, striding down the sweeping steps.

'I'll help,' Jake said, moving after him.

A few moments later Jake was back beside her with the ladder under his arm. He leant it against the outside wall of the house. 'So, is this for me to do a pre-purchase inspection or some minor repairs? I've been waiting all day for you to share your exciting news.'

'You and me both,' Des said.

'Come on back inside and I'll tell you all about it,' Emily said, leading the way. She darted into her room to retrieve the paperwork.

'Hmm, very mysterious,' Des muttered as he and Jake made their way back down the hall to the kitchen.

When they were settled in their respective chairs again, Emily swallowed deeply, cleared her throat, and began speaking.

'So, Donald and Trevor Baker have offered to sell me the house and approximately twenty acres of surrounding land. They want ten thousand dollars upfront – five to each of them – to fund a trip they want to make overseas. They're on the pension,' she explained to Jake, 'so they have to be careful about earning too much.'

The men nodded.

'Then I would have to pay another instalment of ten thousand dollars – again five thousand to each of them – each year for the next nineteen years. It's a total of two hundred thousand dollars. Oh, and I also have to pay all costs associated with the subdivision of the title.'

Jake and her father sat in silence.

Emily put the document on the huge timber table, as if to prove she wasn't making it all up. She frowned thoughtfully, trying to remember whether there was anything she'd forgotten.

'Wow,' Jake said. 'That sounds like a fantastic offer to me.'

'It does indeed,' Des said, nodding.

'Ordinarily it would almost be too good to be true,' Emily said.

'But...?' Jake prompted.

'I don't have much money,' Emily said, the words coming out more like a sigh.

'Hmm,' Jake said.

'I've got around forty thousand. So I can probably make the first two payments, depending on how much subdivision costs are – and providing the roof doesn't need replacing straight away and the wiring doesn't turn to poop.'

'Right,' Jake said. He looked a little uncomfortable; probably from learning such intimate details about her finance.

'So,' Emily went on, forcing herself not to dwell on the negative aspects, 'I want to know what you both think, honestly. Dad, whether you think it's a good idea, generally; if I can find the money that is. Jake, how much I would need to do the place up – if it's even worth it – and if you know how much subdivision costs would be.'

Emily had spoken quickly and was now quite out of breath. She swallowed deeply a couple of times and then sat wringing her hands in her lap. She was eager to hear what they had to say, but also scared of what that might be.

# Chapter Seven

'Dad? Jake?' she asked, looking from one to the other.

Jake indicated for Des to speak first.

'I think it's a great idea – depending on financing of course – and of course we'll help any way we can. Though I would have to do some careful work on your mother,' he added. 'But Jake here's in a better position to give advice. What are your thoughts, mate, from a practical perspective?'

'Well, I'd rather have a good look around the house before I commit to a professional opinion, but my initial thought is that it sounds like a fantastic opportunity. As to the question of subdivision costs – I'm afraid you're probably looking at around fifteen thousand. It's interesting you ask, actually. Anthony – my mate in Whyalla – and I were only discussing subdivision the other night. A lot of the farmers on the outskirts of the city are cashing in on the expansion of the steelworks, so there's land being carved up all over the place.'

'Oh. I had no idea it would be that much,' Emily said, her shoulders slumping in response. 'There's no way I can afford to do it then,' she said quietly. She wished she'd known that before getting her hopes up. She thought of the diamonds, but dismissed them. To part with something Gran had given her would be wrong, wouldn't it?

'We've got a rainy-day account,' Des offered.

'Thanks Dad, but there's no way Mum would agree to use it for this – you heard her when I moved in; she thinks the place is a dump. Anyway, it's not exactly raining.'

'What's a rainy day if it's not helping to get our only child back on her feet and happy?' he said, reaching across the table and giving her hands a squeeze.

'Thanks Dad,' she said, attempting a weak smile. Looking at him smiling warmly back at her, she felt her heart clamp. It was one of the nicest things he'd ever said to her.

'There's always more than one way to skin a rabbit,' Jake said brightly. 'We'll just have to put our heads together and come up with an outside-the-box plan.'

'Or just rob a bank.' Emily groaned.

'Or rob a bank,' Des said.

'If they want their overseas trip within the next twelve months, you'll have to get cracking,' Jake said, poking at the paperwork lying on the table. 'Anthony was saying it takes around six months to complete a subdivision. But if I were you, I wouldn't sign anything beyond a basic agreement of their terms before the subdivision is done and dusted.'

'Six months! I had no idea it would take that long.'

'Well I guess in one way it's good; it'll give you some breathing space to sort out the finance,' he added with a shrug.

'What do Barbara and David think about it — I take it you have discussed it with them?' Des asked.

'They said I should go for it and that they'd even loan me the money if necessary. But I couldn't; it wouldn't feel right to borrow from friends.'

'I agree, but it's very good of them to offer.'

'Pity they couldn't buy the whole farm and then sell off the bit to you. Not that I know anything about their circumstances or anything,' Jake said. 'Just thinking aloud.'

'The old brothers probably wouldn't want to sell everything because it would definitely muck up their pensions,' Des said.

'Hmm,' Emily added.

'But if they did, and invested wisely, they might not even need the pension,' Jake said.

'Ah yes,' Des said, 'but they're of the view that it's owed to them – their right for being lucky enough to be Australian. So they'll have it at all costs, thank you very much.'

'That's crazy.'

'I agree,' Des said, holding his hands up in surrender. 'But it's how most people around here think.'

They lapsed into thoughtful silence until Des broke it a few moments later.

'Actually, on a slightly different tack, Em, there's something you should know,' he said quietly.

'Oh?'

'Yes, about John and the Strattens.' Des shifted in his chair and examined his lap. 'You're going to find out soon enough and I'd rather you heard it from me, as much as I hate to...'

'Dad, come on, you're scaring me,' Emily pleaded.

'They've paid him out of the family company – apparently to the tune of around three hundred thousand dollars. I'm sure my information is reliable.'

Emily felt the blood drain from her face. Out of the corner of her eye she noticed Jake looking very uncomfortable.

'I think I'll go and unpack,' he said, putting his hands on the table. 'You clearly need your privacy.'

'No, don't feel you have to go, it's okay,' Emily said, lifting her hand and touching his arm. 'It's not a secret.'

'I'm really sorry, Em,' said Des. 'I knew it would be a shock, but I didn't think it would upset you this much.'

'It wouldn't have a week ago, but this changes everything,' she said, prodding the paperwork in front of her.

'I don't understand,' Jake said.

'I told you how my ex, John, had ripped me off in the financial settlement – I suspected he had, but I couldn't be bothered fighting him. It was hard enough getting up the courage to leave him, let alone try and fight the richest family in the district for a decent payout. But it's too late now. It's not the money; it's the deceit that gets me. No wonder he was in such a hurry to get me to sign on the dotted line; he was coming into a stack of money. I know it was the wrong thing to do – sign without having a lawyer or accountant go through everything – but I was just so tired; just wanted it to be over and to start getting on with my life.' She smiled sadly. 'What a bloody idiot, right?' she added, with a deep sigh.

'Not at all, not at all,' Des said, patting her hand. 'You did what you needed to do – and that was the right thing for you at the time. There's nothing to beat yourself up over. You were conned, plain and simple. You just need to decide what to do about it now.'

'Nothing. There's nothing I can do,' she said, burying her face in her hands.

One hundred and fifty thousand dollars – half of that payout – would probably have been enough to do the subdivision and most of the renovating.

'If only I'd known before I signed,' she said.

'Unfortunately, my dear, I think that was the point,' Des said, looking sadly at his daughter and shaking his head slowly.

Jake was frowning. 'I don't want to pry or anything, but didn't you and John only recently separate?' he asked.

'Yes, just over a month ago. What difference does that make?'

'Well, I thought you had two years to settle financial matters.'

'I told you. We already have.'

'But if you can prove he lied about his assets…'

'I appreciate your concern, Jake, but it's too late.'

'Listen. What I'm saying is that you might be able to reclaim – there's a two-year window; I'm almost certain of it.'

Emily wasn't sure if he was excited, frustrated, or angry – he was getting quite animated and considerably louder.

'At least ask the advice of a decent lawyer. And if you can't afford to, I'll bloody well pay for it! I don't want to see a friend of mine ripped off.'

Jake's face was now quite red. Definitely angry, Emily decided. She stared at him, wondering at his sudden change in manner.

'Sorry, I just hate to see injustice,' he said, getting up and starting to pace back and forth alongside the kitchen window.

Emily watched him, still surprised at his outburst.

Des cleared his throat before speaking. 'Jake, one of the things we need to remember is that this is a very small district...'

'Why should that make a difference?'

'It shouldn't, but unfortunately it does. If Emily were to go for what you and I know to be her fair share, she'd run the risk of being run out of town – shunned at the very least.'

'You cannot be serious! This is the twenty-first century!'

'But in some ways not.' Des sighed. 'It's hard to believe, but such things do go on.'

Emily looked at Jake's confused expression.

'The farmers around here are like a protected species, and if they're threatened – especially by a woman – they close ranks,' she explained.

Jake's eyebrows rose sharply.

'They won't actually tar and feather you and drive you out into the scrub,' she said with a tight laugh, 'but I have seen people's lives made very difficult.'

'So leave, then. Pack up and leave.'

'But why should she?' Des said.

'If it's what it takes to get her fair share – what's legally hers – why not? You're entitled to something.'

'I already got something – forty thousand,' Emily said quietly.

'Well pardon my French, but that's bullshit! If John has just received three hundred thousand – half of that should be yours.'

Emily shook her head. 'Anyway, it's not just about the money. It's about being able to hold my head up – and my parents being able to as well.'

'You'd give up the chance to set yourself up financially, to make an easier life for yourself, because of what people *think*?' Jake stared at her, aghast.

'Money isn't everything.' Emily hated saying those words when right now the money really *was* everything to her. But she knew the cost would be just too great – financial and emotional. The Strattens could afford the best lawyers, have it drag out for years, whittling away her precious few resources until she had to give in in the end anyway.

It might be gutless for her to let it go – and she might regret it every day for the rest of her life – but she didn't have the energy for a fight. Jake simply didn't understand.

'I'll just have to find another way to make this happen,' Emily said, more to herself than to the others.

'Well, if you're sure,' Jake said. 'You're an intelligent woman – as, Des, you are an intelligent man. If both of you say this is how it works out here, then far be it from me to argue. But if there's anything I can do to help then you only have to ask,' he said, coming back to the table and sitting down heavily.

'Thanks Jake,' Emily said, offering him a tight smile.

'We appreciate it, mate,' Des said.

'All I hope is that what goes around really does come around,' Jake added through clenched teeth, 'and that this John character gets his comeuppance somehow or other.'

'Hear, hear,' Des said quietly.

A feeling of comfort settled upon Emily as she glanced at Jake and then at her father. It felt good to have their support, and to have everything out in the open. Gran was right – a problem shared was indeed a problem halved.

She wasn't at all embarrassed to have Jake know how bad her financial situation was. He wasn't the sort that would pity her.

She'd find a way to make her dream of owning and renovating the house a reality – no matter how long it took. She'd phone Donald and Trevor later and let them know she accepted their kind offer.

Again she thought about the uncut diamonds mixed up with Gran's buttons. Was it something she should at least look into?

*If only Gran was here to ask.*

# Chapter Eight

Emily took the men out and showed them the proposed boundary, then left them to have a good look around without her. She wanted them to appraise the house and surrounds without feeling constrained in their comments.

Back in the kitchen, she began tackling the pile of dishes left over from lunch. She was desperate to return to looking for the diamonds, but forced herself to stick to the task at hand. She couldn't have said why, but she didn't want to tell her father about them yet, and didn't want to risk being interrupted when Jake and Des came back in.

She glanced out the kitchen window. They were apparently in deep, animated conversation, both indicating something with outstretched arms. There was plenty of nodding and agreement going on. Emily smiled at how well they seemed to get along.

Grace, who had chosen to stay outside, was watching their goings-on intently, her head cocked to one side as was her habit. Emily thought she looked like she wanted to round them up. *Well, she is a sheepdog.* She grinned and returned her attention to the dishes beneath the suds in the sink.

She had just finished laying the baking pan on a tea towel to dry when there was a loud noise above her. Startled, she looked up, half expecting a section of ceiling to fall down. But her heart rate settled when the next noises she heard were voices and then the steady sound of crunching and creaking – footsteps.

Ah, Jake and her dad must have gone up onto the roof to check it out.

She hadn't wanted to impose on Jake and didn't want her father going up there alone. But she did need to know how much longer the iron would last before it needed to be replaced.

David and Des had checked for leaks inside the roof space the day she'd moved in, but that didn't tell her the condition of the roof as a whole. She'd seen from up on the hill that it was very rusty, but she'd known of people living under roofs in that state for years, even decades.

The muffled voices accompanying the creaks and groans became gradually quieter as the men made their way to the other side of the house.

Emily had finished drying and putting away the dishes, and had just made a jug of iced lemon cordial when she heard their voices outside in the bathroom.

A few minutes later they came back in chattering loudly, and sat down at the table. Both men's hair was unruly and windswept, and their faces were flushed. Emily was glad she had thought to prepare the cold drink. She put glasses on the table and sat down.

'Well, the good news is we didn't fall through the roof,' Des said, grinning. There were beads of perspiration on his forehead, face and neck, and his wiry grey hair was sticking up all over the place.

'And the bad news is?' Emily asked, not really wanting to know.

'That unfortunately the roof will need to be replaced – sometime in the next year or so,' Jake replied. 'Unless you get a ferocious hail storm – some sections are paper-thin.'

'So how much would a new roof cost me?'

'You'd need around twenty grand,' Jake said.

'Great,' she said with a groan. 'Anything else I need to know?'

'Nope, it's a great place. Bit tired, but structurally it looks pretty safe and sound,' Jake said.

'If I were you I'd do all I could to take the Bakers up on their offer,' Des added.

'That's the conclusion I've come to,' Emily said, feeling neither buoyed nor disappointed.

'Hmm,' Des and Jake murmured in unison, catching sight of the cordial. 'That looks good.

'Thirsty work.' Des reached for the jug. 'Jake? Em?' he asked.

'Yes please. That would be great.' Jake handed over his glass.

Emily handed over her glass with a nod.

'This isn't homemade by any chance?' Jake asked.

'It is actually,' Emily said.

'As good as always, Em,' Des said, emptying his glass and filling it up again.

'It's incredible,' Jake said. 'Is there any limit to your talents? Jam making, cooking, cordial; and that's all I know about. Can't believe that husband of yours let you go.'

'He didn't have much of a choice,' Emily said. She instantly went a shade of deep crimson, which she tried to cover up by staring down at the tablecloth. But it didn't go unnoticed.

'I'm sorry, I shouldn't have said that,' Jake said, looking embarrassed.

'It's okay.' Emily took a sip of her drink.

'Ah, don't be sorry, Jake,' Des said. 'It's true. John Stratten certainly did not deserve my Emily. Good riddance.'

'Not according to Mum,' Emily said, shocked at hearing her thoughts out loud – she thought they'd stayed locked away in her head.

'Emily, dear, sometimes your mother can be a nincompoop,' Des Oliphant said, taking another long slug of drink as if to drive home the point.

'I just don't understand why Mum chose to listen to John and not ask *me* for the truth, Dad. Where's the loyalty?'

Emily saw that Jake was shifting in his chair and looking about for a means of escape again. She felt for him, but she was on a roll and didn't want to stop.

It was rare she had her father to herself, and she needed to get some things off her chest. She'd stayed silent too long, holding onto her feelings and trying so hard not to hurt anyone. And where had that got her?

'If there's something you need to tell me, Em, I suggest you do so,' her father said in a gentle tone. 'Bottling things up is never a suitable long-term solution – it just ends up with an explosion sooner or later.'

'John told Mum I left because he tore down an old cottage I was interested in doing up,' Emily said to Jake.

'It was a lovely old limestone place with brick quoins – lots of potential,' Des said, wistfully.

'I don't understand. He demolished a building because you showed too much interest?'

'Under the guise of needing the space for a hayshed,' Emily added.

'When there were over two hundred other suitable acres around the house to choose from, mind you,' Des said. 'I really didn't want to believe he could be that spiteful.' He shook his head.

'Gosh, sounds like a nasty piece of work.'

'Oh yes. But that wasn't the worst of it.'

'So, um, if you didn't leave because of that, why did you?'

'Because he shot at Grace,' she said.

Two mouths dropped open and wide eyes stared back at her, and then at Grace who was curled up in her bed in the corner, oblivious.

'He *shot* at her? Why?' Jake said.

'His excuse was that he was warning her, joking or something,' Emily replied with a shrug. She was surprised to find her eyes filling with tears; had thought it no longer affected her. 'I just wanted to protect her – I'm the only one who can,' she said, wiping a hand across her nose, which had started to run a little.

'Oh Em, I had no idea,' Des said, reaching across and patting her hand while shaking his head slowly. 'Why didn't you tell me?'

Emily raised her eyebrows and looked at him knowingly. 'And then he had the nerve to rip you off!?' Jake cried. 'I would have thought he'd have wanted to pay you off so you didn't tell anyone what a piece of shit he is. Apologies for the language, but I just can't believe what I'm hearing!'

'No one around here would really care,' Des said to Jake. 'Farmers shoot work dogs all the time – if they get into the sheep, if they don't come when they're called, if they go left instead of right... It's what they do.'

'Sounds barbaric.'

'I agree, but it's apparently quite acceptable behaviour. He would have just explained it away and made out that Emily was throwing a hissy fit. Being a townie – not raised on a farm – her reaction would have been brushed aside as typical.'

Jake's jaw hung open in disbelief. 'So instead, he told your mother you left because he demolished the cottage – like you *had* just thrown a hissy fit? Why not tell her the real story, Em? I don't get it.'

'I guess I didn't want to shatter her impression of him – however deluded.'

'Why ever not? After the way he treated you! I wouldn't mind betting that a man capable of tearing down a cottage out of spite and shooting at your dog just for fun wouldn't have been the nicest of husbands all round.'

'No. No he wasn't, actually.'

At that moment Emily was bombarded with the very vivid mental image of John laying his steel-capped work boot into the kelpie they'd had before Grace. It was the moment she had decided that she could not – *would* not – have children with a man so cruel; she would never have children at all, because marriage was for life.

And now it struck her that she was no longer under that particu-lar obligation either. Emily had so forcefully put the notion of children out of her mind that she didn't know how she felt about it now, other than somewhat unsettled. She was days away from her thirty-second birthday. Would her biologi-cal clock start frantic-ally ticking at some point? God, it was too much to contemplate. She almost put a hand to her forehead, but stopped herself just in time, and instead forced her attention back to Jake, who had just asked her a question.

'Well, why let your mother continue to think otherwise, especially now you've left him?'

'My wife, whom I do love dearly, bless her, tends to get a bit star struck,' Des said. 'When Emily married the most eligible man in the district – supposedly anyway – Enid thought it was the best thing since sliced bread,' he continued. 'Even if Emily had told her the truth, it wouldn't have made any difference. She has the Strattens so high up on a pedestal that she would never hear a word against any of them. In her opinion Emily blew it. John couldn't do anything that would warrant her leaving, because the Strattens have the wealth and social standing Enid has always craved. The wealth I couldn't give her, as it turned out,' he added quietly.

'Money isn't everything,' Jake asked.

'I'm afraid Enid has never quite grasped the concept that money doesn't buy happiness.'

'But surely she can see it now; that his money wasn't enough to keep her daughter happy?'

'No, I'm afraid she just thinks Emily is a fool. Sorry dear,' he added, grimacing at his daughter.

'And I haven't had the heart to tell her that he's actually quite broke – well, he was until the payout from the family company,' Emily said.

'He is? He was?' Des said in disbelief.

'Yep,' she said, taking a sip of cordial. 'Last time I saw the bank accounts they were almost empty.' Emily left it at that. She could have told them about the trips to the casino, the amount he spent on beer, hard liquor, and cigarettes each week, but chose not to.

Emily couldn't believe the frank discussion she was having with her father. She felt a little exhilarated; pleased it was out in the open, but at the same time disappointed. The person who really needed to hear all this – her mother – wasn't hearing it. Again she had the unsettling feeling that everything had changed yet nothing was different.

She and Des reached for the jug at the same time. It seemed they were both trying to fill the awkward silence.

'Sorry,' they muttered to each other.

'Allow me,' Jake said, picking up the jug and filling up their glasses. They settled back into their separate thoughts.

As Emily leant back from the table, the urge to continue the conversation about her mother's issues sat like a heavy cloud over her. But she couldn't ask her father – he was probably already regretting what he had said.

If Enid knew and understood, would it make things better? Or could it actually make things worse? Her mother, after all, was an expert at seeing what she wanted to see and ignoring what she didn't.

Emily hated that about her; the apparent vagueness, like a roller blind coming down when something arose that Enid didn't want to hear, believe or confront.

She supposed she must have got her own forthrightness from her father – though he rarely showed it like he had today. He kept a lid on it when Enid was within hearing. How could someone live like that, day after day, year after year? And why would they?

Emily went over what her father had said and how he'd said it, and thought she detected an undercurrent of guilt – as if Enid was somehow the way she was because of him. Because he hadn't been wealthy enough.

No. It probably had more to do with Enid feeling second best. She remembered their conversation from only a week or so ago, when Des had told her about his first – and possibly only – true love, Katherine Baker; how she'd been killed in a riding accident all those years ago. How sad he'd seemed, sitting under the apricot tree just up the gully. It was as though it had only happened yesterday, not four decades before.

Emily wondered if John was *her* first true love and if she'd ever get over him. But she couldn't imagine he'd still bring tears to her eyes in a year, let alone decades. Perhaps that was the difference with someone dying as opposed to a relationship ending.

Oh, who was she kidding? She had thought she loved him, but really, if she was honest with herself, it wasn't the deep, Romeo and Juliet type of love people talked about.

What would Gran have said about it? The woman who gave up an Indian prince to spend her life in the sticks doing it tough with a farmer. She'd never know.

Again the urge came upon her to look for the rest of Gran's diamonds, but she knew now that she'd never be able to part with them. Their sentimental value was too great. Part of Emily knew it was ridiculous, but another part wondered if they perhaps held some kind of magical power on account of their being from India.

Was it coincidence that she had finally gained the strength to leave John so soon after she'd been given the button jar?

'Gosh, I didn't realise how late it was getting,' Emily said, staring at her watch a little disbelievingly. It was almost six o'clock. 'There are plenty of leftovers for us to pick at for tea. Or perhaps you'd just like tea or coffee and some fruitcake.' She'd meant to get it out just after lunch, but Jake had produced a huge box of chocolates that they'd immediately begun devouring.

'I'd love a cuppa and some cake, but I'm not sure I can fit it in,' Jake said.

'Seriously mate, Emily's fruitcake is well worth finding room for,' Des said.

'It'll still be here later or tomorrow, or possibly next week,' Emily said with a laugh.

'Oh, what the hell,' Jake said. 'May as well go the whole hog. It *is* Christmas after all. I'll have some cake and a cup of Milo – if that's okay – and then later I'm going to sit and do some drawings and notes for your project here.'

'Surely not on your weekend off.'

'Just a few doodles; it's not exactly work. And anyway, I'm excited by the potential; I want to put together some options and suggestions for you.'

'Well, that would be great. Thanks Jake,' Emily said, trying to sound brighter than she felt.

'My pleasure. Anyway, I've got to do something for my keep – I might be imposing on you quite a bit over the next few months. If you let me.'

*I like the sound of that*, Emily thought, and would have said the words aloud if her father hadn't been sitting right there.

# Chapter Nine

Emily would have served the tea and cake in the lounge room, but there were only two old armchairs. Bringing in a hard wooden kitchen chair would completely ruin what little ambience there was. And of course, being a gentleman, Jake would have insisted she sit on one of the comfy chairs. *One day I'll fill the room with decent furniture*, she told herself, and then sighed; there were so many things that would have to come before that, when funds permitted. Why did everything have to revolve around money?

When they had finished their cake and the men had refused a second slice, Emily suggested they go and rest in the lounge while she rinsed the few dishes they'd just dirtied. Jake tried to help her, but she was almost forceful in ushering them out of the kitchen and across the hall.

'Best not to argue, mate,' Des Oliphant said, leading the way.

Emily was glad to be left to her own thoughts for a few moments; she'd join them soon. Bloody John. A few weeks ago she'd been okay with the knowledge that he'd ripped her off, and had pretty much washed her hands of the whole business. But the revelation of just how much – and how badly she now needed the money – made her feel very depressed and angry.

Not that she had any choice but to make the most of things. As Gran had been fond of saying, 'There are plenty of people worse off than you, dear. Count your blessings.'

*And what are they?* She wondered with a stab of self-pity.

Several hundred thousand dollars' worth of uncut diamonds? *That I can't do anything with*, she added bitterly. Why all the bloody torment over money? Maybe it was a sign from the universe. But of what, that it's a cruel, heartless place?

If everything revolved around karma; good begetting good, bad begetting bad, then what the hell had she done wrong? Was it marrying John? Or perhaps leaving him? And why wasn't he being punished, after the way he'd treated her?

She felt the hairs all over her body stand up. A shiver rippled through her for barely a second before leaving again. She was left feeling slightly rattled, but with no idea why.

She forced her concentration back to the dishes in the sink. Emily moved her hands back and forth, enjoying the warmth of the water through her rubber gloves. But thoughts of John didn't stay banished for long. Seconds later he was back on her mind.

This time it was the night of their honeymoon when he'd forced himself on her. At the time she hadn't thought of it as rape. He was her husband. It was his right, right?

She'd pretended to laugh it off – a trick she'd learnt while being bullied at school – but she had felt violated and dirty. Who could she have told anyway? Her mother? And be told simply that it was her wifely duty?

And this wasn't something Emily could share with Gran.

No, she had decided at the time, for now she would just have to grin and bear it. But not long after that, she discovered that it wasn't enough to just 'lie back and think of England'. She had to learn to fake orgasm as well.

John's ego, and, she quickly realised, his own pleasure relied upon this charade. Otherwise he would spend ages humping and heaving on top of her before it was finally over.

Emily wondered if she would ever enjoy sex. Perhaps John had ruined her for any man in the future; she certainly couldn't imagine trusting anyone so completely again.

The thought should probably have made her more melancholy than it did. As it was, she just felt impassive. She shrugged as she stood there at the sink with one hand stuffed inside a mug, staring out the window at the old shearing shed flanked by a scrub-covered hill.

No matter how hard it would be to go it alone, at least she wouldn't have to submit, and then hate herself for the hypocrisy.

*This is good*, she thought. *A vital step on the path of healing – learning to be detached. One can only find true happiness with someone else when one has found it alone.* Or something like that; she couldn't remember exactly how the saying went.

Regardless, the last thing she wanted was to share her heart – actually even just her *space* – with anyone else.

It was lovely having Jake stay, but as much as she enjoyed his company, she was glad it was only for the weekend. She would enjoy being on her own again.

It was the same reason she did not want Nathan Lucas moving in with her, no matter how much money he brought with him. No, she wanted – needed – to be alone. Having him move in for his money would be following her mother's path, and she was past that now, wasn't she?

*Well, I'm getting there.*

A feeling of fierce determination settled upon her. She was going to make it work on her own, whatever *it* was. She felt buoyed, empowered to succeed. And it had nothing to do with John and his money. If only she could figure out where she was meant to be directing this energy.

Obviously there was the house, but there had to be more to it than that. It was a bit melodramatic, but she had the overwhelming feeling that she was on the cusp of something exciting, something big. She sniggered to herself; ah, Emily Oliphant, ever the romantic.

Her English teachers had always said she had an overactive imagination, her Physical Education teacher, unrealistic expectations. Perhaps that was her whole problem.

★

Emily entered the lounge room and smiled. Her father was slumped in the armchair, his legs stretched out onto the floor in front of him.

'Is there anything I can get you while I'm up?' she whispered to Jake.

'Actually, do you have paper and a pencil I can borrow?'

'Sure,' Emily said, and went back to the kitchen to retrieve the requested items plus an eraser and a ruler from the kitchen drawer. She put them on the plain 1960s-style wood-grain laminex coffee table in front of him, and then went to her bedroom and retrieved the novel she was reading.

When she re-entered the lounge room, she smiled at hearing a quiet snore escape her father's lips.

'Here, you sit here – I'd rather use the coffee table to lean on,' Jake said quietly, vacating the second armchair.

'Are you sure?'

'Absolutely. I'm a big one for sitting cross-legged on the floor – I want to do it as long as I can before old age and creaking limbs set in,' he said, grinning broadly at her.

He settled himself in front of the coffee table, directly opposite Emily and with his back to the wall.

'Would you at least like a towel or pillow to sit on?'

'No, I'm fine, thanks.'

After a few moments, Emily was reading silently, her father was gently snoring, and Jake was scratching away on the paper and pausing every so often to rub furiously with the eraser, and then brush off the debris. Glancing at the top of his head, she noticed his thick, short dark hair was lightly dusted with grey.

The first time he noticed her gaze, Jake said he'd vacuum all the crumbs up later. He'd clearly misunderstood her look as concern for her clean floor, when instead it had been pure contentment. *What a perfect day*, Emily thought, before returning to her book and searching for where she'd left off.

It seemed like only minutes later when Jake sat back from the coffee table, stretched, got up, and then laid two sheets of paper on her lap – the first mainly consisting of a list, and the second a rough floor plan. In fact almost an hour had passed, Emily was surprised to find upon checking her watch. It was almost seven o'clock. Her mother would be ringing any minute now to see where Des was. She shook the thought aside as Jake spoke.

'My basic idea for renovating, and proposed budget,' Jake said.

'Wow, thanks,' Emily said, looking at the pages.

'The figures are pretty rubbery, but should give you some idea of what you'd be up for.'

Emily put the list of figures underneath and stared at the house plans. She turned the page around, frowning slightly as she tried to decipher which was the front and which was the back view.

Jake leaned over her shoulder and pointed. 'There's the bathroom under the verandah. If you did it up, leaving it where it is, you would still have outside access, which is always handy. And if you ever did anything with the place that involved the public, you wouldn't have people traipsing through the house.'

'Good idea.'

'I'd extend it back along the verandah so it lined up with the bedroom behind the kitchen here. That way you'd have yourself a bedroom with an ensuite. The good thing is the plumbing is already nearby – saves money.'

'Okay.'

'Another option would be to turn the middle bedroom into a main bathroom and ensuite for the front bedroom. Or you could turn the whole side verandah into wet areas and give all three bedrooms an ensuite. That would be perfect if you ever wanted to run a B&B. It wouldn't be a huge deal to rip up the concrete and lay pipework and then cover it up again, although adding bathrooms can be expensive.'

'Wow, I see what you mean – heaps of options. That's good food for thought.' Emily's head was spinning with the possibilities. If only money wasn't such a problem.

When Des left, the sun was low in the sky and the birds were performing their pre-bedtime ruckus in and around the trees, squawking, fluttering, darting back and forth. Emily and Jake stood on the verandah in the fresh cool air and waved him off.

'What a lovely evening,' Jake said, looking around him.

'Hmm,' Emily replied, vaguely, still staring after her father's ute as if in a trance. The summer sunset glowed amber around them.

'It's getting late. I need something savoury to eat,' Emily said, heading back into the house and down the hall to the kitchen. After a few moments Jake followed her.

'I'm going to have a pick at the leftovers if you'd like something. I love cold roast vegetables – especially in a sandwich with some cheese and mayonnaise. But I'm happy to heat something up for you if you'd like.'

'No, cold is fine with me,' Jake said. 'Do you mind if I get back to the buttons?' he asked a little shyly. 'I'm just dying to know.'

She desperately wanted to know too, but was equally nervous about what they'd find. But she couldn't close the door now it was so far open. They'd gone too far for that.

'Sure,' she said, and retrieved the jar and ice-cream container and put them on the bench.

While she fossicked in the fridge and the cupboards and put everything on the table, Jake resumed sorting the buttons, keeping to their plan of collecting like items and letting the diamonds reveal themselves gradually. They both worked in silence, and Emily looked across the bench a couple of times and noted that gradually the line-up of diamonds had grown. There were now six.

# Chapter Ten

'Got you, you little sucker!' Jake suddenly cried, holding up the seventh. 'Wow, Em, they're all here!'

Emily should have felt pleased, excited – something, anything. But all she felt was a vague twinge of disappointment that there was no longer a great family secret – a secret she'd partially revealed but could reveal no further. Really, what had been the point? To learn something no one else knew?

'It's almost a bit of a letdown,' Jake said, standing back from the bench and staring at the stones lined up in front of him.

'Hmm,' Emily agreed. He'd taken the words right out of her mouth.

'This morning I thought, well I *hoped*, if they were here your life might become a little easier. But I see now there's no way you could ever part with

114

them. I wouldn't be able to. Do you want to at least think about getting them valued?'

'No.' Emily was so frustrated she could cry. Here, right in front of her, was possibly all the money she would need to buy the house and do a fantastic renovation. Yet she was no better off now than before – there was no way she could cash the diamonds in, even if she knew how or where to do it. It was totally out of the question. Gran had held onto them all and entrusted her to do the same. She couldn't – *wouldn't* – let her down.

'Don't just dismiss it out of hand; there's too much at stake. Perhaps there's another way.'

'Like what?' Emily said, responding to his frustrated tone.

'Well, maybe you could borrow against them – not actually have to sell them.'

'Jake, I know you're trying to help, and I really appreciate it, but it just wouldn't be right,' Emily said heavily. 'Gran kept them a secret all these years. What right do I have to expose it?'

Jake nodded thoughtfully.

Despite her deflation, Emily felt an overwhelming sense of camaraderie towards Jake; he seemed to genuinely understand how she felt about the diamonds and why.

'In that case, I don't think anyone else should know about them,' he suddenly said. 'God, I wish I hadn't realised the first one I found was a diamond – if I hadn't done that damned course. I'm so sorry, Em.'

'Don't be, Jake; it's not your fault. And it was – *is* – an exciting find.' And it had been, until she'd had the intervening hours to let the ramifications seep in. Probably best they had, otherwise she might have got all carried away and blurted it out in front of Barbara, David and Des. And then the romance of Gran's secret would have been shattered.

'It's just so frustrating. If you're not meant to use the diamonds, why find them in the first place? It's like a bad joke.'

'Maybe it's a test,' Emily said, shrugging. 'How hungry are you?'

'Not overly. But then I always think that until I start eating your wonderful food.' He smiled warmly at her.

'Well, don't get too excited, it's only cold meat and vegetables and bread, remember,' she said with a laugh.

'Sounds perfect to me. What shall I do with these?' Jake pointed at the row of glossy stones.

'I reckon put them back in the jar and shake it up.'

'I suppose they have been there safely for the past sixty years or so – well, in *a* jar.' He put the stones in one by one before putting the rusting lid back on and tightening it up. He stared at the well-defined layers for a few moments before walking the few steps over to Emily and holding the jar out to her.

'I can't bear to shake it up after all the time we spent sorting them,' he said with an apologetic grimace.

Grinning widely, Emily accepted the jar, turned it upside down, gave it a couple of turns and a gentle shake, and handed it back.

'Actually,' she said, 'I like it better muddled – far too contrived in layers. Much more like Gran this way,' she added with a grin.

'Where do you want me to put it?' Jake asked.

'In the pantry, up the top for now, while I think of somewhere better.'

Since moving in, Emily had often thought of putting the jar on display, but she didn't want her mother telling her how ridiculous it looked. Enid's well-practised sneer could still turn her into a humiliated five year old. Maybe one day she'd get over it, or come up with a clever reason for the jar's public presence. Until then it would have to stay hidden.

They sat down and started assembling their sandwiches in amiable silence.

As Emily bit into her sandwich and watched Jake out of the corner of her eye, for a moment she felt her resolve about saying no to Nathan slipping. She thought how really nice it was having Jake here – male company in general.

She liked how at ease Jake was, but without being too familiar. Without crossing the line. And she liked how at ease she was with him.

But there was something more intense about Nathan – like he was trying too hard to please her. Or was that just because he was desperate for somewhere to stay? He had said there was no pressure.

Looking back, she had to admit to feeling a little of Nathan's intensity rubbing off on her in only the short time he'd been here. She had enough trouble staying calm generally; the last thing she needed was to start feeling on edge all the time again.

This was her intuition speaking, wasn't it? If so, she had to listen to it or else risk being bitten on the arse by hindsight somewhere down the track. She had to stay strong and phone him that night – keep it brief and firm. She had to say no, and get it over with. As soon as she'd finished eating.

'God, I completely forgot,' Jake said suddenly. 'Distracted by those damned diamonds, I mean buttons – must forget all about them. I was going to suggest a bottle of wine. I brought a selection of red and white, but I'm afraid the white will need a spell in the freezer. A nice light Yarra Valley pinot might go very well with this, though. What do you think? Would you like some?'

'That would be lovely, thanks.'

'Back in a sec then.' He leapt up and Emily watched as he left the kitchen on a long stride, enjoying the shape of his behind in jeans that were neither too baggy nor too tight. When she realised she'd bitten her lip she told herself off.

They enjoyed the rest of the meal in easy conversation punctuated by gentle silences, sipping on the wine, which went very well indeed with their sandwiches.

Afterwards they took their glasses into the lounge and were just in time to catch the end of the ABC news. As she stared at the television and sipped her wine, Emily thought about what a nice Christmas it had been. She'd been a little afraid of facing her first Christmas without John. Mostly for fear of being reminded of how much her life had changed since last year. But it had helped that her mother hadn't been there, she mused, instantly experiencing a twinge of guilt.

Emily was feeling a little lightheaded, despite drinking very slowly. She insisted Jake pour the last of the wine into his glass and then politely declined his offer of another bottle while being careful not to discourage him from doing so if he wished. Though she liked that he didn't; it showed restraint.

John hadn't had any restraint, even when he was driving. God, she really didn't miss sitting home alone night after night waiting for the knock on the door from the police to tell her he'd wrapped the ute around a tree. She'd never told anyone; they'd have said she was paranoid and should seek professional help. But she wasn't; knew in her heart of hearts that it was only a matter of time. He'd dodged that particular bullet so many times already.

She'd given up years ago trying to make John understand that his cavalier behaviour could kill someone else as well, destroy someone's family. She only hoped when it happened there would be no one else involved.

'Are you okay?'

Emily looked up at hearing Jake's voice, apparently a frown still upon her face.

'You look worried.'

'Sorry. No, just thinking about something I shouldn't be. How does tomorrow's weather look – okay for an outdoor barbeque?'

'Might be touch and go by the looks of the satellite map.'

'Oh well, we'll just have to play it by ear.'

Emily reminded herself she had to ring Nathan. She wasn't looking forward to it. But she decided it was too early – they might still be having dinner.

Ten minutes later, when Jake was engrossed in the Christmas movie and Emily was pretending to be, her mobile began to ring in the kitchen.

'Sorry,' she said in a loud whisper, and raced to answer it. The number was unfamiliar.

'Hello, Emily speaking.'

'Hi Em, it's Nathan.'

'Oh hi, I was going to call you later – thought you might still be having dinner.'

'Oh, cool. So you've made a decision then?' he chirped.

*Stay firm*, Emily instructed herself.

'I have, and I'm really sorry, but I'm not interested in having a flatmate at present. Sorry.'

'Oh!'

'You did say there was no pressure.'

'I know, and there isn't, but I can't say I'm not disappointed. But it's your choice. No chance of changing your mind?'

*Stick to your guns, Em.*

'No. I'm sorry, Nathan, I really am, it's just that right now...'

'Don't be. Doesn't matter. I'll find somewhere else. Okay, better go. See you round.'

'Okay then, see you,' she said, but he'd already hung up.

Emily stared at the phone for a few moments feeling increasingly annoyed. He'd said he'd wait for her to call him. Yet here he was, less than twelve hours later, calling her for an answer. And not even bothering with any small talk.

Part of her was glad he'd got straight to the point, but that wasn't really the issue. It was rude. She clearly meant no more to him than somewhere to put his suitcase.

Well, at least it was done and she could sit and watch TV in peace.

*But first I am going to quickly ring the Bakers about the house.*

She brought up their number and with a shaking finger pressed Call. It was answered on the second ring.

'Hello, Donald speaking.'

'Hi, Donald, it's Emily Oliphant, over at the old house. Er, merry Christmas,' she added.

'And to you. Have you thought about our offer?'

'I have, and I'd love to accept it.'

'That's great news.' Emily heard a muffled sound, which was most likely him telling his brother.

She took a deep breath. *Now for the hard part.*

'The only thing is, I'd rather not make the first payment until the subdivision has gone through, just in case we strike any problems.'

'I understand. It would probably be a bit risky for you to go ahead without that certainty.'

'But I've been told it could take up to six months.'

'I don't see that being a problem for us. Our trip is almost a whole year away yet.'

'Oh that's a relief. Thank you for being so understanding,' Emily said.

'And thank you for wanting to take care of the house.'

'It's my pleasure. I love it. I'll let you go now. See you.'

'Cheerio then,' Donald said.

Emily hung up and tried to figure out whether she felt relieved or terrified as a result of officially putting the ball in motion regarding the house. She was shaking a little. *It's a good thing. It'll all work out for the best.* She went back into the lounge.

'Well, for better or worse I've just officially taken up the offer of the house,' she announced as she entered the room. Jake looked up.

'That's great news, well done,' he said, smiling warmly.

'Well, time will tell,' she said, and sat down in the other armchair beside him.

# Chapter Eleven

Emily thought she'd never get to sleep; every time she closed her eyes a disjointed montage of the day's events flickered in her mind: her call to Donald Baker about the house; what her father had said about Enid; Nathan's proposition; the diamonds; Jake's reaction to the way John had treated her; John's payout.

And then there were the usual questions that plagued her when she was too tired to keep them at bay: How was she going to make do on her own without a job, without a man? What was she going to do with her life in the long term? Had she done the wrong thing taking on the house? Should she leave Wattle Creek and start afresh somewhere else? Why hadn't she had the guts to demand her fair share from John? Why did everything come back to money? And why did everyone keep saying money wasn't everything and that it couldn't buy happiness?

★

Emily woke feeling bleary-eyed and tired. The last time she'd checked it had been one o'clock. It was now six-thirty. No matter how badly she slept or how late she went to bed, she usually woke at around the same time. And no matter how long she lay in bed or how much she tried to talk herself into it, she could never go back to sleep.

She pushed back the sheet and light cotton blanket, got out of bed, dragged her robe from the hook on the back of the door, slipped her feet into her worn sheepskin slippers, and padded down the hall to the kitchen. She took extra care to be quiet and let Jake sleep on. She let Grace out the kitchen door and stood on the verandah while the dog did her morning ablutions.

'All better?' Emily asked, as Grace trotted past her before coming back inside.

She gave Grace her breakfast and as she watched the small dog eat, wondered, *what now?* She didn't want to risk waking Jake by banging about and packing stuff for their barbeque with Barbara and David. Half his luck if he was still sleeping.

But it didn't feel right to go ahead and have her morning coffee or breakfast without him. No, she should wait. But she had no idea how long he might sleep. What if he was one of those city types who lounged around in bed until eleven? *Don't be stupid*, Emily heard her inner voice say, *he didn't sleep in last time he stayed.* It had been Elizabeth who had struggled to be up before ten and complained loudly about it.

It was weird how she kept forgetting that Jake had been here before. She decided it must be because of the change in dynamic – Elizabeth not being with him.

As much as she liked her cousin, she preferred Jake without her; Elizabeth tended to be way too pretentious and loud when there was someone around to impress.

No one in the family had ever really figured out what her job as a business analyst was all about. But everyone knew she earned stacks of money, drove a flash BMW, and lived in a swanky apartment in Melbourne.

Emily had never been to Melbourne, despite many invitations. She'd never known whether the invitations were genuine – they were almost always issued in front of someone else – and she had never felt comfortable spending the money; hers or John's.

Now she realised that even if she did have the money, she would probably never visit Elizabeth. There would be nothing worse than being paraded around as the country hick cousin. Not to mention being swamped by strangers in a noisy, bustling city, tall buildings looming all around and blocking out the light. The idea of spending time in a place the size of Melbourne was really quite daunting.

She shook these thoughts aside, picked up the pad and pencil from the bench where Jake had put them back the night before, and began setting out a budget – funds in hand, expenses now, and those in the foreseeable future.

It was a list she'd made many times, and she some-times wondered if she did so in the hope that at some point the numbers would suddenly become doable.

This time she added twenty thousand under antic-ipated expenses to cover the re-roofing. She looked at the totals. She could pay for the subdivision, make the first year's instalment on the house and replace the roof, but would then have less than a thousand dollars left. She had to eat. And what if her car died or something?

At least with nothing in reserve, she'd be eligible for Centrelink assistance. That would certainly help. Though the thought of being labelled a dole bludger by her mother made her feel decidedly uneasy.

Would it be worth it if it meant not worrying so much about basic week-to-week expenses? She *was* looking for a job, so it wasn't like she'd be doing anything wrong. The only thing standing in her way would be her pride, which was bloody stupid – cutting off her nose to spite her face, Gran would have said.

It wasn't her fault she'd been diddled by John. Well it was; she'd let him get away with it. But if anyone should look bad, it was him. She was doing the best she could to pick up the pieces and start again. And if that meant having to claim Centrelink benefits for a while, so be it.

But, hang on, anything over five grand in the bank and she'd still be subject to their waiting period: she wouldn't be able to make a claim until she had purchased the property, and she couldn't do that until the subdivision had been done, and Jake had said that could take up to six months.

Bloody hell, it was so damned complicated – all these steps that had to be taken in the right order.

Emily had her pen poised and was frowning when Jake walked in. She looked up and took in his slightly dishevelled appearance. He was wearing blue and white striped long pyjama pants and a navy blue t-shirt. His hair was standing up and sticking out, and there was a thick shadow of stubble on his chin. She smiled as he rubbed at his eyes like a child and squinted at the light filling the room. God, his eyes were gorgeous.

'Why are you frowning on such a lovely morning?' His raspy, deep voice sounded like he thought the day was anything but lovely.

'Oh, just making a few notes and lists of figures.'

'You know, just because you write them down doesn't mean they'll get any better,' he said, smiling warmly at her. 'No matter how many times you write them down, they don't change. Believe me, I've tried,' he said, slumping onto the nearest chair.

'Guess I'm still living in hope.' Emily shrugged and got up. 'Coffee?'

'Oh, yes please!'

'Did you sleep okay?'

'Brilliantly, just needed a few more hours. No matter how late I get to sleep, I always wake up early; it's really quite annoying.'

'I'm the same.'

'Well, it's my own fault; I sat up until midnight making notes in my journal and reading. Just wasn't tired. So now I'll pay for it today.'

'I couldn't get to sleep either – tossed and turned for ages. At least we've got nothing strenuous to do – unless you're driving back to Whyalla tonight.'

'No. Since I know you're an early bird, I'll leave in the morning.'

'I always feel better after my first coffee,' Emily said, filling the kettle.

'Ah yes, caffeine, the wonder drug. I can't seem to live without it these days.'

'Hmm.'

When they were both seated at the table with their coffees, Jake said, 'So, anything other than the obvious troubling you this morning about the figures?'

'Well...'

She hadn't intended to tell him about wanting to qualify for Centrelink, but suddenly found it all spilling out.

'Don't be embarrassed, Em. Seriously, there's nothing wrong with asking for some help when you need it – that's what Centrelink is there for. I doubt you're the sort to stay on it for long. And anyway, I'm sure you've paid plenty of tax over the years. So you shouldn't feel ashamed. Personally, I'd be claiming as soon as you possibly can so you don't completely use up all your reserves. You won't have all this cash in six months when you buy this place. If only you could offload it now; you'd have six months with some money coming in. Hmm,' he added, and began tapping the pen he'd picked up against his hand.

'I wouldn't want to do anything dodgy,' Emily warned.

'God no. I would never suggest anything like that. You could always park some money in one of my company trust accounts.'

'Wouldn't I have to have a legitimate reason – like a deposit or something?'

'Technically, but we could...'

'Thanks Jake, and no offence, but even that's already sounding a little iffy for me. And I really don't want to involve anyone else.'

'Fair enough. But at least let me send you the details of a decent conveyancer. He's not cheap, but he won't rip you off, and he's good.'

'I'd appreciate that, thanks.'

Emily got up from the table.

'Now, I'm more than happy to do eggs for you, but I'm having cereal – muesli.'

'Muesli sounds good. Knowing you and Barbara, there'll be a mountain of food for lunch.'

Emily brought the Tupperware container of cereal, milk, bowls and spoons to the table.

'Yum,' Jake said, 'you'll have to tell me which brand of muesli this is – it's very good.'

Emily blushed slightly. 'Um, actually, it's my own blend. I couldn't find one without those processed little pellets – I find them too sweet.'

'Well at least give me the list of ingredients – or do I have to guess myself?' He picked up the container and stared through the clear window for a few moments before putting it down and continuing to eat.

'Shall I have first shower or would you like to? I don't mind either way,' Emily said when they'd finished eating and pushed their bowls aside.

'You go – I'm determined to discover every ingredient,' Jake said, picking up the muesli container again. 'You can test me when you're done,' he said with a laugh.

'Okay.'

Emily left the room grinning – he really was good fun and so easy to be with.

'I'll give you a hint,' she said a few minutes later as she passed back through the kitchen on her way to the bathroom. 'There are eleven ingredients all up.'

'Right,' Jake said, turning over to a new page on the pad.

*

A few hours later, they were sitting in Emily's car at the place where the five roads intersected at Barbara and David's mailbox.

They'd only been there a few minutes when David's white ute clattered over the cattle grid at the end of their drive and turned towards them. David stuck his arm out of the window, waved, and then indicated that they should follow him.

They turned into the next open gateway along and made their way up a rough track that wound through scrappy bushland, Emily being careful to keep far enough back so as not to be showered in stones from David's vehicle.

'You're bound to get some great shots up here – it's beautiful; like an oasis tucked away.'

'Hmm. Sounds lovely.'

'And thankfully they seem to be out with the forecast.'

'Fingers crossed.' As they shuddered and vibrated over corrug-ated sections, Emily was relieved to see in the rear vision mirror that Grace was still curled up on the back seat and hadn't been flung onto the floor. She was also glad they'd taken her car. Not that she liked the punishment her old Ford was taking, but she didn't want Jake getting into trouble with his hire car company. She cringed every time they hit a particularly deep rut or bounced over a protruding rock. She'd forgotten how rough this track was. *I need a ute.*

'You need a ute, Em,' Jake said.

'Yeah,' she agreed. *Spooky.*

Suddenly they emerged into a lush clearing. David drove around the edge and stopped near the far side against what looked like the opening to a forest. Emily parked and turned off the engine while taking in the scene; gorgeous tall gums surrounded by smaller eucalypts and a variety of native shrubs. They got out and Emily stared around her in awe. It was even more beautiful than she remembered.

'Perfect or what?' David said to Jake, indicating the space with a wide spread of his arms.

'Breathtaking,' Jake replied in a breathy voice.

'How are you feeling?' Emily asked as she hugged Barbara.

'Fit as a fiddle. Just needed a decent night's sleep,' she said brightly.

'That's good to hear. It would have been such a shame to cancel the picnic. I'd forgotten just how perfect this spot is,' Emily said.

'Well, it's very special to us, isn't it darling?' Barbara said, putting her arm around David's waist.

David looked at his wife with a dreamy expression on his face. It was like those looks the leading couple in a romantic scene in an action movie shared – like they were unaware of anything else going on around them; cars blowing up, people being shot et cetera. Emily almost giggled.

'Jake, this is where David took me on our first date, and then a year later, proposed.'

'Ah, well I have to get a shot of you both here then,' Jake said, camera already out and trained on them.

Seconds later he showed them the two photos he'd taken in the viewfinder. He'd perfectly captured their contentment and the beauty of the setting.

'I'll print them out and send you copies when I get back.'

'Thanks, we'll have to get that one framed,' David said, giving Barbara a peck on the cheek.

'Actually, we still haven't seen any of the shots you took last time you were here,' Emily said.

'Oh, I'd completely forgotten. They're on my laptop, but I left it back in Whyalla. I would have emailed some, but I figured you didn't have the internet at your place.'

'You can send them to us,' Barbara and David said at the same time before laughing.

'They're okay photos, but nothing like the real thing right here,' Jake said.

'We'd still like to see them.'

'Okay,' he said, making a show of exasperation. 'I'll bring the laptop next time and subject you all to a boring slideshow. But don't say you weren't warned.'

# Chapter Twelve

They emptied the vehicles and set up their makeshift campsite, and then Jake produced a bottle of sparkling shiraz. Before long, Grace was tucking into a bone nearby and they were all holding plastic flutes of fizzing liquid.

'So what are we toasting to, other than wonderful friends, fine wine, good food, and lovely tranquil settings?' Barbara asked, holding up her glass.

'You've about covered it, my dear,' David said, raising his glass and tapping it against Barbara's.

'Actually, I have something else,' Jake said, looking at Emily.

She gave a small nod of assent.

'In addition to Barbara's eloquent toast, I'd like to raise a glass to Emily.' They all held up their glasses and he continued solemnly, 'To Emily and the great Australian dream.'

'Oh my God, you said yes to buying the house! Did you? Tell me you did!' Barbara leapt up and down, spilling wine all down her arm.

'I did. I rang the Bakers last night. It's official.'

'And you didn't phone me straight away?!' Barbara said, accepting a paper serviette from David and dabbing at the spilt wine.

'You went home feeling unwell, remember?'

'Oh yes, but I would have got off my death bed to hear this news! Oh, well done!' She hugged Emily tightly with one arm, careful not to spill more wine. 'I'm so proud of you,' she added more quietly.

'Thanks. Let's just hope I've made the right decision,' Emily replied.

'Oh you have. You have. Ooh, I'm so excited for you.'

'Congratulations Em,' David said, finally able to get a word and a hug in.

As much as Emily enjoyed their enthusiasm, what she enjoyed even more was Jake enveloping her into a warm embrace and planting a kiss in her hair behind her ear.

'It's going to be great,' he said before letting her go.

Finally things settled down and they were able to focus on organising lunch.

★

Afterwards they all relaxed back into director's chairs and waited for their overfilled stomachs to feel more comfortable and the barbeque plate to cool down.

'I've eaten way too much,' Emily said, patting her tummy.

'That was amazing. Thank you,' Jake said.

'Thank *you* for the lovely wine,' Barbara said.

'Pleasure was all mine.'

They'd only had the one bottle, being careful to not be over the limit to drive. Despite only having a short trip back on quiet roads, Barbara, David, and Emily were all taking extra care.

The recent deaths of two young locals just weeks apart had been a sharp reminder to the whole district that drink driving kills. Wattle Creek's only police officer now drove around with his breathalyser as much as was humanly possible, desperate to stop the senseless loss of life occurring on his patch again.

But as Barbara and Emily had discussed at length, there was probably little point to all his efforts; these things always seemed to come in threes. There would be another fatality. Just when, where, who, and exactly how, was a mystery.

Besides which, it was the middle of the day, and they'd all laughed over the fact that since they'd turned thirty, alcohol with lunch made them just want to curl up and have a nanna nap.

The sparkling shiraz had been the perfect accompaniment to the kangaroo steaks David had brought; the slightly gamey, marin-ated flavour working well with the peppery red.

Barbara and David had initially been a little reluctant to tell Jake it was kangaroo, but he'd picked it straight away; the colour, strong scent, and slightly denser texture of the raw meat.

They'd also had slices of grilled potato, pumpkin and zucchini, and a bowl of Barbara's egg salad. It was a particular hit with Jake, and they had all laughed at his insistence on cleaning the remnants from the bowl with a slice of bread – white bread.

As gourmet as their barbeques were, Barbara, David, and Emily had made a pact that the bread could only be white – the old-fashioned type; squishy, fully processed, and lowest in nutritional value. It reminded them of their childhoods.

Jake had been delighted. 'Haven't had white bread for ages!' he'd exclaimed. 'I'm too brainwashed by nutritional facts to buy anything other than bread full of grains,' he'd added as he'd gleefully grabbed two slices and put them on his plate.

David explained that they didn't normally eat anything but wholegrain either, but that their white bread thing was a deliberate attempt to subvert the whole nutritional do-gooding and gourmet barbequing craze, which they had otherwise fully embraced. White bread was their last connection to times gone by and down-to-earthness, Barbara had proudly concluded, with Emily nodding solemnly in agreement.

'That's bloody brilliant! I love it!' Jake had said, grinning broadly.

Emily had been watching carefully for his reaction, and had been pleased when he seemed to get the joke straight away. He really did fit in well. And having him there meant she didn't feel like the fifth wheel the way she often did when out with Barbara and David.

'Well, I hope you've all left room for pavlova,' Barbara announced loudly, her voice bringing Emily back to the chatter around her.

She looked at the eskies. She couldn't remember seeing a pavlova or a container large enough for one.

'Not here,' Barbara said with a laugh. 'It would have shattered on that bloody track and I wasn't having all my efforts wasted. No, back at the house – it's almost on your way anyway. You're not rushing off back to Whyalla, are you Jake?'

'Not until the morning. And I would love pavlova if Emily's happy to stop in.'

'Are you kidding? I would never pass up the opportunity to have pavlova – especially Barbara's,' Emily said.

'I guess that's a yes then,' Barbara said, grinning.

'Hang on a minute,' David broke in. 'We've brought Jake here so he can take some photos. So you'll all have to wait – come on, mate,' he said, getting up.

Jake followed his lead.

'Ah, very clever,' Barbara said. 'Pretending you need to go off. And it'll be just long enough for us girls to have packed everything up.'

'I'll stay and help,' Jake said.

'No, you go, but don't be surprised if we don't lift a finger while you're gone,' Barbara said. She stretched out her legs and folded her arms across her chest, giving her husband a defiant look over the top of her sunglasses.

'Quite all right my love; you just rest up and we'll deal with it when we get back,' David said, in a patronising tone. He patted her on the shoulder before striding off towards the edge of the clearing.

'Righto, see you in a bit,' Jake said, sounding a little unsure. He waved before turning and setting off after David, his camera slung over his shoulder.

'See ya,' Emily called, grinning. She loved watching Barbara and David's friendly sparring.

'I like him,' Barbara said, sighing and settling back into her chair.

'I should think you should *love* him. He is your husband.'

'Not David, darling; Jake.'

'Barbara!' Emily warned.

'What?! I just said I like him; what's not to like?'

'It's what you didn't say – and you know perfectly well what I'm talking about.'

They settled into silence.

'Hey, did you hear about John being bought out of the family company?' Emily said a few minutes later. 'Dad told me yesterday after you'd left. Apparently somewhere in the vicinity of three hundred grand.'

'David did mention a rumour – I didn't want to say anything until I knew for sure. Half of that should be yours.'

'Don't I know it? But he'll have to live with what he's done. I'm not going to worry about it; it's done now. I just hope what goes around comes around.'

'Me too, lousy bastard. Speaking of money – any joy on the job front?'

'No – you'd be the first to hear. And you know Jake reckons it's going to cost around fifteen grand for the subdivision alone.'

'That's a bugger. Well, our offer still stands.'

'Thanks very much, Barbara. I really do appreciate it, but seriously, I couldn't. Anyway, I'm even more determined to do this on my own now.'

'Good for you. And I totally understand about not wanting to borrow from friends – I'd be exactly the same. It's just that we want to help, that's all.'

'Well you are – you do – just by being here and listening to me whinge and moan all the time.'

'Sounds like you're just going to have to step up the jam production.'

'Actually, Jake got a call from his sister just before we left. Apparently she sold the whole second batch to some little gourmet shop in St Kilda. Remind me to show you the picture of the gorgeous labels she made: Emily's Gourmet Homemade Apricot Jam, they said.'

'She sounds lovely. Fancy doing that for you when you've never even met.'

'I know. But then Jake seems nice; I guess it runs in the family. Hey, I totally forgot to tell you – I can't believe I forgot. Nathan came out looking for somewhere to live – eight o'clock in the morning yesterday, *Christmas morning*, if you don't mind! Was all casual and friendly, asking if he could rent a room, saying he'd leave me to think it over – no pressure, blah blah blah. And *then*, less than twelve hours later, he rings and demands to know if I've made a decision!'

'I'm guessing by your tone you're not having him move in?'

'No, as much as the money would be very helpful, I think I need to be alone for a while – just a gut feeling.'

'Well, you've got to listen to that.'

'I'm glad I had already decided before he rang. He certainly isn't one who likes hearing the word "no".'

'I thought he seemed quite nice at the funeral, but then I wasn't exactly in the best frame of mind to take much notice.'

'He was lovely at the funeral. And he seemed nice as pie at Mum and Dad's that night. Not pushy at all,' Emily mused aloud.

'Just goes to show, doesn't it?'

'Yep. John seemed so nice when I met him too,' Emily said wistfully. 'Why do people have to change?' she added, more to herself.

'They don't change – they just reveal their true character over time. The truth can only be hidden for so long.'

'Hey, that reminds me. You'll never guess what Jake found amongst Gran's buttons.'

Emily watched Barbara's eyes grow steadily wider as she told her about the button jar, the diamonds, and the prince's letter.

'Oh that's beautiful,' she said, bringing her hands to her chest and clasping them when Emily had finished.

'Isn't it? But the frustrating thing is there's all this money sitting there that I can't use.'

'I don't see why not, Em. You're pretty strapped. I'm sure, from what you've told me about your gran, she'd want to help.'

'I couldn't – she's had them for so long.'

'Clearly I'm not as sentimental as you, because I'd use them if I was in your boat.'

'You'd sell them?'

'I'd at least think about it. Why not get them valued and see if you could use them as collateral somehow?'

'I don't like the thought of parting with them.'

'You wouldn't be parting with them if you just put them up as collateral.'

'It'd be too big a risk – she treasured them all those years.'

'Or maybe she totally forgot they were there and if she'd remembered would have kicked herself for not cashing them in and using the money,' Barbara suggested with a shrug.

'Hmm, I hadn't thought of it like that. But how could you forget something like that?'

Barbara shrugged. 'Well there was that story about those people who accidentally donated a suitcase full of money to the Salvos – they'd clearly forgotten. And you did say your gran had Alzheimer's...'

Emily's mind started to spin with confusion. She had been all right about her decision to forget the diamonds when Jake had agreed that there was no way she could part with them. And now here was Barbara, possibly the wisest, kindest person she'd ever met – other than Gran – giving an entirely different perspective.

Perhaps Jake had only agreed out of politeness. After all, they didn't know each other all that well and he was a guest in her house.

Maybe Barbara did have a point. What if Gran had forgotten all about the diamonds? She'd been diagnosed with Alzheimer's disease more than ten years before she died. Or what if she'd never really cared about the diamonds in the first place? What if she hadn't really cared about the prince? All Emily had was one letter – from him.

Emily thought of the times she'd spent with Gran, and smiled at how the old lady still had the capacity to push her mother's buttons. Even right to the end when she'd often almost completely retreat into her teenage years, Gran would smile and wink at Emily when Enid snapped at her or left the room out of frustration.

She didn't know how much of what Gran did was her sense of humour and how much was the disease, but there were definitely times when she was intentionally messing with people, and Emily had been in on the joke. She smiled. Yep, Gran had certainly played on her condition when it suited her.

The last time Emily saw her, the day she gave her the button jar, came to her clearly now, as if brought into focus by the lens of a camera. She saw the serious expression, the clarity in the slightly opaque grey-blue eyes which were, indeed, almost the exact shade of the uncut diamonds. She heard Gran's voice; its measured tone, the words, which at the time had seemed a little odd: 'I need you to have this and take good care of it.'

Her heart slowed but thudded harder against her ribs. Emily could almost hear its hollow beat. *If only she'd said something like, 'Use them wisely' I'd know for sure.* She let out a deep sigh.

'You okay?' Barbara asked, sitting up straight and looking across at her friend.

'Yep, just thinking about Gran. Dear old thing. I miss her.'

Emily felt a heaviness descend. With Gran no longer around there was no way of knowing her wishes, and if she went ahead and let the diamonds' whereabouts be known, there would be all sorts of pressure from her mother and aunt, and probably her cousins too. She was old enough and smart enough to know that the whiff of money would bring out the vultures. *Oh God!*

Feeling a little queasy, she got up and poured herself a drink of water from the bottle in the esky.

'Can I get you some water or something?' she asked Barbara, tossing the question over her shoulder.

'No thanks, I'm good.'

Emily felt a little better after the water, and deciding she'd feel even better if she busied herself, began packing up everything.

'Traitor,' Barbara said, hearing the noise and looking across to see what Emily was doing. 'I was going to leave it for David — teach him a little lesson...'

'Oh. I figured since I was up...'

'Doesn't matter, I guess all good things must come to an end,' Barbara said. She got up with a sigh. 'They're probably sitting behind a tree waiting until we've finished before showing themselves.'

Less than five minutes later, Jake and David emerged. Barbara and Emily, having just finished putting everything beside the ute and car, exchanged looks and burst into laughter.

Jake and David looked at each other and then from Barbara to Emily.

'Something funny?' David asked.

'Nope,' Emily and Barbara said in unison, shaking their heads in an effort to quell giggles. 'Just your impeccable timing.'

David shrugged and lifted an esky onto the back of the ute.

'Got some great shots,' Jake said, lifting Emily's esky into the boot of her car.

'Great. And thanks for that,' Emily said, nodding towards the boot.

'Well, come on, back to the house for pav and coffee,' David said. 'We've worked up another appetite while you lazy things have been sitting about,' he said, putting his arm around Barbara and giving her an audible sloppy kiss on the cheek.

Barbara pretended to scowl at him before they piled into the two vehicles and David led the way back.

As they drove, Jake chattered with excitement about the shots he'd taken. Emily managed to mumble in all the right places and not give away the fact her mind was elsewhere. She couldn't stop thinking about what Barbara had said and whether or not she should try to sell the diamonds.

# Chapter Thirteen

Back at Barbara and David's, they were all engrossed in dessert, the only sounds being murmurs of enjoyment and the clink and slide of forks across plates, when suddenly they were startled by a series of sharp electronic beeps.

'God, I hope that's not what I think it is,' David said, putting down his fork and pushing back his chair from the table.

'That's David's SES pager,' Barbara explained to Jake. 'He'll now go and call in to let them know he's available and find out if they need him.'

Barbara, Jake, and Emily returned to finishing their dessert and coffee.

When Emily pushed her empty plate aside and her chair back slightly from the table, she noticed David standing in the nearby doorway. His face was pale, quite ashen, and he seemed a little perplexed and undecided about something. He looked from the phone in his hand to the door and back again several times.

'Darling, are you okay? You look like you've seen a ghost,' Barbara called.

David continued to stand in silence, frowning and biting on his lower lip.

'Whatever is the matter?' Barbara said, getting up and going over to him.

Emily and Jake exchanged questioning glances and shrugs.

'Um, er,' David stammered, looking right at Emily.

'David, what is it?' she asked.

'John. He's crashed his ute – he's, um, dead.'

Emily felt the colour drain from her face, as if someone had pulled a plug. She unconsciously checked her watch.

'Less than half an hour ago,' David said, misreading her reflexive action. 'I can stay if you want, but they need help to...'

'No darling, you go. We'll be okay. We'll take care of Em, won't we Jake?' Barbara said.

Jake nodded his agreement. He put a hand over Emily's and gave a brief, gentle squeeze.

Emily looked down at his hand and frowned. *How do I feel?* She realised she wasn't actually sad or upset; just surprised, and perhaps a little shocked.

'I'm okay,' she said, trying to sound bright. Instead her voice came across hard and brittle; as if she didn't care.

*I don't actually care.* The realisation brought a new wave of shock and surprise.

She thought of his parents, and wondered whether she should call them. Gerald and Thora Stratten would be distraught. But when she thought about John not being around anymore she felt nothing – not even the numbness of disbelief – except an over-whelming desire to know the details in all their gruesome glory.

*I'd better keep that to myself.*

She'd only left him a month and a half ago, and it wasn't like they'd remained friends or anything. But Jesus, she should feel something, shouldn't she? What sort of person felt nothing upon hearing that her husband – estranged husband – had had a terrible accident and was dead?

'Seriously, I'm fine,' she said, smiling faintly first at Jake and then at Barbara. 'Bit of a shock, that's all. Drink driving, I suppose; it was only a matter of time,' she said with a grimace and tight shrug.

David was still standing in the doorway. He was shifting awk-wardly on his feet, as if trying to decide whether to stay or leave.

'Go David, seriously,' she urged. 'At least if you're there we'll get the full story,' she said.

'Well, if you're sure…'

'Of course. Go!'

'Sorry guys,' David said. He rushed over, pecked Barbara on the forehead, laid a hand briefly on Emily's shoulder and kissed her on the cheek. 'Good to see you again, Jake, sorry I have to rush off,' he said, extending a hand.

'No worries, mate, catch you next time. Thanks for a great day.'

'Well, better get cracking.'

*Not that it'll matter since he's already dead.* But of course the SES had to be there to clean up any spilt fuel, help police cordon off the scene, and keep the rubbernecking public at bay. And to get the body out if it was still trapped.

Emily wondered if at some point it might hit her and she'd get upset; feel *something*. Grace, who had been lying on the floor in the corner, trotted over and stood beside her, looking up with pleading brown eyes. And then Emily did feel something; guilt for ignoring her dog.

It was then that she decided she would feel nothing over John Stratten's death; she would not let him take anything more from her.

Emily was a little taken aback at the forcefulness of her decision; it was as though it had come from a depth beyond her own soul, or from somewhere outside her. The words 'I hope he rots in hell' were, almost as instantly as they were formed in her mind, count-ered by the words 'one shouldn't think ill of the dead'.

*In that case*, she thought, *I will think nothing.*

But almost as soon as she had made this silent undertaking, the questions began to tumble into her mind, one after the other, like falling dominoes winding their way around a room: Where did it happen? Had he been drinking? Did the ute roll? Did it hit a tree? Was there fire? Did he die instantly? Was he alone or was someone with him? Where was he going? Where had he come from?

Ten minutes later, Jake and Emily were at the door, hugging Barbara and saying their goodbyes.

'Now you're sure you're okay?' Barbara said.

Jake responded by putting a protective arm around Emily. 'She'll be fine; I'll take good care of her,' he said.

Emily didn't argue; she liked the feeling of strength in his arm. She didn't even protest when he opened the passenger door for her. As he drove, she cast a couple of glances across at him and noted how nice it was to have someone drive her again, share the burden, if only for a little while.

She felt exhausted, and practically stumbled over the front doorstep when they arrived back at the house. Luckily Jake caught her before she could fall.

She was annoyed with herself for coming across as frail. He'd most likely think it was due to her husband's death – that she was grief-stricken. But it wasn't that at all. She thought she should make that clear, but couldn't find the energy.

'Would you like to go straight to bed or can I get you a cup of tea or something?' Jake asked as he closed the front door on the late afternoon. It was only just past five o'clock.

'I'm fine, Jake. Seriously, you don't have to fuss,' she said wearily. Emily hoped she didn't sound snappy and ungrateful. She made her way to the kitchen on autopilot and sat heavily on the nearest chair.

*Damn, I still have to unpack the car.* She decided to do it after a fortifying cup of tea, when she would hopefully have regained some energy. *Why am I so bloody tired anyway?* She'd done nothing all day but sit around eating and relaxing. Hell, she should be on a sugar high from the pavlova.

'I'll unpack the car after we've had a cuppa,' Jake said, going to the kettle and filling it.

Emily looked up at him, frowning slightly. Had she spoken aloud? Had he read her mind?

'No, I can do it, I'm fine.'

'No offence, Emily, but I don't think you are fine. You couldn't be; you've just heard your husband is dead.'

Emily sighed. How could she make him understand when she didn't really understand it herself?

'My estranged, soon to be *ex*-husband – as soon as was humanly possible. I know I shouldn't speak ill of the dead, but John was not a particularly nice man, and, quite frankly, his death does nothing but help to remove the reminder of what an awful mistake I made. And for that I'm grateful. There, see; I'm a heartless bitch,' Emily said, and shrugged.

Jake stayed silent.

'Honestly, all I feel is slight relief,' she added with another shrug.

'Okay. But you have seemed pretty down since we heard.'

'I don't know; I just feel tired. Not like I haven't had a decent night's sleep, more like I'm losing the will to deal with all this stuff. John's death means I'll have people asking how I feel, telling me they're sorry to hear of my loss, blah, blah, blah. And I'll have to pretend I care. It's just another thing I don't need in my life right now.' She sighed deeply.

'You're sounding overwhelmed,' Jake said, placing a steaming mug in front of her.

'Thanks,' she said, looking up at him. Still looking at him, she began to frown. That was the word; overwhelmed. He was absolutely right; that's exactly how she was feeling.

'It's like I've got so much to think about, deal with. I just want to curl up and wait for it all to go away.'

'Which of course it won't, unless you deal with it. You realise that don't you?'

'Yeah, I just don't know how or what to deal with first,' she said, sipping at her tea. 'I've got no idea what to do with the diamonds – they could give me my life back, but it would be wrong to get rid of them now, so soon after finding them. But Barbara disagrees. She thinks Gran would have wanted to help me. And there's also the possibility that Gran didn't even remember them.'

Jake nodded.

'I also need to sort out the subdivision, but if I go ahead I won't have any money to live on. I can't find a job anywhere, and Centrelink won't help me because I've apparently got too *much* bloody money. It's all such a mess.'

Emily threw her hands up in a gesture of helplessness, and was surprised to find her eyes filling with tears.

Jake got up and brought over a box of tissues from the far end of the kitchen bench.

'Thanks,' she said and plucked a couple out. She wiped at her eyes. She was relieved when Jake began speaking.

'The way I've learnt to deal with stress in my life – and believe me there have been plenty of hairy times – is to figure out what you have some control over and what you don't.'

Emily nodded, dabbed at her dripping nose and tried not to sniff.

'Then you start making decisions around the things you can control and put the other stuff out of your mind until it arises. You reduce the number of things bothering you by putting those you have no control over into a compartment in your brain and filing it under "not my problem". For example,

you have no control over what people think of you
and your relationship with your ex-husband. So you
have to make a conscious decision to take it out of
the pile of things to worry about.'

Emily looked down into her almost empty cup.
In her lap she clutched a wad of wet, soggy tissues.
She wanted to get up and put them in the bin, but
Jake hadn't finished.

'Then take the subdivision; that's something you
can control – in part. You've made the decision to
go ahead. Now you need to get the ball rolling by
making enquiries. I bet if you do then you'll start
feeling a lot better about it. Remember, knowledge
is power. You might find that things start to fall into
place – like maybe the surveying company might
want a significant deposit before doing any work and
that in turn might help sort out your problem with
Centrelink. Seriously Em, I know it doesn't feel like
it sometimes, but things do work themselves out –
and usually for the best.'

'I guess.'

'As for the diamonds, I think you should put all
thoughts of them aside. They've been there for what,
sixty years? Another few won't matter. I do think
that if you are meant to do something with them
then the answer will become clear at some point. But

if you're too stressed, you run the risk of missing it. You're in a better position to listen to your intuition when you're calm and rational.'

'You're right. Thanks Jake,' she said, smiling tearfully at him.

*God, he sounds just like Barbara.*

'You're welcome,' Jake said. 'Now come on, let's get this car unpacked,' he said, getting up.

Lying in bed later, Emily's thoughts returned to John's death. How did she really feel? She was sad for his parents, because although they had their faults, they were human and would be grieving. But she still felt a certain sense of relief at knowing she'd never have to bump into John or some woman he'd shacked up with ever again.

*Shit. What about the funeral?*

Of course she'd have to attend – in a small town everyone attended everyone's funeral. But would she stand beside his family as if she was still a part of it? Would she be expected to play the part of grieving widow? Could she?

Way too much to think about. Emily dragged the sheet and light blanket over her head in an effort to block out the thoughts. When that didn't work, she forced herself to remember Jake's words about not worrying about the things she couldn't control.

And the funeral was definitely something she couldn't control.

No, she'd have to cross that bridge when she came to it.

# Chapter Fourteen

Emily was still tossing and turning when her mobile rang beside her. Barbara's home number was on the display.

'Hi Barbara,' she said.

'Sorry to call so late, but I thought you'd like to know straight away...'

'Oh?'

'...about John – the facts, before you start hearing all the rumours that will be flying about already.'

'Okay.'

'You weren't asleep were you?'

'No.'

'It's just you sound a little vague.'

'Just a lot on my mind. So, tell me what happened.'

'Well it's a bit odd really, given he must have travelled Rowley Road a million times. Seems he lost it in the gravel on the big bend near the pine trees. Apparently it's just been graded, so I guess that wouldn't have helped. He must have been going pretty fast because they said the ute rolled three times before ending the right way up. The bloody idiot wasn't wearing a seatbelt – if he was they reckon he would have been okay by the looks of the damage to the vehicle, which, as you can imagine, is a total write-off. He was thrown clear, and ended up with his head against a concrete strainer post.'

'Was anyone with him? Was anyone else hurt?'

'No, thank goodness.'

'Was he drunk?'

'David doesn't think so. Obviously they won't know for sure until blood test results come back, but David said he couldn't smell any alcohol. So how are you doing?'

'Fine, I'm fine.'

'I guess it's understandable you're a bit quiet, a bit upset. You've had quite a shock.'

Emily felt a stab of annoyance at her friend. *Why does everyone think I should be upset?* She sighed; she really didn't have the energy to go through this conversation again tonight.

But Barbara was her best friend, with whom she could discuss anything, who wouldn't judge. She took a deep breath.

'I'm glad he's gone, actually. How terrible is that?'

'I'd say it's quite understandable, given the way he treated you. To tell you the truth, I'm a little relieved myself.'

'What? Why?!'

'I didn't want you wasting any more negative energy on that bastard. But I wouldn't be your friend if I didn't support you in whatever you felt – whether I agree or not.'

'Thanks Barb.'

'You're welcome. You'd do the same for me.'

'So you don't think I'm suddenly going to melt into a puddle of tears? I think Jake does.'

'Well, you might well fall in a heap at some point down the track, but I doubt it will be over John's death. Actually, you'll probably be a lot better because of it.'

'Why's that?'

'They do say that getting over a break-up can actually be harder than the death of a partner; with a break-up they remain as a reminder. I've heard of psychologists saying that people who've lost a loved one seem to recover more quickly than divorcees because of the more obvious break it creates in the phases of their lives.'

'Makes sense. I must admit I'm glad I'll never have to bump into him or one of his floozies on the street ever again.' An involuntary, audible yawn escaped Emily's lips.

'I'd better let you go. I'll speak to you tomorrow.'

'Okay. Thanks for letting me know straight away.'

'No problem. Sleep well.'

'You too. See you.'

★

Emily woke the next morning with the disconnected feeling of having dreamt a lot but without sense. She lay on her pillows with her eyes closed, trying to conjure back the remnants. Early in the night she knew she'd dreamt of John – terrifying scenes of their life together; the good, the bad, and the downright ugly – ending with a car wrapped around a large gum tree with her trapped in the passenger's side.

She'd woken in fright, sweating, and with her heart racing. A check of the time on her mobile had revealed it was only 3:00 a.m. She'd lain there trying to get back to sleep, trying to think of anything but John, her poor financial situation, what the hell she was going to do with her life, and the many other random thoughts that would pop into her mind if she didn't keep them at bay.

But what was it she'd most recently been dreaming? Whatever it was, it hadn't been about John. She screwed her eyes tighter, trying to search the dark depths of her mind.

And then it came to her: Jake. She'd dreamt about Jake, hadn't she? They were at some function together. She remembered how handsome he'd looked in his dark pin-stripe suit. She'd been wearing tailored black pants with a formal wraparound shirt of deep smoky blue-grey silk in almost the exact shade as the diamonds in Gran's button jar. But why? Where were they? What was the event?

And was he there as her partner or just a supportive friend?

With a sudden pang, she realised she would really miss him when he said goodbye. Not just his cheery company, but on a deeper level, his companionship.

*Oh God. I'm starting to seriously like him.*

*He lives in Melbourne,* she heard her rational self say, *and the last thing you need is another relationship, especially now. He's just a friend; it's only because he's so nice and you're vulnerable that you're getting carried away.*

*Stop it!*

Emily sighed. She could tell herself all this, but the ache in the pit of her stomach told her there was no point pretending. It was probably best that he was leaving that morning. Otherwise she might soon be behaving like a lovesick teenager.

The feeling was familiar; something she hadn't experienced for many years and hadn't thought she'd feel again. But she recognised it immediately; the birth of an intense longing that inevitably progressed into never wanting to spend time apart.

It was the sort of fluttering triggered by the most obscure things; the way someone held their head when deep in concentration or sipped at their mug. The little things that you wanted to watch for the rest of your life. *Love.*

Emily didn't believe in love at first sight; in her mind relationships grew from the inside out as each person got to know and like the other at a soul and values level.

Love happened when there was a strong enough connection that you could enjoy the silence together without the need to entertain, as well as have a healthy debate where each could express their own opinion freely.

It was also about knowing what the other person needed and happily giving it – even when it meant a little sacrifice of your own. Well, that was how she thought it should be. It was what she'd felt in the beginning with John.

So, really, what did she know? She'd been conned by her own feelings before. No, she couldn't allow that to happen again.

John! Oh bloody hell! She'd have to phone his parents and offer her condolences as soon as a civilised hour for calls arrived. Did they even know yet? *Should I be the one to tell them? No, surely the police will do that.*

She hadn't spoken to or seen the Strattens since the split. Would they blame her; be upset with her? Maybe. People reacted to grief in all sorts of ways. But she'd just have to take it on the chin and remain calm and considerate of what they were going through.

Emily heard movement in the next room, a door being opened and closed, and then footsteps and the creaking of floorboards. Jake was up and making his way down the hall.

Ah Jake. She thought of trying to force herself back to the dream in a moment of indulgence. He'd looked very handsome all dressed up in a suit and tie. Not that he didn't look good in jeans, t-shirt and rough stubble. God, how was she going to face him now? She was bound to turn beetroot red.

She got up, dragged on her robe and made her way to the kitchen. She paused in the doorway, watching him filling the kettle at the sink. Her heart fluttered; she loved seeing him so at home in her house. He turned as she entered.

'Good morning sleepyhead,' he said, grinning at her.

Emily grinned back, her heart flip-flopping. She willed her colour to stay neutral. 'Good morning yourself, early bird.'

'Hope I didn't wake you.'

'No, been awake for ages. Had the strangest dream,' she found herself adding.

'Care to share?'

'Not much to tell. You know how dreams are – not really making sense and all over the place.' Emily felt her colour rise. She tried to will it away by busying herself with getting the breakfast things out.

Jake put two mugs of coffee on the table and Emily thanked him. They lapsed into silence, unlike the previous morning when they'd chattered non-stop.

'Oh, I texted my mate Anthony last night about finding you a surveyor. He'll get the ball rolling for you as soon as he can.'

'That's great. Thanks very much.' Emily couldn't muster any enthusiasm. She doubted anything would happen for weeks; everyone was off work for the Christmas/New Year break and most businesses were closed.

'My pleasure.' Jake paused. 'Are you okay, Em? You seem awfully quiet? Understandable, I guess, given yesterday's shock.'

'I'm fine, seriously. It's just that when I've had a really vivid dream it sort of makes me feel weird for a while. I just feel a bit out of kilter.'

'Sort of like you're stuck between reality and the dream?' he asked. 'I get the same thing, though it hasn't happened to me for ages. So, tell me about your dream. Unless of course it was some erotic fantasy in which I featured.'

Emily looked up at him and blushed furiously. Jake was grinning cheekily. Was he flirting with her?

'I knew it; I'm just so damned irresistible,' he said, throwing his arms wide. Emily looked away.

'Don't be ridiculous, Jake. I did *not* have an erotic dream about you.' *May as well tell him.* 'But you did feature. Fully dressed. In a suit actually.'

'Really? How very odd. Must have been a *very* important occasion to get me dressed up. Where were we? We were together, I take it?'

'Yes.' Emily found herself relaxing. 'I think it was the opening of something. For all I know, it's a sign

I'm to open a B&B or something,' she said with a laugh and took a deep slug of her now lukewarm coffee.

'This place would be great for a B&B. As I said the other night, you could fill in the side verandah for ensuites off the rooms on that side.'

'Seriously, though,' she continued, 'do you think dreams are there to tell us things – guide us?'

'God, that's one of those meaning-of-life questions,' he said with a laugh. 'And it's way too early in the morning for *that* con-versation. But I do think you'd be a great host – you're a fantastic cook, and great company.'

'Thanks Jake, I've loved you being here.'

'And I've loved being here.'

They fell into a slightly awkward silence.

'I guess you need to decide just how much you like having visitors – every week or weekend, not just here and there,' Jake finally said, breaking the silence.

'Hmm. You don't think I'm too far from town – off the beaten track?'

'Not necessarily. Some people might see that as a virtue – it's all in the marketing.'

'But would anyone want to be so far from a major city or town?'

'Are you kidding? Of course they would – to see birds, trees, taste your cooking, not to mention your wonderful jam. God, Em, it's what the sea change, tree change, thing is all about – people escaping from their life and re-charging, if only for just a few days.'

'There's actually a retired couple, the Havelocks, setting up a B&B the other side of town.'

'Competition is healthy. And you might be going for different clientele. I imagine an older couple might want older, retired, people visiting. You just choose your market and then target it correctly. For instance, you make it more appealing for middle-aged executives rather than families with snotty-nosed kids. Not that all kids are snotty-nosed,' he quickly added.

'Oh, I hadn't even thought about who. I'm not sure I'd want children running through the place.'

'Well, that's important to know from the start – it'll help you formulate your plan.'

'It's not that I dislike kids, I just don't have any experience with them.'

'I know what you mean. My cousin Milly's kids are pretty good, but just one day with them is enough; I'm always pleased to hand them back. It's exhausting.'

'So you really think a B&B could work here? I'm not too far out of town?'

'You just have to make it worth the effort, that's all. The more cellar doors and antique shops that open up in the area, the more people who will be looking for nice accommodation. And I'm sorry, but the motel in town won't really cut it. I'm sure it's clean and comfortable, but it's hardly a dream getaway. I checked them out online before I rang you, actually.' Now he looked a little sheepish.

'Why?'

'I wanted to visit, but wasn't sure how you'd feel about me staying here on my own. And being Christmas and everything... Anyway, they were booked out all weekend.'

'Well, I'm glad they were booked out; I've enjoyed having you here. I'm going to miss you.' Emily hadn't meant to say the words out loud, but it was too late.

Next moment Jake's hand was across the table and over hers, giving it a gentle squeeze. Emily looked up at him.

'I'm going to miss you too,' he said.

She tried to read his expression. Was it just friendly, was he teasing, or did he seem slightly sad too?

'Oh, look at the time. I'd better get going.' Jake leapt up, breaking the spell and the silent gaze before it could get awkward again.

He collected their bowls, spoons and mugs, and carried them to the sink. Emily followed him as he left the kitchen, collected his small suitcase and strode towards the front door. She felt a pang of sadness watching his back. She had always hated goodbyes.

They hugged on the verandah; Jake, a head taller, with his chin near her hair.

Then he bent down and ruffled Grace's ears.

'Look after your mum, there's a good girl,' he said to the dog before standing up again. He gave Emily a quick peck on the cheek before skipping down the steps to his car and stowing his suitcase in the boot.

He got in, turned on the vehicle, and drove away with a wave from the open window.

Emily continued to stare, long after his car was swallowed up by the trees. Had he lingered just that bit longer than standard friendship? Had he kissed her hair affectionately? Had he held her tighter than when he'd hugged her on arrival?

Grace's claws to Emily's thigh brought her back and she went inside, telling herself the catch in her throat was silly. *God, Emily, it's like you're seeing your husband off to war or something. Get a grip!*

'Such a bloody romantic,' she said aloud. 'Come on girl, let's go find the last of the apricots and make some jam to try and keep our minds off everything.'

In the distance she noticed dark clouds beginning to loom. *That'd be right*, she thought wryly. They matched her mood.

# Chapter Fifteen

While Emily was occupied with gathering the last of the apricots, the bank of heavy purple-grey clouds moved closer. It was only when she finished and looked up to check their progress that she noticed. They seemed to chase her and Grace as they hurried back down the gully to the house.

'Phew Gracie, just in time!' Emily said, a little out of breath, as they closed the door on the black sky and the first large drops began to fall. Soon it was coming down in buckets.

Thankfully she had jam to make to distract her from looking up at the roof for signs of damp. Worrying wouldn't help; she'd just have deal with leaks when and if they happened. She silently asked the house gods for a break.

★

She had just finished filling the jars and was washing up the pans when her phone rang. She dragged off her rubber gloves as she crossed to the kitchen table. Her parents' number was on the screen.

'Hello, Emily speaking.'

'Emily. It's your mother.'

Emily steeled herself for the inevitable. Enid's tone told her she was about to be told off. *What have I done now?*

'Hi Mum. How are you feeling? We missed you on Christmas day.'

'Well, if you were concerned, it might have been nice for you to enquire about my welfare, Emily.'

'Sorry, I've...'

'Anyway, that's not why I'm calling. Now, your father and I have just heard about John's accident. What a terrible tragedy for you. Poor John. Please accept our sincere condolences.'

'Thanks Mum.' *You do realise we were estranged, don't you?*

'How are Thora and Gerald holding up?'

'I don't know. I haven't spoken to them.'

'Why ever not?'

'Uh, well, I'm not really sure what to say.'

'Oh Emily, now is not the time to be selfish. They need your support. They are going through the worst thing a parent can go through and you don't know what to *say*? Oh for goodness sake.'

Emily tightened her shoulders. She was supposed to be a strong, independent woman, not a five-year-old girl. She had to stand up for herself.

'Mum, John and I were separated. You know that. It's not for me to turn up and pretend like everything was fine. How would that look?'

'Like you care, Emily. That's how it would look. Why should Thora and Gerald suffer because of your petty little squabble? They're family; they need us around them at a time like this.'

'Well, *you* call them.'

'I will. Just as soon as I know you've been out to see them!'

'Mum, I'm not driving out to see them.'

'Now Emily... Oh hang on. What is it, Des?'

There was the sound of a hand being put over the phone and a muffled conversation in the background.

*God,* should *I be going out there – pretending our separation didn't happen? I'd look like a complete hypocrite. It wouldn't be right, the estranged wife of their dead son turning up and acting like a grieving widow. No, I won't do it.*

Suddenly Enid was back on the phone. 'Emily, your father is demanding to speak to you. Just think about what I said and for God's sake do the right thing.'

'Bye Mum,' Emily said, but there was no response. Then there was the scratching sound of the phone being handed over.

'Hi Em.'

'Hi Dad.' She let out a sigh of relief.

'Are you okay? John's death must have shaken you up a bit.'

'It has a little. I know Gerald and Thora have lost their son. I just don't...'

'I know, dear heart. You and John and Thora and Gerald have history. Just because your marriage didn't work out, doesn't mean you don't care what they're going through.'

'So do you think I should be going out there to see them?'

'That's not for me to say.'

'I'm not totally heartless. I just don't think it would help them to see me.'

'I tend to agree.'

'Mum thinks I...'

Des Oliphant let out a deep sigh. 'Sweetheart, you and I both know your mum means well, but she has the blinkers on when it comes to you and John.'

Blindfold more like, Emily wanted to say.

'The only person you are answerable to is yourself. You can only do what you feel is right.'

'Thanks Dad.'

'You don't have to thank me. I just want you to be happy — we both do.'

'Mum sure has a funny way of showing it.'

'Take no notice. This has hit her hard. As I'm sure it has you. Grief's a funny thing. Well, you know — not *funny* funny.'

'I know what you meant.'

'I think every new death reminds us of all those we've said goodbye to before. It isn't necessarily the person, but the feeling around death — the memory of the loss and... Oh, listen to me getting all philosophical.'

It made a lot of sense, but before Emily could reply, he continued.

'All I'm saying is, allow yourself to feel whatever you feel, and do whatever you have to do for your own soul. No one else can truly know how you really feel and certainly no one can tell you how you should react.'

'Hmm.'

'I know you have Barbara, and I'm so pleased you do, but if you need another shoulder, you only have to ask.'

'Thanks.'

'And don't worry about your mum. As I've said, we all deal with death and grief in our own way. It's a tricky business.'

'Hmm.'

'Okay then, better go and see if the eye of the storm has passed,' he said jovially. 'Bye for now.'

'Okay, see you. Thanks for the call.'

Emily hung up and was surprised to find herself bursting into tears. And not just a few drops. She plucked tissues from the box. *Oh Gran, I miss you so much.* Her heart ached so badly she could barely draw breath.

Grace appeared beside her and nudged her leg. Emily slid off the chair and onto the floor to cradle the dog in her lap. With her arms wrapped around the puppy, she sobbed into the soft fur on her neck.

'Oh God, Gracie,' she mumbled. 'What would I do without you?'

Soon Grace struggled free from Emily's grasp and sat in front of her mistress, catching the tears that dripped from her chin, her head twisted slightly and her features showing the concerned expression that was so much a part of the border collie. Emily couldn't help but smile. Slowly her tears subsided.

'Mummy's okay, she's just a little sad,' she said. She put her hands around the dog's small face, leaned forward and kissed her on the head. 'Your grand-dad's right; grief is a tricky business.'

Of course she was sad about John – all death was sad. But it didn't mean she was ready to forgive him. Maybe one day, but right now it was all too recent, too raw.

She felt for Gerald and Thora as well, but she couldn't just drop everything and rush to their side like the good little daughter-in-law. It would be too awkward. She'd see them at the funeral, and in the meantime she'd send a nice card and carefully worded note.

Emily felt much better for having made the decision. Although there was a lingering niggle of doubt. What would Gran have said? Damned if you do, damned if you don't?

She got up from the floor and pulled herself together. Outside, the rain was coming down hard.

Minutes later her phone rang again and Jake's name appeared on the screen. Emily was so relieved she almost burst into tears again. It took considerable effort to keep her voice steady.

'Hi Jake!'

'Hi Em, how's things?'

'I'm okay. How was your trip back to the steel city?'

'Fine. No dramas. Anthony and I are off for an early dinner and then it will be a very early night. I'm pretty tired actually. As I'm sure you must be...'

'I am a bit.'

'It's a lot to take in.'

'Hmm.' He was obviously giving her room to talk about how she was feeling, but she didn't want to burden him with it all.

'You don't have to talk about it if you don't want to. But I'm here for you if you do.'

'Thanks Jake, I really appreciate it.'

'Well, I really wanted to just check on you and thank you so much again for a lovely weekend.'

'It was my pleasure. And don't forget you have an open invitation. You're welcome to stay anytime you like.'

'Careful what you offer, Em. I might be there every weekend.'

*And I wouldn't mind if you were.*

She liked the sound of his voice, especially the way he said the shortened form of her name. 'If only I could put you to work for your keep,' she said with a laugh.

'I'm sure it'll all work itself out. At least you've got things moving with the survey – that's a step in the right direction.'

'I hope so.'

As if sensing an awkward moment coming on, Jake started ending the call.

'Well, I'd better get going; Anthony will be here any minute. We're trying the local Chinese restaurant tonight.'

'That sounds nice. Please thank him for organising the surveyors.'

'I certainly will.'

'And thank you so much for calling.'

'You're welcome. You take care of yourself, Em. And remember, I'm here if you need me.'

# Chapter Sixteen

The question of whether to write, phone or visit John's parents in person had started as a niggle, but ended up fully consuming Emily.

That night she tossed and turned well into the early hours, the thunderstorm raging overhead adding to her angst. The whole house rumbled as if a freight train was going through, and lightning lit up her bedroom from behind the ancient blinds and curtains.

Emily spent the night teetering between concern about the roof and what to do about John's parents. At one point, Grace appeared at her bedroom door, scratching and whining to be let in. Rather than tell her off and send her back to the kitchen, Emily welcomed her into her bed.

In the morning she was bleary-eyed and no closer to a decision. She considered ringing Barbara, but she really had to start making these decisions for herself. It wasn't right to rely on her friend so much. Barbara had her own issues – grieving for her father in-law, looking after her husband – and was exhausted from having a houseful of guests stay for the funeral. The fact she had sent a text yesterday rather than ringing told Emily her friend needed some space. Emily had texted back, thanking her for checking, telling her that she was fine, and that she hoped Barbara was too.

That was the thing about great friendships; you could have your space when you needed it and a friend would understand.

So, as much as Emily wanted to consult with her over what to do about the Strattens, she hadn't, and wouldn't. Anyway, she was sure Barbara would just say something along the lines of what her father had said; that, really, it was entirely up to her.

Refusing to give in to the washed-out feeling, Emily dragged herself out of bed, had coffee and breakfast, and set her mind to dealing with domestic duties. Thankfully the dark clouds had temporarily passed, and where she was looked clear for getting some washing dry.

She had just come in after hanging out the sheets, when her phone skittered on the bench beside her and began ringing. The display showed her parents' home number. She sighed. If she ignored it she'd just have to phone back later. If it was her mother, it would be best to just get it over with. As she answered it she sent up a prayer to no one in particular that it be her father; she really didn't have the energy for another tussle.

'Hello, Emily speaking.'

'Now Emily...'

*Oh God, here we go.* She took a deep, fortifying breath.

'...your father and I have been talking and we've decided we can lend you five thousand dollars.'

*What?*

Emily could hear her father in the background. She couldn't make out what he was saying, but the fact that she could hear him at all over her mother meant whatever it was it wasn't good.

'Oh! Wow! Well, thanks Mum, but I don't think...'

'But your father said you were short of money.'

'Well yes I am, but I'm sure I'll manage. I really appreciate the offer, but I'd rather sort it out on my own.'

'What about Gerald and Thora? Have you spoken to them?'

*Why on earth would I borrow money from the Strattens? Has she completely lost the plot?* Emily frowned. How could her mother think her so insensitive?

'Um, no, why would...?' Emily's cheeks began to flame.

'Well he *is* their son, Emily. They should at least be consulted.'

*Consulted? About what? What the hell are you on about?*

'Sorry Mum, but what are you talking about?'

'The funeral of course, Emily! For goodness sake, you really are dense sometimes!'

*The funeral.* Emily's mouth dropped open. Was her mother seriously suggesting she pay for John's funeral? No, surely not.

Jesus, what was the protocol here anyway? Would it be any different if she had plenty of money?

'Emily! Are you still there?'

'Yes, I'm here.' Emily searched her mind for some way to stall things. She could hear her father again in the background. He was now practically shouting.

'Well?'

'Well what?'

'You're sure you don't want the money – it's just that it's in an account we have to give notice on.'

Emily's head was swimming. What was she supposed to say? Why would she pay for his funeral anyway, and why would anyone – least of all her mother – expect her to?!

It wasn't fair. Where was the 'If you're unhappy, darling, then of course you should leave', the 'You have our full support; whatever you need', and the 'We just want you to be happy'? Instead, Enid had given her a lecture about lying in the bed she'd made – she'd as good as sided with John.

Emily felt a sudden feeling of vindictiveness engulf her; she should tell her mother just what a piece of shit her son-in-law had really been.

But no, she acknowledged, calming slightly; she'd just come across as petty. Enid only ever saw what she wanted to see. Her mother would say it was the grief talking and offer some pep talk about time healing all. And Emily couldn't bear that. She was not grieving; she was bloody furious!

'Emily! Emily! Des, are you there? There must be something wrong with her phone,' she heard her mother say to the background. It seemed her father had given up trying to convince her to stop this nonsense phone call.

Emily bit her lip as she tried to find the right tone – firm and rational but holding the fury in check. She took a deep breath before speaking.

'Mum, John and I had separated. You know this. In just under a year we would have been signing divorce papers. So I have absolutely no intention of paying for his funeral. It is not my responsibility.'

'Of course it is; you're his wife. It's your place, Emily.' The unspoken question – 'What will people think?' – hung in the air.

'Mum! You are not listening to me!' Emily shut her mouth and silently counted to five in an attempt to calm herself. 'He'd been with at least one woman since we split up, probably more; let the most recent one deal with it!'

'Emily! What a dreadfully disrespectful thing to say. The man has died; at least show some compassion.'

Emily again toyed with providing a few home truths, but shook the thoughts aside and stayed silent.

'Well, you should at least phone Thora and Gerald.'

Of course she should, and she would. Probably. Maybe. But not for the reasons Enid was thinking.

It would be a difficult phone call to make. She hadn't spoken to either of them since she'd left their son. Now she at least had a valid excuse, and her call would be expected. She felt a ripple of fear make its way through her before disappearing.

'Yes, I will phone them. But it will only be to offer my condolences and certainly not to offer to pay for or organise the funeral.'

There was silence on the other end of the line.

'Mum? Are you still there?'

'Emily, it's me, Dad. Your mother's a bit upset.'

Emily heard a door slam in the background. 'Sorry Dad.'

'Don't be. I did try to explain that it had nothing to do with you, but you know how stubborn your mother can be...'

'Yes.' And now Enid would go off and sulk for not having got her way. Emily had seen it so many times before. Back when she was still living at home, if things hadn't improved after an hour, Emily would seek her mother out and inevitably back down on whatever she'd done to upset her.

With a bit of a shock, Emily realised she'd never actually stood up to her mother and then continued to stand her ground. With the realisation came a little sense of empowerment. She allowed herself a moment of congratulations. Not for upsetting her mother – she actually felt quite guilty about that – but for properly standing up for herself for once. And she was not going to back down this time.

'Em, don't worry about it. I'll try again to make her see sense.'

'Dad?'

'Yes?'

'You don't think I should be paying for John's funeral do you?'

'Not for a bloody second!'

'Even if money wasn't such an issue?'

'Absolutely not! God, Em, don't let your mother's insane notion get into your head. She's just worried about what people will think – you know how she is.'

'Dad, she does know it was definitely over between us, doesn't she?'

'Yes.' He paused. 'Well, I thought so. But I think with his death she's retreated into some sort of fantasy land where the two of you are concerned.'

'Great,' Emily said with a groan. 'She's not, you know, showing signs of, um, Alzheimer's or something, is she?'

'No, I don't think so. I am keeping an eye out because of the family history, but I think this is just a case of wishful thinking and severe disappointment.'

'I hate her being disappointed in me,' Emily said, suddenly feeling vulnerable again.

'You and me both, dear,' Des said with a deep sigh. 'Look, I'd better go. I'll call you later if I get the chance.'

'All right. And Dad, sorry again.'

'There's nothing to be sorry about. I'll speak to you soon.'

'Okay. See you.'

Emily hung up and sat staring at the phone in her hand. Just how had Des Oliphant put up with all the drama all these years? To a degree it was duty – in the sense of marriage vows – but she couldn't help thinking there was a hell of a lot more to it than that.

She shook the frustration aside and went back over the conversation with her mother. The more she thought about it, the more she fumed. She scrolled through her most recent calls log and pressed the send button when she got to Barbara's number. She tried to force herself to breathe slowly and deeply as she waited for it to connect and then start ringing. *Please be there*, she silently prayed to the empty room.

'Hi Em.'

'Sorry, but I need to vent!' Emily blurted.

'What's happened?'

'My mother!'

'Oh. What's she done now?'

'She's just been trying to lend me five grand to pay for John's funeral because it's my place to sort it out!'

'Jesus.'

'Can you believe it?!'

'Well yes, actually,' Barbara said, with a tight laugh, which instantly had Emily feeling a little better.

'Yeah, actually, me too.'

'So I take it you said, "Thanks very much Mummy dearest, but no thanks"?'

'Well actually...'

'Oh Em, please don't tell me you're going to do it.'

'Only kidding. No, I told her there was no way I'd pay for that piece of shit's funeral – well, obviously in language a little less colourful.'

'And?'

'And of course she didn't want to accept that.'

'But did she – eventually – accept it?'

'I'm not sure. She handed the phone over to Dad and presumably went off to sulk. After slamming a door.'

'It's not often your mother doesn't get her own way, is it?'

'Understatement of the century. You know, Barb, I can't remember ever standing up to her like I did just now – and not eventually backing down.'

'Well, it's long overdue. And I certainly hope you don't back down.'

'Not a chance. Why should I spend five grand just to keep my mother happy? Maybe once upon a time, but not now.'

'Good to hear. I've been waiting for you to start standing up for yourself for ages – especially where your mother is concerned. I would have said something before, but you've been too fragile to hear it.'

'I see that now; things are going to change around here. They already are.'

# Chapter Seventeen

Wednesday morning, after another sleepless, stormy night, Emily sat at the huge kitchen table turning her mobile phone over end to end in one hand. She'd never get a decent night's sleep if she didn't contact Gerald and Thora. *And if the damned rain doesn't let up.* The time had come to cease the niggle inside her once and for all. The question was, should she phone or drive out there? What if they weren't home or had the place locked up? She supposed she could leave a note at the gate. And if they were home, would they welcome her or be hostile?

They were, after all, grieving for their son and there was a chance that they might somehow blame her. Would they?

Despite their different backgrounds, Emily had always got along quite well with John's parents. They'd never hung out together just for fun, but there hadn't been the tension she'd heard some people mention when talking about their relationships with in-laws.

But things would be different now. They hadn't called at the time to say they were sorry the marriage had ended, or offered any assistance. Then again, why should they have? They were probably busy with John. But at least it would have showed that they cared.

She'd felt part of their small family, and while she knew she'd left it when she'd left John, she thought they'd at least have spoken to her parents. She wondered whether Enid had phoned them.

Emily frowned. How would they feel about her turning up out of the blue? Well, it wasn't exactly out of the blue – whilst she'd been reluctant to acknowledge it, it was pretty much mandatory that she acknowledge John's death. That much was obvious.

Emily sighed. She really didn't know what the best thing to do was. Phoning would certainly be easier on everyone. It probably wouldn't cut the mustard in her mother's etiquette stakes, but that was too bad.

Emily's finger shook and her heart raced as she dialled the Strattens' number and waited for someone to answer.

'Hello, Thora speaking.' Emily noted how tired she sounded; not her normal carefully clipped accent.

'Um, hello Thora, it's Emily.' There was a pause and Emily wond-ered if she needed to add, 'your soon-to-be-ex-daughter-in-law'.

'Emily, hello. Nice of you to call back.'

Emily recognised the tone at once as a rebuke. *Nice of me to call back?* Had she missed a message? No, she didn't think so.

'Thora, I'm so sorry about John. It must have been a terrible shock for you.' Emily hated the banality of her words, but what else could she say?

'No different for you I imagine, Emily.'

Emily frowned. *What a strange response.* Oh, well, the poor woman was grieving, and could hardly be expected to be her usual self.

She offered a quiet, non-committal, 'Mmm.'

'I must say I am relieved he wasn't another casualty of drink driving, as I'm sure you are – though I wouldn't have been surprised.'

'Uh, yes.' Emily shook her head and tried to under-stand the strange direction the conversation was taking.

'I suppose you want to talk about funeral arrange-ments. Well, you're not to worry about a thing; Gerald and I will organise everything. It looks like next Tuesday will probably be the date.'

'But...' *Why the bloody hell does everyone think I should have anything to do with the funeral?*

'No, we insist; you've got enough on your plate, sorting out John's affairs and coming to terms with it all.'

*But I don't understand. Why should I have to sort out his affairs? It's got nothing to do with me.*

'Actually, there is one thing. We'll need his outfit for the funeral. It'll be easiest if you leave it at the post office for Gerald to collect – by lunchtime Friday at the latest.'

Emily opened her mouth and closed it again. *I have to do what?*

'Now,' Thora continued, changing the subject, 'Gerald will come down once a week – more often when it's hot – to check on the sheep and clean out the troughs for you. We'll talk about the crops later. If there's anything else you need help with in the meantime, you only have to ask.'

Emily's head was beginning to swim. *God, surely they don't expect me to take over the farm. It's their land, isn't it?*

She knew from Des that John had been bought out of his share of the family company, but everything was still owned by the company, wasn't it? The land alone would be worth in the order of a million, not the three hundred grand he'd reportedly been paid.

Emily couldn't shake the uneasy feeling that something wasn't quite right about all this, but she didn't want to look like an idiot by probing further. And if she didn't ask, she wouldn't have any more put on her plate to deal with. Ignorance wasn't exactly bliss, but in this case it was helpful. If the Strattens expected any more of her, they'd have to spell it out.

'I know you have Enid, but if you need some company, you only have to ask. I understand widows usually find nights the hardest to deal with. You're still family, you know.'

*Need company? Still family?*

And then slowly a new realisation dawned for Emily. The blood seemed to freeze in her veins.

*Bloody hell. Do they think we were still together? No, surely not. Do I say something? I can't; not now, not like this. How could they not know? How could he not have told them?*

She shook her head slowly at the irony that John could still cause her such discomfort – even from the steel confines of the mortuary. *Bastard.*

'Are you still there, Emily?'

'Yes, sorry, I'm here. Just a lot on my mind. Thanks for the offer; I'll keep it in mind.'

'It's a lot to take in, a lot to organise, but we know you're a capable young woman – you'll be fine. As will we.'

Emily heard what sounded like a stifled sniffle and then Thora clearing her throat.

'I'd better go; I have to call the undertaker,' Thora added hurriedly.

'Well, please let me know if there is anything else I can do to help.' *What else am I supposed to say?*

'I will; thank you. Bye for now.'

'Bye Thora.'

Emily put down the phone and stared at it for a few moments while commending herself on her decision to phone rather than drive out to see them.

She picked it up again and dialled Barbara.

'Em, hi. How's things?'

'Sorry to bother you, Barb, but I need to talk to someone.'

'What's happened?'

'Well, I've just been speaking to Thora Stratten, John's mother, and you'll never guess what...'

'What?'

'She seemed to have no idea we'd split up.'

'No! You're kidding?'

'I wish I was.'

'But people have been talking about it for weeks.'

'I know.'

'Has she been away?'

'Not that I know of.'

'So what did you say? Did you enlighten her?'

'Nothing really. And no, I couldn't bring myself to – she has enough to deal with right now.'

'You're going to have to tell her sometime.'

'I couldn't do it on the phone. I was just so shocked that she didn't know.'

'Hmm, maybe best to leave sleeping dogs lie. But not forever. You will have to tell them. You know that, right?'

'God, Barb, the last thing I want to do is go back to the farm, let alone sort through his things. And choose his burial outfit – can you believe she wants me to do that?'

'I'll help; it won't be so bad.'

'Thanks, Barb. I was hoping you'd offer,' Emily said a little sheepishly.

'So when do you want to do it; tomorrow, get it over with?'

'That would be good, actually, if you can spare the day. They need the clothes by Friday lunchtime – I have to leave them at the post office. Don't let me forget.'

'No problem. But I'd better go now and sort out a few things.'

'Okay, thanks so much.'

'It's quite okay. I'll pick you up at nine – I'll bring the ute, just in case you find some things you want.'

'Oh, okay, good thinking – thanks.'

'Well, I'll see you then.'

Emily snapped the phone shut. She hated the thought of going back to the farm, let alone going through John's things. The only comfort was the knowledge that he would have hated it even more than her.

# Chapter Eighteen

'Ready to do this?' Barbara called through the open window.

'As ready as I'll ever be. You've no idea how much this means. Thank you,' Emily said, settling herself into the front passenger's seat of Barbara's dual cab ute. 'The things we do,' she added as she fastened her seatbelt.

'Well, you could have told Thora the truth and got out of it.'

Emily didn't reply. She was feeling decidedly uneasy about going out to the farm again, let alone the tasks ahead of them.

'At least it looks like the weather might be kind today.'

'Hmm.'

'Your roof holding up okay? I'm sure I heard hail last night.'

'So far so good,' Emily said.

They drove the rest of the way into town lost in their separate thoughts. Emily's stomach churned. She'd only just got used to being the subject of gossip thanks to her separation from John. It had taken weeks before she could do a trip to town without becoming a quivering mess. Now she was feeling that way all over again. If only they didn't have to stop. But they did; they needed a few boxes to pack up belongings – there were bound to be things that she would want to take home.

The place was abuzz with people stocking up after the Christmas long weekend, scurrying about and enjoying the bright sunshine after the rain. A bout of rain always seemed to put the town on a collective high.

A few times Emily noticed that voices seemed to quieten when she was within earshot. A couple of times she caught the words 'John' and 'his wife'. People who might ordinarily have stopped to discuss the weather or the most recent political happenings were apparently too busy tapping away on their smartphones or studying their shopping lists to utter a word. They seemed to immediately look down upon seeing her.

Emily forcibly kept her demeanour light and cheery and her head held high, despite noting that very few people held her gaze longer than the split-second nod of vague greeting. Barbara didn't seem to notice or, more likely, just chose to ignore it.

When they had finished scouring the town for packaging, Emily went to the post office while Barbara went to the hardware store to pay their account.

She had just crossed the road to come back after checking her post box — empty except for a selection of colourful glossy advertising brochures — when she was accosted by Beryl Egbert.

'I'm so sorry for your loss.'

Emily looked blankly at the stooped old lady for a moment. It took her another second to realise she was talking about John. She made her expression sombre.

'Thank you,' Emily said, forcing herself to sound sad.

'Do you know yet when the funeral will be?'

'I understand it'll be Tuesday. Thora and Gerald are handling all the arrangements.'

'And how are they holding up?'

'As well as can be expected under the circumstances.' Emily felt the desperate need to flee. 'I'm sorry Mrs Egbert, but I really must be going.'

'Of course, dear. I'd better go and get started on the sausage rolls.'

'I'm sure Thora will really appreciate a plate for the wake,' Emily said, offering her a warm smile. The old lady was famous for her sausage rolls, identifiable by random fork marks in the pastry. Emily thought they just might be the best in the district.

It seemed Beryl Egbert was the sign everyone else needed to stop muttering behind Emily's back and offer their condolences to her face. Six old women and three old men approached her with their sympathies during the fifty metres back to Barbara's ute. Emily nodded and muttered her thanks in reply.

Barbara wasn't back when Emily reached the vehicle. While she sat waiting, she wondered why people thought it necessary to offer her condolences. Had they all forgotten she'd left John just over a month ago? Had they forgotten about him gallivanting around town with another woman? Had his death triggered some sort of separation from reality, collective amnesia?

Jesus, she suddenly thought, thank Christ he'd not ended up on life support. Otherwise she might have been expected to sit beside him in hospital, patting his hand as if they'd still been happily married.

And then a funny thought struck her: no doubt the old biddies would have her patting his left hand

and his latest fling stroking the other. Emily shook her head at the absurdity of it all.

One thing was for sure, though; alive or dead, people expected her to behave as the dutiful wife. It was clear now she'd have to at least make some effort to appear as the grieving widow. Not the relieved estranged wife she actually was.

She sighed, hating the hypocrisy she was entering into – had already entered into. But it was easier than pointing out the truth.

And of course there were the sensibilities of townsfolk to consider; a life lost was still a life lost, and everyone deserved to be grieved for, no matter their sins on earth. God, she was well and truly indoctrinated. Perhaps it *was* time to think about leaving the district.

'Sorry about that, took longer than I thought,' Barbara said as she got in. 'The place was packed.'

'No problem, I haven't been waiting long.'


As they headed out on the road that Emily must have driven nearly a thousand times – but not once since leaving John – she wondered how she felt, and decided that empty was the best way to describe it. Empty and numb.

They slowed down when they came to the stretch of road where John had lost his life, both glancing at the shiny new section of wire fence and disturbed earth where the thick round concrete strainer post in the corner of the paddock had been replaced.

Emily noticed Barbara glance quickly at her before returning her attention to the scene outside. The corner that John Stratten had missed last Sunday afternoon was a long, sweeping bend with plenty of warning, plenty of signage, and plenty of visibility. So what had gone wrong?

Emily wondered if he had been doing something as simple as changing the volume or channel on the radio, or lighting a cigar-ette. It made her a little sad to think of something so everyday snuffing out a life.

God, she really did not want to go back to the farm – it was too much like a backwards step. And just when things were finally starting to look a little brighter.

They came around the final bend, and as Emily listened to the fine gravel spraying the underneath of the vehicle, she kept her eyes fixed on the blue-grey-green of the small gums and mallee trees grouped in the corner of the first of John's paddocks.

She'd convinced him that a stand of trees in the corner would offer the sheep protection and better define the boundary. He'd reluctantly agreed, but had left her to plant the five hundred and fifty seedlings on her own. It had taken her a week, and a few days every time she watered them with the fire-fighting unit while getting them established.

Now she was surprised to see how much they'd grown, even in the time since she'd been gone. She should have felt pleased with how well they looked in their nice straight rows, but instead felt an odd sense of sadness tugging at her throat. They were nothing more than a monument to a better time – before it had all gone so horribly wrong.

Emily swallowed hard and turned her gaze back to the front. Just as they turned into the driveway that wove past the house, she saw a series of tall steel uprights framing the landscape like a sculpture. *The new shed.* She frowned at the pile of rubble that remained where the old cottage had been felled. She remembered the afternoon she had come home to find John in his green front-end loader, demolishing the place she had dreamed of doing up – demolishing her dreams. Had he been telling the truth or not about needing the land? She felt a little guilty.

*You left because he shot at your dog, not just because he demolished the cottage*, a voice in her head said. *And because it was only a matter of time before he hit you too. I did the right thing*, she reminded herself. She was glad she hadn't brought Grace today.

'Are you okay?' Barbara asked, putting a hand on Emily's knee.

Emily nodded. 'I wish I didn't have to do this.'

'I know, but if we get stuck in it'll be over before you know it.'

'I doubt there'll be anything I want – not now.'

'Well, you won't know until you look. And anyway, it'll be good closure for you.'

'I thought that was John turning up to my parents' house with all my stuff in a trailer,' Emily said with a wan smile. 'Not to mention signing off on the financials.'

'I guess the universe didn't see it like that, because here you are back again.'

'Well, I bloody well hope this is the last time. Once the funeral is over, I'm done with John.'

'I know you've got bad memories, but it really is quite a nice house. The whole setting is lovely – those gorgeous big gums,' Barbara said, bringing the ute to a stop at the open double farm gates into the large area enclosing the house and a variety of sheds.

Emily gazed around. 'I thought that too when he first brought me here,' she said. 'It took my breath away. I loved the huge gum trees dotted around the old brick-and-stone buildings and flanking the creek. And of course the orchard down the way.' Emily didn't want to go and check – didn't want to know if Stacy had used the fruit or if it had been left to rot; either scenario would probably do her in.

'Isn't it sad how our whole perception of something physical can be completely skewed by emotional stuff?'

'Oh that's very deep, Barbara. But you're right; I thought John was the most handsome man I'd ever met until he started being nasty. That night he turned up at Mum and Dad's with the trailer I couldn't believe I'd ever found him attractive at all. Weird, huh?'

'Hopefully after today and then the funeral you'll feel free of him.'

'God, I'm sick of funerals. Gran's, Doug's, now John's. It feels like the only social activities I've had for ages are bloody funerals.'

'Me too. Other than our picnics with you and Jake, I haven't done anything for ages.'

'That's because there is nothing to do around here,' Emily said.

'Am I detecting cabin fever?'

'No, not really. I love being at the house. And it's not like I've got the money to spend anyway. Sorry, I'm just feeling sorry for myself.'

'You're allowed – but only for a few moments. It sounds like we need to take a day trip to Hope Springs or Charity Flat. We can just window shop.'

'Sounds good. But let's wait until after the funeral when I can finally put John behind me – again,' Emily added with a groan.

'Okay, you're on.'

Barbara put the ute in gear and slowly drove the last hundred metres to the house, and then turned off the vehicle. Emily felt a wave of sadness mixed with nostalgia. Physically, the house and surrounds didn't look a lot different from when John had first brought her here before their marriage. It was still the same double-fronted farmhouse made to look long with the addition of two rooms at the far end, and a large washhouse near the back door. Yet, really, everything had changed. It was impossible to know the heartbreak hidden by those thick walls that were rendered in the same pale grey as the nearby riverbed.

They got out and walked up the sloping concrete path to the back glass sliding door. As she reached for the handle, Emily thought it was lucky that John had never locked the house. Asking Thora for a key would have raised all sorts of awkward questions.

The door shuddered in her hand and squealed and scraped over the dirt and debris in the tracks. A blast of stale air rushed out, carrying with it the unmistakeable odour of cigarettes.

'God, I so don't miss that smell,' Emily said. 'I'd forgotten how awful it was.'

'I thought he only smoked outside.'

'Apparently not anymore.'

'If it's like this after no one being here for a few days, how bad must it have been when he was living here? Jesus, I'm surprised he didn't have lung cancer.'

'Well, lucky for him he crashed his car instead,' Emily said.

She frowned. Her mind went back to the crash scene. She still found it hard to believe it had happened – there of all places – along the fifteen or so kilometres of dirt road.

'What's wrong – other than the obvious?' Barbara asked, looking at her.

'Just thinking about the corner he crashed at.'

'What about it?'

Emily shrugged. 'It just seems weird to me that it happened there, when there are so many much more dangerous corners.'

'I guess his time was just up,' Barbara said with a shrug, and stepped past Emily into the large enclosed verandah. She continued through the open doorway into the big central country-style kitchen.

Emily remained standing at the sliding door, and Barbara looked back at her.

'Sweetie, you'll never know, so don't dwell on it. If there was anything suspicious about the crash, the police would have been all over it and we would have heard. Just let it go.'

'I know. You're right,' Emily said, moving into the house at last, but unable to shake the feeling that there was a whole lot more to the story.

# Chapter Nineteen

Emily stood just inside the kitchen, taking in the scene before her.

'God, he lives – lived – like an absolute pig!' Barbara exclaimed.

Dirty dishes were piled haphazardly in the single sink and on the drainers on both sides. The nearest end of the large timber kitchen table was strewn with newspapers, magazines, envelopes and what looked like business letters.

Tea towels, streaked and smudged with what Emily didn't want to think, were draped over the brown vinyl upholstered chairs.

At the far end of the table, near the sink and stove, sat a plate with the remnants of something brown, which could have been anything from faeces to gravy or barbecue sauce. The only sign of tidiness was the knife and fork lined up across the plate. In front of the plate was a higgledy-piggledy collection of condiments in various shapes and sizes and brands, and an almost empty roll of paper towel.

Emily was frozen to the spot, her senses struggling to comprehend the extent of the filth. She heard the buzzing of blowflies, and suddenly noticed the sickly stench of rotting, decayed food. Its source wasn't immediately identifiable; the stagnant water underneath the pile of dishes in the sink? The rubbish bin overflowing against the nearby wall? Or both? Beginning to gag, she pulled a crumpled tissue from her pocket, pushed it hard against her nose, and bolted from the room.

Back outside she gulped in the fresh air, and was starting to feel better when Barbara joined her.

'Bloody hell, that's bad,' Emily said. 'Maybe we should call in some cleaners and come back when we're not going to catch the plague.'

'I'd rather just get this over with,' Barbara said. 'It'll be much better when we open all the windows and air the place out. Why don't you do that while I get rid of the bin and sort out the dishes.'

'Okay, thanks. I'm guessing by the mess there was no floozy currently on the scene,' Emily said, as she turned and went back into the house. She again found herself wondering whether John had been alone for Christmas, but shook the question aside. There was no point thinking about that now.

She held her breath and rushed through the kitchen into the hall beyond to open the rarely used front door. As she did, she again had the unsettling feeling that things were the same but somehow totally different.

She went through the house and pushed up every grime-covered window and then struggled with, and finally dragged open, the remaining three dirt-sealed doors. She returned to the kitchen where the stale air now held a slightly sickly artificial floral note.

'Good idea,' she said, nodding at the can of Country Fresh toilet spray now standing on the table.

'Well, it took me a while to decide which smell was actually worse. Are you okay?' Barbara asked, half turning from the sink where her hands were buried deeply in thick suds.

'I'm fine,' Emily said, nodding.

'Good. While I finish these, why don't you have a quick scout around and think about anything you might want to take. Then I'll help you go through room by room.'

Emily hesitated.

'What's wrong?'

'I still don't feel right about it; too much like snooping.'

'Well, you promised Thora you'd do it, so there's no backing out now.'

'Hmm. I suppose I'm just feeling a bit overwhelmed.'

'Imagine how she must be feeling. She's just lost her son. You're saving her extra heartache, so feel good about that.'

'Could you imagine her arriving and seeing the state he'd left the place in – she'd have had a stroke!'

'Exactly, which is why we're cleaning the place up. Actually, first can you grab a tea towel; I'm running out of room.'

Emily went to the third drawer beside the sink, pulled out a crumpled tea towel and took a plate from the drainer.

'Makes you wonder, doesn't it, what the police must find on a daily basis,' Emily said. 'Yuck!'

'Which is why our mothers taught us never to leave the house without first doing the dishes,' Barbara said.

Emily dried the dishes and automatically went straight to where they'd always been put away.

'So, does it feel weird being here, especially standing here doing something exactly as you used to do?'

'Yes and no. On the one hand it's like nothing has changed. But when I stop and let myself think about it, it feels totally wrong me being here. I really don't like the idea of going through John's stuff – especially the office.'

'Well, I'm dying to have a good nosy. It's not like he'll know. I bet you'll find a heap of stuff you had forgotten about. Especially when you can take your time and not worry about him getting upset.'

'Actually you're right; there is a set of new towels I wouldn't mind taking – hopefully they're still new.' And there was all the silver and crystal and china; the 'good stuff' as John had called it. She was going to take that if it was still there.

'Believe me, that'll be just the start. Your place really could do with some homey touches. No offence.'

'None taken. But do you think it might be bad luck to take stuff from a bad marriage and use it to start over? I heard that somewhere.'

'I guess it depends on its significance, and the emotion attached to it. How about we just cross each bridge when we come to it? If in doubt, I'll be your voice of reason,' Barbara said. She pulled the plug, rinsed the suds down the drain, dragged off the rubber gloves and laid them over the tap.

'Well, at least the kitchen is looking and smelling a whole lot better,' Barbara said with a nod of satisfaction. She looked around the room. 'I gave the stove top and benches a wipe down, but I'm stuffed if I'm giving the place a full-on spring clean.'

'I reckon I'll wash all the linen, towels, and the tablecloth. It's pretty windy; it should all dry while we're here. And I may as well do John's washing as well while I'm at it,' Emily said thoughtfully.

'That's generous of you.'

'Just seems the right thing to do,' she said, shrugging. 'But I draw the line at taking the curtains down and doing them.'

'All right then. Let's start in the bedroom so you can get the first load of washing on.'

'Okay, let's do it,' Emily said, taking a deep breath and striding forward.

# Chapter Twenty

Opening the wardrobe, Emily was shocked to feel nostalgic at the first whiff of John's masculine, earthy scent. God how she'd once loved that smell...

She shook her head. Scent really was a powerful thing. But she had to focus and get the choosing of the outfit out of the way.

'I wish Thora was doing this. How do you think she would like him to be dressed? What if I get it wrong?'

'There is no right or wrong. Just make a choice. I'm guessing he wasn't a suit man.'

'Well he does own one...'

'Just put him in something that is *him* — favourite jumper, pants.'

'Should I dress him in a jumper if it's the middle of summer?'

'Maybe a nice shirt then,' Barbara said, clearly becoming a little exasperated.

'Okay.' Emily knew just the one – a white shirt with pale grey floral embroidery. She'd bought it for him to wear to a wedding last year.

Upon seeing it he'd turned up his nose and said it was girly. But she'd managed to convince him it looked good. And it had.

Sadness threatened to overwhelm her again as she dragged the shirt off the hanger. It looked clean, but not freshly washed. He'd clearly worn it and then put it away again. Emily deliberated on adding it to the washing pile. Or would Thora appreciate smelling his scent again? Like she had?

Looking around, she noticed Barbara had left the room. Soon she heard the vacuum cleaner start up in another part of the house.

She put the shirt on the bed and set about finding John's charcoal dress pants. Would he need underwear? He'd need shoes – his shiny black shoes were right there – but would he need socks? Unsure, Emily put together a whole outfit, including a pair of boxer briefs and dress socks. She was careful to choose the best, least worn. For a brief moment she considered buying a new pair of each, but dismissed the thought as utterly ridiculous. Thora would have enough on her mind without worrying about him wearing brand-new underwear.

She carefully folded the clothes and put them on top of the shoes in the shopping bag they'd set aside for the purpose. She then stood back and did an inventory in case there was anything she might have missed. *His dress watch.*

She opened his bedside drawer. There sat the heavy stainless steel watch she'd given him as a wedding present. The lump in her throat swelled and tears filled her eyes. He'd loved that watch. Emily carefully placed it on the top of the pile of clothes. She took the bag out into the hall so she wouldn't have to look at it again, swallowed back the emotion and set to work on going methodic-ally through the rest of the bedroom and his things.

Slowly they worked their way from the east side of the house to the west, tidying up and occasion-ally putting aside an item to take with them. Emily had paused in the lounge room. She so badly needed more seating over at her house. And a TV that was made in the twenty-first century and had a remote control would be nice. No, it wouldn't be right. She'd reluctantly torn herself away. They were there to clean up the place, not clean it out.

All this belonged to Thora and Gerald, other than her few things and the wedding presents. Most of the furniture had been in the house prior to her arrival and whilst none of it was particularly valuable, it was old and most likely Stratten family heirlooms.

Thora and Gerald had a houseful of lovely things and there was probably nothing here that would be of any interest to them. But that was for them to decide when they came out after the dust and emotion had settled.

When Barbara and Emily finished, the place would be able to be left for a few months without any problems and electricity wouldn't be wasted running an empty fridge and freezer and appliances left on standby.

Barbara had thought of everything, right down to bringing three huge eskies. Why let perfectly good food go to waste? There would be nothing worse for Thora and Gerald than to be greeted by the smell of rotting meat if the power went off at some point.

When they opened the chest freezer, they found it well stocked with lamb. Someone – Stacy? – had bagged and labelled all the cuts and carefully stacked them. The writing wasn't John's. As she and Barbara stared into the space, Emily knew they were both thinking about the same thing; the message John had given Barbara the day Emily had left him, reminding her to get freezer bags on her way home once she was 'over her little hissy fit'. That day seemed so long ago.

'Lucky you like your lamb,' Barbara said with a kind smile as she shut the lid. They discussed 'borrowing' the freezer to store the meat, but decided Emily could probably fit everything in the freezer part of the old upside-down fridge her father had found her, which was currently almost empty. If not, there was plenty of spare room in Barbara and David's chest freezer.

Emily was surprised at how much she found that she wanted to keep – they had been given so many lovely things for their wedding. On the awful day she had walked out, she'd only had her car boot to carry things in – and no home to put them in anyway.

Feeling so down at the time, she couldn't imagine ever bother-ing with fine dining again. But seeing it all now, Emily quite liked the idea of getting out all the finery next time Jake came to stay. Not to impress him, but just because it added a nice, civilised touch to dinner.

*I really hope he comes back soon.*

Opening another cupboard, Emily ran her hands over a set of thick forest green Egyptian cotton towels that had never been used. She looked forward to relegating her parents' thinning mismatched hand-me-downs to rags for washing Grace and wiping her muddy paws, and mopping up spills.

Every now and then she got quite excited about finding something she'd completely forgotten about. But the feeling was always bittersweet; brief bursts of pleasure replaced soon after with guilt. How dare she enjoy this when a life had been lost?

Well, it wasn't like she'd offered to pick through the spoils; Thora had practically insisted, Emily mentally countered. More than that, she thought, pausing while wrapping a lovely white oval platter with raised, scrolled detail around the edge, she'd *expected* her to do it; like it was her duty.

A heavy, slightly nervous sensation settled in her stomach. Did Thora and Gerald really not know they had split up, or was Thora perhaps just in denial like her own mother seemed to be? Could she, like Enid, have spent the past month or so assuming it was just a tiff and that they'd be over it and back together soon? She might even be pretending nothing had happened at all.

Surely John had called them. Surely he'd been in touch with them for Christmas. He *must* have told them then. Or in the unlikely case that he hadn't, surely they would have heard something on the grapevine. If not about their separation, then about John's dalliance with another woman. No, they *had* to know. Emily tried to shake aside the sickening feeling of disbelief. Talk of the split had gone through the town like wildfire. She sighed. They absolutely had to know.

Suddenly slight relief swept through her as she realised how ridiculous she was being; Thora knew she wasn't living at the farmhouse because she'd asked her how she'd settled in. Hadn't she? Now, what had she said exactly? Emily racked her brain.

No, she had said it was nice to hear from her – nothing about settling in. She took a few deep breaths.

If Thora thought she was living there still, there would be a message for her about John's death on the landline's answering machine. Shit! She had seen a red flashing light when they'd been in the kitchen. She'd ignored it. Emily's heart rate suddenly increased.

She unfolded her crossed legs, got up, and rushed back out to the kitchen. Her finger shook as she pressed the button to play new messages. She waited for the twangy female American voice to tell her there were five new messages and to get to playing the first. The wait was excruciating and she was rocking on her feet, urging the machine to hurry up when Barbara appeared beside her.

'What's going on?'

The first message began to play. Emily put her hand up to silence her friend. As they listened, their mouths dropped open and they stared from the machine to each other and back again:

'Emily, it's Thora here. We've just had the police here about John. I'm calling to make sure you are all right; I'm sure them turning up must have been a shock for you as well. You must be devastated. Please let me know if there is anything we can do. We'll contact the funeral director first thing in the morning as he's a family friend, so please don't worry about that, or the death certificate or anything of that nature. But if there's anything specific you would like to include in the service, please let me know.' At that she let out an, 'Oh Gerald,' and whimpered for a moment before the message ended with a click, the phone clearly disconnected.

The American voice came back on saying the message had been left on Sunday at 7:00 p.m. The second message was from Enid and said she would try her mobile. At this Emily shook her head and wondered if it was wishful thinking or forgetfulness on Enid's part, or if she might in fact be showing the first signs of dementia.

The third and fourth messages were just hang-ups and the fifth message was again from Thora. She sounded concerned, but said that she presumed Emily had gone to stay with her parents, that she and Gerald were there for her if she needed anything, but that they would give her her space. *Oh God, poor Thora.* Emily put her hands to her cheeks.

'Bloody hell,' Barbara said quietly. 'She *does* think you and John were still together.'

'Now what am I supposed to do? How could she not know – it's been right around town and back again?'

'And he's had at least one other woman staying out here since you left,' Barbara said, staring at Emily with disbelief. 'Haven't you spoken to her at all in the last month and a half?'

'No. We never saw much of them.'

'So John wasn't close to his family?'

'No. So what do I do?' Emily said, dragging a chair out from the nearby table and plonking herself down on it. 'I can't exactly tell her now – she'd be devastated.'

'Well, maybe she knows, but was telling herself you'd get back together.'

'But we did the financial settlement – that's pretty final.'

'That's true. Maybe they didn't know about that either.'

'But John was tied up with the family business – surely they would have discussed it. He would have had to, wouldn't he?'

'He was pretty underhanded with you; perhaps he was with them too.'

'I wonder what Thora and Gerald would make of it all,' Emily said.

'You're going to have to tell them, you know,' Barbara said solemnly. 'Not now, though. Not before the funeral. It would be too much.'

Emily looked at her friend.

'God, I'm going to have to stand up there beside them at the funeral and pretend to be the dutiful wife, aren't I?' Emily put her head in her hands.

'I'm afraid so.'

'And just when I've decided to finally get a backbone and stop kowtowing to my damned mother.' The implications began to sink in. 'Not to mention the whole town thinking I'm a complete bloody hypocrite and that I'm sidling up to Thora and Gerald to benefit from his death or something.'

'Well, you'll know the truth. It doesn't matter what everyone else thinks. You'll be doing it for Thora and Gerald, and that's all that matters. After the funeral, when things have calmed down a bit, you can tell them.'

'I just don't understand. How is it that the whole town can know we'd split up, and about his floozy, but his parents didn't?'

'Same way the wife is usually the last to know her husband is having an affair.'

# Chapter Twenty-one

They laid Barbara's plastic-backed red and black tartan picnic rug out on the patch of overgrown lawn under the Hills Hoist rotary clothes line. *I suppose I'll have to mow the bloody lawn as well!* Emily thought as she sat down heavily.

She watched Barbara methodically unpack the large esky and lay everything out. She was trying not to look across at the bones of the new shed and at what lay beyond. Every time she saw the pile of rubble where the old cottage had been, she felt a stab of disappointment and annoyance. This patch of lawn had once been her favourite place to sit at the house, but she'd forgotten the enormous changes to the landscape that had recently taken place.

Soon they were feasting on egg sandwiches — straight from the square plastic box, because thanks to the long grass they were sitting on, the only way to keep their narrow-bottomed cups of apple juice upright was to stand them on the plates.

Emily remembered the once breathtaking scene; a pale stone cottage with red-brick quoins, topped in blemished corrugated iron speckled with rust and pinholes.

It had been flanked across the back and on the western side by a selection of tall, thick-waisted gum trees, all the same species and possibly hundreds of years old. Beyond the trees to the west, a safe distance away, snaked a creek. It now only ran in the wettest of winters or during summer flash floods, thanks to dams which had been dug in the nineteen fifties in the small range of hills at the back of the property. Even still, it was a gorgeous setting. Emily sighed. Well, it had been.

Now there was no cottage. Instead the gums flanked an unfinished steel structure – the damned hayshed – which without its cladding looked more like an uninspired first-year industrial design student's sculpture.

'It's neither here nor there, is it?' Barbara said, following Emily's stare.

'No. I guess he did need the space to build on after all. I must say, I feel a bit guilty about thinking what I did.'

'Why? Because he's dead?'

'Probably.'

'Not that it really matters now, but he clearly *didn't* need the space. Look where he's started the shed. It's right next to the road. There's about fifty metres between it and the cottage.'

'Hmm.' Emily frowned. Barbara was right. 'Perhaps he really did pull it down out of spite.' She remembered her scrapbook, her dream of turning the little place into a B&B, a studio or gallery. And John's smirking words, the afternoon he'd knocked it down: 'Maybe now you'll stop with all this bed and breakfast nonsense.'

'Well it doesn't matter now. You can forget all about it. You've got a great new house – well, an old one, but you know what I mean – that you'll one day turn into a showpiece.'

'Yeah in about a million years,' Emily said, rolling her eyes before taking another triangle of egg sandwich from the plastic container.

'You just have to have faith.'

'In what; the universe, you reckon?'

'And yourself. It'll all work out, somehow, sometime.'

'As in: "It won't happen overnight but it will happen"?' Emily said, raising her eyebrows at her friend.

'Something like that. So, how was it having Jake stay without Elizabeth?' Barbara asked, abruptly changing the subject, as she topped up their drinks.

'Good. He really is such nice, easy company.'

'Any idea when he's coming back?'

'No, I think he's pretty busy.'

'You sound disappointed.'

'I am a little, to be honest. I don't know why,' she said with a dismissive wave of her hand. She gazed back over at the steel structure. 'It was nice to talk to someone who lives an interesting, different sort of life,' she said wistfully. 'Someone who doesn't just see me as John Stratten's ex.'

'So what did you talk about?'

'The house mainly – he's got some great ideas. If only I had the money. Jake reckons it would make a perfect B&B.'

'I agree – and you'd be a great host.'

Emily turned quickly to look at her friend. 'Do you mean that, Barb? Seriously?'

'Of course. You're warm and friendly and welcoming. You love to cook and you're good at it – you could run jam-making classes to entertain visitors.'

Emily chuckled. 'That's what Jake said.'

'It'd be a good drawcard. I can just picture it; city people coming for weekend cooking getaways. Sort of like the Thai cooking schools that have become so popular. Yours could be The Authentic Country Cooking School,' Barbara said, now with her hands stretched out high above her as if holding up a banner.

'Yes, well, I don't know why I'm getting all worked up about it, it's not like I've got the money to do anything.'

'You've got the diamonds.'

'I wish I hadn't found them. I can't do anything with them.'

'Why not? You were clearly meant to find them when you did. And the timing was pretty spooky – right when the offer of the house appeared. You can't just dismiss them.'

'If, as you say, I was meant to put them up for collateral or something, wouldn't this *universe* you're always going on about have me feeling better about it all?'

'Fortune favours the brave, Emily.'

'It's not brave, it's disloyal.'

'Emily, I'm sure your gran would admire your sentimentality, but I think she'd prefer you to be happy – certainly not freaking out about money all the time.'

'I just can't, all right? Please don't let's fight over this, Barbara.'

'Okay. Fair enough.' Barbara backed off.

'God, I wish I had your optimism.'

'Just takes practice – and a few things going right. Don't forget I was raised by a mother who taught me I could be anything I wanted to be.'

'Hmm, lucky you.'

'Though, really, what difference did it make? Here I am, just a farmer's housewife,' Barbara said with a shrug. 'A pretty happy one, granted, but a housewife nonetheless. Not much ambition here, I'm afraid, but I'm fine with that. And so is my mother, for the record,' she added with a wry smile.

'You're lucky. Why do you think people have kids if they don't want them to be happy?'

'Perhaps to shine a light away from their own inadequacies, to compensate for some kind of loneliness inside them, or maybe to try and rewrite their own lives to be better.' Barbara shrugged. 'Any number of reasons.'

'Do you and David want kids?'

'We've actually been trying since we got married. I guess it will happen when and if it's meant to,' Barbara said with another shrug. Emily thought she saw her friend's features cloud slightly and wondered if she wasn't as nonchalant as a moment ago. But she couldn't be sure she hadn't imagined it.

'I think you'd be a great mother.'

'Thanks. You would too, you know.'

Emily didn't know what to say. Instead she changed the subject. 'Gosh. I'm full; I've been stuffing my face with your gorgeous sandwiches and not even thinking how many I've had.'

She lay back on the blanket and stared up at the cobalt-blue sky and the fluffy clouds skipping across it. She hoped that one day she'd be as happy and content as Barbara seemed to be.

'I keep dreaming about Jake,' Emily said suddenly, breaking a lengthy silence.

'Erotic dreams?'

Emily detected Barbara's broad grin distorting the question, and reached out and playfully slapped her arm.

'No, but we're together, at some sort of function. I've had the same dream – well, variations of it – three times now.'

'It must be going to come true then,' Barbara said with a laugh. 'What's it about?'

'I'm not really sure. I can't tell where we are, but we're all dressed up. Pretty vague, I know. But every time we've been in the same outfits. I'm wearing a smoky blue-grey wraparound shirt and black pants and he's in a dark grey pinstripe suit with a tie that matches my top. And does he look gorgeous in a suit...' Her voice trailed off as she thought about how he'd looked in her dream and how he'd felt kissing her cheek and hair the other morning when he'd left.

'Someone sounds a bit smitten.'

'Hmm. It's bound to end in tears. He's probably got a string of women hanging off him in Melbourne – my cousin Elizabeth for one. Beautiful, sophisticated city women...'

'He's not with Elizabeth,' Barbara said. 'Actually, he's not with anyone,' she added quietly.

'Really?' Emily said, propping herself up on her elbow. 'How do you know?'

'He told David the other day when they were off taking photos in the scrub.'

'And...?'

'Sorry, that's it. David said he tried to quiz him, but he clammed up.'

'Hiding something?'

'No, David thinks he's just a private sort of person.'

'Yeah, he is quite quiet about most things except architecture and photography. I love how he's so passionate, but without being arrogant. I just wish he didn't live so far away – I could see us being really good friends.'

'You'd be more than friends.'

'Maybe, probably, in time.'

Mere days ago, Emily would have added that right now another relationship was the last thing she needed, but she was no longer feeling that so strongly. It was as though her grief over the separation had begun to ease with John's death. She was still cautious about getting involved again, but something had changed. It felt almost like she'd been vindicated for her decision to leave her marriage.

'If it's meant to be, it'll be.' They both said the words at exactly the same time and then chuckled at their synchronicity. Emily smiled at hearing one of Gran's well-used quotes come out of Barbara's mouth.

'Come on, let's get back to it. The sooner we start, the sooner we finish.'

# Chapter Twenty-two

The last room to be cleaned was John's office. Emily hadn't gone in there earlier because she assumed the window was still nailed shut as it had apparently been since before John had moved in. Now she stood in the doorway, shaking her head at the scene before her.

There were piles of paper on every available flat surface – the spare double bed, desk, swivel chair, and the two grey filing cabinets.

Loose pages were scattered like crazy paving across the multi-brown swirling pattern of the 1950s carpet.

'Bloody hell.' Barbara said, appearing beside Emily in the doorway and peering over her shoulder.

'I've been standing here for five minutes trying to figure out where to start.'

'So if all the papers are out here, what's in the filing cabinets? Surely he can't have had enough paperwork to fill them as well.'

'They're probably almost empty. I set up a filing system with labels and everything when I first moved in, but I wasn't allowed to actually file anything. John never let me touch his papers — he said they were private.'

'What a mess. How the hell did he do his tax returns and GST Business Activity Statements?'

'Bundled everything up, stuck it in a box, and sent it off to the accountant's poor office drudge to deal with.'

'Would have cost him a fortune.'

'Probably.'

'Now there must be some sort of system here in all this chaos,' Barbara said, stepping around Emily and into the room. 'Let's start with the desk. A lot of it seems to be in piles, which suggests at least some form of collation.'

'Hmm.'

'Ah, this looks like bills to be paid,' Barbara said, picking up a pile and flicking through it.

'Do I bundle them up for Thora and Gerald to pay? Oh shit, I can't do that; they think we were still together. I suppose that means they're my responsibility. Jesus.' She put out her hand to Barbara, who handed them over with a grimace.

'Maybe you can wait until after you've told them. When things have calmed down a bit.'

*Sure. Hi Thora, forgot to tell you that John and I had separated before he died. And by the way, he left a few bills for you to pay.*

'Bloody hell!' Emily said when she saw the figure on the first invoice. She sat down on the bed on top of another pile of papers and went through every page.

'There's tens of thousands' worth here. And some of them are on final notice,' she said. 'How could he have let things get this bad?' Again the question of whether John's death had been an accident flickered in her mind. 'I'll just have to pay them, I suppose – and quickly by the looks of it.' Emily frowned. *How am I going to pay them when I'm not a signatory to his accounts? Hmm, tricky.*

She remembered how humiliated she'd been the day she'd gone into the bank to change her address details on her personal accounts. The teller had informed her – in front of half a dozen waiting customers – that John had cut off her access to their joint accounts. She'd wanted the ground to open up and swallow her, and had been too ashamed to set foot in the place since.

But it looked like she probably would at least have to go in and discuss all this with someone in there. And she wondered how sympathetic Nathan Lucas would be. *Oh God, can it get any worse?*

Emily checked her watch and was surprised to find it was already a quarter to three. They had to get to the post office by five. She looked back to the task before her and felt overwhelmed.

'Perhaps I should go through all this paperwork on my own – it might take days,' Emily said.

'I'm not leaving you to do it on your own. We either start now, or come back tomorrow. Personally I'd rather knock it over now, but it's entirely up to you,' Barbara said.

'Thanks Barb, I really appreciate your help, but I just can't see where to start and my brain feels completely fried. To be honest, I'd forgotten there was even an office to go through. If I'd known it was going to be this bad I never would have agreed to do it.'

'Well, let's at least have a quick look and get an idea of how much there really is to do. If he's kept absolutely everything, it might be a matter of just chucking most of it out,' Barbara said. She sat down at the desk and pulled some blank paper from the stash in the ink jet printer. Next she began rifling through the desk drawers.

Emily looked around at the work ahead of them. *I guess I'll have to get everything together for his final tax return as well.*

'I reckon stack the papers, keeping them in their bundles, so we have some space to work with. I'll do some labels to make sorting easier. Doesn't he have any bloody marker pens?!' With a loud bang, Barbara shut the first of the three drawers at the side of the old pedestal desk and opened the next one down.

'He did have, because I bought them – they probably ended up in the shed.' Emily sat down on the bed and began gathering the various piles and laying them on top of each other in a criss-cross pattern.

'That's better,' she said when she'd finished and the bed was tidy except for one thick stack of papers. It was amazing how much more doable things could seem by just starting with one simple task. 'Did you find a marker?'

She waited a few moments.

'Barb?'

'Huh?'

'The marker pen; for writing the labels – did you find one?'

'No, but I found this,' Barbara said. She swivelled the office chair around to face Emily. She held out a stapled, crisp unfolded wad of paper and a business envelope.

Emily accepted the items with a frown.

'It was already open,' Barbara added.

'What is it?'

'You'll see.' Barbara swivelled back to face the desk and continued going through the drawer.

Emily stared at the typing on the envelope: LAST WILL AND TESTAMENT OF JOHN EDWARD STRATTEN.

She remembered the day they'd visited the Strattens' family solicitors in Adelaide on the way back from their honeymoon on Great Keppel Island. They had made the wills deliberately simple. Neither document listed any items, just a general statement that everything was to be left to the other person. But that was over three and a half years ago. So much had changed since then.

When she had walked away from her marriage, changing her will had been the last thing on Emily's mind. Of course it had to happen sooner or later, but there were many more pressing things to deal with: like finding somewhere to live.

Was this *really* John's last will and testament? And why was it out of its envelope?

When they had arrived home, John had put both wills in the desk drawer, sealed. She had promptly forgotten all about them.

Again the circumstances of his death niggled at Emily. Could it have been suicide? She tried to force the question aside. There was no point wondering, because it could never be proven. As Barbara had said, if the police – or attending CFS or SES or anyone else – suspected anything, something would have been said and the whole town would be talking about it. *So stop it, Emily, you're just being melodramatic!*

'I wonder if this is really his last will and testament,' she said aloud.

'No idea, but yours is here too – still sealed. So, are you rich?'

Emily's head began to swim as she tried to grasp the consequences.

*We were separated. And had signed off on the financials. Surely that changes everything. But what if...?*

She'd heard of people inheriting nothing but debt. Her heart began to race and her armpits became sticky. She'd have no idea of the true situation until all the bills were paid and paperwork sorted through. And God only knew what other bills were lurking in the mailbox or still on their way.

'I doubt it; probably in debt to the hilt more like,' Emily said, finally answering Barbara, who had turned back around and was looking at her with patient expectation.

Barbara offered her friend a sympathetic smile but stayed silent.

'Jesus, what a mess,' Emily said, rubbing a hand across her face. 'This could change everything. Before it looked like just a matter of paying the bills and handing over the paperwork. Now it seems I'm going to have to properly tidy everything up. I'm exhausted just thinking about it.'

'Do you think you should advise the solicitors of his death?'

'I'm pretty sure Thora said she was taking care of that, along with the death certificate and the funeral. Well, looks like I'll be back out here all day again tomorrow.'

'You mean *we'll* be back out here all day again tomorrow,' Barbara said.

'I can do it; I've burdened you enough.'

'Emily, I wouldn't dream of leaving you to do it on your own. And together we'll get it done in half the time. Then maybe we'll make the pub for a late lunch as our reward.'

'Okay, but it will be my shout – it's the least I can do. You're the best,' she added, getting up and giving her friend a hug.

Barbara shrugged her off after a few moments. 'I keep telling you, it's not a problem – it's what friends do for each other. And as I also keep saying; I know you'd do the same for me if our situations were reversed.'

'Well, I really do appreciate it.'

'I know you do. Now let's finish packing up the other stuff so we only have this to deal with tomorrow.'

'Actually, if I stick all this paperwork in a box I can sort through it at home. It'll save us coming back.'

'But you're exhausted.'

'I'll feel better after a nice hot shower. And there's nothing worth watching on TV at the moment.'

'Well if you're sure.'

'Yep.'

'Shit, we'd better get cracking if we're going to get the bag of clothes to the post office before it shuts,' Barbara said, getting up. 'Thank goodness I packed the ute as we went,' she added.

They turned off lights and closed doors as they threaded their way back to the kitchen. Emily put their handbags in the top of the box of paperwork, Barbara grabbed the last esky, and they left, sliding the glass door shut behind them. Emily hated leaving the house unlocked, but she didn't have a key.

As she walked down the path, she felt a heavy sadness descend. It wasn't dissimilar to how she'd felt the day she'd left John and her marriage. Though today she was a lot calmer and there was no need for urgency.

It was as if she felt sad for the house being left all alone. Ridiculous, she told herself, and hurried to catch up with Barbara, who had already put the esky in the back of the ute, strapped it down, and was getting into the vehicle.

Emily sat with the large box of paperwork at her feet. She wasn't looking forward to the hours it would take her to sort out everything, but it had to be done. She still couldn't believe John hadn't told his parents they'd separated.

They drove in silence, Barbara concentrating on getting them into town as quickly as possible whilst carefully negotiating the gravel road.

Emily stared out the window, not really seeing the blurred scenery rushing by, as questions fired back and forth in her brain: Why had his will been opened? When had he opened it? Was there a more recent will? And if not – if she *was* still his sole beneficiary – what exactly had she inherited?

And why the hell hadn't he told his parents? Was it because he thought they'd get back together?

# Chapter Twenty-three

Back at home, Emily sat on the hard lounge-room floor with the unpacked piles of paperwork fanned out around her. The boxes of crystal and other household items she'd brought back from the farm would have to wait; right now she was desperate to know where John's finances stood.

Grace lay with her head on her paws, watching her. The little border collie had been really excited to see her mistress after being confined alone in the yard all day, but when she'd tried to curl up close to her, Emily had scolded her for upsetting the papers and pushed her away. The dog had been sulking ever since.

Despite having apologised instantly and profusely, Emily felt dreadfully guilty every time she looked at her.

She'd overreacted; she was tired and frustrated at having John back in her life again. She stared at the paperwork, trying to figure out where to begin, her eyes and brain refusing to focus. Maybe Barbara was right; she shouldn't be doing this tonight.

She was still staring at the blurred patches of white on the floor when her mobile skittered and began to ring. Her parents' home number was on the screen. It had to be her mother because it was the night her father would be at a Lions Club meeting.

*That's all I need.* She sighed, took a deep breath, and pressed the green button to accept the call.

'Hello, Emily speaking.'

'You sound tired,' Enid said. 'I didn't get you out of bed; you're not sick are you, only it is very early…'

'Hi Mum, no.'

'No, what Emily?'

'No to all of the above – not in bed, not sick, just tired after a very long day.' As the words came out of her mouth, Emily wished they hadn't. Infuriatingly, it turned out this was one of the rare times Enid was actually listening to every word her daughter said.

'Oh, why is that? You're a lady of leisure; what could you have possibly been doing that has you exhausted? Not climbing up ladders working on that dreadful old house I hope!'

'No.' Emily quickly racked her brain for something to say that wouldn't sink her into an abyss of further questioning. She really didn't want to talk about John, but she had to say something.

'Just weary. There's a lot to organise and think through for the subdivision.' Well it was sort of true. She'd heard from the surveyor. She couldn't believe they would be there Saturday – New Year's Day. She'd queried it, but was told it was either that or in around three months' time. Thank goodness for knowing people who knew people. So the ball was well and truly in motion. She was still plagued with doubts about whether she was doing the right thing, but she told herself that the surveyor actually being available at that time of year was a good sign.

'Surely you're not seriously going ahead with all that nonsense. There's no point in...'

While she half listened to her mother offering all the reasons why she shouldn't buy the house and do it up, Emily found herself indulging in a little guilty glee over doing something entirely off her own bat and of which her mother so clearly disapproved.

It still hurt her terribly not to have her mother's support, but accepting it was just the way she was helped. As did becoming closer to her father in recent times, and seeing that Des didn't always share Enid's viewpoint. For the longest time she'd assumed they were of one voice.

She'd only recently discovered – now that she was seeing more of Des away from his wife's shadow – that he actually had a really healthy, positive outlook on life, in contrast to Enid's glass-half-empty attitude.

'Are you there Emily?'

'Yes, I'm here.' Emily forced her attention back to the present and her mother's voice in her ear. What she said next surprised even her. 'Thank you, Mother. Your objection is duly noted, but as it is my money and my life, it is my decision. And I have chosen to go ahead with my original plan. Was there anything else or did you just phone to remind me of your lack of support?'

'Oh well, I wouldn't put it quite like that,' Enid blustered. 'I just need to know you've thought all this through. Buying a house is a very big responsibility, you know.'

Emily had to bite into her cheek hard enough to wince to stop the retaliation bursting forth in a torrent.

'I know,' she said through gritted teeth. 'Now, was there anything else?'

'Well, about your birthday dinner tomorrow night – would you like roast chicken, lamb, or pork?'

*Oh shit! I completely forgot!* Emily suddenly felt that she didn't want to do what she did every year – birthday and New Year's Eve dinner at her parents' house. Too much had changed.

'Um, I can't do dinner tomorrow night. I'm sorry; I should have told you sooner. I've had so much to think about that I totally forgot.'

'But we always have dinner for your birthday. You're deliberately being difficult because I disagree with your silly plans to buy that dreadful rundown old house. Now come on, Emily, this really is very childish.'

'I could make it for lunch,' Emily offered. *I said I'd have lunch with Barbara. Fingers crossed she's busy.* 'But I have other plans for the evening.'

That was her first outright lie. Actually, for the first time in years, she had no firm plans for New Year's Eve. Usually she and John ate dinner with her parents and then headed out to the local pub where there was a DJ or live band. Invariably John wrote himself off with his mates and became even more belligerent than usual while Emily had to watch on, waiting until he was ready to go home – usually in the vicinity of 4:00 a.m.

Each year she would stand, or sit, unable to hear herself think, let alone speak to anyone else, and shake her head wondering at what point he would grow out this ridiculously juvenile behavi-our. They were over thirty for goodness sake! She'd bite her tongue lest she get branded a 'party pooper', 'stick in the mud', or be labelled with some more colourful alcohol–induced epithet. She certainly wouldn't miss that this year.

*Would it be too weird to spend New Year's Eve alone in front of the television watching the fireworks?* God, that would mean she had joined the ranks of her parents and their generation! Emily returned her attention to her mother's voice on the other end of the phone.

'Oh, with that lovely Nathan Lucas I hope. Or perhaps Jake? Such a pity I wasn't able to make Christmas lunch and see him again.'

'No. Not Nathan and not Jake.'

'Well, who with then?'

It was at the tip of her tongue to say, 'None of your damned business,' but instead she said, 'Barbara and David Burton, actually.' Emily hated lying, especially when it meant implicating someone else; it usually ended badly. She didn't know what Barbara and David were doing, and supposed they must have been invited to the home of someone she wasn't friendly with. They probably hadn't wanted to embarrass her by mentioning it.

But if she rang Barbara as soon as her mother hung up she might just get away with this one. There was every chance Enid would phone Barbara and try to get her to change her plans – or at least have them join forces.

'But you said you had forgotten.'

*Oops!* Emily suddenly had a burning need to not have her mother win on this. *I forgot to tell you I wasn't coming. Not that it was my birthday.*

'Mum it's my birthday, and I'd like to have dinner with my friends. As I said, I can come down for lunch.'

'Well, I have other plans for lunch as it happens, and I really don't like to muck people around by...'

'We don't have to do anything.' *I'd actually prefer it.* 'I've had plenty of birthdays already and I'm sure I've got plenty more to come.'

'Well if that's what you'd prefer,' Enid said with a huff, clearly miffed.

'It is. And if there's nothing else, I've...' Emily was about to say, 'I've got a heap of paperwork to sort through,' but just stopped herself in time. Any elaboration was bound to elicit further enquiry. 'I've got to go.'

'Right, well then.' Emily could almost hear the unspoken words, 'If that's the way you want to be,' hanging in the silence.

'Okay, bye then, see you soon,' she said brightly, and then pressed the button to end the call. She rolled her eyes at Grace, who looked as bored with the conversation as she had been.

Emily sat for a few moments feeling the frustration coursing through her. But she had stood up for herself again, and she was quietly pleased with having done that.

It was odd how she was suddenly objecting to things she'd put up with for so long. Maybe Barbara was right that she was finding her true self now she was alone.

Emily stretched out her arms high and wide above her head. As corny as it was, she felt a bit like a butterfly emerging from its cocoon and spreading its wings for the first time.

The buzz of the phone on a pile of papers interrupted her reverie. She crossed her fingers, hoping it was not her mother calling back. She needed a bit more time before another round with Enid. The number on the screen was Barbara's.

'Thank God,' she said, looking to the ceiling as she pushed the answer button.

'Hi Barb.'

'What have you found in all that paperwork?'

'Nothing yet – I've only got as far as spreading it all out on the floor. I was just about to start going through the first pile when my mother rang.'

'Oh, and how is Enid?'

'Look Barb, I need a favour.'

'Oh. Right. Name it.'

'I had to tell a lie to get out of dinner tomorrow night…'

'Well I hope you said it was because you're having dinner with us.'

'I did actually. I just don't feel like going, but I couldn't bear to hurt her feelings.'

'Uh-huh! See what I mean about the universe working its magic?'

'How do you mean?'

'Well I'm ringing to invite you to dinner tomorrow night. Sorry, bit short notice… But anyway, nothing fancy; just a roast or something. It *is* your birthday, right?'

'Er, yes, but how did you know?'

'You mentioned it once and I somehow seemed to have remembered. Probably because it's also New Year's Eve.'

'Hmm.'

'We never do anything for New Year's Eve anymore. I think the whole thing is ridiculous. Can't stand being around all those drunk people.'

'Me too. John always insisted on going to the pub and getting plastered. So I certainly wasn't going to miss that this year. But what's all this got to do with the universe?' she asked.

'Well, it made sure you were available to accept my invitation, silly. So will you come? I just had an inkling that you might need to stay away from Enid, this year of all years.'

'Thanks, Barb, I'd love to. And you're absolutely right. I was quite prepared to sit here alone; I just didn't want to go to Mum and Dad's. I did offer to do lunch instead, but thankfully she already has plans. Also, I got another lecture about what a bad idea buying this place is – I certainly don't need that on my birthday.'

'What *is* her problem?'

'What do you mean?'

'I don't understand why she doesn't want you making your own decisions.'

'She's always been like that. Sometimes I think she only objects to something because she wasn't the one who thought of it. If *she'd* found the house it would have been a great idea.'

'Well, it's her problem, not yours, Emily, so don't worry about it.'

'Easier said than done. I think I'm well-conditioned in that regard.'

'It'll take time, but I will re-program you if it's the last thing I do!' Barbara said forcefully.

They both chuckled.

'Meanwhile, figuring out John's finances should keep your mind off your mother for a while.'

'I'm too tired now. I think I'll just go to bed and tackle it in the morning.'

'There's no rush, you know. Most of the bills will probably be local and everyone around here knows he died. That's sure to buy some time.'

'I know, but I really want to know how much he owed. And to what extent I'm going to be affected.'

'Fair enough. But remember, you don't know for sure that it's anything to do with you. Just promise you won't stress over it.'

'I'll try not to – can't promise though,' Emily said.

'Well on that note, I shall bid you good night. Sleep well. We want you bright-eyed and bushy-tailed on your birthday,' Barbara said with a laugh.

'You too. And don't remind me – another year older,' Emily added with a groan. She disconnected the call and tucked it in her pocket. 'Come on girl, bedtime,' she said to Grace, unfolding her legs and getting up.

But as she stood over the paperwork spread before her, the curiosity got too much and she sat back down again. Grace gave a big harrumph of exasperation and copied her mistress.

'Sorry Gracie, but I just have to know.'

# Chapter Twenty-four

Emily woke on her birthday feeling bleary-eyed. Despite promising herself a good night's sleep, the need to know had kept her up late going over the paperwork. She'd gone to bed feeling confused and dazed. It was just like the diamonds all over again; the promise of potential riches that were out of reach.

On the one hand, if she was still John's legal beneficiary, all her money problems would be over. She'd be able to afford to do up the house.

But on the other, they had split up and finalised their relationship via the financial settlement. Surely his parents were, therefore, the correct beneficiaries? Was there another, more recent, will? Was that why the one Barbara had found was out of its envelope? Part of Emily hoped so – it would mean she could stay right out of it and leave it all to Gerald and Thora.

And if there wasn't and it was legal, would it be *moral*? Would using the money bring her bad luck?

Emily shook it all aside. At some point she would have to have a very difficult conversation with John's parents. And that was a discussion she didn't want to think about.

It seemed the town gossip had got it right for once. John Stratten had been paid out of the family company to the tune of around three hundred grand – two hundred and eighty-five thousand dollars to be precise. After the small balances in the various bank accounts, and John's outstanding bills were taken into account, it looked like there would be almost two hundred thousand left.

Emily had sat there stunned, looking at the figures, and had been about to phone Barbara with the news when she realised it was after midnight.

Two hundred thousand dollars might almost be considered a fair price for the way he'd treated her. The way he'd treated Grace. Would Thora and Gerald agree if she came clean? Could she even tell them the whole truth about their son? Should she?

*What if I tell them and they don't believe me?*

The money might almost make up for having to stand alongside his parents at his funeral and pretend to still be part of their family. She wished they could hurry up and get it over with.

Emily forced thoughts of John and the Stattens from her mind. Tuesday would come soon enough. Meanwhile it was her birthday, and she was determined to enjoy it.

The good thing about having changed her plans with her parents was that it meant she didn't have to drive all the way down to Hope Springs, spend a few hours avoiding contentious topics, and then drive back again.

On the other hand, it meant that her mother would probably still be sulking, and that made her feel guilty and a little sad. Enid might even come down with another of her 'heads'. *Why can't I just damn well celebrate my birthday how and with whom I like, without all this emotional upheaval?*

Guilt gnawed at her, but not enough to phone and reinstate their original plans.

No, Barbara was right; her current feelings were only due to years of conditioning. Emily hadn't done anything wrong; she was just standing up for herself. If only she had done that years ago, and with John as well. *Oh John.* She sighed. *Don't let it ruin your day. Nor let your mother for that matter. You've made a good step forward. Leave it at that.*

Rather than dwell on her troubles, she decided to go for a walk.

Emily took a different route to normal, going out the back of the house across to the shearing shed. Out in the open, away from the shelter of the small hill behind the house, it was a lot windier than she'd realised. She didn't mind walking when it was cold and wet or even quite warm, but she hated being pummelled by wind.

Instead of climbing through the fence and adding a large paddock to her distance, she walked briskly along it until she reached the copse of gums, and then turned into them to make her way back.

She enjoyed the murmur of the trees around her and the flashes of sunlight lighting the otherwise shaded track. Emerging from the trees she paused to take in the white house awash in sunlight, and took a deep breath. It really was beautiful – and would be even more so when it was given the makeover it deserved.

She hoped Barbara was right; that things really would be okay. Some things were already; she could see that. She really did have a lot to be grateful for on her thirty-second birthday. Even if she couldn't afford to renovate once the subdivision went through, at least the house would be hers.

Grace was happily snuffling in the grass nearby. If it hadn't been for the little dog, who knew where she'd be?

*Today*, she told herself, pursing her lips, *is going to be a great day, and tomorrow the start of a great year.* She nodded her head once to cement the thought and strode forward.

★

Emily had just finished eating breakfast and was putting the kettle on for a fortifying coffee before unpacking the boxes of household items they'd brought back from the farm, when she heard a friendly double-toot of a car horn. It sounded like Barbara's car.

She opened the front door just as her friend was stepping onto the verandah.

'Happy birthday!' Barbara cried, wrapping her arms around Emily.

'Did I know you were coming over this morning? You'll be sick of me by tonight,' she added with a laugh as they made their way down the hall to the kitchen.

'Never! And, no, we hadn't planned to catch up this morning. But I have to confess to my curiosity getting the better of me about the paperwork. And clearly you did that rather than unpack,' she added, nodding at the couple of boxes on the floor. 'So...?'

'Not before I've had my first coffee for the day,' Emily said, and set to work preparing two mugs while Barbara hovered about, clearly anxious to hear what she had learnt.

'Ah, that's better,' Emily said, finally seated and taking her first sip.

'Well...? I'm dying to know what...' Just as Barbara started, Emily's mobile skittered on the bench.

'Hi Jake,' she said, exchanging raised eyebrows with Barbara.

'Hi Em, just wanted to see how everything is going. Did you manage to get hold of the surveyor?'

'Yes, thanks. Believe it or not, he's actually coming out tomorrow. And there's been a bit of a development on a different front too,' she said, turning away from Barbara. She'd wanted to tell her friend the news first.

'Oh?'

'Well, fingers crossed; there might just be a way I'll be able to afford the renovations. I won't know for sure for a while yet, but...'

'Oh. So you've decided to sell the diamonds after all?'

'No.'

'Then how? Don't tell me you won the lottery,' he said with a laugh.

Emily began to wish she hadn't said anything.

'There's a chance I might have inherited John's estate.'

'Really? But I thought...'

'Apparently he hadn't changed his will after our separation. It looks like I might still be his sole beneficiary. If I am I'll probably inherit enough to get the renovations done.'

'That's amazing.'

'I must admit it's all come as a bit of a surprise. I still haven't totally got my head around it. And it's certainly not a done deal.'

'Well, you've got my number if you need any help at all. I'll give you a good deal if you want me involved.'

'Thanks, I really appreciate it.'

'How are Barbara and David?'

'Great. Barbara's here right now, actually.'

'Oh, well I won't keep you, just wanted to say hi really and see how everything was going.'

'Thanks, that's lovely of you. I'll speak to you soon.'

'Okay. Say hi to Barbara for me.'

'I will. See you.'

When Emily turned back around, Barbara was staring at her with her mouth open.

'You've inherited enough from John to do the full renovation?! When were you going to tell me this?'

'When I got half a chance,' Emily said with a laugh.

'What about John's parents? Have you spoken to them about the will?'

Emily winced.

'Don't take this the wrong way, but you really need to talk to them before you go getting too far ahead of yourself.'

'I know. I just...' *It's nice to dream.*

'So how much are we talking?'

'Around two hundred thousand. Give or take,' Emily said with a shrug.

'Oh my God. That's fantastic. If it happens. See, I told you things would get better.'

Emily couldn't disagree with that.

'So I guess that means we'll be seeing a whole lot more of Jake?'

'Of course I want him to be involved,' Emily said, 'I'm just not sure yet how much that will cost me.'

'Oh, I'm sure he'll do you a good deal,' Barbara said.

'That's what he said. But it's business, Barb, I don't want any special favours.'

'I know, but he's so nice...'

'Hmm.'

'There she goes – all dreamy again. You do realise you get this serene, vacant expression every time his name is mentioned, don't you?'

'He's just a friend.'

'Methinks the girl doth protest too much. You're in love.'

'Barb, you can't be in love with someone you've only met twice and haven't even slept with.'

'Why ever not – there's a century's worth of romantic novels based on that very notion.'

'Seriously, though, I am very fond of him, and I can't wait to see him again. But I don't think I'm in love with him.'

'Whatever you say, Emily,' Barbara said, collecting the mugs. 'Can I get you another coffee while you sit there daydreaming?' she asked, ducking away from the pen Emily launched at her.

'Yes thanks,' Emily said before lapsing into deep thought about Jake: *God, I miss him. But does that mean I'm in love with him?*

*I don't know.*

Regardless, she did trust him, and she definitely wanted him to be at the centre of the project to renovate her house. *Could it really happen?* She could just picture the two of them poring over plans on the kitchen table, walking around in hard hats and commenting on goings-on, choosing taps and tiles together...

'There's that look again,' Barbara said, reappearing with two full and steaming cups.

# Chapter Twenty-five

Barbara left two hours later after helping unpack the boxes and sharing an early lunch of ham and salad sandwiches, leaving Emily feeling tired but happy.

She had put the empty cartons out in the shed and just finished the dishes when she heard the crunch of car tyres on gravel.

*Another visitor?*

She cocked her head to listen and Grace did the same thing before trotting out into the hall. Emily followed the dog and opened the front door to find her father standing with his arm raised and hand clenched about to knock.

'Dad! What are you doing here?!' Emily cried, pulling him into a hug. As they embraced, Emily stood on tippy toes to see if her mother was waiting in the car. Enid never wasted time and energy getting out of the car unless she had to, and when visiting without an appointment always sent her husband ahead to knock on doors.

Emily had always hated this embarrassing habit of her mother's – if the person was at home, there were always a few awkward moments while everyone at the front door turned and watched Enid's journey from the car. She'd often wondered if she did it because she was lazy or whether she just wanted the attention – or perhaps a bit of both.

But there was no Enid waiting in the car today. Did she really have a lunch to attend or was she sulking?

'I've come to surprise my only child and wish her a happy birthday. What else would I be doing here?' Des said, sounding a little indignant.

'Sorry, but you know what I meant,' Emily said, feeling chastised.

'It wouldn't be a surprise if I made an appointment, now would it? So, sweet pea, happy birthday. I hope it's a day filled with joy, followed by a year of happiness.'

'Thanks Dad,' Emily said. They hugged again, and Emily felt herself choking up as she replayed his words in her head. It was a rare moment to hear Des Oliphant sounding so soppy and sentimental.

'Right, so, any chance of a coffee?' he asked, wringing his hands. 'Or are you just going to keep me standing out here on the doorstep?'

'Of course, come in.' *That's more like the Dad I know and love*, Emily thought with an inward smirk as she stepped aside to let him in.

Once seated, Des pulled an envelope from the front pocket of his navy work shirt.

'Sorry it's not very exciting, but we decided it might be just what you need at the moment.'

'Thanks Dad,' Emily said, smiling at her father.

Inside the envelope was a card with the standard 'Dear Emily', 'Happy Birthday' and 'Love, Mum and Dad' in her mother's neat, compact handwriting. *Well, that's something anyway.* Inside the card was a plastic gift card emblazoned in the bold blue of Mitre 10 hardware stores.

'Perfect,' she said, with a hearty nod. 'Actually, speaking of this place – which we weren't really, but are now – I've got a bit of news.'

'Don't tell me the subdivision has come through already?'

'No, that could take months. I've only just organised the survey. But...'

'You've officially started seeing that nice Jake fellow and he's...'

'Dad! Shh. I'm trying to tell you something serious!'

'Sorry.' He made a motion of zipping his mouth, turning a key and then tossing it over his shoulder. Emily rolled her eyes at him.

'I was over at the farm yesterday — John's place. Barbara and I were cleaning the house up and going through the paperwork for his parents.'

'That was awfully nice of you. Why would you…?'

'Let me finish. When I was speaking to Thora the other day, she didn't seem to know about our separation.'

'You can't be serious.' He stared at his daughter with wide, disbelieving eyes. 'How can she not have known?'

'I have no idea, Dad.'

'But the whole town…'

Emily held up a hand and shook her head. 'It's weird, I know. But it was pretty clear that she thought I was still living there. I don't know whether she's trying to ignore the truth like Mum, or if John didn't tell her, or what. But I could hardly tell her she'd have to deal with her dead son's effects, now could I? She would have wanted to know why, and it would have raised all sorts of questions. I decided I could at least help wind things up, tidy the house.'

Des looked doubtful. 'Okay.'

'Anyway, I was going through the paperwork in John's office and I found our wills. He hadn't changed his. It looks like I'm still the sole beneficiary of his estate.' *If there's not another will.* Emily ignored the nagging voice in her head.

'Are you sure about this?' Des asked.

'Yes, totally, he hadn't changed it. I've still got to find out – I'll probably have to see a lawyer about it – but it looks like I'll have enough money to be able to do the house up – properly – when the subdivision goes through and I actually own it.'

'But won't his parents object, contest it or something? I'm not sure how these things work.'

'Well, as far as they're concerned, we never split up.'

'That may be so, but they are going to find out sooner or later. And I imagine they might be pretty upset. How much are we talking?'

'Around two hundred grand once his bills have been paid.' *If it's all above board.* Emily wished her conscience would shut up and let her dream – at least for a while. 'He must have changed his mind on buying the tractor, because there's no record of the down payment. Or perhaps it was just a rumour after all.'

'Bloody hell, Em. This all sounds terribly far-fetched.' Des shook his head slowly before picking up his mug.

'Doesn't it just?'

They both sipped their coffees in silence until Des spoke a few moments later. 'So then that would mean you now own the farm too,' he said thoughtfully.

'No, I'm pretty sure that's owned by the family company, and kept by Gerard and Thora when John was bought out.'

'I don't think you have that right,' Des said, his forehead creased. 'Not unless things have changed. As far as I know, John inherited the farm when he was a kid – around twelve years old. Some kooky old uncle who wanted to stick it up the family, I believe.'

Emily's mouth dropped open and she stared at her father as he continued.

'His parents were livid – Gerald had assumed it would just go to him. And of course the irony was that *he* had to run it because John was still at school. Just goes to show that one should never assume.'

*Hmm.*

'So do you seriously think the farm has been in John's name all these years? Why wouldn't he have told me?'

'Did you ever ask who owned it?'

'No, I just assumed...'

'Ah, see, there we go again – assumptions. And he probably assumed you knew, or that it didn't warrant mentioning. Really, why would it?'

'So why wouldn't Thora and Gerald have told me?'

'That little word again, Em. They probably assumed you knew.'

'So how do I find out for sure – without actually asking them?'

'You didn't find title deeds then?'

'No.'

'Probably in a bank vault somewhere.'

'Oh God, they could be anywhere.'

'Does the family have a particular firm of solicitors they use?'

'Yes, they're in Adelaide – they did our wills. Thora did say they would handle the death certificate and not to worry about that side of things.'

'Ah, well, in that case it's all sorted. They'll be in touch. Don't worry; I'm sure you'll be notified in due course. Meanwhile, what have you got planned for your birthday?' Des asked, clearly signalling the end of the discussion.

But Emily's mind was still on the farm.

'Em?'

'Sorry?'

'Your birthday. What have you got planned?'

'Just dinner with Barbara and David tonight. I'm sorry I upset Mum, but it's been such a crazy time...'

'No need to apologise. It's *your* birthday to spend as and with whom you wish.'

'Thanks Dad.'

'So Mum isn't sulking is she?'

'Why would you think that?'

'Well, she didn't come out with you.'

'She had an early lunch out – some last-minute thing – and is now most likely back at home busily cooking jam for the local show. Seems like she's taken a leaf out of your book.'

'But she's never...'

'I know. I don't know what's got into her lately. All these new hobbies. Anyway, I've been deputised,' he added, puffing out his chest and pretending to pluck at imaginary braces. 'But I thought you'd have spoken to her by now. I'm sure I heard her leaving a message earlier this morning.'

'Oh.' It must have been while she was out on her walk. Emily hadn't noticed a message when Jake rang. All of a sudden she was annoyed at herself for being so petty, and for getting things so clearly wrong. She forced the thoughts aside.

'Dad, what the hell will I do with a farm?'

'Sell it, lease it out, I don't know. You could become a farmer,' he said, shrugging. 'Don't worry about it until you know for sure – the solicitors should let you know in writing if...'

'I suppose so,' she replied.

With solicitors in charge it could take months. She hoped she hadn't jinxed things by jumping the gun and telling Jake and Barbara how much money she'd inherited. *Well, how much she might have inherited.* She'd better not tell anyone else. And she'd better not say anything about the farm just yet.

'Dad, probably best not to tell anyone about this; don't want to count my chickens and all that.' *Little bit late for that, don't you think?*

'Fair enough. My lips are sealed.' He started to mime zipping them again but stopped. 'But I can't exactly *not* tell your mother,' he said with an apologetic grimace.

'Okay, but make sure it goes no further. God, she'll be ropable when she finds out how much I'm going to spend on this place.'

'It's your life, dear. She knows that. Just doesn't always accept it. Well, I'd better be off. You have a great night and a happy New Year's Eve.'

'Thanks. You too.'

# Chapter Twenty-six

'Birthday girl, come on in, come on in!' Barbara cried, as she flung the front door wide. They hugged tightly before breaking away. Emily then accepted David's hug and peck on the cheek.

'Happy birthday, Em.'

'Thanks David,' she said, making her way down the hall towards the Burtons' kitchen. She really was so blessed to have friends like Barbara and David. She felt as comfortable and welcome here as she did in her own house.

'Hold on,' Barbara said, grabbing her elbow from behind as she was about to pass the dining room. 'We've decided to go all posh on you tonight – crystal, silver, Wedgwood, the whole bit. Packing up everything at the farm the other day got me all inspired.'

'Ooh, what fun! But you should have told me;
I'd 'ave worn me taffeta,' Emily said, smiling and
putting on a broad Cockney accent.

'Oh come now darling, not *taffeta* posh,' Barbara
replied, in a very toffy English accent.

Emily loved it when they played around and did
silly voices. She paused in the dining-room doorway,
looking over the fully set table. Cut crystal wine
and water glasses sparkled and silver cutlery shone
in the flickering light of the silver candelabra's three
candles. The scene was so overwhelming she forgot
about her accent. 'Barb, this looks great. You've gone
to so much trouble.'

'Ah not with the food, darling – peasant fare
tonight I'm afraid; we can only do so much.'

Emily bit her bottom lip to stop herself from
exploding into laughter. 'Was that *pheasant* fare,
*pleasant* fare or *peasant* fare you said?' she asked,
continuing their charade.

'Oh God, not you too,' David said, rolling his
eyes. 'I've had this one pretending to be posh all
afternoon.' But he was unable to hide his grin. 'I'll
get the champagne.'

'Strawberries; don't forget the strawberries,'
Emily and Barbara both called at the same time, still
in their respective put-on accents. They looked at

each other and burst into uproarious laughter. Tears were streaming down their faces and they were both standing with one hand on the polished back of a dining chair and holding their stomachs with the other when David returned.

'Your drinks, my ladies,' David said, bowing and adopting a plum inflection of his own.

'What fun,' Emily said. 'We should do this more often.'

'No thanks, it took me ages to polish the silver,' David said, pouting. They both waved his objection away.

'Well, we can do it at my house now I've got all the good stuff. David, you'd be butler, wouldn't you?'

'Yeah, sure, why not? There we are,' he said, carefully extracting the cork with a satisfying pop. He poured three tall glasses of sparkling white wine.

'It's a pity Jake couldn't be here,' Barbara said. 'He would have fitted in with our silliness rather well I think.'

'Did you invite him?' Emily asked, accepting a glass from David. She had the uneasy feeling that she was the last to know something that was about her.

'Of course. Cheers,' Barbara said, raising her bubbly and ignoring Emily's frown.

'Happy birthday, Em.' All three clinked glasses, muttered 'Cheers,' and took their first sips.

'Yum,' Emily said. And then she added, 'You didn't tell him it was my birthday, did you?'

'Well, I *was* trying to convince him to come. Not that it mattered in the end; he couldn't make it,' Barbara said, flapping a dismissive hand. Emily thought her friend was looking a little flustered.

'Is he still in Whyalla or did he go back to Melbourne?'

'Dinner with a client – no idea where that might be,' David said quickly.

'Oh well, he is very busy. And he was just down here,' Emily said, trying to hide her disappointment and the uneasy feeling that was becoming stronger. *He didn't even wish me a happy birthday when he phoned.*

'But he did send a present,' Barbara said, putting her glass down on the table and crossing to the sideboard, where Emily now noticed a long skinny box adorned with a purple ribbon and bow. Barbara picked it up in both hands and held it out to Emily.

*What? Wow! But oh God, now I'm going to have to reciprocate, and I don't even know when his birthday is... This is why there should be a blanket rule of no exchanging gifts after people turn eighteen.*

David pulled out a chair from one end of the table and indicated for her to sit. Emily concentrated on untying the bow holding the lid on the box.

Putting aside her issues over gifts, Emily allowed herself to be genuinely excited. It really was lovely of Jake to have sent her something. There was nothing like an unexpected present from someone who clearly had good taste.

Inside the box was a large postal tube. Shooting Barbara and David a quizzical glance, she lifted it out, pulled a red plastic stopper from one end, and extracted a roll of stiff paper. There were five separate sheets in all, though she had trouble keeping track because they kept rolling back into themselves. Her breath caught as she realised exactly what Jake had sent.

'Oh wow,' she said. 'He's done plans for the house – proper plans; with measurements and everything.' She put her hand to her now burning cheeks and instantly the unfurled pages sprang back together again. She stood up and stared at the roll, feeling a little overwhelmed at Jake's generosity and thoughtfulness. David reached around her and secured the corners with four heavy silver coasters from the other end of the table.

David and Barbara stood either side of Emily as she slowly and carefully perused each sheet, placing a hand here and there to hold down the pages as she repositioned the paperweights.

The first sheet was a floor plan, and it took Emily a few moments to ascertain which was the front and which was the back of the house. The plans were for the option of creating three bedrooms with ensuites – turning the house into a B&B – that he'd mentioned Christmas night when doing his rough sketches. The following four sheets showed the outside of the house from each side. Jake – well, she assumed this was Jake's work, though where he had found the time she had no idea; he'd only been gone four days – had even taken the trouble to add touches of colour. How lovely of him to do this for her…

Suddenly Emily was gripped with worry; he'd almost certainly expect her to engage him as architect now he'd put this much effort in. And she'd seen his work on his website; it looked very expensive – way out of her league. He'd won major awards for goodness sake. But how could she turn him down now?

Another thought struck her; was this actually a birthday present at all? Barbara had said it was, but maybe she'd just assumed. It had been wrapped in a ribbon, but there didn't seem to be a card. And if Barbara was right, why hadn't Jake mentioned her birthday when he'd called that morning?

Perhaps this was his response to the news of her possible inheritance and that she'd be able to do up the old place after all. Maybe this was his way of getting in first to stake his claim for the business. She really should have kept her mouth shut.

She hated to think that the kind, gentle, seemingly genuine man she had shared her house with on two occasions could be so calculating. But then she'd been taken in by John all those years ago.

A new thought popped into her brain; why had he sent the plans to Barbara and David and not her? That was a bit odd. At that moment David and Barbara's home phone began to ring. Emily checked her watch; it could only be telemarketers calling so close to the dinner hour.

David answered the phone and handed the portable handset to her.

'It's for you.'

Emily accepted it with a puzzled frown.

'Hello, Emily speaking,' she said, a little tentatively.

'Hi Em, it's Jake. Happy birthday! Did you get my present?'

Emily was opening and closing her mouth as the polite interval in which to answer slowly evaporated.

'Hello? Are you there?'

She finally found her voice.

'It's so lovely of you to call – and to send the plans. We're looking at them right now; they're lovely, thank you,' she finally blurted.

'My pleasure. I'm so disappointed I couldn't be there to help you celebrate.'

'Where are you?'

'About to go into dinner with a client.'

'But it's New Year's Eve!'

'Well, you know what they say – no rest for the wicked,' he said with a laugh. 'I really wish I could have been there with you guys.'

Emily looked from Barbara to David. Both her friends grinned back, and looked to be very pleased with themselves.

'That's okay, it's not exactly a milestone or anything.'

'Oh come on, every birthday is worth celebrating. Maybe next year.'

*I'd like that.* But Emily didn't have time to dwell.

'The reason I called – aside from wishing you a happy birthday – is to make sure you understand the plans. Well, not the plans themselves – I'm sure you can work them out – but the meaning behind them. I don't for a second want you to think this is any more than a gesture on my part – a gift. You shouldn't feel bound to accept any help from me in a business capacity...'

Suddenly he stopped.

'Oh listen to me rambling on like a lunatic. I'm just trying to say that I don't want you feeling obligated to me in any way.'

At that moment Emily realised that she'd very much like to be obligated to him – and in every way. The suddenness and forcefulness of the thought crashed through her and made her blush deeply.

'And, for the record, the plans have nothing to do with our conversation about your inheritance this morning – or the diamonds – so please don't think this some kind of strategic business move or anything. I've actually been thinking about doing them since that first weekend when Elizabeth and I visited.'

*Before I even had an inkling the place could be mine,* Emily thought.

'I always thought the place was lovely and had great potential. And after our conversation on Christmas Day I decided to draw them up properly.'

Time was weird; it felt like finding out she could buy the house had happened both yesterday and months or even a year ago – just like leaving John, his death, and everything else that had happened.

But all these things had been stuffed into only a little over six weeks. Mind-blowing really. She shook her head and refocused on Jake just as he finished speaking.

'Okay?'

'Thanks, I understand what you're saying.'

'That said,' he added, 'I would love to be involved in the project – as project manager maybe?'

'I'd love that, but I don't think I could ever afford you, Jake. I've seen your website,' Emily said, and then added a laugh to soften her comment.

'That's just the power of marketing, my dear. I'm sure we can come to some mutually rewarding arrangement. Now I must let you go and get on with your dinner. Sorry to keep you; I just wanted to call and clarify things. Happy birthday again. Sorry I didn't mention it when I rang earlier, but I didn't want to ruin the surprise.'

'Thanks again so much for the plans – they're lovely – and for calling.'

'You're more than welcome. I look forward to discussing them with you in person soon.'

'Okay, bye.'

'See you soon,' Jake said, and hung up.

Emily felt heavy with disappointment as she handed the phone back to David. *How soon is soon?*

Hearing Jake's voice had stirred a deep longing in the pit of her stomach.

'Right, this calls for more champagne,' David said, clapping his hands, and left the room.

Emily sat down and stared at the plans while trying to decipher her feelings.

'Having him call wasn't meant to upset you,' Barbara said, dragging out a chair and sitting down next to her.

'It hasn't. I think it's more surprised me, because until now I didn't realise how much I felt for him. I hardly know him, but God, Barb, I miss him.'

Barbara raised her eyebrows and grinned knowingly at her friend.

'Yes, I know. You were right, I was wrong – I'm quite possibly in love with him.'

'Then why are you so glum?'

'Because I wish he was here.'

'I'm sure he'll be back soon.'

'But whenever that is, it'll only be a visit – he lives in Melbourne, remember?' A strange expression crossed Barbara's face and Emily was about to ask, 'What's that look for?' when David reappeared beside them with the champagne bottle with rubber stopper tucked under his left arm, a small plate in each hand, and another balanced on his right arm.

Each dish held a small salad of baby spinach, chicken, roast pumpkin and fetta. She was so swept away by the beauty of the presentation that the question on her lips left her.

'Entrée is served,' David said.

'Thanks darling,' Barbara said, relieving him of the plates.

'God Barbara, this is superb,' Emily said after her first mouthful.

'Sorry, but I can't take the credit – entrée and dessert are all David's work.'

'Well, aren't you a dark horse!?'

'Not all beer and barbeques is our David, hey darling?' Barbara said, smiling fondly at her husband, and patting his hand.

'Too much *MasterChef* and *My Kitchen Rules*,' he said with a dismissive wave.

'And to think, only a few short weeks ago he was complaining about my viewing tastes,' Barbara said.

Emily smiled at her happy friends' gentle sparring. She and John had been like that once, briefly. She could imagine having such fun with Jake.

By ten o'clock Emily was having trouble staying awake, but she managed to make it to midnight, when they celebrated by pulling the strings on a couple of party poppers, cheering, and hugging.

After a week of late nights and early mornings, of stress and anguish, she'd had a lovely relaxing birthday – much better than she had ever had with John – but again Emily wished Jake had been there to stop her feeling like the fifth wheel.

*Maybe next year.*

# Chapter Twenty-seven

Emily followed her morning routine of getting up early and letting Grace out, but instead of sitting at the table with her mug of steaming coffee, she decided to take it back to her bedroom. She wasn't hung-over from her night with Barbara and David, or even all that tired. She just felt like indulging herself, which she rarely did.

And it was pouring with rain outside again. It was nice listening to it beating down on the iron roof, and she'd managed to stop herself worrying about the damage it might be doing. *What will be will be.*

She put her mug down with a thud on the wooden chair she used as a bedside table and climbed back into bed, wondering why she didn't do this more often. Grace leapt onto the bed and curled up at her feet, instantly warming them.

Emily pushed the pillows up to support her and retrieved her mug. Leaning back into the plushness, she wallowed in a feeling of deep satisfaction. Why was she up before seven every morning, even weekends, when she didn't have a job to get to – or anywhere else to be for that matter?

The answer came to her as she took a deep sip of her coffee: because that was the way her mother had raised her. *Yes*, Emily said to herself, scowling. *I have been well and truly indoctrinated.*

She then found herself wondering whether the yearning she felt for Jake – which seemed to be getting stronger by the day – was due to her mother's brainwashing as well; the idea that she had to have a man in her life. Deep down, was her desire for him just an expression of some pathetic unconscious fear of being alone?

She certainly wasn't remotely interested in sharing her space with a man twenty-four seven – which was most of the reason she'd turned down Nathan Lucas. Some occasional company would be nice though, and Jake was so intelligent and such a good conversationalist...

She bent down to retrieve the tube of plans that she'd left propped up between the bed and the wall.

It really was so terribly generous of him to do that for her; no doubt it would have cost thousands if she'd had to commission them herself. And to organise sending them to Barbara and David. It really had been a lovely surprise.

Emily folded her legs and then unrolled the plans across them. They were perfect. She pictured herself chattering with guests sitting around the large table in her freshly renovated kitchen while she cooked them a hearty breakfast. If only she could start searching for paint colours, tiles, fixtures and fittings.

But she'd been raised to be cautious. And while she'd arranged the survey in preparation for the subdivision, she agreed with Jake's initial advice that she wait until everything was in her name – signed, sealed, and delivered – before starting any actual renovations. She wouldn't make her initial payment to the Bakers until the subdivision was completed, and that might be months yet.

But it would be worth the wait. With a couple of hundred thousand to spend, the place would be a showpiece. Not that that was the aim. The point was to save the old house. And somehow indirectly make up for the stone cottage John had destroyed. If she hadn't shown an interest in it, she was sure it would never have crossed his radar. If only she'd kept her mouth shut and her aspirations to herself.

A quiet voice somewhere in the depths of her mind piped up, saying, 'But that is what a good marriage is about; sharing dreams and working towards them together, as a team.'

Emily found herself sinking into melancholy as she wondered whether John had had any regrets, or seen the errors of his life flash before him as he lay dying.

*Stop it, Emily.*

She pushed the plans aside so she wouldn't drip coffee on them, took up her mug again, and forced her mind to focus on how peaceful Grace looked slumbering at her feet.

★

Emily was startled to hear banging on the front door. The rain had stopped and the house was eerily quiet. She heard a bark and then the sound of claws on the floorboards.

'Hello, anybody home?'

She sat up and wiped her eyes, groggily. Somewhere along the way she'd slumped down. The male voice was familiar, but she couldn't quite place it.

She must have fallen asleep. How long for? A quick check of her clock radio told her around half an hour had passed. She wished the caller would go away; maybe they would if she pretended she wasn't there.

'Em, it's me, Jake. Are you here?'

*Jake!*

She sat bolt upright and began searching frantically as if for some magic solution to enable her to appear at the door not looking like she'd still been in bed. She patted at the bird's nest that was her hair. It wasn't like Jake hadn't already seen her in her just-got-out-of-bed state a couple of times before. But something felt different this morning.

'Coming,' she mumbled.

'Em!' He sounded quite insistent now. Odd for Jake.

'Yes, I'm coming,' she called in a voice barely able to reach the bedroom door, let alone make it down the hall and penetrate the heavy door.

She dragged her robe from the chair and left her bed in one flowing movement. She stuck her feet into the sheepskin slippers and wriggled her toes down until they were secure, and shuffled out to the front door, pulling her robe shut and tying the belt as she went.

'Happy New Year!' Jake said.

'What are you doing here?!'

She'd meant to sound pleased to see him, but her tone suggested she was anything but. Her brain was going a mile a minute. Clearly he'd still been in Whyalla last night after all. Now she thought about it, there had definitely been some caginess from David and Barbara. You don't flit back and forth between Whyalla and Melbourne in a couple of hours without a private jet, and she was pretty sure Jake's company didn't have one of those. No, her friends had known exactly where Jake was.

'Surprise,' he said, cringing and shrugging. He then threw his arms out, as if to try and lighten the obvious tension. But it didn't work; they continued to stand, both looking awkward, with an open door and Grace between them. 'I'm so sorry,' Jake finally said, breaking the silence. 'I didn't think for a second that you'd still be in bed.' He looked her up and down.

'That's all right. I was just having an indulgent lie-in.' She wanted to pull him towards her in a big hug, kiss him passionately on the lips, tell him she was glad to see him and that she'd really missed him. Instead, she stood looking at her feet, which were making little shuffling movements of their own accord.

'If it's a bad time, Em, just say – I can come back later. Or not,' he added, looking crestfallen. 'Hi Gracie,' he said, bending down and patting the dog.

'Sorry? No, don't go. Sorry, come in,' she said, stepping aside to let him pass. As she shut the door, Emily fought the urge to bang her head into it. *What the bloody hell is wrong with me?!*

As she turned back, she fell into Jake, who had turned towards her.

'Oh!' she said, blushing at the unexpected contact. 'Sorry!' She grasped at the tops of his arms to regain her balance. Jake held her arms in return. They stood locked together, less than a full reach apart. Looking up, Emily noticed an odd expression on Jake's face – as if he was inspecting every one of her creases and freckles and taking note of their size and shape.

She looked away, feeling self-conscious. Her heart rate was suddenly dangerously high and she was beginning to sweat. She made to pull away.

'Oh no you don't,' he said, and gently eased her towards him. Embarrassed, Emily continued to avoid his gaze. Then his index finger was lifting her chin and his lips were brushing hers with the softness of a feather. Emily responded by opening her mouth slightly. He kissed her more firmly, and soon his tongue found hers. Her legs felt weak.

'Oh Em,' he muttered into her mouth.

Emily groaned back in response. She was aware of the intense heat filling the tiny space between them. Jake pulled her to him. Their kissing became heavier, more urgent, and Emily found herself panting slightly. She was disappointed when, a few moments later, Jake stopped kissing her passionately, pecked her on the lips and then on the nose, and pulled her back into a tight hug.

'Sorry, I got a bit carried away,' he said into her hair.

She wanted to say he could get as carried away as he liked; she didn't mind. But instead she concentrated on the feel of his strong arms around her and his sweet, musky yet masculine scent, all the while willing the ache of frustration in her groin to dissipate.

'I had to see you,' he whispered. 'I've missed you so much it hurts.'

The words were almost lost in her hair. Emily felt the molten tingling in her lower stomach increase.

'I know it's too soon, and please don't be scared, but, Em, I love you.'

Emily stiffened slightly. Had she heard correctly? Had he really used the 'l' word and her name in the same sentence?

He had. The realisation came upon her like a rolling bank of storm clouds. She clung to him harder, fighting back tears.

'Oh Jake.' Her voice was a sigh. She wanted to tell him she wasn't scared; that it was the nicest, most perfectly timed utterance she'd ever heard. But doing so now wouldn't mean as much – it would seem like an afterthought, an automatic response. And it wasn't. Warmth flooded through her like a gently bubbling volcano, filling her with happiness.

Emily was as surprised as Jake by what she did next. She pulled away, grasped him by the hand, led him into her bedroom and over to the bed.

Jake read her cue and pushed the mass of house plans onto the floor before gently laying her onto her back. They embraced and kissed for a few minutes, their desire becoming more urgent.

Just as Emily was willing Jake to take it to the next step and tear off her robe, he pulled away. She tried to pull him back, but he was stronger. He gave her a final kiss before rolling off her and propping himself up on one elbow. Emily groaned in frustration. She was so desperate for him she thought she might explode. You had to admire his self-restraint; she couldn't have done it, wouldn't have.

'I don't want us to rush things. I didn't tell you I love you so you'd sleep with me. I just wanted you to know how I feel.'

Emily felt a mild stab of annoyance at herself. If she were really honest, she had felt some sort of need to respond, to go one up on him. Deep down she was glad he had put a stop to proceedings, even if she did feel a little bit rejected.

'God you're gorgeous,' he said, staring at her and slowly shaking his head. He brushed a stray hair off her face. 'And please don't think for a second I don't want to, because I do, very, very much. But I just don't want to jinx us by rushing in.'

Emily wriggled so she was lying on top of him, slid her hands under his back and pulled herself closer. She kissed him on the lips before folding her arms across his chest and meeting his gaze.

'I'm so glad you're here, Jake. And I think I love you too.'

'Think? You *think*?!' he said, smirking at her and trying to sit up. After a struggle, he managed to rise enough to peck her on the lips. 'I'm only teasing. You're in a different place to me – emotionally – which is why I don't want to rush it. God you're beautiful, Em,' he said, putting his hands to her face and pushing back her fringe.

Tears prickled behind Emily's eyes. *Damn it*, she silently cursed as the first one sprang forth.

'Oh Em, don't tell me no one's ever told you you're beautiful before,' he said, kissing away the tear.

As she shook her head in response, the tears began to flow freely. *Damn it.*

'Oh come here.' He held her tight and she let herself sob for a few minutes.

Gradually she pulled herself together and then, after turning away, wiped her eyes with her sleeve. 'I don't know what's wrong with me; I've dreamt of this and I wanted it to be perfect,' she said with a sniff.

'It is perfect. You've had so much to deal with, I'm not at all surprised you're a little emotional. It's actually quite nice to see you a little vulnerable, Em. It shows you're human. Because you sometimes seem way too tough,' he added more gently.

'Do I? Really?'

'A little, but you've had to be. But I'm here now; I'll take care of you.'

Emily felt herself flinch at hearing the last words.

Jake obviously saw it too. 'Not that I think for a second you need taking care of, Emily Oliphant.' He was grinning at her. 'Now, you get dressed and I'll get my bag from the car. By the way, the button jar looks great there by your bed.' He gave her a final peck on the lips and left the room.

Emily stared after him with a blissful smile plastered across her face. Just how perfect was he? He didn't think her silly at all for having it out on display. And yes, he was right; the small wooden chair beside her bed was the perfect spot for the button jar.

She'd brought it in after her first sleepless night tossing and turning over what to do about contacting the Strattens. Now it was the last thing she looked at before going to sleep and the first thing she saw in the mornings. She liked the idea that Gran watched over her while she slept. Not that she'd ever tell anyone; it sounded so lame and childish.

Sometimes she put the large, heavy, rattling object in her lap and ran her hands over it, searching for answers like a clairvoyant might with a crystal ball or some other talisman. She could never see into the future, but she would often conjure up an appropriate saying of Gran's, and remember the sound of the old lady's voice.

As she undressed and then plucked items of clothing from the pile beside the bed where she'd stepped out of them the night before, her thoughts again turned to Jake. Just thinking about him made her all gooey inside. She felt like a teenager again. Could he be her Mister Right?

*Jumping the gun a bit, aren't we? You haven't even seen him naked.*

God, the thought of sex (with anyone) was actually quite terrifying. What if he didn't like her naked? What if he didn't like sex with her? What if she didn't like sex with *him*? What if they just didn't fit together?

*Oh, for God's sake, stop it!* she silently told herself. He was a good man; they would sort through all that other stuff together.

# Chapter Twenty-eight

They moved around the kitchen as if they'd been sharing the house for years, and there seemed no need to discuss who was to do what. Jake went straight to the pantry and retrieved coffee, tea, and sugar. Emily filled the kettle and then collected mugs from the cupboard and teaspoons from the drawer. Coming together at the bench they shared a smile, acknowledging the ease of their existence.

'You must have got up early,' Emily said, leaning back on the bench and waiting for the kettle to boil. 'Have you had breakfast?'

'No, but you haven't either by the looks of the empty sink.'

'Very good, Sherlock. So, cereal, toast, or shall we celebrate with eggs?'

'Eggs, definitely. But I hardly think *not* having sex is worth celebrating.' 'I was thinking of us – the fact you're here, the first use of the *l* word, silly. Anyway, restraining ourselves was your idea, remember,' Emily said, making to hit him with a teaspoon. 'Men,' she said, rolling her eyes. 'Always a one track-mind.'

'Hmm, I didn't detect any disinterest from you earlier, young lady,' he said, raising his eyebrows.

'I actually have some bacon and some tomatoes if you fancy going the whole hog – so to speak. I decided to splurge a little bit, since I might not be quite so hard up now. I'm going to treat myself to bacon and eggs on weekends.'

'Lucky for me I'm here on a Saturday.'

'I would have made an exception for you anyway, you know. To prove I can be a little flexible and spontaneous.'

'You don't need to prove anything to me. I had a little taste of your spontaneity half an hour ago, and I'm hoping to put your flexibility to the test in the not too distant future.'

'Oh very funny,' Emily said, pouting. 'I meant…'

'I know what you meant.'

Suddenly he was pulling her to him and putting his lips to hers. Emily's groin began humming as his tongue probed between her lips and found hers. When they pulled apart a few minutes later they were gasping for air.

'Hmm, I'm way out of practice; can't seem to breathe and kiss,' Jake said, giving her a final kiss and releasing her.

Emily wondered just how out of practice he was. Had it been as long for him as it had been for her? John had long since stopped pretending that sex was anything beyond him getting his end in and relieving himself. Kissing had gone by the wayside around a year into their marriage. Emily hadn't complained; gone was the intimacy, but so too were the stale cigarettes, beer breath, and stubble rash. And it certainly meant it was over with a lot quicker.

'Penny for your thoughts, my darling,' Jake said, running a hand gently through her hair.

'Oh, nothing really.' Emily fought for something innocuous to tell him but failed. She turned back to the bench and busied herself with making the coffee.

'How 'bout you do the eggs and toast and I'll do the bacon and tomatoes,' Jake said. 'Team effort.'

'Okay, but I'm not used to cooking with someone else, so I might get bossy or crotchety or something.'

'I consider myself duly warned. But I do want to pull my weight. I'm not having you doing everything.'

As they worked on their separate tasks, Emily and Jake moved around each other and the kitchen like dancers performing a ballet. Occasionally they would meet at the bench or stove. At those times they would look at each other and smile.

'I take it you and John didn't cook together,' Jake said at one point.

'No.'

'Ever?'

'No. Not together. At home he considered it the woman's job to cook, and out camping, the man's. Just old-fashioned I guess,' she added with a shrug, feeling guilty for getting so close to speaking ill of the dead.

'Did you love him?'

Emily stiffened, and continued staring at the eggs in the pan.

'I must have; I married him.'

'I can't imagine you putting up with being taken for granted.'

Emily wanted to say, 'Well I did,' but instead said, 'Can we please not talk about this?'

'Okay, sorry. I can get a bit nosy. This bacon's done. Do you have some paper towel to drain it on?'

'Middle shelf of the pantry. Around my chest height and to the right.'

After lingering over breakfast, they cleared the table in silence; a couple of times Emily looked across at Jake, marvelling at how well he just seemed to slot into her house and routine.

When she started the dishes he appeared beside her, put his arm around her shoulder, pulled her to him and pecked her on the lips, and then grabbed the nearest tea towel. He then leant with both elbows on the bench, staring out of the window while Emily got things organised in the sink.

'It's such a lovely spot,' he said.

'Hmm,' Emily agreed.

'Hey, look,' he suddenly said. 'You're being surveyed.' He raised a hand in greeting at the man walking past, dressed in high-visibility work wear, and carrying a large yellow tripod. The man gave an energetic wave back. 'I still can't believe they're here on a Saturday, and on New Year's Day, for goodness sake!'

'All thanks to your friend, Anthony. It was today or wait for months. No rest for some.' Emily felt a little overwhelmed. Finally, a major step in her grand plan was actually taking place. It was a sign her life was really getting better. *Wow, it's really happening, and fast*, she thought, feeling like tears would well up if she dwelled on it for much longer. And then Jake was at her side, holding her close. Had she spoken her fears aloud?

'It's probably pretty overwhelming for you to see your dream finally starting to take shape – especially after the rough trot you've had,' he said, holding her tight to him.

Emily nodded against his chest. It felt so good to be held. 'It is a bit.' It was sort of the truth. But what was really overwhelming her was the thought of coming clean with John's parents after the funeral and potentially having the dream snatched away again.

'Well, let's get these dishes done and have another cuppa. I'd suggest champagne to celebrate, but it's still a bit early for that.'

Emily resumed scrubbing dishes while Jake chattered about the various projects his company was working on. She loved how animated he was – a clear sign of his passion – but after a while she found herself shutting out his voice and thinking about her own things.

She wondered how long it would take to hear from the lawyers about John's estate. Should she phone and see where things stood? No, that would make her appear greedy. She'd find out soon enough. When she was meant to. *Time will tell.*

Emily forced John from her mind and was annoyed to find thoughts of her mother taking over. Other than the very brief birthday message she'd left yesterday, Emily hadn't heard from her since their argument on Thursday night. It was probably a good thing.

Her father had mentioned a new hobby – making batches of jam for the local show in a few months. Emily wondered if her new interest had something to do with her own jam being well-received in Melbourne. If not, it was one hell of a coincidence. Enid Oliphant, despite having a mother who excelled in the culinary crafts, had never shown a bit of interest in following in Gran's footsteps. Until now, it seemed.

It had taken a long time for Emily to connect the dots and see the competitive streak her mother seemed to have fostered towards her. She hadn't given it much thought until recently, when Barbara pointed out that Enid had had her hair cut in a very similar style to Emily's. It was only a few weeks after Barbara had cut her straight shoulder-length mouse-brown hair into a neat bob.

Emily wasn't usually all that fussed about appearances – hers or those of others – beyond looking tidy. And as her mother's hair was grey, she hadn't grasped the similarities as quickly. But having once been a hairdresser, Barbara was more observant, and as soon as she mentioned it, Emily could see it too.

Even so, she had tried to brush it off as coincidence. But Barbara, determined to prove her point, had added that Enid's hair was also that bit shorter at the back, like Barbara had done Emily's. At hearing that, she'd felt a dawning of realisation, and a whole lot of things that had happened over the years suddenly made sense.

Barbara had gone on to explain that she thought all the quizzing her mother did over her life showed that Enid was very insecure about how independent Emily was. Emily had laughed at that and reminded her friend what a mess her life was in since she'd left John. To which Barbara had said that that in itself showed strength.

It was funny how people saw things in completely different ways. When Emily left John, she had half hoped he would come after her, apologise profusely, promise to change his ways, and beg her to come home. Where was the strength in that? But when she'd tried to explain, Barbara had said the strength lay in not going back to him when things were tough – not giving in. Emily thought that was more about stubbornness and pride than strength.

'There you go again, off in your own little world,' Jake said, cutting into her reverie.

Emily realised she was staring out the window and hadn't washed anything for goodness only knew how long. The drainer was empty and so were Jake's hands.

'Oh, just thinking about life, you know,' she said with a shrug. 'The way things change.'

'Far too deep and heavy,' Jake said with a laugh. They stood side by side for a few moments, looking out the window. The two surveyors were now walking up the hill beyond the shearing shed.

Emily ran her hands around the bottom of the suds-filled sink and was surprised to find it empty. She couldn't even remember washing the cutlery. All that was left were the two frying pans, which she'd leave to soak for a while.

'More coffee?' Jake said, turning away from the window.

'Hmm, thanks.' Emily felt slightly dazed as she left Jake to the coffee-making and sat at the table.

'Are you okay?' he said a few moments later, putting a mug down in front of her. 'You look a little pale.'

'I'm okay. I just feel a bit weird.'

'Sick?'

'No, a bit out of kilter – you know, just odd.'

'Probably because all this is finally becoming very real,' Jake said, making a sweeping gesture with his arm. 'Totally understandable – it's a pretty big thing. Not to mention me turning up out of the blue.'

'Hmm. I guess that must be it. But it is great to have you here.'

# Chapter Twenty-nine

About an hour later they were at the table discussing the plans when they heard Barbara's voice echoing down the hall.

'Yoo-hoo! Em, are you home?' The rain had stopped to reveal a perfect cool summer day. Emily had left the front door open after Jake had arrived to air the house.

'Coming!'

Grace bounded out of the kitchen and into the hall, skidding slightly as she took the corner too fast. Emily skipped after her, and Jake loped along behind.

'So what are you doing here?' Emily asked after they'd all exchanged more New Year greetings and hugs. As she suspected, Barbara didn't seem at all surprised to see Jake, and Emily thought she caught a look pass between them. Again she felt a slight niggling of jealousy and unease that they had been talking behind her back. She blinked away a frown and returned her attention to Barbara.

'Bernice at the post office thought this looked important,' Barbara said, dragging a thick, long and narrow business envelope out of her handbag and handing it to Emily. In the top left corner were the logo and address details of the law firm who had done Emily and John's wills.

'Why was she open on New Year's day?'

'She wasn't. I bumped into her in the street and she asked if you were with me or in town. When I asked why, she said that something had come in for you late yesterday. Lucky I've got the spare key to your box in my handbag!'

'That was very good of her,' Emily muttered, staring at the article and turning it over in her hands a couple of times. Her heart began to race. She took a deep breath before sliding her nail under the seal.

'Ah the quaint ways of the country, where everyone knows everyone,' Jake said, shaking his head. 'Anyway, how about we do this inside rather than at the front door. Barbara, would you like to come in for a coffee?'

'Oh shit, I'm so sorry, yes, come in. I didn't mean to keep you standing there.'

'Well, I can't actually stay for long, but a cuppa would be nice, thanks.'

They trooped down the hall and into the kitchen, Grace leading the way and Emily straggling at the back, consumed with dread over what news the envelope might contain. She sat down while Jake and Barbara stood together at the sink – an obvious ploy to give her space. She stared at the envelope as though it were some foreign object she'd never seen before.

'So, what does it say?' Barbara asked a few minutes later, taking the chair beside her.

'No idea.'

'Come on, you can't put it off forever. And anyway, it can only be good news, can't it?'

'Hmm, I think so.' *Lawyers don't write to tell you you* aren't *a beneficiary, do they?*

'So what's the problem?' Jake said.

'Scared, I guess.'

'Of what?!' Barbara and Jake cried at the same time.

Emily shrugged. How was she supposed to tell them that she was scared of more change? That she'd gone through too much already. Yes, she might soon have John's money to do the renovation, but what if the letter said she had to sell the farm, dispose of all the machinery and stock? What if there was a huge tax bill or something she didn't know about? And then there were his parents... She didn't think she had the capacity to deal with anything else right now.

Even the thought of going ahead with the renovation was starting to feel like too much, made all too real by the sight of the two surveyors wandering around. *If only I could just find a normal job, and have a simple life for a while.*

Well, she could put the renovation on hold, she supposed, but it would be just putting off the inevitable; she couldn't live like this forever. It was one of those no pain, no gain scenarios.

Emily felt exhausted just thinking about it. Her life was too damned complicated. Bloody John. That's why she'd married him in the first place – to have a nice simple life as a farmer's wife. But then he had to ruin everything by turning out to be a complete prick! *Bastard.*

Emily ripped open the envelope with such force it almost tore in two. Jake and Barbara exchanged concerned glances.

'Right,' she said, trying to flatten out the wad of papers on the table. She quickly flicked through the pages, scanning their contents. But the legal speak meant she had to go back to the start and read slower in order to fully understand their meaning.

'Oh,' she said, as she read the second page.

'What?' Jake and Barbara said.

'No. How the hell am I meant to...?' Emily muttered.

'What?' said Jake.

'What does it say?' said Barbara.

'Are you going to tell us or just have us die of curiosity?' Jake asked.

Emily read silently for another minute, then looked up and glanced from Jake to Barbara and back again. She opened her mouth to speak and then closed it again, her brain spinning too much to formulate words. She tried again.

'According to this, I'm John's executor, and the *sole* beneficiary of his will,' she finally said.

'But that's good news isn't it?' Jake said, clearly confused.

'Yes it is,' Barbara said, 'Emily here just hasn't figured that out yet.'

'We were separated – I'm sure the last thing John would have wanted was me owning everything.'

'Well, then he should have changed his will,' Jake said.

'Or at least told his parents,' Emily muttered, barely audibly.

'What about his parents?'

'They apparently hadn't caught up with the separation,' Barbara said.

'But how could they not if everyone around here knows everyone's business?'

'*That* is the question of the century,' Barbara said. 'Emily is going to tell them after the funeral, when things settle down a bit.'

'I just couldn't bring myself to tell them straight after John's death. They'd already lost John, and I didn't want to hurt them even more. But it's going to look really bad now that I'm sole beneficiary — they'll think I did it because of the money. Do you think they might contest the will?'

'I can't imagine anyone contesting a will unless they were really hard up financially,' Jake said thoughtfully. 'Most people wouldn't want to bother with the trauma of it, not to mention the cost involved.'

'Well, until I come clean about the separation, I won't know what they think. And I can't do that yet. Meanwhile, I'm going to be responsible for settling his affairs. I'm going to have to run the farm, pay his bills, sort everything out. What the hell do I know about running a farm?'

'No one says you have to actually *run* it, silly,' Barbara said. 'You could sell it.'

'I can't sell it until I know whether it's part of the estate – or whether it's still part of the family company. Oh God, it's doing my head in already,' Emily said, putting a hand to her brow.

'Actually, David is looking for a bit more land. Maybe he could take a short-term lease,' Barbara said with a shrug, looking a little sheepish.

'Really? God, that would be a weight off my mind.'

'Why couldn't you just leave it for a while until you decide what you want to do?' Jake asked, looking from Emily to Barbara.

'Weeds mainly,' Barbara explained. 'If they're not kept on top of they'll take over and be twice as bad the following year. And they're worse than usual, thanks to all the summer rain we've had. Whoever crops it will have to think about rotation, what crops where et cetera. And the stock will need to be drenched, not just checked. Even though seeding won't be for a few months, there's still heaps to do over summer,' she concluded.

'Oh, I had no idea. I can see your reluctance now, Em. It sounds like an awful lot to deal with,' Jake said.

'Exactly.' Emily said. *Bloody John. Even after death he's landed me in the shit.*

'So who's doing all this at the moment?' Jake said.

'Well, it's all been put on hold, which is fine for a week or two. John's father has been keeping an eye on the sheep and the troughs.'

'So why couldn't he just take it over?'

'It's too far away from their main farm – too much travelling. It's okay for checking the sheep once a week, but not really practical for bringing machinery back and forth for cropping.'

'Which is why David is perfect – only around twenty minutes up the road from the far southeast corner of our place and going the back roads. Of course we'd do it all by the book – get a proper contract drawn up and everything.'

'It's a hell of a lot to take in,' Emily said, shaking her head.

'So are you still going to have enough to do this place up?' Jake said.

'I won't know for a while, but I think so. According to this, there was a life-insurance policy with me as beneficiary too. I vaguely remember John's parents saying just after the wedding that they'd taken out policies in both our names, in case something happened and there were kids to raise.'

*Not that there were.*

Goodness knows how much Gerald and Thora had spent on keeping the insurance policies current. *But how could I tell them that I was never having children with a man who was capable of beating his dog and then shooting it because it didn't come quickly enough? He was their son.*

Emily felt hot and clammy and a little queasy in the stomach. She'd essentially been deceiving them for the past several years. But which was worse? Lying by omission, or telling the truth and letting them know what kind of person John really was?

'Just how much are we talking?' Barbara asked.

'It looks like I'm pretty much set for life if I'm careful.'

'Jesus.'

'Wow, that's great,' Jake said. 'So why aren't we jumping around with excitement and cracking open a bottle of champagne?'

'I feel so guilty.'

'Why? It was John's choice to make you bene-ficiary, to not change his will when you split up,' Barbara said.

'Exactly,' Jake said, nodding in agreement.

'But...' She took a deep breath. *How can I tell them?* 'I'm not sure that I actually ever really loved him.

Not properly. I think I loved the *idea* of him and the life he could give me.' God, she really shouldn't be saying this in front of Jake, but it was too late now. She swallowed hard.

'I left him, and now it looks like I end up with everything. It doesn't seem fair. He'd be devastated if he knew. And the town,' she added. 'What will everyone else make of all this? They thought it was bad enough me leaving him.'

'You can't feel guilty, Em. It's the way it's meant to be. It's karma; you haven't done anything wrong. You're a good person; you deserve this,' Barbara said.

'I wish I could just wake up in a few months to find this place fully done and the change of ownership dealt with.' *And to have got out of having* the *conversation.*

'You just need to relax and let it settle in your mind, and then you'll be able to go through and tackle each issue, one at a time. You're a smart girl, you can do it,' Jake said.

'Why don't I help you out by mentioning the farm stuff to David right now? There's no pressure – but he's bound to have some good ideas on where to start in sorting everything out.' Barbara got up and gave her friend a hug. 'You'll see; it'll all work out fine.'

'Thanks Barb.'

'We'll discuss it later,' Barbara said. She then hugged Jake and said, 'I'll leave her in your capable hands. I'm so glad you're here.'

'I'll see you out,' Jake said.

Emily knew they'd be discussing her out on the front step, but she didn't have the energy to join them. Her brain ached, and she felt like going back to bed for a week. Only three hours ago she'd woken up feeling so positive. But now her world had been completely rocked. If only she'd spoken to Gerald and Thora before. She laid her head on the table and awaited Jake's return.

'I'm sure all this calls for another fortifying cuppa,' Emily said when he did, 'but I'm awash – I'll be peeing for the rest of the day if I have another. But can I get you something?'

'No thanks, couldn't fit any more in either. Do you want to go for a walk or something? Get some fresh air?'

Jake placed a hand over her two that lay linked on the table. Emily stared at it, enjoying the warmth and sense of comfort. Part of her wanted to be left alone to process everything in her own time. But how could she tell him that? God, why did everything happen at once? She'd just been enjoying the prospect of getting to know him on a more intimate level, and now there was all this other stuff to deal with.

She smiled at picturing Gran with her lopsided grin saying, 'Well dear, it doesn't rain; it pours.'

*Ain't that the truth?*

'What are you smiling at?' Jake asked.

'Gran used to say, "It doesn't rain; it pours." You know? I think she'd find all of this quite funny – she had a quirky sense of humour.'

'I sensed that from the whole button jar thing.'

'Oh, why's that?' Emily asked, frowning.

'Well, the fact that she chose to keep the diamonds in there. It's like the ultimate contrast: mixing the most commonplace with the most precious. And the fact that she gave it to you knowing you'd figure out her secret.'

'But I didn't. You did.'

'You would have eventually. Anyway, I'm sure she knew you'd treasure it for the memory rather than what it contained.'

'Wow, it's almost like you could have known her yourself. You know, she was from a really wealthy family – hence spending time overseas and having the opportunity to meet an Indian prince – but she chose to walk away from that to marry the man she loved. She could have gone to university and become anything, but she chose to be a farmer's wife. And Grandpa was quite poor; not someone they thought was right for her by any stretch. He just had a small scrub block when they met. He told me she always worked alongside him like a man – got stuck in and got her hands dirty – despite coming from a life with servants. They were such a great team,' Emily concluded wistfully.

'I take it you didn't have that kind of partnership with John?'

Emily thought about all the hope she'd felt before her marriage; that they'd be true partners, standing shoulder to shoulder, sharing everything.

'No. Apparently a woman's place is in the kitchen,' she said with a wry smile.

'You're kidding!?'

'Unfortunately not. Actually, do you fancy taking a drive?' she said suddenly, swiftly changing the subject.

'Sure, where?'

'I wouldn't mind checking on the farm.'

'You mean right now?'

'Yep, if that works for you.'

'Certainly does.'

'You might like to bring your camera – there are some nice spots worth capturing.'

'Okay, brilliant. I'll just go and get some gear together,' he said, getting up.

'You do that and I'll pack some food in case we get hungry. I'm not sure how long we'll be gone.'

# Chapter Thirty

They were halfway to the farm when Emily started to feel seriously jittery. She'd told Jake to bring his camera, promising sights worth seeing and exploring. Inviting him was beginning to feel like a very bad idea.

How stupid was she to bring the new man in her life to the old man in her life's home? *What was I thinking?* Clearly she hadn't been.

*Get a grip, Em. John is dead. You have every right to be there. And you have nothing to feel guilty about. When we arrive, you'll swap the car for the ute and give Jake a tour of one of the loveliest properties in the district.*

Emily gave a sharp nod of agreement, tightened her hands on the wheel, pursed her lips, and focused even harder on the road beyond the windscreen.

'Are you okay?' Jake asked, turning from watching out the side window towards her.

'Yes, why?'

'You seen awfully tense. We don't have to do this – not now – if you don't feel up to it. It's fine to change your mind.'

Emily's hands relaxed on the wheel and some of the tension in her shoulders eased.

'Thanks, I am feeling a bit weird, but I think I need to do it. I'll have to sometime.' She smiled wanly at him.

The longer she stayed away, the longer she could put off thinking about the decisions she would have to make – the umpteen different things she'd have to deal with. But it was only putting off the inevitable, and in doing so, increasing her stress and fear. *Just like not speaking to his parents. I'll do it after the funeral*, she told herself forcibly, and pushed it from her mind.

Decisions would have to be made about the running of the farm, and quickly, or else she'd lose a whole year or more if the crop rotations and other schedules were mucked up. She didn't have a clue about any of it, but could remember John once yelling at her for querying why something had to be done right *then* and in *that* paddock. It was in the first days of their marriage, and he'd treated her like a backward child; the 'townie' that she was. It was the first sign she'd seen of his cruelty, and his refusal to have her involved in any aspect of the farm.

Gran had been right, she thought, bringing herself back from thoughts of John. The old woman had always told her that the best policy was to deal with things as they arise, and never to put off hard decisions. Doing so just ate away at the soul and made the decision harder.

*If only I'd followed that advice when it came to leaving John*, Emily thought wistfully. It all seemed so obvious now. But she'd been under so much pressure to stay – mainly from her mother. And of course there was Gran's view that one must give things a damned good shot – see them through.

Emily chuckled to herself. The old dear had had a quote or snippet of advice for just about every little situation, and some of her sayings contradicted others. No one could follow *all* Gran's advice – it just wasn't possible – and trying to do so was bound to do your head in.

'What are you laughing about?' Jake asked, grinning at her.

'Oh, I was just thinking about my gran again.'

'So, what's so funny?'

'I've just realised that it would actually be impossible to follow all her advice.'

'Oh?' Jake frowned, clearly perplexed.

'Well, take my marriage.' For a second Emily doubted her choice of example, but she forged ahead anyway. 'If I was being true to myself by leaving John, I couldn't also be sticking it out and seeing things through to the end, could I? It's paradoxical.'

*Just like how I can't tell his parents about our separation now, because they'll be devastated that John never told them – and because it'll mean telling them how he treated me. But if I don't tell them then I'll be lying by omission and getting rich under false pretences – if they find out from someone else they'll think I've been deceiving them in order to get my hands on John's estate. If only money wasn't involved.*

'Hmm, I see what you mean. Which is why only you can know what is right for you, Em. Only you can live your life. Everyone else will have an opinion, but ultimately you're the one responsible for your own actions – and your own happiness.'

'I'm sure that was probably one of Gran's sayings as well,' Emily said, rolling her eyes.

'I'm serious.' He put a hand on her thigh as if to prove it.

'I know. I just can't believe I didn't see before how ridiculous it is, trying to follow all her advice.'

'It's not ridiculous. She was obviously a very wise woman, and a big influence on your life. But maybe you've been using your memory of her as a bit of a crutch and this realisation is a sign that you don't need to anymore.'

'What, like a sign from the universe?' She resisted again rolling her eyes.

Jake shrugged. 'If you like.'

They lapsed into silence, Jake focused on taking in the surroundings, and Emily processing what he'd said. She felt a little disloyal questioning her recollections of Gran. But the old lady had had dementia – and God only knew how long she'd had it before being diagnosed.

Emily was suddenly struck with the thought that possibly nothing Gran had said to her since she'd been fifteen could be relied upon. She felt a lump beginning to form in her throat. An image of Gran, with her lopsided grin, appeared in her mind, plain as if she'd only seen her yesterday. As it became clearer, she realised she was seeing the day Gran gave her the button jar.

She frowned, watching the scene unfold, while she struggled to focus on the road ahead.

Now she saw Gran looking quite perplexed – confused – as she handed over the jar; hardly urging her to take good care of something precious. The old lady didn't have a clue that she was essentially handing over the family jewels.

Replaying it in her mind, Gran didn't seem to know what she was doing, or even who Emily was. Why had she been so convinced that Gran had singled her out? She'd spent so long looking to the buttons for answers. How could she have been so pathetic, so naïve? Even John had seen it. He'd teased her about it. But that had made her seek the solace of the button jar even more.

Slowly the answer came to her. She'd been hearing what she wanted to hear; it was the universe protecting her during a tough time.

But the diamonds tucked in with the wooden, plastic, and metal buttons were real. What did that mean?

Nothing more than proof of some family secret that had almost gone to the grave with Gran. Emily felt like she was back at square one. Did that mean Gran had given her the jar on purpose, knowing the diamonds were in there? What if she'd just disposed of the jar, dismissed it as the lifetime's hoard of a mad old woman – like her mother would have?

And what if she did sell the diamonds – if she wasn't so damned sentimental? Emily's head spun.

*No. Everything has happened the way it was meant to. I was meant to get the diamonds. I was meant to keep them and not sell them. I was meant to remember Gran's sayings. And they were meant to help me through this traumatic time.*

With all the mess going on in her mind, Emily knew three things for sure: Gran was the wisest woman she'd ever met; Gran had had a great life, not regretting for a second choosing love over money and status; and she, Emily, had wasted far too much energy and time worrying about what her mother wanted and expected from her.

From now on, she thought as she turned off the main dirt road and onto John's – no, *her* – property, she was going to do her own thing; live her life her way – whatever that was.

She was feeling more buoyant as she pulled up beside the huge corrugated-iron implement shed with its six sliding doors. She got out and went over to the third door from the left and gave it a hefty tug while making a mental note to sort out some way of locking it up. And the house.

*Things are going to change around here, and John can't do a damned thing about it.* It occurred to her that his parents could probably do whatever they liked, but she shook it aside. *Until I tell them, let me have this little fantasy. And maybe they won't care. Yeah, right!*

Jake was standing beside her as she stared into the dark shed. Grace trotted off ahead of them, the tip of her wagging tail disappearing into the darkness. They could hear the scratch of her nails on the concrete. Emily frowned at the empty bay, and then brought a hand to her mouth.

Of course! The ute was now mangled and sitting in the wrecker's yard. How could she have forgotten? She felt her knees go weak.

'What's wrong?' Jake asked, laying a hand on her shoulder.

Emily turned to look at him, her face white and drawn.

'I completely forgot about the ute. I was going to swap vehicles to drive us around the farm. But John was driving it when he died. I can't believe I forgot. We'll have to do a bit more walking than I'd originally planned.'

Slowly her colour returned and she got herself together. She pulled the door closed until only a small gap remained.

'Gracie, come on, quick, we're going now,' she called loudly. After a few moments Grace trotted out, tail bouncing, and Emily finished closing the door.

They walked the few metres back to the car in silence, Emily busy making another mental note; replace the ute.

'Are you sure you're okay?' Jake asked when he, Emily and Grace were settled back in the car. 'We don't have to do this if you don't want to.'

'No, I do. I'm fine. I just got a bit of a shock.' She laughed self-consciously. 'Yet another one.'

Jake looked at her calmly. 'As long as you're sure.'

'Totally. I'm looking forward to having a good look around.' And at that point Emily realised she actually was.

It had been a couple of years since she and John had gone on a proper tour of the property; just driving around checking things out and stopping wherever took their fancy for a barbeque. Emily had put the small gas stove in the boot, but it just wasn't the same as cooking chops and sausages over real coals on an old plough disk. But you couldn't do that with the summer fire restrictions currently in force.

*Another time*, she thought, pausing for a few moments to think where the plate would be located, and failing.

She started the car, turned it around, and drove back the way they'd come.

'Looks like a nice solid old house,' Jake said, nodding at the house as they passed it.

'It has its good points. Great kitchen, but not really a patch on where I'm living.'

'So I suppose you'll rent it out then?'

'I suppose so. Remind me to show you through when we get back.'

Emily paused at the end of the driveway, considering whether to go right or left. In the paddock ahead was the pile of stone from the ruined cottage, and the uprights of the half-finished hayshed. She winced at the sight.

She wondered fleetingly if the stone from the cottage could be salvaged and the structure rebuilt, before dismissing the notion as utterly ridiculous. She had to get over it; harbouring such resentment wasn't healthy. At least she didn't have to look at it every day through her kitchen window – that she couldn't bear.

'Was that *the* cottage?' Jake asked, pointing to the rubble.

'Yep.'

'Sacrilegious. I'm not surprised you were devastated.'

Emily shrugged. 'At the end of the day, it was only a cottage, I guess.'

'She says to an architect who specialises in preserving old buildings,' Jake said, laughing. 'It could be rebuilt, you know.'

'Really?'

'Of course.'

'It'd be a pretty big job.'

'Yes, but not impossible. You'd have to separate the useable stone from the debris, clean off the old mortar, and then you could rebuild. It would have started out as a pile of rocks in the first place.'

'Hmm, I hadn't thought of it like that.'

Emily turned right and halted the car at the steel mesh gate into the paddock next door. She was glad when Jake leapt out of the car, saying, 'I'll get it.' Hopefully that would mean an end to the topic of the cottage.

'If I hadn't seen it for myself, I wouldn't have believed someone could be so spiteful,' Jake said, as he settled back into the car after shutting the gate. 'To go to the trouble of tearing down the cottage and then put the shed nearby – not even use the site,' he said, shaking his head.

*And there you have it*. Emily pursed her lips and put the car in gear.

# Chapter Thirty-one

Although she was careful to take the rough track slowly, Emily cringed every time she felt the bump and thud and twang of stones underneath the car. The heavy, fertile soil John had often bragged about was also home to sharp brown rock.

'I wonder where the stone for the cottage came from – it's not indigenous by the looks of this,' Jake said, nodding at the rough, stony track ahead of them.

'Nearer the coast I'd reckon. We're only thirty kilometres inland. All the old cottages, schoolhouses, and churches around here are built from limestone. I guess it was easier for the early settlers to come by.'

'It's certainly easier to work with,' Jake replied. 'Often just a matter of plonking a rock in and filling up the gaps with mortar. And it's easy to break if you need it smaller. The iron in this stuff was probably too difficult to work with back then,' he added, again nodding at the track. 'Wow, it's a lot more undulating than it looks.'

Emily turned the corner of the paddock and drove alongside the dense scrub, beyond which rose a small range of hills. She stopped the car about halfway along the paddock where a narrow track disappeared into the scrub – a path worn smooth over many years by sheep making their way down onto the flat to graze or drink from the trough against the road.

'Sorry, we'll have to walk from here. Bring your camera,' she added, turning off the car and getting out. 'Gracie, you stay right here beside me,' she commanded with a point to her leg. The dog immediately fell in alongside.

Emily felt pleased to be showing Jake around. Gone was the unease she'd felt in the car. This really was an exciting new beginning. She indicated for him to go first, and held back enough so she wouldn't get hit in the face with tree branches.

She remembered the day John had brought her here; proud to be showing off his little piece of paradise.

She felt a similar pride, though she reminded herself that *her* little piece of paradise was the twenty acres twenty kilometres or so back over to the west.

This was just an asset she would have to decide what to do with. Would Thora and Gerald demand she hand it over to them? Could they?

About a kilometre in, the scrub opened up into a lush clearing with a natural soak and a small creek running through it. Up here there was still a trickle of fresh water, unlike the dry creek bed where the cottage had been.

Emily tramped along in silence, lost in her own thoughts, reminding Grace to stay beside her every so often. She had no idea where on the property the sheep were, and she didn't want to disturb them.

'Wow, this is gorgeous,' Jake whispered, stopping at the edge of the trees. 'Look.' He indicated forwards with his head.

Ahead of them were about a dozen kangaroos, lying stretched out in the sun.

'Grace, stay,' she hissed. The dog was crouched low beside her, her tail still.

Jake carefully put down his bag, squatted, and removed his camera.

The kangaroos were now flicking their ears back and forth – their presence had been detected. A couple of them lifted their heads and looked directly at them. Jake would have to be quick if he was going to capture this.

He began clicking away, and continued as one by one the kangaroos got up and then slowly and gracefully hopped away into the scrub and out of sight. They didn't seem too startled, just not at ease with human company.

'I won't be allowed to say this once I become a landowner – farmers and wildlife aren't supposed to get along – but aren't they majestic creatures?'

'Gorgeous,' Jake said, nodding.

'I hope you got some good shots.'

'Certainly did,' he said, standing up. 'Here, have a look.' They leant in together to look in the viewfinder.

Emily was impressed with what he'd taken, but was distracted by his proximity. *God, he smelled good!*

'I don't know how you think you're going to top this spot,' Jake said after he'd put away his camera. He wrapped his arms around her. They kissed while Grace snuffled around in the scents left by the kangaroos.

'Shall we keep going?' Emily asked after they had regained their breath.

'Sure. I'd like to see how it looks from the other side,' Jake said. He set off, skirting the natural clearing. Emily followed with Grace trotting beside her.

★

'How far back does the property go?' Jake asked.

'About the same distance as back to the car and across a few kilometres. I'm not very good with distances. It's around four thousand acres all up, but only half of that is on this side of the road. Come on; I'll show you as much as I can – we'll find somewhere for our barbeque along the way.'

'Surely there's nowhere else as picturesque as this,' Jake said, as they started walking back.

'You'll just have to wait and see.' She grinned. The spot she had in mind would take his breath away. He'd seen the oasis-type settings so far – David and Barbara's and now hers – so it was time for something different.

It felt odd thinking of the property as hers. Though, technic-ally speaking, it had been hers while she'd been married. Not that John had ever let her feel that it was.

After returning to the car, they continued around the property until they could see the back of the house and surrounding sheds in the distance. They had come full circle after going through a number of steel mesh gates and quite a few of the much more difficult and dangerous wire or 'cocky' versions. Between them they had managed to get the notoriously tricky gates opened and closed without injury.

Again they parked near the scrub at the base of a rise. Emily unloaded the boot and between them they carried the esky, small gas barbeque and bottle, and a backpack containing a ziplock bag of dog biscuits, a large bottle of water, two dog bowls, cutlery, hard plastic plates, and a tartan picnic rug.

Grace raced ahead and disappeared off into the scrub. The hill was quite steep and a little rocky, so they stayed silent while they watched their feet and tried not to appear out of breath. When they got to the top, the view was just as beautiful as she remembered it.

Stretching out before them were miles and miles of farmland and scrub. The patchwork of browns, greens and pale yellows looked like a magnificent quilt. In the distance, the farmland gave way to a wide strip of pure white sandhills, announcing the rich blue-green of the Spencer Gulf.

They were blessed with a cool, clear day. The white-painted grain silos were clearly visible, stretching up and seeming to join the cobalt blue sky with the farmland and the nearby ocean. The first time Emily had seen this view she'd marvelled at how it seemed to encompass the whole cycle of farming life.

'My God. It's beautiful. I didn't think you could top the oasis earlier, but bloody hell!' Jake said in a breathy voice.

Emily grinned at him. 'Glad you like it.'

Jake got out his camera and began frantically snapping away as if he was concerned the view might disappear at any moment. Emily smiled. He was like a kid let loose in a candy store.

'It must have been hard to leave all this behind,' Jake said, peering into the lens and making adjustments. 'Do you miss it?'

'Not often,' she replied with a shrug. 'Too many bad memories, I guess.'

But she hadn't felt at all uneasy driving around. In fact, she had to admit that she felt really quite at home. Being here had always felt right, it was just that so much had happened.

Her feelings about the place had been shifting since the day she and Barbara had come over.

As Emily unpacked the lunch things, she tried to get her thoughts in order. She loved where she was living, and she'd gone past the point of no return on that. She'd given her word to the brothers, and the surveyors were there right now.

But what if the farm did come to her? Could she see herself living here again?

This house was already done. Could do with a spruce up, but certainly didn't need a full renovation. Emily bit her lip. *I don't know.*

At least she would have somewhere to live while she renovated. No need to beg for the use of her parents' caravan.

'Here, let me do that,' Jake said, taking the barbeque from Emily and setting it up in a matter of seconds.

'Thanks,' she said, leaving him to light it while she got Grace some food and water. She smiled at the dog stretched out on the rug; the picture of contentment.

'You're awfully quiet,' Jake said, turning back from the barbeque.

'I've just been thinking about what you said.'

'What's that?' he said, diving into the esky.

'If I do end up owning this, do you think I should give up on my place and move back here?' As she said it, Emily felt guilty about the plans he'd drawn up potentially being for nothing.

'I guess it depends on how you feel.'

'It's weird; I don't feel at all like I thought I would. Driving around today I've actually felt quite at peace with the place.'

'I don't know, Em. I can't advise you one way or the other. Both places are bound to have pluses and minuses – you just have to weigh them up with how you feel inside. But don't waste energy worrying about it…'

'I know, I know, the universe will sort it out the way it's meant to be,' she cut in, a little exasperatedly.

'Exactly. Give it time. Meanwhile, just enjoy this view. You can't read the signs if you're worrying too much.'

# Chapter Thirty-two

'Thanks for bringing me here, Em,' Jake said, staring out to the paddock stretched out below them. 'It's so peaceful. The perfect place to celebrate New Year's Day. Look at those sheep; not a care in the world.'

'I've always thought that about sheep,' Emily said. 'John hated them. Working with them drove him mad; he'd get into such a rage every time.'

'I wonder why he bothered then.'

'Money, I guess.'

Grace chose that moment to get up from her snooze. She crouched down, head and tail lowered, and stared at the large white dots slowly moving around in the distance. She was noticeably quivering all over.

'You stay here, Gracie. No rounding up of sheep for you, my girl,' Emily warned, giving her a pat. But the little border collie seemed to shrug off her attention and remained totally fixated on the sheep.

'Does she know how to round them up – like properly?' Jake asked, turning the sizzling chops.

Emily glanced at him as he squatted over the barbeque. His jeans were stretched tight across his backside and his rugby top covered his lean back without disguising its definition.

'No. Well, I don't know. She's never been taught, but she seems to think she does. Grace! Sit. Down. Now!'

Again Emily was ignored. This time she pulled at the dog's collar, dragged her close and pushed her into a sitting position. Grace very reluctantly complied. She whined in objection before lying down with a sigh, resting her chin on her paws.

'Good girl,' Emily said, and released her hold on the collar. 'Right, lunch.'

'Great food; I'm full,' Jake said, putting his plate aside and lying back on the rug.

'Hmm. How is it that something so simple can taste so good?' Emily said, leaning over him to put her own plate out of reach of Grace. Cooked bones were a no-no for dogs.

'Must be the good company and the lovely tranquil setting,' Jake said, grabbing Emily and pulling her down on top of him.

They kissed, quickly becoming lost in the moment. When they finally withdrew and sat back up, it was Jake who noticed Grace was missing. 'Where's Grace?'

'Oh God.' Emily looked around the immediate area, and then stood up for a more distant view. 'Look,' she said, pointing ahead with one hand while the other shaded her eyes.

Jake stood up and put a hand to his forehead to block out the bright afternoon sun. 'Wow. How clever is that?'

There, far below them, were the sheep they'd been watching earlier, only now they were in a tightly formed bunch and moving *en masse* towards them.

Emily laughed. 'I suppose I should be angry.'

'Are you sure she isn't trained?'

'It must be in her DNA or something,' Emily said.

'Amazing.'

'Hmm.' Emily was too impressed to call the dog back.

The sheep were now just below them on the last flat area before the scrub and the hill. They watched, mesmerised, as the sheep began circling. Occasionally they caught glimpses of Grace, who was running around circling the large group.

'Now what's she doing?'

'Looks like keeping them in the circle or stopping them moving. You probably know as much about this as me.'

'But you're a farmer,' Jake said, staring at her.

'No. I was *married* to a farmer – who wouldn't let me help him, remember? I'm just a townie.'

'Oh.'

'So what do you reckon we're meant to do with all these sheep staring at us.'

'No idea.'

They started to giggle. After a few moments they both began calling Grace and slapping their thighs. 'Come on Gracie. Good girl. Clever girl.'

The dog looked from them to the sheep and back again, clearly very reluctant to leave her charges. She swayed back and forth as if being physically torn between her job with the sheep and loyalty to her mistress. She moved to where she was halfway between the sheep and Jake and Emily, and stood looking back.

'You can leave them now, girl. Come on,' Emily called.

With one final glance at the sheep, Grace seemed to give a shrug of her shoulders and bounded up the hill. Her tongue was hanging out and she was panting when she got to the top, but she looked very pleased with herself. Farmers often talked about decent work dogs being worth three men and how they absolutely loved working sheep; it was fun to them, not work. Emily had never really believed it; had actually thought it a bit cruel how hard they were worked and treated. Now she could see how wrong she'd been.

She and Jake bent down and made a huge fuss of Grace. There was no point telling her off; the dog clearly thought she'd been doing the right thing rounding up the sheep for them.

'Was that fun?' she said, ruffling the dog's ears. Grace was squirming about, lapping up the attention. Emily realised she hadn't seen her this excited since she'd left John and the farm, and felt a stab of guilt. She thought she'd been doing the right thing keeping Grace as a pampered pet, but what if in her perceived kindness she was actually being cruel? At least Grace had her for company and wasn't left alone every day. But maybe it wasn't enough.

Grace kept looking back and checking the sheep.

'I think we'd better get going; she's clearly not going to let this go, and I didn't bring a leash.' Emily could also now see why most farmers kept their dogs chained up or in pens – another thing she'd previously considered cruel.

'You hold on to her and I'll pack up,' Jake said.

Emily felt guilty watching Jake struggling back down the hill to the car carrying everything except the backpack, which was all she could manage while keeping a tight hold on Grace's collar. She was glad when she had her in the car and could straighten up properly – she was getting a definite crick in her back.

'I'll give you a massage later,' Jake said, noticing her stretching.

'I'd like that,' she said.

He hadn't said it in a provocative way, and nor had she, but Emily imagined how good it would be to feel their skin together, not to mention having those lovely strong hands kneading her...

She pictured them starting with a soak together in the big claw foot bath. Perhaps she'd light candles too. Did she have any? Yes, but only plain ones kept in case of blackouts. Emily made a mental note to invest in some scented and coloured candles.

*No*, she told herself, trying to rid her mind of the image and her groin of its humming. *We're taking it slowly.* A massage didn't necessarily mean naked, and it wouldn't necessarily lead to sex. Besides, she was *so* not ready to be seen in all her nakedness.

But then she sighed. It was going to happen sooner or later. Jake would see her little pot belly and thick, dimpled thighs; there was nothing she could do about them. No diet, starvation, or punishing exercise regime had ever made a difference. She wondered how she measured up against her stick-thin cousin Elizabeth, or all the other sophisticated Melbourne women he'd most likely dated. Oh well, if he didn't like what he saw – a slightly stout size twelve – then there was nothing she could do about it.

She hoped he would like what he saw, though.

'What a perfect day,' Jake said, smiling at her. 'Thank you.'

'My pleasure,' Emily said, beaming back at him.

'I think someone's a bit pooped,' he whispered, indicating towards the back seat with his head.

Emily glanced in the rear vision mirror and smiled. Grace was fast asleep across the back seat with what looked like a grin on her face.

'You're going to have to get her some sheep to play with,' Jake said.

'Hmm.' Emily replied absently. She was thinking that John would have had a fit. The thought caused a shudder to run through her.

'You okay? Someone walk over your grave?' Jake asked.

Emily remained silent a few more moments thinking that was exactly what she was feeling.

'Sorry? No, I'm fine. Just a lot on my mind,' she finally replied.

Again she wondered whether the lives of townies and farmers really could be successfully blended. As a townie, there was so much to learn about life on the land, and she'd been willing to learn. If only John had been willing to teach her, instead of shutting her out.

Had she overreacted about him shooting at Grace? It had been the last straw, the action that finally made her mind up to leave him. Maybe he had been only warning her off, as he'd said. But if so, why then hadn't he demanded she listen to him all those weeks ago; made her understand? Why hadn't he fought for them?

*Because he didn't want to.*

Maybe she'd given him the out he'd been waiting for. Emily felt a stab of anger towards him for giving up so easily, but a stronger stab at herself.

*You wanted him to be the knight in shining armour, but he didn't know.*

Emily sighed. It didn't matter anyway; he'd had his face firmly planted in the bosom of Stacy the buxom barmaid.

*Exactly! But why the hell do I still feel so guilty?*

Jake interrupted her thoughts. 'Are you sure you're okay? You're scowling. Have I done something to upset you?'

'No. As I said, I've just got a lot on my mind.' The words came out snappier than she'd intended. She cast a glance at him. He looked decidedly crestfallen.

She remembered Barbara saying, 'Men are actually a lot more sensitive than we give them credit for.' Why did life have to be so damned complicated? Having Jake turn up and tell her he loved her should have been magical. Now, instead, she had a bloody farm to sort out and a renovation to get underway. And all she could think about was John. It should have been an exciting time, but it felt as if the sky was falling in on top of her. Was she having some kind of emotional breakdown?

'I got some great shots,' Jake said, in an obvious attempt to lighten the gloomy mood in the car.

'That's great,' Emily said, failing to sound enthusiastic.

Emily knew Jake was confused about how she was behaving and was wanting to fix things, but she couldn't find the words to do anything about it.

'You must be exhausted trying to process all this,' he said.

'I'm okay,' she snapped slightly. *Why do men always diagnose brooding as tiredness or hormones?*

'Well, I'll cook tonight – you can sit back and relax.'

'I'm not really hungry.' Emily cursed her sudden cruelness. Where was it coming from? She loved him, didn't she? So why was she being so horrible? Jake was trying to get through to her and she wasn't letting him. She sighed deeply.

'I'm sorry, Jake. You're right; I am tired. It is a lot to process. I know the possibility of inheriting all of this should be good,' she said, 'but it's making me think about things I don't want to think about. It's making me question everything.'

'You mean whether you did the right thing leaving John in the first place? What might have been?'

Emily nodded.

'Maybe you need to talk about it; let it out.'

He was probably right, but it didn't seem right or fair to unload onto him about her ex. Wasn't that one of the absolute no-nos of a first date?

'Probably.'

'Barbara told me he really wasn't very nice. And from what you've said…'

'Aren't we all guilty of that sometimes?'

'Yes, but she said he could be cruel. And the cottage…'

*God, just how much has Barbara told him?* Annoyance crawled slowly up her spine. She tried to push it back.

'So why did you stay?'

'You've met my mother,' she said, offering him a weak smile.

'Please don't tell me you stayed because of your mother. You're smarter than that.'

'It's different out here,' she said with a shrug. She tried to sound nonchalant, but his comment had hurt. She felt rebuked, and didn't like that he seemed disappointed in her.

'Oh don't give me that crap about what other people think. As I said, you're smarter than that,' he said, becoming a little exasperated.

'Obviously not,' Emily said quietly. His words had cut too close to the bone. And she didn't like feeling ganged up on. As silly and nonsensical as it seemed, that was exactly how she was feeling. Just what had Barbara said to him behind her back? The more she wondered, the more annoyed she became.

Just as they got back to the farmhouse, her mobile began to ring. *Saved by the bell.* She pulled the car to a stop and dug in her pocket for it.

'Hi Barbara,' she said, frowning slightly as she stared at the steel skeleton of the half-built hayshed.

'Not Barb, me,' David said brightly.

'Hi David, what's up?' She brightened.

'I'd like to talk about leasing the farm — if you want me to.'

'Oh, that's great.'

'Barbara told me about the letter from the solicitors. Executor and likely beneficiary. Congratulations.'

'Thanks.'

'You don't sound so excited.'

'I am, it's just that it's given me a whole lot more to deal with than I need right now. Everything seems to be happening so quickly, and John's not even in the ground yet.'

'Well, hopefully I've just given you one less thing to worry about. We'll do it properly of course; commercial rates, with a proper contract and everything.'

'That is a huge weight off my mind, thanks.'

'Thank you! I've actually been looking for some more land. I've drawn up the paperwork; I can bring it over now it you like.'

'Already? Wow, you don't muck around! What lawyer works that quickly and on a public holiday?'

'None that I know of,' David said with a laugh. 'I've actually drafted the contract myself based on the other two properties we're leasing. Piece of cake, really. I'll explain it all when I see you. Are you at the house?'

'Not *that* house. On my way back from the farm, actually. Give me about half an hour.'

'Okay, see you then.'

'See ya.' Emily hung up and put the phone in the car's console.

'Is David going to lease the farm?'

'I hope so. He's coming over to talk about it.'

'That's one less worry on your mind, then.'

Was Jake having a dig at her? Emily knew she should feel more jubilant – it was, after all, a major concern off her mind – but she just didn't. At least David's phone call had put an end to the interrogation, and for that she was grateful. But she was still annoyed at him – and at Barbara.

'Do you think I should pull that monstrosity down or finish it?' she said, pointing at the steel structure before putting the car into gear and moving forward.

'Depends if the farm needs a hayshed or not. Probably better to ask David.'

'It's just so bloody ugly. Makes a dreadful view from the bedroom,' she said.

*Oh well, it's not like I'll have to wake up to it every morning.*

She looked at her watch. 'Oh, I was going to show you through the house. There really isn't time now. Sorry.'

'No worries, there's always next time.'

'Hmm.' Emily was now wondering if there would be a next time. She was again feeling crowded.

As they turned onto the road, she looked wistfully at the house.

'So before David rang, you were about to explain why you stayed married to John when he was cruel.'

'No I wasn't. You told me I was stupid to stay.' She knew her chin was set stubbornly like her mother was prone to do, but she didn't care.

'Emily, I did *not* say that. I said you're smarter than that. It was a compliment, not a criticism.'

*Well it bloody well felt like a criticism to me.*

The only response she could find was a shrug.

'I think it would be good for you to talk about it.'

'Well I don't.' She would have folded her arms across her chest to force home her point if she weren't driving. Instead she gripped the steering wheel tighter.

'Of course it's your choice, but I don't think bottling everything up is healthy, Emily.' His tone suggested annoyance, and casting a sideways glance she noticed his arms were now crossed.

*Is this our first fight? God, we haven't even slept together yet.* Why was it happening now, when they'd been getting on so well?

*Just a tiff,* she told herself. *We'll be okay.* Jake would cook her dinner, give her a massage, she'd apologise for being a grump – blaming it on the stress – and they'd make up. Maybe even in bed, properly.

They just needed the change of scene to jolt them out of it.

But their journey back to the house continued in steely stubborn silence.

# Chapter Thirty-three

Back at the house, they unloaded all the lunch things onto the kitchen floor.

'No, it's easier if I do it,' Emily said, as Jake started to empty the esky. Damn it, she was still snapping at him; why was she still being like this?

*Because you're cranky at Barbara too.*

'I'll put the kettle on then shall I?' he asked.

'Not for me, thanks.' Emily felt terrible; he was clearly trying to build a bridge. Part of her wanted to wrap her arms around him, tell him she was sorry, beg his forgiveness and have this silly tiff over and done with. But it wasn't that simple. Emily had inherited her mother's gift of sulking and – while not to the same extent – a bit of her self-righteousness.

The cuddles, apologies and begging were up to Jake. But judging by the polite indifference he was now showing her, he wasn't about to do any of these things. He shrugged and proceeded to fill the kettle, seemingly oblivious to her iciness.

Perhaps he was from the school of men who put everything down to hormones, and thought that one must just steer clear until the storm passes. She wouldn't have picked it; he'd seemed so understanding previously.

She glanced up at him a couple of times from where she was unloading the contents of the esky onto the floor. He didn't seem at all perturbed. Maybe a little tired, but certainly not like he was brooding, or was even aware of the tension in the room. His nonchalance annoyed her even more.

She watched as he took up his mug, grabbed his camera bag from the table and opened the door, holding it that bit longer for Grace to decide to follow him outside.

'Traitor,' Emily growled to herself as she slammed the lid down on the empty esky. She watched as Jake settled himself on the verandah in the late-afternoon sun, with Grace beside him and her head in his lap. She scowled.

Unpacking done, she sat down at the table, feeling like a cup of tea after all. But she didn't want to get up and make one now after shunning Jake's offer. Then she'd have to admit that she had changed her mind.

God, she was suddenly exhausted. What a roller-coaster of a day. She laid her head in her arms on the table and closed her eyes. David would be there soon. And after that she'd go and have a soak in a nice hot bath full of scented bubbles – on her own.

*But I can't really do that with a guest in the house.*

An hour ago she'd been imagining sharing a romantic bath with him. Now all she wanted was to have the place to herself.

A commotion outside brought her head up from the table. Jake was pacing with his phone to his ear. Grace was looking up at him, her head following his back-and-forth movements across the short section of verandah.

'Christ, are you sure?' she heard him say. And then he was at the glass kitchen door, struggling to turn the handle with a mug dangling from his other hand. Emily leapt up to help. He passed by without acknowledging her and put his mug on the sink.

'Well, book my flight, but you'll need to give me two hours to get back to Whyalla.'

Emily stood staring at him.

'Yes, yes, I'm on my way. I just have to throw my bag in the car.'

*What, he's leaving? I didn't mean...*

'Thanks Sim, see you soon.'

Emily frowned at him as he ended the call and then stood for a few moments looking confused and running a hand through his hair. His face was a ghostly white-grey colour.

'What's wrong? What's happened?'

'Look, I'm really sorry, but I've got to go. There's something I need to deal with back in Melbourne,' he said, and left the room.

Emily followed him out, and, not knowing what else to do, hovered in the hall wringing her hands. In less than a minute he had his small suitcase and car keys in hand, and was out the front door.

Outside they stood apart, neither of them wanting to make the first move or knowing what it should be.

'Sorry it had to end like this,' he said, gripping her by her upper arms and pecking her firmly on the cheek. 'But I really do have to go. I'll call you.'

'Okay,' Emily said, nodding. She waved him off and then watched until his car was out of sight.

*Sorry it had to end like this?*

Emily had the sinking feeling Jake had literally just driven out of her life – for good. He hadn't even kissed her goodbye properly. And it was her fault.

No, it was Barbara's. If she hadn't spoken to Jake behind her back it wouldn't be like this. She had no right to talk to him about John. And he had no right to ask. Emily was too angry to cry beyond the couple of tears that had already escaped.

She went inside and slammed the front door, causing Grace to leap in fright and give a little yelp. Ordinarily she would have reassured the dog, but not today. And where the hell was David anyway? Pfft! She checked her watch. It was almost an hour since they'd spoken.

Emily stood in the hall turning this way and that a few times, looking for something to do to distract her. She went into the bedroom, tore the sheets off her bed and stormed out to the outdoor washhouse.

As she loaded them into the washing machine, she caught a whiff of Jake's aftershave. She ignored it and threw in some detergent, slammed the lid shut, and leant back on the machine. She was surprised to find herself slightly out of breath.

Suddenly the lump in her throat burst and tears poured down her face in a torrent.

Why did everything have to turn so bad when it had finally started to go well?

She had to pull herself together. David was bound to turn up any second, and the last thing she wanted was for him to see her like this. She dragged a tissue out of her sleeve, blew her nose loudly and wiped her eyes as she crossed to the outdoor bathroom.

She checked herself in the small mirror above the sink – she looked a bloody wreck – and proceeded to run water into the basin to wash her face properly.

Half an hour later she was at the kitchen table, tapping her fingers on a mug of steaming Milo and looking from her watch to the phone. She was beginning to worry about David. If he'd changed his mind he would have called. God, she hoped nothing had happened. She sighed deeply and picked up the phone.

'Hi Em,' Barbara said.

'Hi,' Emily said coldly.

'How's it going with Jake?'

'He's gone.'

'What? Did something happen?'

'Barbara, David said he was dropping in some paperwork, but I was expecting him over an hour ago. Do you have any idea how much longer he'll be?'

'I was just about to ring you, actually. He got called out with the SES. Hey, are you okay? You sound down. Did you and Jake have some sort of fight?'

'Sort of.'

'Oh I'm sorry. So bad that he left?'

'Apparently,' Emily lied. 'Barbara, why did you tell Jake things about me behind my back?'

'Things? What things?'

'How cruel John was, for one.'

'It just came up in conversation. Why?'

'It doesn't matter.'

'Well, clearly it does. What's wrong?'

'What's wrong is you meddling in my life.'

'But I…'

'I'd thank you not to discuss my personal life with anyone, if you don't mind.'

'But…'

'Tell David to post the paperwork when he can.' Emily hung up. Her face was burning and tears were again blurring her vision. Grace snuffled at her leg, and, for the second time ever, Emily pushed her away.

The phone began ringing. Barbara's name glowed on the caller ID. She let it go to voicemail. Less than thirty seconds later it rang again. This time David and Barbara's home number was backlit. She left the phone on the table, grabbed her hat from the back of a chair and called to Grace, who was eyeing her warily from her bed in the corner.

'I'm sorry, Gracie, I'm just a grump. Come on.' The dog appeared obediently at her side, but was still a little hesitant. As she opened the door a blast of warm evening northerly wind blew in. She pursed her lips. The temperature wasn't too stifling, but she hated the wind.

Emily thought about going back inside, but Grace was already running ahead of her up the hill.

*I suppose I owe the poor little thing some fresh air after growling at her like that.*

And she always felt better after a walk.

# Chapter Thirty-four

The next morning, Emily woke at her usual time. She was feeling surprisingly well-rested and quite okay until she stood at the sink, waiting for the kettle to boil, and began going back over the day before.

She'd fought with Barbara. The thought caused her stomach to sink, leaving her aching. And of course Jake had left – called suddenly back to Melbourne – with the two of them barely on speaking terms.

Well, there was nothing she could do about it now. Barbara had done the wrong thing talking to Jake about her and Jake shouldn't have been so damned nosy. *I have nothing to apologise for,* she thought, setting her jaw in defiance.

God, she really hoped it wouldn't affect any business relationship with David. An SES call-out. Emily wondered what had happened; how serious it was; who was involved.

She shivered slightly. Someone else had died; she just knew it. And she was bound to know them; you always did, living in such a small place.

Why hadn't Barbara called again later, using that nugget of gossip as an excuse? Emily checked her voicemail. Nothing. There was a missed call from Jake, but no message.

*Should I call Barbara?*

No. That would be giving in, and it was too soon for that. Anyway, they'd been in each other's lives so much lately it was probably good to have some time apart. It wasn't like she didn't have a whole heap of stuff to deal with at the moment.

*No, it's probably all for the best*, she concluded.

Emily poured hot water into her mug, unable to shake the hollow feeling. She went back to her bedroom, sat in bed propped up by pillows sipping her coffee, feeling anything but relaxed. There was so much to do; she should just get up. Anyway, David was bound to turn up this morning with the papers.

She got up and got dressed. Back in the kitchen she got out a pad of paper and a pen, and began writing down everything she had to do for the Bakers' house – *my house*, she thought with a smile – and to settle John's estate; breaking down everything into small, individual tasks.

She'd go to Mitre 10 this week and look for tiles, taps and basins. It was too soon to be hunting for finishes, but it was what she felt like doing – and she had the gift card from her parents to put towards it.

*It's finally happening*, she thought, with her pen poised against her lip.

As soon as the estate was settled she'd have plenty of money in the bank, and a whole heap more when John's life insurance paid out. *Fingers crossed Gerald and Thora don't object.* The surveyors had been and surveyed. When the subdivision went through, she would be able to pay the Bakers' first instalment and sign the contract for the purchase. Then she could get the house plans finalised.

*I will use Jake. Forget the money; he deserves the job after all the work he's done.*

He would remain professional, wouldn't he? Yes, absolutely. Nothing to worry about there.

The thought of calling him made Emily feel a little queasy. Why couldn't she be feeling jittery and nervous about calling him after a weekend of passion? Why couldn't it have been like that?

*No*, she thought, returning to her list, she could probably submit the plans to council as they were and then see if they needed more information later. That step was a little way off anyway. Meanwhile she'd go shopping for fixtures and fittings. That would be fun – just what she needed right now.

Emily was still engrossed in her list when she heard a banging on the front door, and then David's voice calling her name.

She opened the door and called an automatic bright, 'Hi David,' before she'd fully seen him. His bland 'hi' in return caused her to study him more closely. He looked terrible; tired and pale.

'God, David, have you been up all night?'

'Yeah. Can I come in?'

'Sorry, yes, of course.' She stepped aside and shut the door behind him, and then strode down towards the kitchen.

'Have a seat. Coffee?'

'Please.' He slapped the yellow manila folder he'd been holding on the table, dragged a chair out, and sat down heavily with a sigh.

'No offence, David, but you look like shit,' Emily said with a laugh as she put a mug in front of him.

'I hear you and Barbara have had a tiff,' he said, taking a sip and meeting her gaze over the rim of his cup.

Emily looked away. 'Sort of,' she mumbled.

'Oh well, not for me to get in the middle of, except to say Barbara's pretty upset about it.'

'Hmm. So what was the SES call-out last night?'

'Oh my God, you don't know. I thought Barbara would have told you.'

'What's happened?'

'Trevor and Donald Baker – they died yesterday.'

'Both of them?'

David nodded. 'Tragic accident; should never have happened,' he said, shaking his head slowly.

'How?'

'Trevor was feeding the sheep a round bale of hay and somehow managed to roll the tractor over onto himself. It looks like he hit a greasy patch of dirt on the side of the hill and the weight of the bale on the front caused it to topple over. If only they'd put a rollover protection cage on...' Again he shook his head.

'So what happened to Donald?'

'They think he had a heart attack. It looked like he'd been trying to pull Trevor out. He was lying nearby.'

'Oh God; that's awful.'

*Will this affect the house?*

It was awful that this should be her next thought. *Donald and Trevor are* dead, *and all I can think about is the roof over my head.*

But she had their approval for the subdivision, and they had agreed on the price and instalments once that was done. *It should be fine.*

'Poor Gary Smith is pretty shaken up – he found them. I don't think that's something you ever get over,' he said. 'It won't affect you buying this place, will it? You've got everything in writing, right?'

'It should be fine,' she said, mentally crossing her fingers.

'Well I guess that's something.'

'They were such nice men – bit gruff when you first met them, but hearts of gold really. They were so good to let me move in here when I was so desperate. They were going to take a holiday to Ireland with the money from the first instalment,' she said. 'I guess that won't be happening now,' she added, pointlessly.

'I'm sure they were really pleased to know you were going to do the place up.'

Emily studied her mug. She felt really sad that they wouldn't get to see the house in all its glory.

'So where are you at with it all?'

'Surveyors were here yesterday,' she said, without enthusiasm.

'And Jake too, I hear,' David said, raising his eyebrows. 'Where is he anyway? Barbara said he looked quite settled when she dropped by. You didn't have a tiff with him as well, did you?'

'He got called back to Melbourne – not sure what the story is.' She spoke quietly, and avoided looking

David in the eye. 'So that's the paperwork for the lease then?' she asked, pointing towards the folder. She was grateful for the opportunity to change the subject.

'Yes.' David dragged the folder towards him, pulled out two stapled documents. He then went through each page, explaining the terms. 'We can discuss the sheep once you've spoken to Gerald and add a clause about them if necessary. I'd be happy to take them on. Or not. It's entirely up to you.'

'Oh. Okay.' *Oh God, Gerald and Thora. Right after the funeral.* Her heart raced with nerves, causing her to shift in her chair. She took a deep breath and told herself to focus on one thing at a time.

Beyond the mention of a thirty-five-thousand-dollar fee per year for use of the land, not much else made sense to Emily. The sensible thing would be to get a lawyer to take a look over it – or at least an objective third party. And Gerald.

She hesitated. *How much did John make from the land? More than thirty-five grand, surely. But do I really want to quibble with friends over a few thousand dollars? What's important is that someone takes over and a whole year of productivity isn't lost.*

And David would do the right thing by her – they were friends, he and Barbara. Their little tiff was just that, and would soon blow over.

'I'll leave this with you to look over. Give me a call when you know what you want to do about the sheep.'

'Okay. Thanks.'

*Damn sheep*, Emily thought. She really would have liked to have had this totally dealt with and off her radar.

'Well, I'd better be off,' he said, and got up.

They made their way down the hall to the front door.

'Ring Barbara, Em. Don't let this fester too long,' he said, on the threshold.

Emily nodded to appease him, though she had no intention of calling Barbara – at least not today.

*I'm not the one who needs to apologise. She's the one who spoke to Jake behind my back.*

'And you go and get some sleep,' she said, hugging him tightly.

Back inside, she sank onto the kitchen chair. A potential big problem had been dealt with – well almost. What a huge relief. The next big item on her to do list was to go to the bank and sort out being a signatory to John's accounts. She felt a little uneasy about setting foot into the bank after the last time. And seeing Nathan Lucas again. But it had to be done. *I wonder if he's found anywhere to live yet. Perhaps he might like to rent the farmhouse.*

She thought of poor Trevor and Donald, how she'd barely known them, and how kind they had been. She would be forever grateful to them for allowing her to stay in the old house in her time of need.

They had been another saving grace. She smiled sadly at the small black and white border collie lying in the corner.

# Chapter Thirty-five

With nothing much else to do, Emily decided to spend the New Year's public holiday Monday cleaning the house. She hoped the noise of the vacuum cleaner would take her mind off Jake and Barbara, and distract her from brooding about John's funeral the next day. She had just unplugged the machine after doing her bedroom and was about to drag it down to the lounge room when she heard a knock on the glass beside the front door.

*I must get a proper knocker before someone puts their hand through the leadlight*, she thought, as she made her way out into the hall.

Who was it anyway? Barbara? Her heart rate quickened. No, the tentative knock wasn't really her. Though it might be now things were different between them.

Emily opened the door to find Tara Wickham standing there. *Donald and Trevor's relative, the financial planner.*

'Oh. Hello. Tara, I'm so...'

Emily stopped herself. She'd been about to say, 'I'm so sorry for your loss.' But it suddenly dawned on her that while Tara didn't look comfortable, she didn't look particularly grief-stricken. What if she didn't know about the Bakers' deaths? Emily thought it highly unlikely; it had happened two days ago. But she wasn't about to make things more awkward than they had to be. As practically a complete stranger, it was certainly not her place to tell her.

What did Tara want? Had she run out of petrol or something? She couldn't be there on professional business, because Emily had made it clear during her previous visit that she wasn't interested. Well, Jake had on her behalf. *Please don't tell me she wants a shoulder to cry on because we've met once before. No, surely not.*

Tara had turned up out of the blue a couple of weeks before Christmas – during Jake's first visit with her cousin Elizabeth – claiming that she was lost and was looking for her cousins' house. Emily remembered how taken aback she'd been, catching the woman looking the house up and down as she'd made her way down the hall and into the kitchen. She'd had a bad vibe about her and she now felt her hackles rise again.

'It's Emily, isn't it?'

'Yes,' Emily said, holding out her hand. She tried to replace her frown of annoyance with a warm, welcoming smile.

Tara seemed a little reluctant to take the proffered hand.

'What can I do for you? I don't have any need for a financial planner,' Emily said. It was a bit blunt of her, but no point everyone's time being wasted with a spiel.

'I'm not here on business.'

It was only then that Emily noticed Tara was dressed casually in jeans and a t-shirt and remembered that it was actually a public holiday.

*So why the hell is she standing there looking my house up and down, running her fingers over the paint on my door surround?*

'So what can I do for you?'

If Tara was there for a cup of tea and an attempt to become her new best friend she'd be sorely disappointed. She might get a cup of tea, but only because Emily had been so well trained.

'May I come in please?' Tara asked.

'Well, I really don't see the point. As I've said...'

'It's about this house.'

'What about it?' Emily stood her ground.

'Donald and Trevor Baker were my cousins. I'm sure you've heard about their sudden deaths.'

She nodded.

'I'm the executor and main beneficiary. I've inherited this house as part of their estate. I'm here to talk about it.'

'Oh, but...'

Emily felt the blood drain from her face and her arms go cold. *There must be some mistake.* Of course this woman was mistaken; didn't know about Emily's arrangement with Donald and Trevor. *If she's the executor of their wills, of course we have to talk about it.* She relaxed slightly.

'I think there's been a bit of a mix-up. I had – I *have* – an agreement with them to buy this house and twenty acres around it. The surveyors were here on Saturday.'

'Of course I'll reimburse you for anything you've spent so far...'

'No, you don't understand. We had an agreement...'

'So you said. But their wills make no mention of it.'

'Well, there's a handwritten offer with their signatures.' *Oh God, why didn't I go out and sign it myself?*

'I know. I've seen it. But my solicitor tells me it's not legally binding. Not, er, worth the paper it's written on, I'm afraid.'

*She's managed to speak to a solicitor on a public holiday weekend? On the New Year public holiday weekend? Seriously!?*

Tara was now smirking. 'So do you think I can come in now?'

Stunned, Emily reluctantly stepped aside. As she followed her down the hall, she noticed Tara appraising the house as she went, just like last time. She wanted to tell her to stop it; it was rude.

Emily motioned for her to sit and took her own seat. There was no way she was going to offer her tea or coffee. She'd hear her out, though. Maybe Tara would still sell her the house.

'You've really made yourself at home since I was here last,' Tara said, looking around the room and taking in the crystal glinting behind the glass cupboard doors. The slight sneer to her mouth told Emily the words, 'I don't see why' weren't far from her lips.

'Yes, I love the house. As did your cousins,' she added, but not sure really why she'd felt the need.

'If it meant that much they would have been living here themselves, or at least not let it get into such a dilapidated state.'

Two fair points, Emily had to concede. 'So are you planning to live here yourself?' she asked.

'God no! Not nearly salubrious enough for me! No, I'm going to put the farm up for sale – in its entirety.'

Emily felt her dream collapsing like a house of cards in front of her. It wasn't fair; just when everything was finally starting to go right again.

Grace chose that moment to let out a loud yawn. Tara glared at the dog with undisguised loathing. Emily wanted to throw her out right then and there, but it seemed *she* was the trespasser now.

Should she be getting a solicitor's opinion of her own? Probably, but she didn't know one she could just call, especially on a long weekend.

'But what's your objection to me having the house and twenty acres?'

'No objection,' Tara said, shrugging her shoulders. 'You can take it up with the new owners in due course.'

Emily could see there was no point trying to reason – she'd clearly made up her mind.

'You'll need to be out by Friday – Saturday morning at the absolute latest.'

*Four days!? Oh Christ!* 'And if I'm not?'

'And if you're not, I'll have the police arrest you for trespass, squatting, whatever,' Tara said with a dismissive wave. 'I'm sure the folks of Wattle Creek would love to see you paraded through in handcuffs.'

'But I don't understand. If you're selling the place, why can't I just stay until the new owners make a decision? It might take ages to sell. I'm still paying rent.'

'Do you really want to know?' Tara got a strange look on her face.

*No.* 'Yes.'

'Because I don't like you.'

And there it was. Emily stood there opening and shutting her mouth like a goldfish feeding. *You're throwing me out because you don't like me?*

'Well, I'd better keep going – see you,' Tara said brightly, leaving the room. 'No need to see me out; I can find my own way.'

Emily shuddered as the front door slammed. She waited until she heard the car leave before making her way down the hall to her bedroom and throwing herself on the bed.

She rolled over and stared at the button jar. She itched to pick it up, ask it to give her some advice. But she resisted the urge.

What advice was there? 'Suck it up, princess, the dream is over?' Not quite one of Gran's quotes, but it was about right. She almost snorted. All of these quotes and relying on the universe to make everything all right was a load of crap. Look where it had got her. She was back almost exactly where she'd started.

Bloody Barbara and Jake and their bloody advice! Grace hopped onto the bed, lay down beside her, and pushed her head under Emily's chin. It was as if the dog was saying, 'It's okay, Mum. We'll be okay.' Emily wanted to cry, release some of the tension and helplessness she was feeling. But there were no tears, not even a lump forming in her throat. Instead her mind started trying to cut a path through all the debris.

*Jesus. What am I meant to do now?*

She considered phoning Barbara, but the thought was fleeting. It was up to Barbara to make the first move to repair their friendship. And anyway, she wasn't sure she could bear Barbara saying, 'Trust the universe, you'll be fine,' or something equally wishy-washy. She felt the overwhelming urge to slap the next person who said that sort of bullshit to her.

No, she'd better do something useful like start packing. Tara had clearly made up her mind and there was no point wasting energy trying to get her to change it.

The idea of packing everything up again was daunting. Emily felt tired just thinking about it.

She wished it was all a nightmare she would wake from. But of course it wasn't; this was very real. She patted the dog and let out a loud sigh before sitting up.

'Come on Gracie, we'd better get started,' she said. She glanced at the vacuum cleaner, where she'd left it to answer the door. 'But if she thinks I'm going to finish cleaning, she can bloody well think again!'

Back in the kitchen, with notepad and pen in hand, Emily wondered if she should phone her parents.

*No.*

As much as she wanted her father's sympathy, the first negative comment from her mother would probably send her over the edge. She'd lost her best friend, the possibility of romance, and her dream house in one fell swoop. And she still had the funeral and then the Strattens to deal with. She was feeling far too vulnerable to risk a conversation with Enid.

She'd been a bloody idiot trusting people's word and not seeking professional advice. Not once but twice. The last thing she needed was Enid pointing out what a fool she'd been!

No, she'd start packing; one room at a time. It would keep her mind off John's funeral. At least there was the farm to go back to.

*Lucky I didn't offer the place to Nathan after all*, she thought bitterly.

For a moment she wondered if Tara would replace her with other tenants. Perhaps she'd just wanted *her* out, specifically.

She went out to the shearing shed to retrieve the boxes of newspaper and bubble wrap that she'd put there a few days before. Dark clouds were looming, gathering thick and heavy overhead. She'd better phone Two Men and A Truck and see if they could move her Friday morning. Their ad had caught her eye in the last bundle of junk mail she'd received in her post box. She now almost snorted at the thought that Barbara would say that was a sign. Everything was a fucking sign if you looked hard enough!

Thankfully the guys who ran Two Men and a Truck were quite recent arrivals in town and hopefully wouldn't know the ins and outs of her life with John Stratten. Not that she could afford to be picky. No. Gran would say, 'Beggars can't be choosers, my dear.'

*Thanks Gran, real bloody helpful.* She silently cursed and then looked up suddenly at hearing a loud crash of thunder, followed by another, and then the tinkle of hail on the roof.

*Fine. Whatever. Do your worst.* With a scowl firmly in place, she prepared to start packing.

# Chapter Thirty-six

Emily stared at the boxes and piles of newspaper and bubble wrap on the floor around her and could not find the energy or inclination to tackle the mammoth task. *Perhaps after a mug of Milo.* But she couldn't even make herself get up to get it. She sat at the kitchen table feeling stunned. Her mind couldn't think past what Tara had said. She wanted to be angry, but all she felt was shock, self-pity, guilt and sadness.

The house would be sold and then torn down, she just knew it. And it was her fault. If she hadn't been there, hadn't upset Tara just by being alive, it would not be under threat. Could she fight this? *Should* she fight this? She loved the house; not just its bricks and mortar, but its soul, its connection to her father, and most of all for being her haven when she'd needed it. She had grown there, felt safe there.

And now her time there was up. It wasn't fair. No, it wasn't. But it was reality. She'd already been humiliated when she'd dared to leave John, and she was facing worse once news of her being his executor and beneficiary got around.

Was this a sign she needed to leave this place? Not just the house, but the district? Was this what the fight with Barbara was about – the universe giving her a clear path, setting her free to move away unencumbered?

Where would she go? Adelaide? Melbourne? Just the thought of being in a city that size gave her goose bumps. All those people swarming around her, invading her personal space.

She liked that here in Wattle Creek she could stop on a corner and chat to people she knew. Sure, there hadn't been so much of that lately, but things would settle down again; someone would do something worse and deflect the gossip away from her.

Was there a life with Jake in Melbourne awaiting her? She could at least go and see how the land lay with him. And Liz had said before she left John that she was always welcome to stay with her. Should she take her up on her offer?

But would that just be running away and not facing up to things? There was a lot to be done here wrapping up John's estate. Could she do it from Melbourne, or perhaps hand it over to Gerald and Thora? Maybe she should just tell them and walk away with nothing; start again somewhere.

*Perhaps this is karma.*

Had she brought all this on herself? Was she getting all she deserved? Suddenly the walls were closing in on her. Emily needed air.

She stumbled out of the kitchen and made her way slowly up the gully with Grace trotting alongside. When she got to the orchard, she sat with her back against the tree where her father had sat the day he told her about his first love Katherine and his connection to the house. Instead of scurrying off after scents, Grace curled up in front of Emily and laid her head on the cross of her ankles.

*I can't fight her. How can you fight someone doing something just because they don't like you?* There was nothing to leverage or work with. Even if there was, Emily didn't think she had the strength. She was tired. Not sleepy tired, not the sort of tired from over-exerting muscles, but a weariness that went right to her soul. Something like she imagined soldiers must feel; battle fatigue.

She'd been through so much recently. It was hard to believe how much. She needed a break. But how do you have a break from being you? It was one thing to escape from a familiar landscape, but her problems would all still be here when she came back. If she left before sorting out her friendship with Barbara and talking to Thora and Gerald, she'd have all that waiting for her when she returned.

She understood how people could disappear, just drop out of society. But there was no way she could do that. As much as her mother drove her mad, Enid was just Enid. She could never hurt her like that.

And the thought of never seeing her father again made her heart clench painfully and the tears start to roll slowly, one after the other, down her cheeks. They had become so close recently. If there was any good to come out of all this then it was her relationship with Des. And Grace. And Barbara and David. And Jake. She felt sure they would come back to her when the dust settled. She was lucky she had people who cared, which was a lot more than many people had.

And, okay, so she'd just been evicted. But she wasn't out on the street; she had the farmhouse to go back to. Even if Thora and Gerald didn't agree with her inheriting their son's estate when they learnt of their separation, they would never see her homeless.

Emily felt bad for the house, but she couldn't fight Tara. Maybe someone else would do the place up.

She had to think that, believe that. It was not life and death. She had John's funeral to get through, and a very difficult conversation to have with his parents. It was going to be very awkward, but it was not mortally wounding. She had to pull herself together and deal with things like the strong, independent woman she was learning to be.

She eased Grace into her lap and hugged her tightly. As much as she didn't want to comply with Tara, she knew she had to. She didn't need more angst in her life. And she certainly didn't need to be the centre of any more gossip. She just wanted a quiet, calm life. Preferably with Jake in it. Really, she only had herself to blame. If she'd sought legal advice and got things signed off properly, she wouldn't be in this mess. She should have learnt that after the settlement fiasco.

Emily let go of Grace, uncrossed her legs, and got up. She made her way slowly back down to the house. Inside she put the kettle on.

She sat with her hands wrapped around a mug of Milo, waiting for the boost of energy she needed to start the packing. Instead, her tired mind moved to thoughts of John's funeral the next day. How was she going to stand up there beside Thora and Gerald with the whole town watching, knowing they were being deceived? The Strattens were very fair people. She wasn't close to them and she found them a little stand-offish, but they had never done the wrong thing by her. They were private people who did a lot for their community. Thora had raised tens of thousands of dollars for charity through her famous garden parties. As far as Emily could see, Thora and Gerald had never deliberately hurt anyone. Whatever John's issues with them, they were his own, just like hers with Enid.

*So how can I knowingly throw them to the wolves tomorrow? And stand by and watch?*

Without knowing exactly what she was doing, Emily grabbed her keys and phone, took David's lease from the manila folder and the lawyers' letter from the table, and stuffed the documents into her handbag as she strode down the hall. She pulled the front door closed behind her and put the bewildered dog beside her in the yard, barely noticing the rain now pouring down upon her. She got drenched in the short dash to the car. But she didn't care.

The sudden downpour had made the already damp driveway greasy, and a few times the car slid in the mud. Emily's heart raced as she fought for control, being careful to steer out of the slide and not brake, just as her father had taught her many years ago.

She sweated under her t-shirt and light woollen jumper, causing an odour of wet sheep to surround her. She was grateful for having to concentrate so closely on the road; that meant she didn't have the chance to run through scenarios for what she would say when she arrived at Thora and Gerald's. She just hoped they would be home and not with a houseful of guests.

# Chapter Thirty-seven

When she pulled up on the wide gravel driveway in front of the sprawling modern brick house, Emily realised she had only been there a handful of times in all the years she'd known John. To say he hadn't been close to his parents was the understatement of the century.

Thora opened the door as Emily raised her hand to knock.

'Emily, how nice to see you. Come in.'

*No going back now.*

Emily noticed Thora's slightly raised eyebrows. She must look an absolute fright. Here she was with wet hair plastered to her head, standing on the doorstep in her rattiest jeans and an out-of-shape jumper with holes and frayed edges. And in front of her was Thora Stratten, dressed neatly in capri pants and a knitted top, with not a hair out of place. She probably didn't even own a pair of jeans.

'Hi Thora. Thanks.'

As she moved into the hall and offered her cheek for the customary air kiss, Emily was stunned to instead be embraced and held in a tight, lingering hug. She hoped she hadn't just put muddy brown streaks down Thora's cream top.

'Come through. We were just having a quiet drink.'

Emily wondered what the time was. Had she rudely turned up right on lunchtime? She felt as if she'd lost a chunk of time. No, it must be mid-afternoon. 'Gerald, Emily's here,' Thora said as she ushered her into the plush formal lounge room off the hall.

Gerald Stratten stood and also greeted her with a warm smile and hug. 'Have a seat,' he said. 'We were both just having a drop of brandy in a glass of milk. Very soothing,' he added sadly, nodding at the glasses on the coffee table. 'Would you like one? Or perhaps tea or coffee. Or something else?'

Brandy in milk sounded like a very good idea. She certainly needed soothing; her heart was racing at a furious pace and her brain was feeling addled.

Did she nod to the offer of brandy? Or perhaps she answered. She couldn't remember, but Gerald left the room.

'And darling, get Emily a towel for her hair, there's a dear,' Thora said to his retreating back. For a split second Emily wondered if she should go off and tidy herself up properly. But she stayed put, feeling very self-conscious and really wishing she had thought to get changed and not let herself get wet.

Enid would have had kittens if she saw her like this, but beyond the initial slight amusement at the corners of her mouth, Thora didn't seem offended by her dreadful appearance. They spoke haltingly about the recent wet weather and Thora was telling Emily about the weeds taking over her garden when Gerald reappeared with their drinks on a tray and a thick fluffy white towel draped over one shoulder. After putting down the tray he handed Emily the towel. She looked at the towel in her hand, suddenly unsure if the correct protocol was to take herself off to the guest bathroom.

'Dry your hair, dear, before you catch your death,' Thora said. She sounded so much like Gran, Emily felt a wave of sadness and nostalgia wash over her. But she was soon distracted by the blush making its way up her neck.

'I'm so sorry about turning up like this. I must look a fright,' she said helplessly.

Gerald and Thora just smiled politely and turned their attention to their drinks. Emily swiped the towel across her hair while their attention was diverted. And as she ruffled her locks she wondered how to begin the conversation that had to be had.

'Now, everything is organised for tomorrow,' Thora began. 'The outfit you chose was just perfect. I think John...' Gerald squeezed his wife's hand as she choked up. She shook her head as if shaking the tears aside, and continued. 'The church ladies are doing the...'

Emily's heart rate rose. She needed to get this over with. But she couldn't interrupt Thora, whose words just sounded like white noise in her ears. Despite sitting there nodding and looking intently at Thora, she was only taking in the odd word here and there. She finished with her hair and draped the towel around her shoulders, not seeing anywhere more appropriate to put it. All around her was polished timber and leather.

When Thora finally took a breath, and before she could go on to give the names of the hymns that had been chosen, Emily took her opportunity and leapt in.

'Thora, Gerald, I'm so sorry, but there's something you need to know.'

Her earnest tone caused them to look up quickly. Emily took a long sip of her drink. The brandy making its way through her felt good. After a moment she forced her eyes up from her glass to meet their gazes. The world seemed to have stopped. The room that had been warm and inviting was now eerily quiet. Was it suddenly a few degrees colder? She took a deep breath, put down her glass, began picking at the frayed bottom edge of her jumper.

'I know the funeral will be daunting, it will be for all of us. But we'll get through it together,' Thora said.

Emily shook her head. She took another, deeper breath, pushed her jumper away, clasped her hands together and looked from one to the other and back again.

Gerald put his hand over his wife's.

'I don't know how to tell you this. I really thought you already knew.' Emily fiddled with her jumper again; stuck her finger into one of the holes. She nibbled on her lip.

'Knew what? What did you think we knew, dear?' Thora asked. She spoke so kindly and looked so fragile, Emily felt the desire to flee and not hurt her.

'I had left John,' she said.

'I'm sorry, left him where?' Thora said, clearly confused. 'Were you meant to be in the vehicle with him? Well, thank goodness you weren't.'

Gerald had a knowing expression. He squeezed both of Thora's hands. 'It might be best if you just come out with it,' he said quietly. Emily could almost hear the unspoken words: 'Dear, we've lost our only son; there's not a whole lot that could hurt us now.'

She found herself wondering if she was sitting where the policeman had sat when he gave them the news. She took a deep breath.

'Thora. John and I had separated. I had moved out. I thought you knew. I can't believe he didn't tell you.' She was rambling. She forced her mouth shut.

'Oh well, no marriage is always smooth. I'm sure...' Thora said.

'No, you don't understand,' Emily persisted. 'We were going to get divorced.' *There, I've said it. It's out now.* There was no sense of relief, no feeling of being unburdened.

Thora looked sad and confused. Gerald looked sad and... Knowing? Had he known? Something? Anything?

'But I don't understand,' Thora said.

'Darling. What she's saying is that they had separated...'

'Why?'

*Why did we separate or why didn't John tell you?* There were so many questions. Emily took another deep breath. She wished she hadn't come. This was even harder than she'd imagined. She'd rather be yelled and screamed at. There was a thick, awkward silence as she tried to sort out the jumble of words and threads in her mind.

'We weren't happy – hadn't been for a long time,' she finally said with a sigh.

'All marriages take work; it's about compromise, *making* it work.'

Emily looked down at her hands. How much should she tell them? The man, her estranged husband, their son, was dead. What was the point of dragging up all the gory details now? 'The thing is, I just wanted you to know because otherwise tomorrow you'll...'

Thora suddenly brought her hands to her face, as if finally understanding. 'The whole district knows, don't they?' she said, aghast.

Emily nodded solemnly.

'Thank you for telling us,' Gerald said. 'It must have been difficult for you to come out here. And you didn't have to. But we're grateful that you did. Thank you.'

'I'm not sure how it went wrong,' Emily said, feeling the need to explain. It was a lie; of course she knew where it had gone wrong. It had gone wrong from the start, when he hadn't wanted to share the running of the farm; had tried to keep their worlds separate.

It was all becoming very clear, as she sat there looking at this impeccably dressed woman in her impeccably decorated room. John Stratten had chosen a townie over all the farmers' daughters, because he wanted a wife like his mother. She'd gone about it all wrong; wanting to – expecting to – stand beside him and toil the land together.

'Was he cruel to you?' Thora suddenly said.

Emily saw a montage of their life together flash through her mind. She nodded. 'He wasn't very nice at times, no.' *Oh, God, please don't ask me for details.*

'No one should be expected to put up with a husband who is cruel,' Thora said simply and quietly before picking up her drink off the table.

Emily blushed. Had she heard right? Was Thora letting her off the hook – just like that?

'I can only apologise. He was an only child. We overindulged him. In things, not love. We were too distant, maybe too cold. I can see that now.' Tears dripped from her chin.

Emily's heart went out to Thora. Had she had the Strattens wrong all this time? Had she been blinded by John's views, too eager to show him her loyalty? She felt a big sense of sadness and guilt that she hadn't made more effort. 'Please don't... As adults, we make our own choices. The thing is, we chose to separate. *I* chose to leave him.' She took a deep breath. *Here goes.* 'So I have no right to inherit anything of his.'

'Of course you do,' Gerald said, without hesitation. 'He was your husband. You deserve it.' He paused, obviously considering his next words. 'You mentioned choices. If John chose not to change his will then that was his choice. It is not for us to question.'

'But...'

'Emily, I can only imagine the cruelty my son inflicted on you – emotionally, and, heaven forbid, physically. He was our son. We loved him, but we knew him. I hoped he would have found his way with you, but clearly not. And I wish we had shown you more support. But what is done is done. We wish you peace. If you want to sell the farm or keep it, that is entirely up to you. I am here if you need any help.'

'Thank you.' The words seemed so insignificant. All the pressure of the last few days left her so forcefully that she almost wept. 'Can I at least give you the insurance? You paid the premiums all these years.'

'And why do you think that was, dear?' Gerald said.

'I have no idea.'

'In case his recklessness ended in his death and you had children to raise,' Thora said, so quietly Emily had to strain to hear.

'But I don't have...'

'It's not your fault you were not blessed, dear,' Thora said through a veil of tears.

*Oh God.*

'I'm so sorry. I'm so, so sorry,' Emily said, burying her head in her hands. She began to cry, slowly at first and then heaving, racking sobs. Suddenly Thora and Gerald were on either side of her and the three of them were crying and hugging.

Eventually the tears subsided and they separated. Emily felt totally spent. And guilty. Why hadn't she just come to them to start with?

'Would you like another drink?' Gerald asked, breaking the silence that was about to become awkward.

'Thank you, but I'd better not since I'm driving. And I really should go,' Emily said, getting up. She glanced at her watch. Where had an hour got to? 'I've actually got a lot to do,' she said, dragging the towel from her shoulder and handing it to Thora. 'I've been living at the old Baker place, but now they've died, I have to move out. I'll be moving back to the farm. If that's okay with you...' They were all now standing facing each other across the coffee table.

'Of course. It's your house, your farm,' Gerald said with a reassuring smile. 'Whatever you decide is up to you,' he said. 'But if I can be of any help...'

'Actually yes,' Emily said, remembering the document in her handbag. 'I need some advice. David Burton has offered to lease the farm. He's drawn up a document, but I... Could you take a look before I sign it?'

'Of course,' Gerald said, holding out his hand. He pulled a pair of glasses from his top pocket and put them on.

There were a few murmurs and a lot of nodding as he quickly read through the few pages. Emily and Thora looked on silently.

Finally Gerald took off his glasses and handed back the pages. 'It looks fine to me. All above board, as you'd expect from David. It's a standard lease agreement. One of the farming groups had it drawn up a few years ago, and most of us have used the same one at one time or another. You should be fine to sign it. It might be a good idea to get him to take over the sheep as well – there's another lease document that can be used as an addendum to this one. I'm sure David will have a copy.'

'Yes, he mentioned it. I just wasn't sure if maybe you…'

'Dear, I'm winding things up here so I can retire; I don't want to take on more sheep, or land. You'll be in safe hands with David. Hand it all over to him for now. Here, sign it now and then you can go back that way and put it in their post box at the cross-roads.' Gerald produced a pen from his other pocket and handed it to Emily. 'Thora darling, could you get an envelope from the office and some paper?'

Thora nodded, got up and left the room. Gerald and Emily sat back down and she signed the paper-work. 'Thank you so much. I really appreciate your advice, and help,' she said.

When Thora returned, Emily accepted the envelope with thanks, slid the signed paperwork inside, wrote a quick note to David saying she'd like him to take over the sheep as well, and slid that in too. As she sealed the envelope and wrote David's name on the front, she felt the tension leaving her shoulders. It was a huge relief to have it dealt with, and with Gerald's blessing and approval.

'Thank you, it's a huge weight off my mind,' she said, tapping the envelope. 'I'd better get going.' They all made their way out into the hall.

'Dear, even if you had divorced our son, we still would have thought of you as family,' Thora said as she enveloped Emily. 'We still do,' she added in a tight whisper. Emily almost erupted into tears again.

'Yes. So please don't be a stranger – after tomorrow's over and done with,' Gerald said a little gruffly, as if trying to keep the emotion at bay.

Emily nodded.

'Would you like us to pick you up, or will you go with your parents?' Gerald asked.

'Thank you, that's very kind. But I'll go with Mum and Dad.'

'Okay. Well, we shall see you there then,' Gerald said, opening the door for Emily to leave.

'Thank you for being so understanding,' Emily said, turning on the front step.

'Drive safely on the wet roads,' Thora said with a weak smile.

Emily got in the car, turned it on, and drove away. She returned Gerald and Thora's wave, thinking it seemed way too jolly given the circumstances.

★

It was as though she was teleported back to the Bakers' house. One minute she was leaving the Strattens' and the next she was letting Grace out of her yard and giving the wet dog a cuddle, with scant memory of the journey. Though she did recall standing at Barbara and David's post box and wondering for a moment if she should drive up the driveway, before sliding the envelope in and getting back in the car.

She hung her legs over the verandah feeling dazed, and struggled to grasp what had gone on, what had been said.

All she knew was that she was free. She could inherit John's estate unencumbered. And she had sorted out leasing the farm to David.

But none of it felt good. She felt numb. And fully aware that she had a horrible day yet to get through. At least she might have spared Thora and Gerald some embarrassment.

# Chapter Thirty-eight

After sitting up late packing boxes, Emily was so exhausted she could barely see straight. When she finally crawled into bed, her whole body ached so much it was impossible to isolate any particu-lar area of painful muscles. But somehow sleep evaded her.

As the early hours became morning, she lay awake, taking an inventory of the past day and making a mental to do list for the one to come. A quiver of nervousness ran through her, followed by the deeper twang of angst.

*John's funeral.*

She checked her watch — six-thirty. In around seven hours she would be expected to stand up in front of the whole district and play the grieving widow. Christ! Her heartbeat began to race. Her stomach began to churn to the point she thought she could probably be sick if she let herself. She ignored it all and got up to let Grace out. Giving up on sleep, she decided take her morning walk a little earlier. Hopefully expending the energy would calm her down.

*Business as usual*, she told herself. Though with her hand shaking on the doorhandle and her breathing ragged, Emily knew she was kidding herself. She strode up the gully after Grace who had bounded off ahead.

*Just take it one hour at a time. You'll be fine*, she told herself over and over.

Emily reminded herself she was doing this for Gerald and Thora. They had made all the plans. All she had to do was turn up and stand beside them. It didn't matter if she was vague or forgetful or anything; this was a funeral, it was expected, almost mandatory.

*This is not about you.*

Emily allowed herself to cringe on John's behalf at his parents' choice of venue; he had been a very reluctant churchgoer. Oh well, it wasn't as though he was in a position to object. And it was what was expected in the small town. Gerald and Thora were old school through and through, and had certain expectations to uphold.

Most of John's friends would skip the church part of it anyway; catch up with proceedings at the cemetery. They'd stand with their heads bowed through the short ceremony, then file past the hole with their heads bowed and chuck in the single carnation offered by the funeral people. Then they'd go off to the pub and get shitfaced – send their mate off in style – while the older women caught up over cups of tea and the older men the odd beer in the bowls club the other side of town.

At least John's death hadn't involved drink driving. It meant the wake wouldn't be the complete farce it usually was – mourners drinking to farewell a mate who had died because of alcohol. Could no one else see the irony in what they were doing? One day one of them would kill themselves driving home from a funeral. Maybe then the stupidity would end.

Every time she heard of a young life cut short from drink driving, she thought about writing to the local paper. But as much as the local copper and the paper's editor went on and on about stopping the needless waste of life, you weren't allowed to point out the obvious. Doing so meant you were being disloyal. Country people were meant to stick together, no matter what.

Emily's sneakers stamped hard on the sharp rocks and uneven ground that was firm but still damp underfoot. She strode on autopilot, following her usual route, deep in thought.

Damn John for putting her in this position; for not telling his parents they'd separated, and then for bloody dying on her. How inconsiderate! It was doing her head in. She had to stay calm, stay dignified, and just get through the day. For Gerald and Thora. It annoyed Emily that, really, she was doing this for John and her mother as well. But that couldn't be helped.

And damn Tara Wickham for making her move just when she'd got settled and when her life was finally starting to look okay again.

Emily hadn't worked off all her frustration when she arrived back on the verandah. She slammed the door behind Grace, filled the kettle, and thumped it down hard on its base.

She was just pouring out some muesli – even though she wasn't hungry, she'd never get through the day without breakfast – when her mobile rang. Barbara or Jake wishing her all the best for today? She hadn't heard from either of them since Saturday. No, it was her parents' home number.

*Bloody hell, that's all I need!* she thought as she pressed the button to answer.

'Hello, Emily speaking.'

'Emily, it's your mother.' Emily rolled her eyes.

'Hi Mum.'

'Now, I'm just ringing to check you're all organised for the funeral.'

'Er, yes.'

*What am I meant to have organised? Don't I just have to turn up? Oh, hang on, this is her way of asking, 'You're not going to embarrass me by not showing up, are you?'*

*No Mum.*

'I know this must be hard for you. We haven't really spoken properly since...'

Emily cut her off. 'Yes, I'm all organised.' Well, technically, she still had to iron a shirt to wear with her black skirt suit. 'Was there anything else you wanted?'

'No, that was all.' She hesitated. 'Well, we'll see you just before one-thirty at the Uniting Church then?'

'Yes. See you then.'

Emily hung up and sat staring at her breakfast. She looked from the bowl of cereal to the carton of milk in front of her and back again with disinterest. But she had to eat. It was doubtful she'd be able to force down any lunch. So breakfast it would be. The last thing she needed was to pass out and make a spectacle of herself at the funeral.

*The way my luck is going I'll probably fall in the bloody hole!*

Emily filled in the time before getting ready for the funeral with packing more boxes. She was still angry about it, and bitterly disappointed, but tried desperately to push those particular thoughts aside whenever they came up. She was trying to look on the bright side. *At least I have somewhere else to live.*

She wondered what the Wattle Creek locals would make of Tara's swift actions. The bush telegraph worked with amazing speed when it wanted to. By the end of the funeral, everyone would know she'd been turfed out of Donald and Trevor Baker's house – if they didn't already know.

Her father would be so hurt that she hadn't told him or asked for his help. But it would hurt more if he knew that the reason she hadn't called was to save herself from the negative comments and gloating that would inevitably come from her mother.

Would other people be sympathetic towards her and appalled at the speed at which Tara had got her hooks into her cousins' assets? Yes, they'd be appalled at Tara; there were certain protocols to be observed around death.

*But will they be sympathetic to me?*

That was the big question. Six weeks ago she'd been the talk of the town, thanks to her audacity in leaving John Stratten. And now, barely a week after his death, she was preparing to move back into his house. It had only taken Emily four days to dig up John's will and learn that she was his beneficiary. Whether or not she deserved it for the way he treated her, it sure wouldn't *look* good to those who knew about the split.

*But it wasn't like that. I never asked to inherit his farm and his money. And I wouldn't be moving back if I had any choice.*

Would that make any difference in people's eyes? Probably not. But what really mattered was that Thora and Gerald knew the truth. Idle gossip she could live with; she had before.

God, she wished she could just pick up the phone and call Barbara. Oh how she missed her friend. They'd been almost inseparable until now. So, really, it would be too awkward that almost three whole days had passed without seeing or talking to each other.

Anyway, it was still up to Barbara to apologise for talking to Jake behind her back. Maybe she had phoned and not left a message. Emily had kept her phone turned off a lot of the time lately unless she was making a call herself – there would be no record of missed calls when the caller didn't leave a message. Now she regretted doing that. What if Barbara and Jake had been calling without leaving messages? She sighed. Well, there was no way of knowing now.

Anyway, Emily sure as hell didn't want to hear Barbara's bolstering mantra about how everything would turn out fine and that she just had to have faith, blah blah blah. Her dream of renovating the Bakers' house was shattered and she was gutted, end of story. And returning to the farm felt like a bloody big step backwards. At least Barbara couldn't nag her about inheriting under false pretences.

As Emily ironed her shirt, she wondered for the umpteenth time in the last few days what had been so urgent for Jake to have to leave so suddenly. She remembered how ashen his face had looked.

She then wondered if he'd actually started a client file on her or if he'd just done the drawings as a one-off. Should she phone his office and tell them the project had fallen through?

If she did, Jake would want to know what had happened; offer his sympathy. As much as she liked his attention, Emily really didn't want his – or anyone's – pity.

And anyway, what would she say to him – about them? She'd have to admit she'd totally overreacted. She could see that now. She'd been feeling guilty about the inheritance, frightened of approaching Gerald and Thora. She didn't want to talk about her past with John – she was trying so desperately to forget it – and didn't want to start making comparisons. Telling Jake all she'd gone through would mean doing that. She just wanted to move on, get over John, and chalk that up to a mistake.

*And how am I going to do that when I'm back in his house?*

Emily got dressed, shut Grace in the fenced-off yard, got in the car, took a deep breath, and set off for town.

As she turned onto the main road from the dirt driveway, something shifted inside her. All of a sudden it was as though everything around her was happening in slow motion – only it wasn't. It was almost like she was watching from beyond, like an out-of-body experience, but that wasn't quite it either. She wasn't hovering above looking down; she was in her driver's seat driving. Everything was just a little fuzzy; not quite right. The car radio sounded muffled, a distorted echo. She felt slightly puzzled as she watched the road before her and behind in the mirrors, her right hand on the wheel and her left automatically moving to the gear stick and back again.

She was making all the motions, knew it was her, but her mind couldn't quite connect the dots.

The weirdest thing was that she didn't feel the slightest bit anxious. She felt fine, better than fine; she was calm, perhaps too calm if anything. Her heart thudded slowly and gently under her ribs; gone was the jittery nervousness that had plagued her all day and made her feel queasy. She wondered if this was what taking valium or a type of sedative was like. Was it some kind of seizure or psychotic episode?

With all these thoughts going through her mind, her calm demeanour remained unchanged, her expression blank and solemn.

Emily arrived at the Wattle Creek Uniting Church with ten minutes to spare. She parked, locked the car, and made her way to the small stone vestibule where Gerald and Thora stood with the two men from the funeral company. They exchanged greetings and embraced. Emily was vaguely aware of being introduced to the two funeral directors as John's wife, and shaking their hands. She felt numb.

She allowed herself to be ushered into the church and seated in the front pew. Nearby, a highly polished mid-brown timber casket adorned in shining gold handles and knobs was resting on a stainless steel stand with wheels.

Emily fiddled with a printed order of service that she didn't remember being handed. She heard the faint shuffling of feet and murmurs of voices as the church filled up behind her. When a hand squeezed her left shoulder, she half turned and returned her father's nod. There was something she'd forgotten.

*Oh, that's right, I was meant to meet them outside. Sorry.*

Still she remained silent and expressionless. She turned back to the front.

Half an hour later, Emily and the Strattens followed the casket out into the sun. They waited beside the black mourning car as people spilled out from the church and neighbouring hall. The two funeral men organised the six pallbearers, then folded the steel gurney and stowed it in a concealed compartment underneath the hearse.

Emily looked down as she felt Thora grasp her hand tightly. She gave a reassuring squeeze and offered a grim, sympathetic smile in return before letting go.

When the pallbearers set off, the younger of the funeral men appeared and opened the doors for them to get in.

They did a U-turn and quickly caught up to the casket, which was being carried at walking pace by six of John's friends. Emily could hear Gerald, Thora and the young funeral man talking around her, could see their lips moving, but she remained silent, gazing out the window and feeling nothing.

At the end of the street, the shiny brown casket was placed into the hearse, which was already parked at the kerb. Emily wondered how it had got there without her realising, but then everything seemed to be happening without her realising.

The few kilometres to the cemetery seemed to take forever. Once there, they waited in the car while the casket was unloaded. Then the six young men carried it down a gravel path between the headstones.

Emily, Gerald, Thora and both the funeral men followed the procession to a hole with fresh brown dirt heaped up nearby. She looked vacantly at the funeral man's hand on her elbow as he eased her into position beside the Strattens.

Emily experienced a strange sense of déjà vu; Gran being placed in the ground. But it passed quickly.

She stared at the jagged pieces of gravel at her feet until someone nudged her forward and offered her a small hand trowel containing dirt. She turned the small implement and watched the brown earth tip onto the large wreath and the box beneath. It sounded like a long and gentle sigh.

She accepted a single carnation, tossed it in and turned away with Thora and Gerald, vaguely aware of the nods of acknowledgement from those lining up for a flower and the chance to utter their last words to the deceased. Emily just looked to the ground.

One by one the people dispersed into the grave-yard to visit the departed or made their way back to their cars. Emily, Gerald and Thora resumed their positions in the funeral car and awaited the return of their driver. They must have spoken and she must have replied, but afterwards she couldn't recall with any certainty what was said.

At the wake, Emily nodded and thanked those around her for their kind words. But she couldn't seem to feel anything; not anger, not sadness, not nervousness – nothing.

Later she watched herself hug her parents and John's parents goodbye at the door, get into her car – which had somehow made it from the church to the bowls club the other side of town – and begin her journey home. All still on autopilot. Had she seen Barbara and David at all that day? Had she spoken to them? Her inability to answer these questions didn't cause her angst or her heart rate to rise. She just shrugged it off and stared vacantly at the road beyond the bonnet.

As she turned onto the long, pot-holed driveway, all around her became clear again and the music playing on the radio crisp and melodious. It was as if she'd shaken off a heavy coat, emerged from a cocoon, or something. Part of her wished she could have stayed in that state forever. It was nice to be numb, and not to have to think about or deal with anything. She could see why people got hooked on sedatives. Only she hadn't taken anything. It was all just way too weird. Would Barbara say it was the universe protecting her?

As the car bumped and shuddered its way along the track and under the dark, shadowy canopy of the avenue of trees, Emily began to feel really sad about losing Barbara's friendship. The longer time stretched, the harder it would be repair. But it was up to Barbara to apologise. Emily had principles to uphold, and she didn't like being spoken about behind her back. The town and its gossip train was one thing, but you should be able to count on a friend not to do that. If you couldn't, then they weren't a true friend.

She pulled up the car and sat looking at the house she would soon have to leave. The first tears for the day began to fall.

# Chapter Thirty-nine

The removal truck idled nearby, waiting for her to take off in her own car and show the way.

Emily would have liked to spend more time in the empty house saying goodbye. It had all happened so fast. She felt an odd sense of guilt and hollowness; like she was letting the house down. She wanted to tell it she was sorry, that she wished things had been different.

Instead, she only paused on the verandah long enough to swallow back the lump forming in her throat and the unshed tears. She then locked the door, pushed the key under and gave it a good shove. She heard it skid a little way down the shiny hall floorboards.

'Come on Grace. This is it,' she said, patting the dog from her squatting position before standing up. She had to consciously tell herself to take deep breaths as she walked to the car on heavy, shaking legs. *God I hate goodbyes*, she thought as she got into the car and put her seatbelt on.

Lucky Jake had left in such a hurry. *Oh, Jake.* She missed him with an ache she wouldn't have believed possible if she wasn't experiencing it. So much had happened since Saturday. She'd been so busy, but the yearning had been there the whole time. Could he be her Mister Right?

She frowned as she drove past the idling truck and entered the canopied driveway for the last time. *I shouldn't have let him go.* But she hadn't had a chance – he'd been called away. *I hope he's okay. I really should call.* But, again, the time for polite enquiry had passed. Anyway, as excruciating as the wait was, if it was meant to be, it would be, right? *Do I really believe that?* She wasn't sure, but thinking it helped.

Emily knew in her heart she loved him, deeply. She didn't yet know if it was as a friend or a life partner – they hadn't had the chance to get that far. But she knew that he would be in her life, somehow, forever. He was someone she could truly trust.

*So why did I get so prickly when he asked about my life with John? Fear?*

Sometimes she could be her own worst enemy. She laughed tightly and rolled her eyes.

*Jesus, Em. Stop with the psychoanalysis. You've got enough to deal with today. Let the universe sort it out, and stop bloody worrying about stuff you can't do anything about.*

As she turned onto the bitumen main road she forced herself back to the job at hand – moving back into the farm; her farm. Not John's. *Mine.* And, even better, guilt-free and with Thora and Gerald's blessing.

While it didn't have the same depth of character as the Bakers' house, the place she was returning to did have its redeeming features, namely a bathroom *inside the house.* And the heating lamps on the ceiling would come in very handy when the cold weather returned.

It would also be nice to put her feet on thick wall-to-wall carpet when getting out of bed. And she wouldn't have to wonder every time it rained whether this was the shower that would make its way through the delicate roof above.

It would take a while to get unpacked and re-settled, but she couldn't afford to waste any time. Having spent money on the surveyors and the removalists, her savings were being quickly eaten up. At least she could get the survey costs back – she'd damn well be forwarding the receipt to Tara as soon as it arrived. She'd be okay when John's money came through, but in the meantime things were as dire as they had been when she'd first discussed the purchase with Barbara.

God, there was so much to do. She hoped David would agree to take on the sheep. She didn't know anything about livestock, and it would save poor Gerald from having to check on them all the time. At some point there were all the sheds to be gone through. And she'd have to do some serious setting up of books if she were going to run a business – the farm. Even though she had leased the land to David, there was still a considerable amount of responsibility on her shoulders. It was quite exciting, if somewhat daunting. She felt a little guilty at feeling so committed to this new life when only days ago she'd been committed to the other house. But none of this had been her doing.

First things first: she really had to get herself made signatory to John's bank accounts in order to get the bills paid.

She'd been putting it off, but now the funeral was over, there were no excuses left.

★

It was nine o'clock when Emily collapsed into bed after a long hot shower, pleased with herself for making the bed her first task after the removalists had unloaded everything and left. She had got a lot done, but each room in the house still had a few boxes waiting to be unpacked. She'd had all the furniture and whitegoods from the Bakers' place put in the washhouse and out of sight – it was mostly stuff Des had picked up for her from the shack sale, and she wouldn't be needing it now.

Later on she'd take a load to the op shop to be put to use by someone else. But for now there were more important things to put her limited energy towards.

She lay back and stared at the button jar – in full view and pride of place on the tallboy – wondering how she really felt being here in the same bedroom she had shared with John.

*The last time I slept here was the night before I left him.*

She half wished she'd had the removalists set her up in the spare room next to John's office at the other end of the house. As it was, in the morning she'd open the curtains to the ugly view of the partially built hayshed and the demolished cottage in the distance.

Well, she was stuck here for now.

Emily still wondered why wanting to run the farm in partnership with John had been such a problem for him. It made her angry. It was true they were from two different worlds, but why should that matter? It hadn't mattered for her grandparents.

Prior to marrying Grandpa, Gran never even had to do her own washing, let alone sit on her hands and knees and scrub the floor of a shearing shed. But she had done it all without complaint. Grandpa always said she gave as good as any man. He'd been proud of his wife, and had had no qualms about telling anyone who would listen.

So although farming didn't exactly run in her blood, it *could* be learnt. John had just been too short-sighted to see that.

Well, thanks to him, she might soon have the best of both worlds; a country life with no neighbours for miles and a small but adequate and steady income. But she'd have to do something with her life; other-wise she'd be bored within weeks.

Emily turned on her side and looked down at where Grace was curled up in her bed on the floor under the window. She couldn't see the dog in the dark, but could sense her presence.

*What do I want to do with my life? Study?*

There were all those ads about universities offering distance education; she could get a degree. But in what?

She rolled onto her back and stared up at the ceiling. Really, this was no different to before, except soon she would have the money to relax and bide her time. Waiting for a while to see what panned out made sense. And she could afford to do that now.

# Chapter Forty

When Emily woke the next morning, it took her a few moments to realise she was back at the farm-house. She heard a shuffling noise beside the bed and leant over to find Grace peering up at her over her paws.

'Have you got a cuddle for Mum? Come on, up you hop,' she said, patting the edge of the bed. Emily didn't feel ready to get up just yet, but the dog sat at attention. She clearly needed to go out.

'Oh all right,' she said, and threw back the covers.

Emily sat on the back step wrapped in her robe and with her feet in her worn sheepskin slippers while Grace went about her business and then snuffled about. It was quite cool for the middle of summer. She smiled, seeing that the dog's routine seemed the same as it had been at the Baker place. Grace didn't seem too unsettled. She couldn't say the same for herself.

Though, to be fair, it wasn't being back at the farm that was unsettling her; it was her next trip into town. It would be the first time since John's funeral that she would be stepping into the lions' den. That's how it felt; appearing in public alone to be scrutinised and spoken about behind her back – or to her face – by the townsfolk. All comments would have been halted, like an armistice, for the funeral. But that was over now; the gloves were essentially off.

Everyone would now know that she had inherited the farm and that she had moved back in. Opinions would be flowing back and forth. There was a snowball's chance in hell that people would be happy about her change of fortune. No, she was a woman, and a townie at that. She had no right to own farmland, let alone work it.

And then there were the circumstances. At least Thora and Gerald knew the truth about everything now. They were really the ones who mattered. Everyone else would eventually find something else to talk about, stretch the truth about, or completely make it up. The only good thing about being the centre of negative gossip – *and let's face it*, Emily thought, *good news dies a pretty quick death out here* — was that eventually it ceased. Emily just hoped that time would come quickly; that the whole town would decide John was a nasty piece of work and that his widow was entitled to everything for her years of torment. *Yeah, right! And pigs might fly.*

Widow. Yes, she was no longer his estranged, soon-to-be ex. She was his widow. A much more satisfactory tag, to be sure. *Oh God, here I am sounding just like my mother — in my own head!* But oh, what a mess! Being the widow was a hell of a lot more complicated than waiting for the twelve months to elapse and send in divorce papers for rubber-stamping. If only she could do it all online.

Most of it she probably could. But the first thing she needed to do was start sorting out the finances. To do that, she needed to become signatory to all the accounts again. And to do *that*, she would have to front up at the bank in person with all the correct paperwork and ID. The thought of stepping back in there after her humiliation last time gave her goose bumps. But it had to be done, and soon, if she was to start getting on top of things.

At least Nathan would be a friendly face. Well, she hoped so. He hadn't seemed the sort to get offended too easily or hold a grudge. And all she'd done was turn down his request to rent a room from her.

But she couldn't shake the feeling that perhaps she'd hurt him with how abrupt she'd been on Christmas night. Was that another reason why the universe had had her turfed out? Bad karma? She wasn't sure she believed in it, but she was beginning to see how people could. No doubt about it, if you looked hard enough, you could see a reason for everything.

Emily sighed. She hoped Nathan was okay. She'd need a friendly ally in the months ahead – especially one who wasn't a true local. And she liked him, just not in the way their mothers had hoped.

Grace appeared beside her.

'All finished checking everything out?' Emily said, and then got up and let the dog back inside.

Emily decided on a hearty cooked breakfast; she'd need all the help she could get later. While she stood at the stove in front of the sizzling pan, she ran through what she had to do in town other than buying the paper and sorting out everything with the bank. She'd see how that went before deciding whether to brave the supermarket as well. She could always pop over to Hope Springs for groceries if necessary.

*Or I could just escape to Melbourne for a few days until things die down.*

Gosh, where had that come from? Emily stared at the bacon which was about to turn from crispy to burnt. Could she just get on a plane and turn up at a huge city like Melbourne?

*Could I be that spontaneous? All on my own? Eek!*

Her attention was caught by Grace slurping water from her bowl nearby. Emily dragged the pan off the hotplate and looked down. She couldn't go anywhere. With Barbara out of the picture, there was nowhere to leave Grace. Her parents were out of the question. Enid would never allow Grace inside. And she couldn't subject her to her mother's sneers of distaste anyway. Des would be great with her, spoil her rotten, but Enid wouldn't have a bar of it. And she couldn't ask her dad to come and babysit her here. Emily's heart sank slightly. No, it looked like she would have to stay here and suffer through the gossip until someone else did something worthy of attention – a good old wife-swap scandal would be just the shot.

She smiled as she spread butter on her toast that had become cold, and then heaped a small mountain of food upon it.

★

Emily was a bundle of nerves when she walked into the bank later that morning. She looked around. Sam was standing at the counter, the same teller who had caused her so much embarrassment last time. At least he had the good grace to blush and avert his eyes.

'Emily!'

She turned to see Nathan at the door of the glass-walled assist-ant manager's office on her right.

'Shit. I was meant to get back to you with that information, wasn't I? I'm so sorry. I completely forgot.'

'Hi Nathan,' she said, moving towards him. 'It's okay; I…' In seconds he was embracing her and pecking her on the cheek.

'Haven't by any chance changed your mind on having me move in?' he said jovially.

Emily cringed at his choice of words. Great! Three heads were visible behind the long counter. They would now most likely think she and Nathan were an item. 'And so soon after her husband's death too.' She could almost feel the air crackling with gossip.

Nathan saw the emotions cross her face. He instantly became professional. 'I take it this isn't a personal visit.'

'Sorry, no. Actually I'm in need of… I'm my…' *estranged, now dead husband's? No,* '…late husband's executor and I need to be added as a signatory to his accounts. I have all the paperwork here – well, hopefully everything I need.'

'Gosh! I don't know what to say. What a strange situation to find yourself in. I heard that he'd died. Sorry for your loss, though I'm not sure in the circumstances... I didn't manage to get along to the funeral. How was it?'

'Hard. Weird,' she said, shrugging.

'Sorry, that was dumb of me to say. And I'm sorry for not calling. I should have...'

'Don't be sorry. Seriously. What is there to say? As you rightly point out, I find myself in a very strange situation.'

'Well, I can certainly help you with sorting out some banking details. Come on in.'

'Thanks.'

'Take a seat.'

Emily was both relieved and disappointed when he closed the glass door behind them. What would everyone think now? But at least their conversation would be private. Well, unless Sam or one of the other two could read lips.

'Right, what paperwork do you have?'

Thankfully Nathan had access to everything they needed on the computer screen at his desk. Soon she was signing the forms he printed from the small printer nearby. He stepped out to take a copy of the law firm's correspondence for their records.

While he was gone, Emily glanced around his office. There were no personal items, nothing to tell her more about him, but she wasn't surprised. He wouldn't have had much of a chance to settle in with all the recent public holidays.

'Right. That's all done. Is there anything else I can help you with today?' Nathan said, as he re-entered, closed the door, handed her back her paperwork, and sat down behind his desk.

'No, I think that's all. Thanks very much. Now I can start getting some bills paid and some order into the...' *Shut up Emily, you're rambling.* 'Oh, never mind,' she muttered as she gathered her things and stood up.

'Hang on, before you go.'

Emily sat back down on the edge of the chair with her papers and handbag on her lap. 'Yes?'

'What, no friendly chitchat? Just business?'

'Oh, well, I'm sure you're very busy,' she said lamely.

'Do I look busy?' he said, sweeping an arm across his desk, which had almost nothing on its polished faux-wood surface. And the stack of aluminium document trays weren't exactly overflowing.

She settled back into her chair a little. 'So, how are you settling in?'

'How do you think? Thanks to you not wanting me, I'm back living with my parents.' He paused, and Emily tried to read his face. Then he smiled. 'I'm only teasing. Lighten up.'

She tried to keep her expression neutral.

*My husband has died — the husband I left — and now my landlords are dead as well, and I've just been turfed out of my new house, only to end up back at the farm I... Excuse me if I'm a little serious, but my life's not exactly a barrel of laughs at the moment.* She opened her mouth to say as much, but Nathan got in first.

'Okay, that wasn't fair,' he said, holding up his hands in surrender. Sorry. You've clearly got a lot going on. Speaking of which... What are you going to do with your husband's place? Are you looking for a tenant?'

Emily only just managed to stop herself laughing out loud, but couldn't stop the wry smile that quickly spread across her face.

'What. What's so funny?'

Emily rolled her eyes and shook her head slowly.

'You haven't heard? I've had to move back there. The brothers who owned the house died...'

'God, people are dropping like flies around here. But hang on, weren't you meant to be buying that place? Don't you have an agreement?'

'Apparently not worth the paper it's written on. The old brothers didn't change their wills, and I was an idiot and didn't get proper paperwork drawn up. I was waiting until the subdivision was done. Their cousin, who also happens to be their executor and beneficiary, turned up and turfed me out. She's putting the whole farm on the market. I moved yesterday.'

'Oh, I'm so sorry.'

'Yeah, well, apparently it wasn't meant to be. She doesn't like me.'

'Are you going to try and fight her? At least look into where you stand legally?'

'Honestly, I don't have the energy. And, really, it's my own fault it all fell apart.'

'Don't be too hard on yourself. Maybe you're right and it just wasn't meant to be. So why do you think the niece doesn't like you.'

'Because she told me.'

'But what's not to like?'

Emily rolled her eyes at him, but blushed despite her best efforts.

'Seriously, why?'

'No idea.'

Nathan gave up. 'Well, I really am sorry to hear about your husband. Sounds like he's left you in a bit of a mess.'

'Thanks. I'm sure it'll be fine.'

'If you need any help, you know where I am,' he said, smiling warmly.

'And I'll keep my ear out for accommodation,' she said, getting up.

'Thanks, I'd appreciate it. This living with the parents isn't quite, well, you know.'

'When I get settled I'll have you out for dinner – get you away from them for a night.'

'That sounds great,' he said, his whole face lighting up.

'Just friends,' she added, feeling the need to keep things clear.

'Of course.'

'Well, I'd better get going.'

Emily stepped out of his office into a bank full of people. All three tellers were serving and three people stood behind each counter waiting to be served. And of course they all turned and looked just as Nathan embraced her and kissed her on the cheek. *Brilliant, just bloody brilliant!*

She blushed another shade darker when he called out to her as she moved towards the door.

'See you soon.'

Emily noticed raised eyebrows being exchanged and heard an 'ooh, did you hear that' stage whisper and a few other muttered comments as she fled.

Next she braved the newsagent. Thankfully those who usually congregated out front to chat had already left and she only had Bev behind the counter to contend with. She had picked up the paper and was looking through the public notices at the announcement of the Bakers' funeral – Saturday morning – when the news-agent cleared her throat loudly.

'I hear you're living back at the Stratten place,' she said.

Emily nodded, then looked up, held her gaze and said, 'Yes, that's right,' her steely look offering the unspoken question, 'And what of it?'

'Such a tragedy. Sorry for your loss,' she replied, her words becoming quieter and quieter.

'Thank you,' Emily said as she handed over some coins and tucked the paper under her arm. 'Have a great day,' she said cheerily and turned around to leave.

Three people had come in after her and she heard one of them hiss, 'She got *everything*, you know.' Emily heard more whispering behind her as she left.

She collapsed into the driver's seat of her car. The groceries would have to wait. There was long-life milk in the cupboard if necessary and there was plenty of food for Grace. She'd deal with the supermarket another day.

# Chapter Forty-one

It took Emily the rest of Thursday afternoon and late into the night to get everything unpacked and into position. On Friday she woke with a sense of enthusiasm. She was aching all over but pleased that she'd got it all done. And sorting out the bank stuff was a huge weight off her mind. It meant that the day was her own, to do with as she wished. She'd start with getting some fresh air and stretching her legs. Last night's forecast had been for a pleasant twenty-five degrees. Perfect.

She got up and pulled the curtains back, and stood there in her light summer pyjamas. She frowned at the pile of rubble from the cottage and the ugly steel structure in front of it – a blight on the gorgeous landscape.

She folded her arms on the top of the oak tallboy and moved her gaze back inside to the button jar beside her with its kaleidoscope of colour.

She took a deep breath. Thankfully she no longer had the cloud of financial worry hanging over her – the pressure of having to make decisions quickly. Once everything was sorted out, it looked like she'd be set for life if she was careful. That was a huge relief. And, she reluctantly conceded, all thanks to John. But idleness just wasn't in her make-up. Gran used to live by the saying, 'I'd rather wear out than rust out.' Emily was the same way; couldn't do nothing for too long. She had to do something. But what?

She picked up the jar and rattled it, smiling at the comforting sound. She looked hard for one of the diamonds, but none were to be seen. Thank God she hadn't had to part with them. Just knowing they were there had been a source of comfort. Is that what had got Gran through all the droughts, loss of crops, through frosts, flooding, and locusts? Had Grandpa ever known?

Feeling the frustration growing, Emily put the jar back down. She'd never know the answers; she should just stop wondering.

'Come on Gracie, let's go for a walk.'

She got dressed and left the house. They paused before crossing the road, Emily smiling at Grace sitting and looking both ways before bounding off and disappearing from sight. She followed the dog towards the steel monstrosity and the ruin beyond it. The pain of seeing the remains of the stone cottage had eased. It had started to the day she'd shown Jake and he'd said it could be rebuilt. She doubted she would ever do it, but it did provide a bit of comfort knowing it was possible.

*Oh Jake.* It had been almost a week and her heart still pulled every time she thought about him. But the feeling obviously wasn't reciprocated. He still hadn't called.

'Oh well, they say time heals all wounds,' she said aloud with a deep sigh as she opened the steel gate and stepped through. She really would have to at least phone his company sometime and let them know the project was off. No, she corrected, she'd have to phone *him*. As hard as it would be, the closure would probably be a good thing.

She scowled at the steel structure as she approached it. That's what she would do today; start taking it down. She could get the front-end loader out – it couldn't be *that* hard to drive and operate the bucket on the front, could it? The frame looked just like a giant meccano project – how hard could it be to take apart? Her eyes travelled downwards and settled on the uprights disappearing into the concrete footings.

She nibbled at her lip. If she could get everything down there would still be four uprights. She'd need a jackhammer for the concrete, and she was pretty sure John hadn't had one of those in the shed. She looked back up and sighed again. It was awfully high – would the front-end loader's bucket go that high? Could *she* go that high? She could at least try.

'Come on Gracie,' she called. The dog paused in her snuffling and looked at her with head cocked to one side as if to say, 'But we just got here, I'm not finished.'

Emily started walking back. Grace would catch up, she always did; didn't like being apart from her mistress for too long.

Back at the house, Emily shut Grace in the yard, much to the dog's disappointment.

'For your own safety. Don't want you getting squashed under a wheel,' she said, as she walked away.

Emily climbed up into the smaller of the green tractors, the front-end loader. Her heart was racing a little with excitement.

*Yes, I can do this.*

She settled into the seat and looked around her. God, it wasn't like a car at all. There was a key to turn it on, a panel of instruments up front, and clutch and brake pedals on the floor. But that was where the similarities ended. To her right were a number of levers, some with numbers and some without. Nothing was familiar. She couldn't even tell which were for driving the tractor and which were for working the bucket out the front. She cursed herself for not taking more notice when riding with John.

When they had first started going out, she'd spent hours perched on the arm of his tractor seat as he worked the land. It was so satisfying to start at the fence and watch the paddock slowly changing, lap by lap, until the point where the corners were all that were left and the tractor would be driven out across them – the headlands they were called – signalling the end.

Seeding had been one of her favourite things about living on the farm. She loved the hum of tractors in the distance in winter, barely detectible in the cold, still night air, the lights dotted about as far as the eye could see. She especially enjoyed seeing the change of colour of the earth to rich dark chocolate as the machine passed over it, the small, even mounds and furrows and the deep, fresh, earthy scent.

The hours of tractor driving had been considerably shortened now they sowed directly rather than ripping up and working back as they used to. These days it was all about keeping the soil as healthy as possible and not overworking it. It made sense; farming was really just gardening on a huge scale, and it was important to keep a good layer of mulch – the previous year's stubble – to add nutrients to the soil and help keep the moisture in.

Could she learn how to be a farmer and run it on her own? It wasn't like you needed brute strength. There were so many machines to do the heavy work. Hmm. Maybe if someone taught her how to drive one of these bloody things! And she took some bloody notice!

She reluctantly got out, slammed the door shut, and climbed back down.

Emily frowned and looked around the shed for another option. She spotted a collection of ladders leaning against the wall. She opened the boot of the car and slid the longest ladder into it. Quite a bit hung out, but if she drove carefully, and hoped the boot didn't try and close on it, she'd get it over there. Next she searched the workshop for two large shifting spanners and some rigger's gloves. Feeling better, she got in the car and drove carefully across to the steel structure. She sat for a few moments looking up. It was very high. Should she be doing this? Yes. She was sick of feeling useless when it came to this farm. She'd at least give it a damn good shot.

Emily unfolded the ladder to its full length and leant it against the nearest upright. God, it was higher than she'd thought. *Stop being a scaredy cat.*

She forced herself to keep looking up to keep the fear of heights at bay. Once at the top, she realised there was a bit of a gap between where the ladder ended and where she needed to be. *I can do this*, she told herself as she stretched across to a beam. Once up, she took a brief look down. Her stomach lurched. Too high. Maybe she'd better go back down. No, not before at least trying.

She patted her pockets and realised she'd left both spanners hanging on the hook on the ladder. She'd totally forgotten to bring them up with her. *Damn it!* She sighed with exasperation and started to look at where to put her feet to get down.

It was a long way just to the ladder. *I don't think I can do it.* The realisation seeped in slowly. Fear gripped her, and then her heart began to race. Jesus, she was stuck up here. *No. You got up here, you can get down.* But the ladder was so far away and there was such a small space to put her feet. And it would be out of sight when she tried. *Shit! Right, just calm down. You're safe here, just sit for a bit and think.*

From her perch atop the frame, Emily looked across at the rubble of the cottage. Where would one start rebuilding it? She wished she'd asked Jake more questions that day. Could she ask him now? Could that be her way back to him? Hmm.

Yes, damn it, she would call him. *As soon as I get down from here.* It would be difficult, but not as hard as leaving John.

*And then I'll phone Barbara. Enough is enough.*

Something out of the corner of her eye caught her attention.

When she looked across to her left, Emily saw a white ute with a rotating orange light flashing on top and hazard lights blinking. Behind it, a green tractor was turning the corner. The two vehicles were about a kilometre away. Someone was moving machinery. The big yellow tank behind the tractor was a boom sprayer. That was the trouble with a good burst of summer rain; a mass of weeds sprang up and then had to be sprayed.

She waved one arm while holding on tightly with the other. She could only hope whoever it was would look at the steel structure and marvel at its ugliness long enough to see her sitting up there.

'Here! Over here!' she yelled.

*They can't hear you, they're miles away and in cabins with the radio most likely blaring. Idiot.*

Emily thought about taking off her top to wave, but didn't want to let go with both hands. Oh God, what was she going to do? There might not be another vehicle along this road for days.

She watched the ute and tractor make their way slowly towards her. She waved frantically until her arms were too tired. Tears threatened as she imagined being stuck there all night.

Suddenly the tractor turned in towards the house. David?! That meant Barbara was most likely driving the ute as escort. She could hear the throaty diesel engine idling nearby. He'd stopped by the house. *Turn off the engine so you can hear me!*

'Help! Over here! Help!' Tears began to fall. The frustration was killing her. She looked down at the ladder. She had to do it. She just had to. But it was such a long way down.

There was a change in noise as the tractor was turned off.

'Help!' she yelled again, but the ute was still idling; there was still too much noise. She thought she could hear Grace barking, but that could have been her brain playing tricks on her. She was finding it more and more difficult to stay calm. She had to get David or Barbara's attention before they went down into the paddock, or left altogether. She focused on breathing in and out slowly.

Suddenly the ute's engine noise increased. It was no longer idling. *No, don't go.* She couldn't muster the energy to yell. There was no point anyway; they couldn't hear her.

Emily noticed a flash of white out of the corner of her eye. She turned, careful not to lose balance. Oh please, let it be, she thought, as the ute made its way up the road towards her.

David and Barbara leapt out of the vehicle below her. Emily was so relieved she let go and wobbled slightly.

'Don't let go!' Barbara and David yelled in unison.

'I can't get down.'

'I sort of figured that,' David said. 'What are you doing up there?'

'Can you just get me down?'

'I'm trying to work out how to do that. Just let me think a minute.'

*Well, hurry up!*

'Are you okay?' Barbara asked.

'Yep, just stuck.'

'I'll go and get the front-end loader. Back in a sec.'

Barbara stayed standing below and David leapt into the ute and drove off back to the house.

'How did you find me?' Emily asked.

'Grace,' Barbara yelled back. 'She kept racing to the corner of the yard and barking her head off. It was so out of character we thought we'd better check it out. And then we saw your car. How long have you been up there?'

'No idea. Too long.'

They both looked towards the house at hearing the tractor start up.

Before long David had Barbara in the cab and was in the bucket and using hand signals to guide the machine close to Emily. Minutes later she stepped down into his arms.

'Thank you,' she said breathlessly, and then sat down in the bucket as David had Barbara lower them.

When she was finally back on solid ground, Emily burst into tears. 'Thank you so much.'

Barbara got out of the tractor and came over.

'Hi Barb,' Emily said sheepishly.

'What the hell were you doing up there?'

The greeting was tense, but not as bad as it could have been.

'I...' She was about to explain when David spoke.

'I'll take the loader back and leave you in Barbara's capable hands.'

'Thanks so much. Again.'

'No worries. You okay if I go and get a bit of spraying done?' he asked. 'You two have probably got some catching up to do.'

'Sure, go for it. Great.'

'Thanks. Darling, I'll call you later,' David said, giving Barbara a kiss. Emily and Barbara watched in silence as he climbed back up into the cab, put it in gear, and drove off with a wave of his hand.

Barbara was the first to break the silence. 'Don't suppose I could use your loo before I head off?' she asked with a wince. 'The trip down took way longer than I thought it would. And then all this excitement...'

'Of course,' Emily said. 'I really need a cuppa if you'd like to join me.'

'That would be great.'

Suddenly Barbara pulled Emily into a hug. 'I've missed you so much. I called, and when you didn't call back...' Her words came out in a torrent. 'I can't believe you got up there by yourself. Seriously, what the hell were you thinking? You could have been killed! What would you have done if we hadn't come along?'

'Well, thank God you did.'

'Thank God you're okay. I don't know what I would have done... If it wasn't for Grace, who knows what might have happened.'

*She saved me. Again.*

Emily hugged her friend back, feeling her chest tighten. 'Oh God, Barbara, I behaved like a complete idiot. And I'm not just talking about this,' she said, waving an arm towards the shed skeleton. 'I'm so sorry. Can we go back to the house, have a cuppa and forget it – accept that I've been a complete idiot and move on?'

'I can if you can. As long as you promise I'll never have to rescue you from up there again.'

They broke apart, dragging the backs of their hands across their cheeks and wiping their eyes as they did.

# Chapter Forty-two

Back at the house, Emily gave Grace a lot of attention while Barbara looked on. 'I'll just get Grace a bone before I do anything else,' Emily said. She raced inside to the fridge and tossed the grateful dog her treat.

'Right, now my conscience is clear for a cuppa. Come on in,' she said.

'You're living here?!' Barbara asked, looking around the kitchen with wide eyes.

Emily silently retrieved coffee and sugar from the pantry, milk from the fridge, and mugs from the cupboard above the sink. She flicked the switch on the kettle and it roared into life.

'Didn't you hear?' she said, leaning against the bench while waiting for the kettle to boil.

'Hear what?'

'Jesus, what happened to the bush telegraph?' Emily said, shaking her head. 'You'd better sit down.'

She poured the water into the mugs, added milk, and put the carton back in the fridge while Barbara took the two steaming mugs to the table.

★

'You're kidding!' Barbara said when Emily had explained about Tara's visit and her sudden eviction. 'You had a bad feeling about that woman right from the start. See, I keep telling you you've got to listen to your intuition,' she said, sipping at her coffee. 'But you had an agreement with Donald and Trevor, aren't you at least going to try and fight it? You love that house. *I* love that house.'

'I know. But I didn't get things signed off properly. Tara's right that the agreement isn't worth the paper it's written on. We had a verbal agreement, but I can't prove that. And I'm too tired to fight anymore. Anyway, there's not a whole lot to work with when someone evicts you because they just don't like you.'

'Hmm, I see your point. Not fair about the house, though – that's just plain rotten.'

'I know. But maybe this is how it's meant to be,' she added with a shrug.

'And for the record, you should have called us rather than pay removalists – we would have moved you.'

'I know. But you've done so much for me already. And it all happened so fast, and...' Emily said lamely.

'We're friends, Emily. We'd do *anything* for you. So what does Jake think about all this?' Barbara said, changing the subject. 'I bet he's disappointed.'

'Well, I need to call him,' she said, looking a little sheepish.

'How is he?'

'Um, we haven't actually spoken since Saturday. He took off suddenly after a phone call and I haven't heard from him since.'

'That's weird. I had you two pegged for happily ever after. You seriously haven't heard from him?'

'He called twice but never left a message. I didn't call him back,' she said, staring into her mug.

'Well, something serious must have happened because he seemed way too well-mannered to not do things properly.'

'My mother would say the same about me,' Emily said, raising her eyebrows and then rolling her eyes.

'And how is Enid? I bet she's thrilled you've finally given up the silly notion of doing up that dreadful old house,' Barbara said, doing a fine impersonation.

'Um...' Emily stared into her mug.

'You haven't told her, have you?'

'Nope. I saw them at the funeral but couldn't tell them. I feel terrible not telling Dad the truth, but I just couldn't deal with Mum gloating over me having to give up the old place.'

'No offence, Em, but there seem to be a few things you're avoiding dealing with.'

'Well, you'll be pleased to know I went and saw Thora and Gerald the day before the funeral.'

'And...?'

'They were amazing, actually. I won't bore you with the details, but they've given their blessing for me to inherit everything. Gerald even took a look at David's lease document before I signed it.'

'That's great. I thought you looked on reasonable terms with them at the funeral. Though I have to say you seemed a bit vague, which is quite understandable.'

'Honestly, it was weird. The whole day it felt like it was happening to someone else – like an out-of-body experience or something. It's done, thank goodness, but now I'd rather just forget it.'

'Well, you did well.'

'Thanks. Oh, and I've been to the bank and sorted out being signatory again. So I guess you could say I'm officially getting my shit together on a few things.'

'But not when it comes to your mother.'

'I know,' she said, taking a sip of coffee. 'Gutless, huh?'

'Not necessarily, but sometimes it's better to just let the shit hit the fan and move on rather than putting it off. And it's usually not nearly as bad as we make it out to be.'

'I know. I had myself tied up in knots before I saw Thora and Gerald. And then it turned out fine.'

'Exactly. Want to call Enid now, while I'm here? Get it over with?'

'Maybe, but should I call Jake first?'

Barbara shrugged. 'That's entirely up to you.'

They startled slightly at the unmistakeable sound of the heavy glass sliding door being opened.

'Yoo-hoo! Emily, are you here?'

*Speak of the devil and she shall appear.*

'In here,' Emily called, leaping up from her chair. 'Mum, Dad, hi,' she said, exchanging air kisses with her mother and a brief but tight hug with her father. 'Cuppa? Kettle's just boiled. Another one Barbara?'

Barbara nodded.

'Yes thank you,' Enid said, huffily. 'How could you have not informed us you were moving house? We went for a drive to visit you and you weren't there. It's only because we bumped into lovely Nathan Lucas outside the newsagent that we found you at all!'

'You've seen Nathan?' Barbara asked with raised eyebrows.

'Yes, he did the paperwork at the bank for me yesterday,' Emily answered simply, ignoring Barbara's expression.

'And why can't you answer your damned mobile phone?' Enid continued, ignoring Barbara and Emily. 'We phoned you an hour ago. It went to voicemail. For goodness sake, Emily!' She dragged a chair away from the table and sat heavily onto it.

'Sorry. It all happened rather quickly,' Emily muttered, trying desperately not to roll her eyes. *And as for not answering my phone, well, I was most likely stuck up on a steel structure.* But she sure as hell wasn't going to confess to that.

'Well, thank God you've finally come to your senses and given up on that awful old house. Ghastly thing.'

'Actually, it wasn't my choice. I loved that house.' Emily was suddenly on the verge of tears. She swallowed hard and willed the tears not to come as she prepared the four mugs of coffee and then delivered them to the table.

'Well, no point crying over spilt milk. You can't make a silk purse out of a sow's ear, you know,' Enid said haughtily, lifting her mug and taking a sip.

*Any more pearls of wisdom for me, mother?*

Des Oliphant smiled reassuringly at his daughter and reached across and patted her hand.

'And anyway,' Enid continued, 'just think what a better catch you'll be with a whole farm to your name.'

Emily frowned, wondering what the relevance was – she'd had the farm before Tara had turfed her out.

'So how do you come to be living here?' Des asked.

Emily flapped an arm. 'Apparently Trevor and Donald left everything to their cousin Tara. She kicked me out.'

'But didn't you have an agreement?' he said.

'Yes, but I never actually signed it.' *Yes, I am an idiot.*

'So you didn't seek legal advice?' Enid chimed in.

Emily's head started to spin. She wanted to say, 'Why do you care; you hated the place and thought I was making a mistake anyway.' Instead she sighed and said, 'No. She turned up on Monday morning and told me I had five days to get out. Then there was

John's funeral on Tuesday, and everything with his estate to be dealt with. With all that's been happening, I just…'

'You've been through a lot. I understand. But couldn't you have at least asked her for some more time?' Des said.

'Dad, she really wasn't interested in negotiating,' Emily said wearily. 'Anyway, it's over now.'

'But she shouldn't be allowed to get away with bullying you. Aren't you going to fight her?' Enid said.

Emily squeezed her eyes shut and tried not to scream. You just couldn't win with Enid. Damned if you do, damned if you don't.

'Mum, it doesn't matter. It's done. I'm just relieved it happened when it did and not halfway through the renovation – that would have been messy.'

'But…' Enid started, then stopped when her husband laid a hand over hers.

'Enid, I'm sure Emily did the right thing for herself,' Des said, quite forcefully.

Emily cast a covert glance at Barbara, who mouthed the words, 'You can't win,' and shook her head. Emily rolled her eyes in consternation.

'Well, I can't believe you moved back here without at least telling us,' Enid said, thumping her mug down on the table. 'How embarrassing to have to be told by someone else. And in the street. We saw you at John's funeral on Tuesday. How could you not have said anything then?'

'Like I said, it was all very sudden,' Emily offered with a shrug.

'We could have helped.'

'I'm sorry, Mum. It was something I needed to do on my own,' Emily said.

Enid responded by letting out a harrumph and folding her arms tightly across her chest.

'So David's taken over the cropping?' Des asked of no one in particular.

'Yes,' Barbara said. 'We've just brought the tractor and boom sprayer down now. Actually, that'll be him,' she said, reaching into her pocket. 'I've got to go down and pick him up,' she quickly explained. Her mobile began ringing as she dragged it out. 'Excuse me.' She turned away from the table.

'Hello darling. Yes, be right there. Okay, due South. Got it. See you soon.' She hung up and addressed the group around the table. 'Sorry, but I'd better get going. Em, can you come along and make sure I don't get lost?' Barbara stared hard and knowingly at Emily.

'Um, well...' Emily looked beseechingly at her parents.

'You go,' Des said, getting up. 'We're on our way to visit some friends anyway. Come on Enid.'

Enid was clearly miffed at being ushered out so abruptly, but Emily wasn't going to let that spoil her pleasure at reuniting with Barbara. If she put her life on hold every time Enid was displeased with her, she'd never get anything done.

Emily air kissed her mother's proffered cheek and hugged her father. As they separated, he squeezed her shoulder and said, 'We'll talk later.'

'Thanks for dropping by. I'll see you soon.'

Grace leapt onto the ute's tray and Emily clipped her to the short chain before opening the passenger's door and getting in.

'Thanks so much for rescuing me. Again,' Emily said, pulling the door closed behind her.

'It had to be done,' Barbara said, beaming back at her.

'God I've missed you, us, this,' Emily said, throwing her hands up and then slapping them on her thighs.

'Me too,' Barbara said, turning on the vehicle and putting it in gear.

Emily didn't say it, but she really had started to fear that they'd never repair their friendship. And just a few words had been said and all was well again. *Ah, communication.*

Talking had definitely not been John's strong suit. He was more about action – like ripping her off in the separation, and destroying the cottage, and taking pot shots at Grace. But he'd somehow neglected to change his will. *And where would I be now if he had?*

'Are you okay?' Barbara asked. 'You suddenly look all sad.'

Emily nodded, realising she could erupt into tears if she let herself. She swallowed hard. 'I was just thinking that if John hadn't died I'd be back where I was when I left him: no money, no job and nowhere to live. It doesn't seem fair. But he's gone, and I'm back on the farm, and it looks like everything might be all right.'

'Well, I do keep telling you that everything happens for a reason.'

'I am actually starting to see that.'

'Good. So what's the story with Jake? He's a good guy, Em, and I know it's probably way too soon for you, but I reckon you'd make the perfect couple. And for the record, I wasn't meaning to talk about you behind your back. I just wanted him to know to go carefully, that's all. I'm sorry.'

'You've got nothing to apologise for. I overreacted. I can see that now. You were just being my friend and looking out for me.'

'Yes I was. You need to understand that when friends talk about you amongst ourselves it's because we care, not because we want to undermine you or pick on you.'

'I know. I get it now.'

'Well as long as you do. Because sometimes, Emily, you are your own worst enemy.'

'I know. Can we just put it behind us and move on? I feel like such an idiot.'

'Consider us moved on. So, what are you going to do about Jake?'

'Well, when I was stuck up on that bloody steel monstrosity, I had decided to call him when I got back down, but I think I've chickened out now. It's been too long.'

'It's never too late, Em. You can't use that as an excuse.'

'You didn't see the way he took off. He couldn't get away fast enough.'

'You said it was something to do with a phone call. Maybe it had nothing to do with you.'

'So why hasn't he left a message to explain?'

'Perhaps it's too personal or too complicated to leave in a message. And why haven't *you* called to check that everything is okay?' Barbara looked at Emily with raised eyebrows.

'Okay, both fair points.' Barbara was right. She'd been too wrapped up in her own problems to think about what Jake might have been going through. It was selfish.

'Anyway, regardless of any personal involvement – or not – between you, at the very least you need to tell him the house project is off.'

'I know.'

'Do you want me to call him for you?'

'Thanks, but no. As much as I'd love to pass the buck, it's something I really have to do myself.'

'Come on then, just call him now. Right now.'

# Chapter Forty-three

Emily's heart rate increased as she pulled the phone from her pocket. She brought up Jake's number and sat staring at it for a few moments. She jumped slightly when the phone started vibrating and then began to ring.

'Bloody hell,' she said, almost dropping it. She frowned at the unfamiliar mobile number.

'Just answer it, Em.'

Emily snapped back into focus and answered with a tentative, 'Hello?'

'Is that Emily?'

'Um, yes.'

'Emily, it's Simone Lonigan here. Jake's sister.'

'Oh. Hi Simone,' Emily said, her eyes growing wide as she looked at Barbara.

'I hope you don't mind me calling you – I got your number from the file at work.'

'Yes, about that, I meant to...'

'I'm not calling about the house.'

Something in her tone made Emily ask. 'Is every-thing okay – with Jake?'

'No, not really. He has no idea I'm calling you, but I need your help.'

'Oh?' Emily frowned back at Barbara's question-ing expression and shrugged.

'Has he told you what's been going on here the last few days?'

'No. He was with me on Saturday when he got a phone call. He left without telling me what it was about. I haven't spoken to him since.'

'Oh God, so you don't know anything.'

'Please tell me. What's happened?' Emily felt worry beginning to course through her.

There was a pause and an audible sigh before Simone spoke again. She sounded a little calmer. 'There was an accident on one of the building sites...'

'Oh God, is he, is he...?'

'Jake wasn't involved. He wasn't here. But some scaffolding collapsed and one of the guys was badly injured. It happened late on Friday – New Year's Eve day. He had surgery and they thought he had a reasonable chance. That's why we didn't let Jake know until Saturday – didn't want to drag him back unless we absolutely had to. Sadly, Shane died on Tuesday.'

'Oh no. That's terrible. I'm so sorry.' *Jake must be a mess.* Emily wondered why Simone was giving her this level of detail. Perhaps she was in shock and just needed to tell someone. She waited her out.

'Jake's taken it really to heart, even though he wasn't there and the scaffolding company made the mistake. It was on his site; that's what matters to Jake. He's never had a serious injury on any of his sites before. The thing is, he's so depressed. He's hardly left the apartment, won't talk to anyone. Hasn't even been into the office. It's hit him really hard.'

'So what can I do?'

'I know this is a big ask, but could you come to Melbourne? I'll pay for your fare. It's all I can think of. He loves you, Emily. I know he does. And he needs you. He's just too damned proud to ask you himself.'

*And I love him.*

'I know he might not like me interfering, but I've never seen him like this before. I'm worried that if we don't pull him out of this state he'll have a breakdown or something.'

'Of course I'll come. And there's no need for you to pay for the tickets. When do you think?'

'Well, that's the other thing. The funeral is tomorrow at four. I think Jake should go – it'll give him closure.'

'Is he planning on going?'

'Um, I'm not sure if he's decided. But I'm hoping between the two of us we can convince him.'

'Is that a good idea?'

'I'll take the blame if it all goes pear-shaped, Emily, but please, we've got to do something.' Simone sounded close to tears.

'Okay. If you think it's the right thing to do, count me in.'

'Oh thank you. Look, I originally booked Jake's flights back and forth between Whyalla and Melbourne, so it'll be easy for me to just book it here. I'm online now. Do you think you could get to Whyalla today in time for a five-o'clock flight?'

'Um,' Emily said, buying time as she stared at her watch and tried to make calculations of what had to be done and how long everything would take. 'Yes, I could make five.'

'Oh, that's great. Thank you. I'll pick you up, and you can stay with me. You've no idea how much this means to me – and will to Jake; you'll see.'

'I hope so,' Emily said.

'He'll be fine. Seriously, he loves you, Em.'

'And I've got a pretty soft spot for him too,' she said, not trusting herself to use the same words.

Emily listened to the clicking of a keyboard in the silence.

'Right,' Simone said. 'I've got you from Whyalla to Adelaide – leaving at five – then a forty-minute wait in Adelaide, and then landing in Melbourne at 9:25.'

'Right, okay, thanks.'

'No, thank *you*. I can't wait to meet you; I only wish it was under different circumstances. I'd better let you go and get organised.'

'Yes, I've got a bit to sort out,' Emily said with a nervous laugh.

Emily hung up and stared at the phone, her mind spinning with things that had to be done. It was now eleven. She'd have to leave no later than a quarter to three. It seemed like plenty of time, but God, she'd never done anything so spontaneous in her life. Just thinking about it was bringing on a headache.

'Are you going to tell me what's going on, or just sit looking at that damned phone?' Barbara said, bringing Emily's focus back into the ute cabin.

'That was Simone; Jake's sister.'

'I gathered that much,' Barbara said, exasperated.

'She's booked me to fly from Whyalla at five...'

'What? Tonight?!'

'Yes. There was an accident on one of the building sites. Someone died. Apparently it wasn't Jake's fault or anything, and he didn't know the guy very well, but he's taken it to heart...'

'Poor Jake. That's awful.'

'Simone is worried he's getting too depressed. She thinks my being there might help bring him out of it.'

'Hmm, makes sense,' Barbara said, nodding. 'Well, all you have to do is throw some clothes and toiletries in a bag, lock up the house, and then drive to Whyalla. We'll take Grace home with us.'

'Oh thanks, Barbara, that'd be brilliant. You're the best.'

Barbara waved the words away. 'So we'll pick up David, head back to the house, collect Grace's things and then leave you to pack. Oh, or would you rather I drive you to Whyalla so you don't have to leave your car in long-term parking?'

'Thanks, but David needs you to help him move machinery, and anyway, you'd have to come back up and collect me. I don't know how long I'll be gone. No, I think it's best if I take my own car. But thanks all the same.'

They left the track and stopped beside the tractor where David stood waiting with his thermos and small esky in hand. With the back seat of the dual cab ute covered with various items, Emily shuffled into the middle position close to Barbara. Anyway, it was only a short trip back to the house. David paused to pat Grace, who panted eagerly on the back, and then leapt into the vacated space.

'Great to see you guys are finally friends again,' David said, as he shut the door behind him. "bout bloody time. She's been like a bear with a sore head, Em.'

'Me too,' Emily said.

'Now, change of plans, my darling,' Barbara said, turning the vehicle around and heading back the way they'd just come. 'We're stopping by the house to collect Grace's things – she's coming to stay for a few days while Em goes to Melbourne.'

'Oh, a romantic sojourn?'

'Not quite,' Barbara said.

'Oh, right,' he said, and fell silent.

'Barbara can fill you in later,' Emily said to him. 'So what do I need to do other than pack and lock the house and drive to Whyalla?'

'Make sure you've got enough petrol in the car. How about I check the oil, water and tyres, and fill up with fuel while you get Grace packed,' David said.

'Oh, would you? That would be great.'

'I'm not in a huge hurry; it's getting too windy to spray today. So we can hang around until you leave if you like.'

'Oh that's brilliant. That way Barbara can make sure I don't forget anything. Being spontaneous is not really my strong suit.'

'So when did all this get decided?'

'Around five minutes ago.'

'No wonder you're in a bit of a flap.'


Back at the house, Emily went to her bedroom and started putting clothes out on the bed. Barbara began gathering Grace's things while David went and sorted out Emily's car.

On her way to the bathroom to collect her toiletries bag, Emily paused to pat Grace, who had long ago finished her bone and was on her bed by the sliding door, surrounded by two bags of bowls, food, blankets, and toys.

'Don't worry. We're not moving house again, Gracie. You're just going on a little holiday. I'll miss you terribly,' she said, ruffling the dog's ears. Grace continued to lie on her front paws looking forlorn.

'Come on, Gracie,' Barbara said, pausing on her way past. 'Stop moping. We'll have fun. And your mum Sasha will be so pleased to see you. She's been all lonely without you.'

They moved back towards the bedroom.

'That's so good of David,' Emily said, hearing her car being moved over to the fuel tank behind the main shed.

'Yes, he is a dear, isn't he? Just like Jake will be to you, in time,' Barbara said.

'Let's just hope he doesn't resent my turning up uninvited.'

'It'll be fine. I think it's lovely that Simone cares enough about her brother to go out on a limb like this.'

'Hmm, I can't wait to meet her. I think I'm in love with Jake,' she added absently.

'I *know* you're in love with Jake, Em. Blind Freddy could see *that*.'


By two-thirty, Emily's small carry-on suitcase was packed and ready. She'd switched off the lights, closed the curtains, and used the key she'd found in one of the kitchen drawers to lock the glass sliding door. All that was left was to put her bags in the car and leave.

'Thanks so much for this, you guys,' she said, hugging David first and then Barbara. 'And you be a good girl for Auntie Barbara and Uncle David, Gracie,' she added, squatting and ruffling the dog's ears. She lingered, not wanting to leave.

*Why are goodbyes so hard? It's only a few days, for goodness sake!* She was grateful when Barbara broke in.

'Go on, quick, go, before we all get weepy.'

Emily grinned gratefully at her friend, gave her another quick hug, and hurried to the car.

# Chapter Forty-four

The first few kilometres were tinged with sadness – she didn't like leaving Grace behind, nor Barbara now they were finally back on track. And it didn't feel right to be missing Donald and Trevor's joint funeral the next day. After the Baker brothers' generosity towards her, she had wanted to say a proper goodbye. But it couldn't be helped; Jake needed her.

Once she turned off the dirt and got up to speed on the open highway, she began to feel better, even quite liberated. She was off on an adventure. Melbourne! Wow! She'd never been there before. Wouldn't Elizabeth be surprised?

*And Jake.*

She hoped he'd be pleased to see her – wouldn't think she was intruding. She felt a little nervous at just turning up, but reminded herself that Simone

491

had invited her. If it all went badly she could just hop back on a plane.

*Listen to you; the great jetsetter.* She laughed. *'Just hop on a plane,' says the girl who hasn't been further than Port Lincoln in years.* What an adventure. Though she did feel a little jittery about the thought of being in a big city.

*

Emily parked her car in the medium-term car park, checked in with plenty of time to spare, got a pre-packaged chicken sandwich from the tiny kiosk, and sat to eat it while she waited for her flight to be called.

She contemplated the sandwich. She wasn't very hungry – was too on edge, and had had a quick bite of lunch with Barbara and David a few hours before – but she didn't want to feel washed out when she arrived in Melbourne and met Simone for the first time. No, she'd better keep some light food in her stomach. But first she should just call her parents and let them know she was heading interstate. Emily took out her mobile phone and dialled their number. As always, she held her breath and hoped her father would answer.

'Hello, Des speaking.'

'Hi Dad, it's me.'

'Em. Hi.'

'Look, I'm really sorry about earlier.'

'It's okay. Well... I think I can understand why you didn't want to tell your mother, but you could have told me.' Emily felt stung by the dejected tone in her father's voice.

'Honestly Dad, I really couldn't have coped with Mum picking up the phone and, well, gloating. I just didn't need it. I had a lot to do in a short amount of time. It was pretty stressful.'

'I know, but we could have helped. As your gran used to say, "A problem shared is a problem halved."'

*No, you're not listening. I didn't want Mum involved.*

'And if you didn't want our help, you could have simply told us at the funeral.'

'Dad, I can barely even remember *seeing* you at the funeral, it was such a blur. All I can say is I'm really sorry,' Emily said. She felt herself choking up.

*Oh God, don't cry. Not here in public.*

'It's okay. You have had a lot on your plate. I'm sorry, I really didn't mean to put more pressure on you.'

At hearing this, Emily's heart clenched and tears filled her eyes.

'Dad, can we talk about this another time? I'm calling on the mobile, so I'd better keep it short. I'm in Whyalla airport on my way to Melbourne,' she blurted.

'What? But...'

'Jake's been involved in an accident. Well, not actually involved. He's fine. Well, not quite fine. One of his subcontractors has been killed. His sister rang and asked me to come to Melbourne because he's not coping so well. This all happened just after you and Mum left. I dropped everything.'

'What happened? Is he okay?'

'I don't know, Dad. That's what I'm going to find out. I'm not sure how long I'll be – as long as needed I expect. I'll call you when I know more.'

'Okay. But is there anything we can do? What about Grace – is she with Barbara and David?'

'Yes, they were still there when I got the call. It all happened in a bit of a rush. I threw some clothes in a bag, jumped in the car, and here I am.' She looked down at the sandwich shaking in her trembling hand.

'You'll miss Donald and Trevor's funeral,' Des said, as if thinking aloud.

'Yes, and I feel terrible about it. But Simone is really worried about Jake and thinks I can help.'

'Well, hopefully you can, whatever it is he needs help with.'

'I'll be there with Donald and Trevor in spirit,' she offered lamely.

'It can't be helped. That's the best you can do in the circumstances.'

'Hmm.'

'Well, give Jake our best. I'll let you get off the phone. Just keep in touch.'

'I will, but it probably won't be until the morning. Thanks Dad. And again, I'm really sorry about... everything.'

'It's forgotten. You just focus on getting to Melbourne and sorting things out with Jake. Safe travels.'

'Thanks Dad, bye for now.'

Emily hung up and took a few deep breaths. She focused on her sandwich so the threatening tears would not have a chance to fall. She wished her dad was here beside her. She prised the first of the two triangles out and took a bite. Not bad, she thought, nodding approvingly, and sank her teeth in with more gusto.

She had finished and just returned to the same seat after washing her mayonnaise-smeared fingers in the bathroom, when her flight was called. She made her way towards the gate, her heart rate increasing slightly. Having only flown a few times before, Emily was both excited and nervous – not so much from fear of crashing, but from unfamiliarity with protocols; which side seat 13A was on, for starters.

At the gate, a young woman checked her boarding pass and directed her onto the noisy tarmac, where she joined a small group. It was sunny and warmer than she'd thought. She took off her light hoodie and hung it over her arm. She wondered if she'd packed the right clothes for Melbourne's weather, which was said to consist of four seasons in one day. *How the hell do you pack for that? Oh well, too late now.*

Settled in her seat against the window, Emily read through the safety card and then watched the suitcases being thrown into the hold below while trying to remember if there was anything breakable in her toiletries bag.

A few minutes later she studiously observed the safety demonstration and then flicked through the newspaper she'd found in the seat pocket in front. But she couldn't focus.

*Relax. You're just nervous.*

She'd have to calm down or else she'd be a mess by the time she met Jake's sister. And she wanted to impress her. Well, not impress her; but give a good impression. She imagined Simone Lonigan was a sophisticated city woman like Liz. What would such a person find interesting about a country girl like her?

*What if she doesn't like me?*

Emily started to think about the impulsiveness of her trip. She'd never done anything so rash in her entire life. But she was doing it for Jake. With a bit of a start, Emily realised there wasn't much she wouldn't do for him; as she'd once thought he felt about her.

Why hadn't he shared his pain, confided in her? And why the hell hadn't she phoned him to ask if he was okay? She felt her face begin to burn with shame.

*I was afraid.*

Afraid that he had left because of her; that he didn't like her as much as she liked him. Emily's heart ached. She should have been there for him this past week. Turning off her phone had been childish. She'd been sulking, selfishly wrapped up in her own petty problems, which were very minor when put alongside the fact that someone had actually died.

*Oh well, at least I'm doing something about it now.* Better late than never, Barbara would say.

Oh Barbara. She smiled. It felt so good to have their friendship renewed. She'd been a fool there as well. But it was in the past now – she would never let anything so ridiculous happen again.

After a forty-minute stopover in Adelaide and another uneventful flight, Emily landed at Melbourne airport. Bright lights lit up the tarmac outside the plane's windows.

As she stood up and joined the queue to disembark, Emily wondered if she'd recognise Simone. She'd seen her photo on Jake's website that night at Barbara's. It was a head-and-shoulder shot, so she had no idea how tall or slim, or otherwise, she was. All she could remember was that she looked warm and friendly, and had straight dark brown hair just shorter than shoulder length and that it flicked out at the bottom.

*Did she say she'd be there to meet me, or was I meant to catch a cab?* Suddenly Emily couldn't remember. She began feeling panicky. Tiny beads of sweat began prickling in her hairline.

*Calm down.*

Emily told herself to breathe, slowly and deeply. Instantly her thoughts became clearer. Of course Simone was going to meet her – she hadn't given Emily an address to make her own way. She thanked the flight attendant at the exit and walked out of the aircraft and up the long ramp on heavy legs. Despite dozing for much of the second flight, she felt exhausted.

*It's okay. It's just the stress. You'll be fine.*

As she emerged into the terminal she heard a voice calling her name.

'Emily, over here!'

A young woman of around her own medium height but of slightly slimmer build, dressed in jeans and a plain pale pink t-shirt was waving her arm and clearly looking in her direction. *How did she know what I look like?* Emily suddenly thought. But she didn't dwell.

Emily walked towards the woman who, she now saw, looked uncannily like a feminine version of Jake. They shared the same shade of brown hair and had similar skin tone. Her face, while daintier, had a similarly strong jawline and chin. But most obvious of all was the wide, beaming smile that lit up her whole face. The woman rushed forward, still waving.

'Simone?'

'I knew I'd recognise you!' Simone said, pulling her into a tight hug. 'It's so wonderful to finally meet you – I've heard so much about you. Thanks very much for coming. Do you have a bag to collect?' she asked.

'Yes,' Emily said, nodding. 'Carousel two I think they said.'

'Come on, this way.' Simone led the way and Emily had to almost run to keep up as she darted her way through the terminal like she'd been there a hundred times before.

Fifteen minutes later they had collected Emily's bag, walked to Simone's small white BMW sedan in the car park, and were on their way. Emily tried to pay for the parking but Simone insisted.

'You must be exhausted,' Simone said, as she negotiated her way out and into the traffic.

'I am a little, actually,' Emily said.

'It's all the air-conditioning, it dehydrates you. And of course you had the drive up to Whyalla first. Jake told me what an absolutely boring drive it is – nothing to see but red dirt and blue-grey saltbush.'

'It is a bit,' Emily said, already feeling comfortable with Simone. She seemed to be as down-to-earth and friendly as her brother.

'I've made a lasagne and salad. I hope that's okay. I didn't think you'd be up to going out and it is rather late.'

'Sounds perfect,' Emily said, noting the sudden grumble of her stomach.

'Jake didn't say you were vegetarian or anything.'

*So he's told her about me.* Oddly, she liked the idea that he had talked to his sister about her. *I wonder what else he's said.*

'How is Jake? Does he know I'm coming?'

'Not yet. I've invited him over for breakfast. I thought we could try to talk him into going to the funeral together.'

'Doesn't he want to go?'

'I don't know. I don't think even *he* knows. He's not really in a very good place for making decisions at the moment. I just want to point out the options and let him know we're there for him. I think going to the funeral will be good for him. I don't want him looking back and regretting that he didn't put in an appearance.'

'So what actually happened? You said something about scaffolding collapsing.'

'Not sure really. The workplace health and safety people are investigating, but we know it wasn't our fault. The scaffolding crew set up the structure that collapsed. We had nothing to do with it, except that it was on our building site and the poor guy was a subcontractor of ours. We'll find out in due course.'

'That's awful,' Emily said. 'Imagine the poor man's family. Jake probably feels responsible.'

'Exactly. I think he's afraid of facing them.'

*I can relate to that.*

The mood in the car was sombre – Emily remembering her own reluctance to visit John's parents – when Simone abruptly changed the subject. 'Hey, I absolutely loved your jam.'

'Thanks so much for doing all that for me. It was very good of you.'

'The pleasure was all mine. I loved doing it. I can just see you as the next big thing in jams and preserves.'

Emily couldn't find any reserves to show her enthusiasm. She was too worried about Jake – selling jam was the last thing on her mind.

'Are you making some more again soon? It's just that my friend Billy is really keen. Did Jake tell you? I sold her the entire second batch for her shop in St Kilda.'

'I don't know, Simone,' Emily said wearily. 'So much has been going on. I've just had to suddenly move house. My head's all over the place at the moment. I did make a small batch with the last of the fruit, but I didn't even think to bring it.'

'You haven't given up on the house that Jake did the plans for, have you?' Simone said, staring at her. 'I love those barley twist columns.'

'It's a bit of a long story.'

'Sorry, I didn't mean to pry.'

'It's not that – I'm just tired, and worried about Jake. Are you sure he's going to be okay with me turning up out of the blue like this? I don't know if he told you, but we had a bit of a tiff before he got called back. It was totally my fault – I see that now. I overreacted over something – something quite trivial, especially compared to what he's been going through.'

'I'm sure it wasn't trivial at the time. You don't strike me as the melodramatic type.'

'That's very kind of you to say, but I don't know what I am anymore. It's been a rough few months,' she said, smiling weakly at Simone.

'Well, I know Jake cares very deeply for you, and you wouldn't be here if you didn't feel the same for him.'

'I do. I really do.'

'Then that's all that matters,' Simone said, sounding triumphant.

# Chapter Forty-five

'Here we are. Welcome,' Simone declared, bringing the car to a halt outside a row of single-storey terraces in the narrow one-way lane they had turned into. Emily hadn't been able to follow the many twists and turns they'd taken, but they were clearly just on the outskirts of the city. Lots of tall buildings loomed very close overhead.

Simone insisted on unloading Emily's suitcase from the car boot and carrying it for her. She opened the nearest iron gate with a squeak, then led the way up a brick path to a Victorian-style tessellated tile verandah and a front door painted gloss black.

'Now it's nothing flash,' Simone warned over her shoulder as she put the key in the lock. 'I bought it as a renovator's delight years ago, but beyond a few cosmetic touches, it still has all its original charm,' she said with a chuckle. She opened the door.

'It's lovely,' Emily said. First she took in the white decorative ceiling with its ornate central rose, and then she let her eyes roam along the periwinkle blue walls where three large canvases were hung evenly across most of the hall's long right-hand side. Emily looked closely. Each of the bright yellow paintings showed a single flower in full bloom; the first a daffodil, the second a tulip and the third a rose. The colours tied in perfectly with the honey-coloured polished floorboards.

'You did these, didn't you? I recognise the style from the gorgeous labels you did for my jam – Jake showed me a photo on his phone.'

'I wanted some decent-sized canvasses, but couldn't afford the work of real artists,' Simone said with a shrug.

'They look like the work of a real artist to me. Do you exhibit?'

'You're being way too kind,' Simone said with a little laugh. 'I'm not an artist, I just did them to brighten up the walls.'

Emily noticed her blush ever so slightly.

'You're in here,' Simone said, opening the second door along, turning on the light, and entering with Emily's suitcase.

'I wish I could put rooms together like this,' Emily said.

There was a feature wall in charcoal grey, perfectly matching the colour of the toile upholstery of the padded bedhead beneath it. Above the window was a pelmet in the same toile fabric, and the curtains matched the grey quilt cover. Beside the window was a wingback chair upholstered in thick, sumptuous ruby-coloured corduroy. On it was a cushion in grey and cream toile.

There was another large canvas above the bed, this time a field of poppies, the colour of which perfectly matched the chair and scatter cushions on the bed.

Emily shook her head in wonder. Some people just clearly had a knack. 'You should be working as an interior designer or an artist, rather than in an office.'

'I can't take all the credit; I did have a colour consultant come in. I wanted bold feature walls, but I just didn't trust myself. I thought there were all these rules around use of colour, but she said, "If you want a bright purple wall in your house then do it. If you don't like it it's easy enough to paint over again."'

Emily felt like throwing herself onto the pillow-laden bed and going to sleep, but instead she put her handbag down on the floor beside her suitcase, and followed Simone out.

'I'll just show you the rest of the house so you have your bearings.'

They went through the door at the end of the hall into a lounge room that spanned the whole width of the house. The room was painted in warm green, and had a feature wall in a darker shade. Again the colour tied in perfectly, this time with the floral tiles surrounding the original-looking fireplace. An ornate gilt-framed mirror occupied the space above the fireplace. On the longest wall and wrapping around the corner was a large cream leather chaise sofa. Above it, instead of more canvases, there was a series of three large black and white photos in matt black frames – sections of old buildings taken at odd angles.

'Are these some of Jake's photos?' Emily asked.

'Yes. Aren't they great? He did them for my birthday last year.'

'Lovely. He's very clever. What are they of?'

'They're three of my favourite Melbourne city buildings. The first one is the Gothic ANZ Bank on the corner of Collins and Queen Streets, the second the old Customs House building on Flinders Street, and the third is three thirty-three Collins Street.'

'I love old buildings.' Emily was reminded of the loss of both the limestone cottage and the Bakers' house. She shrugged off the thought. 'This whole place is great. I don't know why you say it's a renovator's delight,' she said brightly, shaking her head with wonder. 'It's just gorgeous.'

'Thanks. Paint masks a multitude of sins. I was a bit gung-ho when I moved in and I started with the easy bits first, which just so happened to be the front section of the house. Great for first impressions, but I'm afraid it goes downhill very quickly from here,' she said, continuing diagonally across the lounge room to a door on the far side.

They entered a small dining room that contained a lovely old timber dining setting and sideboard. Easing the relative drabness of the plain off-white walls and timber furniture was a selection of canvases in varying sizes, colours and floral designs.

'As you can see, this is my dumping ground for paintings that I don't know what else to do with,' Simone said with a laugh.

'Well, you can dump them at my house any time,' Emily said.

'You're welcome to have one.'

'Oh I couldn't,' Emily said.

'Of course you could. It would be my pleasure if you like them that much.'

'I think you should keep them and one day exhibit,' Emily said, slightly changing the subject.

She didn't want to just take advantage of Simone's generosity. The woman had already given her so much by selling her jam. But more important than the money was that Simone had given her hope when she'd been at her lowest ebb. And all without having even met her. Emily wished she could somehow return the favour.

They moved into the tiny kitchen and poked their heads into the incredibly cramped bathroom that opened from it. The room held nothing but a blue enamel bath with shower over it, a matching pedestal basin with a small mirrored shaving cabinet, and a toilet at the end of the bath beside the basin. There was no way two people could fit into the bathroom at once. The only spare floor space was taken up with the opening of the door.

'See what I mean? An absolute disaster. All of this back section needs to come off and be started again. But it's going to cost a fortune. The bank is happy to lend me the money, but I can't quite get my head around living on a building site without a kitchen and bathroom for six months, especially during winter. Maybe I'll bite the bullet next summer,' she said with a shrug. 'Meanwhile, at least there is an inside toilet,' she added. 'When these places were built the toilets were all out the back. The nightsoil man used to come along the back alleys and take it away.'

'So you live alone?' Emily asked.

'Yes. I've got a newish boyfriend, but we only really see each other on weekends. So far it seems to suit us. He's away this weekend,' she added. 'Well, that's the end of the tour. Outside is just a small slab of concrete and then a huge brown iron fence. I'll show you in the morning. I'll put dinner in to heat – it'll take around twenty minutes,' she said, going into the kitchen and turning on the oven. 'You're welcome to have a shower. Not that I'm saying you need one, but I always feel so grimy after travelling.'

'I think I will, thanks.'

'You'll find everything you need behind the door in your room – towels, bathrobe, slippers...'

'Thanks.' Emily made her way back down to the hall and into the spare room. She closed the door and sat on the end of the bed.

The set of towels on the antique-style rack, in a charcoal colour perfectly matching the feature wall, seemed too well-presented to be used. It was all so perfect, but unlike being in similarly well-decorated homes – her Aunt Peggy's for example – she felt totally at ease.

She extracted her toiletries bag from her suitcase, got undressed down to her underwear, and dragged on the plush, freshly laundered robe – again in charcoal. She pulled it tightly around her, enjoying the softness on her skin, and took a deep whiff of its apple scent. She put fresh underwear in the side pocket of her toiletries bag, tucked it under her arm, took the face washer and one of the towels from the rack, and headed back down to the bathroom.

Simone turned from tossing a fresh salad in a white ceramic bowl. 'Find everything you need?' she asked, smiling warmly.

'Yes thanks,' Emily replied, closing the bathroom door. She couldn't wait to get under a hot shower.

Simone was nowhere to be seen when Emily emerged, nor did she encounter her on her trek back through the house to the guest room. She dressed in jeans and t-shirt and emerged ten minutes later feeling considerably refreshed.

She wandered back down to the kitchen, which smelt strongly of garlic and baked cheese, and suddenly felt hungry.

'Better?' Simone said, appearing behind her.

'Much. Thank you. I think it even increased my appetite,' she added with a laugh.

'Good to hear,' Simone said, moving into the kitchen. 'You take this lot to the table and I'll bring the lasagne and garlic bread,' she said, handing Emily a pile consisting of plates, cutlery, napkins, and a bowl of salad with stainless steel servers protruding from it.

Having distributed the bits and pieces around the table, Emily stood while Simone put down the steaming dish of lasagne and took the foil-wrapped bread from the top and put it on the extra plate.

'Would you like a glass of wine?'

'Actually just water for me would be good, thanks. But I can get it.'

'Glasses are above the sink.'

Emily returned with two tumblers of water to find Simone had put the perfect-sized slice of lasagne and a small pile of salad on her plate.

'It smells divine.'

'It's one of my all-time favourites. Cheers,' she said, raising her glass towards Emily. 'Thanks for being here.' They clinked.

'Thanks for inviting me,' Emily said, smiling back.

'To Jake,' Simone added.

'Jake,' Emily affirmed with a nod.

★

It was eleven by the time they'd put the plates in the sink – Simone was adamant that they were not doing any dishes at that hour – covered the dish containing the leftover lasagne with cling wrap and put it in the fridge. Both women were unsuccessfully trying to hide yawns.

'You're welcome to sit up and watch TV,' Simone said, 'but I'm off to bed.'

'Thanks, but I'm exhausted. What time is Jake coming for breakfast?' Emily asked, as they made their way through the lounge room and into the hall.

'I told him nine-ish, so that means he'll be here right on the dot. Always punctual is our Jake. I'll be up about seven. Maybe you'd like to go for a walk? I go most mornings. But no pressure, we can see how we feel in the morning.'

'Sounds good. At home I don't often sleep beyond six-thirty.'

They were now standing outside the door to Emily's room.

'Well, goodnight then,' Simone said. 'And, again, thanks so much for coming all this way; it really does mean a lot.'

'It's my pleasure. And thank you for everything.' She thought about adding, 'Jake's so lucky to have you as a sister,' but her throat contracted and she felt a wave of emotion overcome her. Her tiredness had caught up. 'Good night then,' she said, turning the handle and entering the room.

In her room, Emily put her light cotton shortie pyjamas on and pushed her feet between the tightly tucked crisp sheets. 'Goodnight Gracie,' she whispered into the dark room, and tried to ignore the slight feeling of homesickness and focus on snuggling down.

She had just got the thick feather pillows arranged perfectly when she realised she hadn't cleaned her teeth. Too bad, she thought, running her tongue around in her mouth. She didn't fancy traipsing back through the house now all the lights had been turned off. She just hoped she wouldn't need a wee during the night and get disorientated.

That had happened once during a sleepover at a friend's at high school; she had ended up stuck in their walk-in pantry unable to find the door out.

Her so-called friend had told everyone at school the next day and Emily had been bullied about it for a whole term. Ever since then, she'd felt uneasy when staying in unfamiliar houses. Not that it was something she had to deal with very often.

She heard footsteps outside her door followed by a gentle tapping. She lifted her head off the pillow.

'Em, I've put night lights on in case you need to use the loo – there's nothing worse than bumbling around disorientated in a strange house.'

'Thanks very much,' she called. She smiled, and settled back down. *Now* Simone had thought of everything.

# Chapter Forty-six

Emily awoke from a deep sleep. She opened her eyes, looked about to get her bearings, and then stretched. God, the bed and pillows were comfortable. She checked her watch; a little after seven.

For a moment she was surprised she'd managed to sleep in half an hour past her usual wake-up time. Then she realised it was half an hour later there in Melbourne, which meant she'd actually gone to bed half an hour earlier than usual. She smiled at thinking that Grace would have been at her to be let out by now. If she were at home. But she wasn't; she was in a big city far away.

A wave of homesickness swept through her, but she pushed it aside. She was here for Jake. And Simone was being lovely to her. Grace was fine being taken care of by Barbara and David. *Pull yourself together.* She reminded herself to phone her parents a little later. If she timed it right they'd be out at the funeral and she could just leave a message. *Fingers crossed*.

She threw back the covers, got up, and put on the bathrobe and slippers.

Simone was in the kitchen doing the dishes.

'Good morning,' Emily said.

'Good morning. Did you sleep okay?'

'Like a log. That is such a comfortable bed.'

'That's good to hear.'

'I'll help you with those,' Emily said, 'I just need to use the loo first.'

'There were hardly any; they're almost done.'

When she came out Simone was nowhere in sight so Emily went back to her room, dressed in the same clothes as last night, put on her runners, and draped her hoodie over her arm. She emerged to find Simone wearing track pants with a matching zip-up hoodie and a plain baseball cap.

'You look like you're keen for a walk. I was just coming to check.'

'Yep, ready to go,' Emily said. 'I usually go in the mornings at home.' She slipped her arms into her hoodie and then zipped it up.

'Great. I want to pick up some croissants for breakfast. There's a lovely little bakery-café around a ten-minute walk away.'

'What a lovely street,' Emily said, as they walked along the tree-lined pavement past row after row of single-storey terraces. 'I can't believe how close to the city you are,' she added, gazing up with awe at the skyscrapers looming above them.

'It really is the perfect spot; it only takes twenty minutes to walk right into the Bourke Street Mall. Not that I do all that often.'

'Gorgeous old houses,' Emily said.

'Yes, hard to believe they were once workers' cottages. I was lucky I got in when I did. Prices have skyrocketed in the past few years.'

They turned left at the end of the long street and approached a café where a mass of lycra-clad men and women sat around small tables sipping at cups. Groups of bicycles leant against walls, trees, or lay in jumbled piles on the ground barely off the footpath. This was something Emily had never seen outside the one bakery-café at home. She smiled and almost laughed out loud at picturing how the old biddies of Wattle Creek would react to such a scene.

They would stand about tut-tutting for a while before someone was dispatched to speak to the local police officer – being as it was outside of council office hours. Upon being informed it was not a criminal matter, they would then set up a committee to raise funds for a bike rack to deal with this dangerous blight on the street – all before the first latte was consumed inside. That was how things were done in a small town; everyone minding everyone else's business.

They stepped inside onto the black and white chequered tiles and joined the end of the queue.

Emily's mouth had been watering for a croissant since Simone had mentioned that's what they were having for breakfast. Croissants were few and far between in Wattle Creek, and she hoped the bakery wouldn't run out. While they waited, she glanced around the sea of French-style ornate wrought-iron tables and chairs. What she couldn't believe was how many fit-looking people – dressed in proper bike riding gear – were tucking into big breakfasts.

*I suppose they must burn it all off on the bikes.*

Then Simone was turning away from the counter carrying a large paper bag with a few spots of grease already seeping through.

With all the constant small shuffles forward that she'd been making with everyone else, Emily hadn't realised how close to the counter Simone had got. She'd wanted to pay for the croissants. That was what house guests did, right? Oh well, she pushed the thought aside. She made a mental note to mention the airfares later.

Outside, Emily breathed in the fresh air.

'Phew,' Simone said. 'I'd forgotten just how busy it gets on a Saturday morning – I tend to come down here later if I do; usually just stay home to read the paper.'

'Someone should tell them they're undoing their exercise with all the bacon and eggs,' Emily said, as they turned back into Simone's street.

'Yes, and how ridiculous do middle-aged men with pot bellies look in lycra?'

Emily laughed and shook her head.

As they got closer to Simone's cottage, her heart began to flutter; soon she would see Jake.

Right on the dot of nine, there was a tap at the front door. Emily's heart leapt into her mouth. She'd been sitting at the table reading the paper, constantly checking her watch and getting more anxious and excited as the hands moved closer to nine o'clock. And now he was here.

Simone put the tray of croissants in the oven and went to let Jake in. Emily stayed where she was, listening to their voices as they greeted each other. Jake sounded tired and flat, not at all like his usual jovial self.

At first he didn't see her when he entered the room just behind Simone. *God, he looks so thin*, Emily thought, *and pale and drawn*. She stood up, and he stopped dead in his tracks, gaping.

'Hi Jake,' she said, her legs suddenly feeling weak. She dipped her head shyly.

'Jake, darling, I think you know Emily,' Simone said, giving him a gentle push forward. He strode towards Emily and then gathered her into his arms. His grip was not nearly as firm as she remembered; everything about him seemed wan.

'What are you doing here? I didn't know if I'd ever see you again,' he whispered into her hair. Then he was silent and Emily could feel his chest shuddering. Was he crying?

'It's okay, Jake. It's not your fault,' she whispered. As she did, she realised how ambiguous her words were – though very apt. She felt her own eyes fill with tears, and her throat constrict. She took her hand from his back and stroked his hair. 'Simone called and told me what happened. I wanted to be here for you.'

'Oh God, I've been such a fool. Look at me, I'm a blubbering mess,' Jake said, releasing her a little. He kissed her softly, and then held her by her shoulders at arm's length, gazing at her.

Emily's heart twisted painfully as she studied his eyes, which had none of the mischievous twinkle she'd been so taken with the first time they'd met. The pain and anguish of the past week had taken their toll.

'Thank you for being here – it means a lot,' he said, kissing her on the forehead and then releasing her. He dragged the sleeve of his navy blue light knitted jumper across his face.

'And thank you, Sim,' he said, offering his sister a wan smile and giving her a hug. 'Can I help you with breakfast?'

'No, it's all sorted. You guys sit. Back in a sec.' Simone winked at Emily before disappearing into the kitchen.

Jake and Emily sat, and he reached across the table and took hold of both of her hands.

'You really are a sight for sore eyes, Em. I'm sorry I left so abruptly. I called that night, but I wasn't sure what to say. And then it all got a bit… God knows what you must have thought.'

'It's okay, Jake. I behaved badly. I'm sorry I was so touchy about you asking about my life with John. It's just that I want to make a fresh start and not dwell on it.'

'I understand that. I was really just trying to understand you better so I'd know how to treat you...'

'Just be yourself Jake. We all have a history. How we are together is what matters. So what's been going on?'

He sat staring at the table and fiddling with the butter knife set in front of him.

'Well I'm sure Simone filled you in on most of it – that one of our subcontractors was killed?'

Emily nodded.

'Thankfully we weren't at fault. I can't imagine how the poor scaffolding people are feeling,' he said, shaking his head. 'But it is my fault he was there; he was working on one of our sites. I didn't know him very well – had only met him a couple of times – but he seemed like a good guy. It seems to have hit me rather hard,' he offered with a helpless shrug.

'I wish I'd been here for you.'

'I wish so too, but that's my fault for not confiding in you. At least you're here now.'

'Thanks to Simone,' Emily said. 'She's great; we've really hit it off.'

'I'm so glad; she's really very special to me,' he said quietly, with a smile that was more of a grimace.

'I can see why. You're both so lucky to have each other.'

Jake didn't say anything. He continued to stare at the table. Emily's heart ached to bring him out of whatever it was; put the light back in his eyes again. But she didn't have any idea how. Would it just take time?

'Are you going to the funeral?'

'I don't think I can.'

'Simone and I think it might be a good idea if you did – you know, for closure. It does help, you know.'

'Hmm. I guess.'

'You don't have to talk to anyone. And it'll be hard, but I think you'll regret it if you don't at least go and pay your respects.'

'Will you come with me?' he asked, looking back up at her, his face clouded. Emily's heart wrenched; he looked like a sad, fearful little boy.

'Of course, if you want me to.'

Just then Simone entered wearing an oven mitt and carrying a tray with three slightly browned croissants on it. In her other hand she held a large plunger of coffee.

'Tuck in while they're hot. There's plenty more in the kitchen, so don't hold back. There's sliced cheese and ham and plenty of jam. None of Emily's though, I'm afraid,' she added.

'How is the jam-making business, Em?' Jake asked, putting a croissant on his plate. He unscrewed the lid from a jar of blackberry jam.

'Not happening at all, actually. I did make a small batch after you left, but I've run out of fruit now and... Oh God, so much has happened. I'd completely forgotten you didn't know.'

'Know what? What's been going on?'

'Well, the house project is no longer, I'm afraid, after you went to all the trouble doing the lovely drawings. And I've moved back to the farm.'

Simone poured three mugs of coffee.

'God, what happened?!'

'The Baker brothers died suddenly last week – an accident on the farm – and they hadn't changed their wills to reflect our arrangement. You remember that woman who turned up when you and Elizabeth were visiting that first time? Tara Wickham, the financial planner?'

'Yes.'

'Well, it turns out she's their main beneficiary. She turfed me out – didn't want a bar of selling the house and twenty acres.'

'But you had a deal with them,' Jake said.

'With only their signatures on it. We had *verbally* agreed to going ahead with the actual sale after the subdivision had gone through. Yes, I was an idiot not to have it all done properly,' she added with a helpless shrug. *God, just how many times do I have to admit this out loud? Enough already.* She almost rolled her eyes.

'Ah, yes, I remember. But why did she make you leave so soon? Surely she would have wanted the rent while she was sorting things out.'

'You'd think, wouldn't you? But no, apparently not. And she wanted me out so soon because, and I quote, "I don't like you."'

Emily blushed slightly. It was embarrassing, even more so saying it out loud. She wished now she hadn't said it. *What must they think of me?*

'Really? That's terrible. I don't like the sound of her at all,' Simone said.

'God, Em, I'm so sorry. And it's probably all my fault. Remember how I got into it that day with her? Oh, I feel terrible.'

'Don't. It was just a healthy debate, if I recall. And she probably doesn't even remember it.'

'Well, we don't know what else is going on in her life,' Jake said thoughtfully.

'Whatever it is, there's no need to take it out on Emily,' Simone said. 'So you just moved out, when she told you to? You're more tolerant than me. I would have dug my heels in and said, "Make me!"' She let out a little laugh.

'I thought about it. But being in a small town… It's a bit complicated, but she could have made my life a bit difficult, and I've been the focus of enough gossip lately. It's a long story,' she added wearily. 'I'm disappointed, of course, because I really loved the place and was so looking forward to doing it up – with Jake's help.'

'Well, lucky you had the farm to move back to. So John's parents were okay with all that in the end?' Jake asked, looking a little sceptical.

'Yes. I finally told them about the separation and everything. I fully expected them to contest the will or something. Which would be completely under-standable given the circumstances. But they were amazing. Really supportive, actually.'

Simone looked puzzled.

'My estranged husband – Jake probably told you he died recently,' Emily explained to Simone. 'Well it turned out he hadn't got around to telling his parents we'd split up, or changing his will. It was all looking a little messy there for a while,' Emily explained.

'Golly. And I thought living in the country was supposed to be the quiet life,' Simone said, shaking her head with amazement. 'Sounds like a lot more goes on out there than here in the big smoke!'

'It does sound a bit melodramatic, doesn't it? I think — well, I hope — things will settle down for me now.'

'Yes, hear hear,' Jake agreed.

Emily smiled at them. 'Thanks.'

'But oh, Em, I'm sorry that I haven't been there for you either. But at least you had Barbara. Sim, Emily's friend Barbara is an absolute brick; you'd love her, right Em?'

'Er, yep,' Emily said, trying to avoid eye contact.

'What, has something happened to her? Are she and David okay?'

'We just had a bit of a falling out, that's all. It's okay now, but...I behaved like an idiot there too, I'm afraid.'

'Well, these things happen. As long as it's all been sorted out now.'

Emily nodded. 'Yes, actually, that's where Grace is.'

'And how is the lovely Grace?' Jake brightened a little more at mention of the dog, and a smidgen more colour entered his cheeks.

'She's great,' Emily said, smiling warmly. 'Simone, you should have seen these two together; they got on like a house on fire,' she said, ripping a piece from her croissant. She slathered jam on it and put it into her mouth.

Simone slapped her hands down on the table as if she'd suddenly had a good idea. 'I know,' she said, 'why don't you go back with Emily, Jake, recuperate in the fresh country air for a few weeks, play with the dog, do some photography? You're not much use at work at the moment anyway,' she added.

He looked sideways at Simone. 'Thanks a lot.'

'Seriously, you need some time away from everything. What do you say?'

'I'd love to. But, um, I haven't been invited,' he said.

'Oh for goodness sake; it's an open invitation, you know that,' Emily said, looking at him. She wished she'd thought of it first. 'I'd love you to come back with me – and to stay for as long as you like. But it's entirely up to you.'

'Simone?'

'I just want you to get better; you've been so down. I'm sorry if I've overstepped the mark. I just didn't think you were in the right frame of mind to decide it for yourself,' Simone said.

'No, you're right. I think it's a good idea, and I'm so glad you called Emily when I couldn't.' Jake patted both the girls' hands. 'I'm lucky to have people in my life who care about me.' He smiled sadly at Simone and then Emily.

'All that matters is that you go and clear your head,' Simone said. 'And I couldn't think of a better person to recuperate you than Emily.' She got up from the table and pretended to wipe her hands. 'Well, it seems my work here is done. Who's for another croissant and more coffee?'

'Yes, coffee thanks,' Emily and Jake said in unison.

'Fancy going me halves in another croissant, Em, or do you want a whole one?'

'No, a half would be great. Let me help,' Emily said, getting up, retrieving the coffee pot, and following Simone out to the kitchen.

'Well, so much for needing all my powers of persuasion,' Simone said, putting two more croissants on a tray and sliding it into the oven.

'Hmm,' Emily said. 'He obviously trusts your judgement.'

'He loves you.'

'You think so?'

'Absolutely.'

'I see what you mean about his emotional state – he's not his usual self at all,' Emily said.

'Well, hopefully that will change with some fresh country air and good old-fashioned TLC. And time.'

Emily might have skipped back into the dining room if it weren't for the pot of hot coffee in her hands. She returned Jake's smile as she sat back down. No words seemed necessary. They were silent as they put milk and sugar into their mugs and glanced at different sections of the paper.

A few minutes later, Simone reappeared carrying the hot tray. Jake broke a croissant apart and put half on Emily's plate and the other half on his own. They settled back into silent consumption.

'So, are we all going to the funeral, or would you rather it be just you and Emily? I don't mind if you do, honestly.'

'Not at all. More the merrier. Oh, no, that's a terrible thing to say,' he said, looking stricken. 'I meant, safety in numbers.'

'We know what you meant,' Simone said, laying her hand over his.

'When would you like to get back home, Em?' he asked.

'Whenever you want to go.' *The sooner the better.* 'I'm sure it will take you a few days to sort things out with work and everything – I'm happy to wait if you'd like to travel together.'

'How does Monday sound? Thanks to Simone here, the business hardly needs me. And I'm sure you're keen to get back to Grace and get yourself properly settled. Being available by phone will be fine for a while.'

'Perfect. I probably should at least phone Elizabeth while I'm in Melbourne,' Emily said, thinking aloud. She didn't feel any enthusiasm for catching up with her cousin, but it was the right thing to do.

'She's in London – won't be back until Thursday week. Conference about the aftermath of the Global Financial Crisis,' Jake said. 'She emailed me. Don't worry; between the two of us, I'm sure we can keep you entertained for the weekend. It's only tomorrow really.'

'I would have loved you to meet my friend Billy,' Simone said, 'in case you decide to get back into making jam. She's the one who's just started the boutique produce shop. But unfortunately she and her partner, Tom, have gone away.'

'You would have liked them, Em. They're nice, but Billy can be a little full-on,' Jake said. 'Let's keep things low-key for Em on her first trip.'

'Fair enough. It's probably quite a culture shock for you.'

*Bless you for being so thoughtful.* 'It's okay. Really, I'm fine,' Emily lied with a shrug. She felt far from fine; she was missing Grace and the sanctuary of the quiet farm. She was relieved she wouldn't have to sit down to lunch with more new people; she was feeling far from bubbly and sociable.

'Why don't we have a quiet lunch somewhere, just the three of us, and only inflict the city properly on Emily to drop by my place,' Jake said to Simone, and then to Emily, 'I'm sure you're finding Melbourne pretty overwhelming after Wattle Creek.'

'Well it *is* very different from what I'm used to,' she said with a laugh, attempting to appear upbeat. She didn't want to sound like the country bumpkin, but she couldn't help what she was. 'But I would love to see where you live.'

'Actually,' Jake said, checking his watch, 'I'd better get going if I'm to get organised before the funeral. I'll come back and collect you both at three.' He drained his mug and got up. 'Em, are you happy for me to book flights for both of us for Monday?'

'Yes, thanks. And that reminds me. Simone, I still owe you for yesterday's flights. Can we go via an ATM?'

'Sure, but why don't I give you my account details and you can do a direct deposit when you get back home? Safer than carting cash around.'

'Okay, great, thanks.' Emily tried not to shudder at the thought of pickpockets and having her handbag stolen. But that's what happened in big cities, wasn't it? Monday couldn't come soon enough. Hopefully there were plenty of flights available. She mentally crossed her fingers.

Simone and Emily walked Jake out to his car – a silver Volks-wagen Golf hatch parked behind Simone's BMW. Out on the nature strip he hugged Simone.

'Thanks for breakfast Sim, and for bringing Em.' He kissed her on the forehead and released her. Then he pulled Emily towards him.

'Thank you so much for being here. I really do love you. We'll work out fine, we just need more time together.'

Emily's heart soared as they waved him off.

# Chapter Forty-seven

Emily found it very unsettling to be attending a funeral for someone she didn't know; she felt like she was intruding. She wondered how Donald and Trevor's had gone – it would have finished a few hours ago. Everyone would most likely still be at the wake.

She'd left a message on her parents' answering machine telling them she'd arrived safely, all was fine, and that she'd be back late Monday and would be in touch then. She didn't mention she was bringing Jake with her; that would be sure to cause Enid to check flight times and turn up with a welcoming casserole the second they arrived home. Her mother would probably start dropping in regularly when she heard he was there. Oh well, she'd just have to be strong and re-draw the boundaries if necessary. But Emily couldn't think about that now, she had Jake to take care of.

Cars lined the streets for miles back from the church. By the time they arrived, they were starting to puff from having to jog to avoid being late.

They joined a throng of people outside the large bluestone church. Many were men ranging in age from their early twenties to late forties. Emily assumed them to be construction workers that Shane, the deceased man, had worked with over the years. Jake nodded, shook hands, and mumbled quiet greetings to a few. He clearly knew some of the mourners, but not very well. She knew he liked to be hands-on with his business, but she imagined there wouldn't be much need for him to interact with labourers on a day-to-day basis.

The church was already overflowing when they arrived and a young lad in a black suit was setting up speakers on spindly tripods for those unable to be accommodated inside. Emily gazed around, taking it all in. She'd never been to a city funeral before, where so many apparent strangers stood in silence waiting for the service to start.

At most of the funerals she had attended, everyone huddled in groups chatting before the service, swapping their woes or elation at the progressing season, the change in commodity prices, or sharing gossip; filling in time before proceedings got under way. Country funerals often tended to be quite upbeat; a social occasion attended by all.

She and Simone stood on each side of Jake, and he put his arms around their shoulders. He kissed them both on the side of the head.

'Thanks for this, you guys,' he said in a slightly croaky voice.

He was back to looking fatigued and drawn – even worse than when he'd turned up for breakfast. He kept wiping the palms of his hands down his trousers. Nerves, stress; poor guy, Emily thought.

It was cool in the shade of the church surrounded by stone and concrete. She pulled her light jacket tighter and checked her watch – the service should have started a few minutes ago.

Finally a voice boomed from the large black box nearby. The service had begun.


It lasted about twenty minutes, and followed the format Emily was used to; sermon and eulogy divided by two hymns. The eulogy contained a few amusing anecdotes about Shane's larrikin nature, and a summary of his short life. At least he hadn't left a girlfriend, wife or partner and kids behind.

She found herself thinking the same about Donald and Trevor, even though they were so much older. She closed her eyes and offered a silent goodbye and apology for not attending their joint funeral. She thanked them for giving her a place to live at a time when it felt like her whole world was collapsing.

And then those outside were parting like a sea as the casket was wheeled out and then carried down the steps to the waiting hearse. There was an announcement that the burial was to be in the churchyard behind, and an instruction to follow the hearse on its short journey.

Jake, Simone and Emily joined the crowd walking slowly after the car.

A few hundred metres in, the hearse stopped and the pallbearers assembled behind it. In front, a large group of men in white hardhats and brightly coloured safety vests lined the path to form a guard of honour.

As the casket was carried through the two rows of men, each man took off his hat, put it to his chest, and bowed. Emily choked up at the sight. She stole a glance at Jake and saw him wipe a tear from his cheek. She put her arm around him and offered a sympathetic smile.

They hung back against the huge pine trees that flanked the perimeter of the large graveyard and watched as the throng fell in behind the casket.

While she couldn't see the actual grave plot, Emily thought she could smell the damp, slightly acidic scent of recently excavated earth. It was something she recognised all too well.

Around ten minutes later the minister declared, 'Ashes to ashes, dust to dust.' The service was over. The mourners formed two long lines and began shuffling slowly forward to pay their final respects.

'Go on,' Simone urged Jake.

'But it will take forever,' he said. He looked hesitant, but also like he wanted to participate.

'We've got all day.'

'If you're sure?' He looked from Simone to Emily.

'You take all the time you need,' Emily said kindly. 'Would you like us to go with you?'

'No, I think I need to do this bit alone,' he said.

'We'll be right here,' Simone said, giving his arm a squeeze.

They watched as, with head lowered, he slowly made his way towards the end of the closest line, nodding greetings to people as he went.

★

When he returned ten minutes later he looked totally bereft, and had two lines of shiny tears staining his face. Emily put her arm around him, but he didn't respond; just stood limply beside them. Soon more people with drooped heads, tear-streaked faces, and grim expressions began to flock past.

'We'd better get going – the traffic will be bedlam,' Jake said with a sigh.

'Are you sure there's no one you want to catch up with?' Simone asked, looking around.

'No, I'd like to just go if that's okay,' he said quietly.

'Of course. Come on,' Simone said. She and Emily fell in on either side of him as they strode out of the cemetery, taking a shortcut back towards the car rather than going all the way around to the front of the church and down the street. They walked in silence.

Emily was trying not to think about her gran and John. She needed to stay strong and supportive for Jake. *God I miss home.* She thought of the comfort she got from the button jar and wished she had it with her.

They slumped into the car, Simone in the back and Emily beside Jake in the front. She closed her eyes for a moment and drank in the comforting warmth from the lovely bright sunshine coming through the windows. In a few minutes it would be too warm, but for now it was nice. Jake sat with his hands on the steering wheel. She put a hand on his thigh and turned to him.

'Are you okay?'

He nodded. 'Yes.' He nodded again, more emphatically. 'Yes I am. You're right, both of you,' he said, looking at Emily and then Simone in the rear vision mirror. 'I did need to go. Thank God Shane didn't have a partner or kids,' he added, shaking his head sadly.

*Thank God for small mercies*, Emily thought. Another one of Gran's sayings.

'What do you want to do now?' Simone asked.

'Head back to your place. Beyond that, no idea,' Jake said.

'Why don't you stay, hang out? We can order pizza later and watch a DVD or two. What do you say?'

'Sounds like a plan.' He turned the key and put the car in gear.

There was a lot of traffic around them and they had to wait ages before being able to exit their cramped parking space. They snaked their way through the narrow streets and finally back onto the freeway. Once they were in the steadily flowing traffic, their trip seemed to go very quickly.

Emily had closed her eyes and was just beginning to fall asleep from the gentle movement of the car when she felt the vehicle stop and heard doors being opened. She reluctantly got out and followed Simone and Jake inside the house. They gravitated towards the kitchen where Simone filled the kettle.

'Right, who's for a cuppa?' she asked.

'Tea, thanks,' Emily said.

'Me too,' Jake said.

'I'll get it; you two go get settled in the lounge.'

Emily followed Jake and sat down at the other end of one of the two plush floral couches.

'You okay?' he asked, touching her hand.

'I'm fine,' she said with a sigh. 'Just a bit sad and reflective – funerals will do that,' she added, offering him a wan smile. 'God, I'm sick of funerals. That's the fourth one in the last two months.'

'Well, I really appreciate you being here for me.'

'I always will be, Jake,' she said, looking directly into his sad hazelnut eyes.

# Chapter Forty-eight

'How do you think he is?' Simone asked as she closed the front door later that night.

Emily shrugged. Jake had seemed a little brighter, but the shadow of sadness was still well and truly upon him. 'Probably okay, considering,' she said.

'Hmm.'

Lying in bed ten minutes later, Emily thought about what she could do to help him once they got back to the Eyre Peninsula. If only there was a project the two of them could do together. She'd love nothing more than to work side by side with him on something.

But he'd probably need some space – both physical and emotional – to process things.

She decided she would set him up in the spare room. As much as she wanted them to fall straight into a passionate love affair, it wouldn't be right.

For things to work out with Jake, their relationship had to evolve without being used as a crutch for his current delicate emotional state – or hers. She vowed to stay strong and keep the physical side of things at bay until he seemed more himself. Tough, but it had to be done. And with that thought, she rolled over and went to sleep.

\*

The next morning Simone showed her more of her suburb, pointing out landmarks and favourite spots. She showed Emily the Queen Victoria market, right on the edge of Melbourne's CBD. It seemed to go on forever; a city in itself! Emily tried to show some enthusiasm, but she couldn't shake the growing feeling of homesickness. She was missing Grace and Barbara and David.

As much as Wattle Creek's small-town ways drove her nuts, it was familiar, and, on the whole, friendly. She liked being able to walk down the street and not have people literally bumping into her. Despite having Simone beside her, she was feeling lonely, as well as sad. And stressed; people were rushing about every-where. *Why is everyone in such a hurry on a Sunday? And how can this walking possibly be considered relaxing?*

At home she enjoyed the exercise value of walking at a brisk pace, but relaxation was also an important part of her daily walk. Here she had to keep her wits about her, checking all the time she wasn't about to bump into someone or get hit by cars or cyclists. They were everywhere!

And the noise! Here, instead of the rustle of trees, squawk of birds and flapping of wings, was the hoot of car horns, shout of traders, squealing of trams on tracks and dinging of their bells. It was all quite nerve-racking.

Emily was relieved when finally Simone announced they were heading back. Not only was she struggling with the noise and activity around her, the place smelt weird; sort of dank, mouldy. Sour. And of car exhaust fumes.

She counted the hours until their flight and then felt a little guilty. She'd enjoyed spending time with Simone, but she couldn't wait to leave this big, scary city. She really couldn't understand why people would choose to live in such a place. Perhaps if you liked to shop and had money to spend... She found herself wondering why Jake lived in the CBD. He didn't strike her as a huge shopper.

Back at Simone's they showered and dressed, and had just settled in to read the Sunday paper when the doorbell rang. Emily checked her watch; surely it wasn't that late already. But it was. He was right on time.

Jake drove them to a café on the edge of a park. *More bikes and lycra-clad riders!* He said the suburb was Malvern, which meant nothing to Emily. She hadn't been able to follow their direction and was feeling quite disorientated. The city skyline was still quite close, but she had no idea which side of it and Simone's house they were. All the shiny, tall buildings looked the same.

Emily was relieved to enjoy her warm chicken salad. She'd been too self-conscious to ask what 'reduced balsamic vinegar dressing' was. As it turned out, it was thick and dark, the colour of treacle, but with a totally different, tangy flavour. *Er, vinegary*, she thought wryly.

An hour later, Jake drove them right into the city to show her his apartment. Whilst Emily had already seen quite a few trams, now that they were rumbling and rattling right next to the car she found their proximity quite scary. A few times she closed her eyes. Jake had laughed, saying that at least you knew where they were going to be thanks to the tracks they ran on.

But as he turned right from the left lane, she almost squealed. God, it was terrifying. Jake laughed again and explained that the 'hook turn' was unique to Melbourne and took some getting used to. As far as Emily could see, you only had a split second in which to do the manoeuvre when the lights were orange and just before they turned red. At the same time you had to make sure there were no trams coming or cars running the red light across your path. Crazy!

Jake had it all in hand, but she was still a nervous wreck when a few minutes later they drove down a ramp into an underground public car park. Jake explained that he rented it because his apartment block, being older style, didn't come with parking.

They rode the stainless steel lift and came out onto the street beside the entrance to a sandwich shop.

'Not far,' he said, leading the way. Emily had never been in an apartment complex before, so was quite excited. She was keen to see how Jake lived.

Less than a hundred metres away he approached an old-style wood and glass door, inserted a key, and stood back, holding the door open to let them in.

'Wow, it's gorgeous,' Emily said. With its black and white tiles, ornate ceiling and light shades, marble and iron hallstand and wall mirror, the foyer looked like a hotel from an old movie.

Jake led the way into an old-style lift with wooden outer doors and steel concertina doors inside. The lift shuddered its way slowly upwards, stopping at the fourth, and last, floor. Again, Jake opened the doors and stood aside to let them pass him into the hall. There were two doors. Jake unlocked the one with a large black 42 on it.

'Welcome,' he said, closing it behind Emily and tossing his keys into a wooden bowl on a small hall-stand very similar to the one in the foyer downstairs.

The black and white tiles carried on into a long galley-style modern kitchen of pale timber cabinetry and granite bench tops with a multitude of brown and cream colours swirling across its expansive, bare surface.

Parallel to the bench was a large, rustic table of aged timber planks on sturdy square legs.

The lounge room to the left was carpeted in charcoal grey slightly tinged with chocolate. A modern low-line cabinet sat against the wall, with a few framed photos on it. Above, mounted on the wall, was a large, black, flat-screen television.

Two taupe-coloured suede sofas – again low-lying, with modern, clean lines – and a steel and glass coffee table were the only other items adorning the generous space.

On the wall opposite the television was a series of large framed photographs of old buildings taken at unusual angles, even more beautiful than those she'd seen at Simone's. In one the view was up into an elaborate wrought-iron staircase from below. Emily stared at the photos open-mouthed.

'Wow, they're fantastic,' she said, breathily.

'Thanks.'

'You really should be exhibiting – and Simone. That's one of yours too, isn't it?' she said, pointing towards the kitchen. On the wall behind the table there was a square painting of bunches of red and green chillies on a bush. The style was unmistakably Simone's.

'Yep.'

'I love it. I'm going to commission you to do something for me when I decide what I want.'

'No problem. Just let me know.'

'I'll just give Em the tour,' Jake said.

'I'm going to watch the city playing,' Simone said, opening one of the glass doors onto a small balcony. The noise that rushed in from outside was quite overpowering. Emily was surprised at how quiet the apartment was with the door closed. You could almost forget how busy it was outside.

'Come on, this way,' Jake said, leading her away from the open-plan kitchen and living area and into a hall. More of Jake's photos lined the bright, white walls. The two bedrooms and study opening off the hall were also carpeted. Emily presumed the larger of the made-up bedrooms to be Jake's, though other than the open, filled suitcase on the floor, there was nothing to indicate he occupied it.

Everything about his home was sparsely decorated and immacu-late, but still warm and inviting. Other than the black and white tiles in the entrance hall and the ornate ceilings and cornices, which were clearly art deco inspired, it was quite modern.

The dressing of the rooms seemed very similar to that at Simone's home, and Emily wondered if she'd had a hand in Jake's decorating too.

'I have the very talented Simone to thank for the finishing touches; I wouldn't know the right ottoman or throw rug if I fell over it,' he said, as if reading her mind. He gave a restrained laugh, and Emily smiled warmly back. Clearly he was being modest. She could see that slowly but surely he would eventually come back out of his cocoon. But it would take a while.

The study had an old-style leather-covered pedestal desk with a brown leather studded chair behind it, and a bank of timber bookshelves lining one wall right to the ceiling.

The tour only took a few minutes, and then they were back in the lounge room. Jake opened one of the glass doors onto the balcony and they stepped out to join Simone. They were greeted by the noisy hustle and bustle from the street, along with cooking smells and the slight odour of car pollution.

'I love the view from up here, but it's so noisy. Is it always like this?'

'You get used to it,' Jake said. 'After a while it fades into the background. I actually find it quite soothing. And I love being able to shop and eat just metres away from home and then close the door on it when it all gets too much. It's the best of both worlds. City living's great, Sim, you should try it,' he said, giving his sister a friendly, gentle shove to the shoulder.

'I'll take your word for it.'

Emily peered out to the narrow city lane below. Everything seemed very grey – the stone of the nearby buildings, the roadway, the pavement. She could imagine so much drabness might make one quite despondent in the depths of winter. She understood Melbourne's winters were generally a lot greyer, colder, and wetter than South Australia's, which were hard enough to bear.

After a few moments they went back inside. Jake put on a pot of coffee while she and Simone settled onto the expanse of taupe suede. With the balcony doors closed, it really was quiet; there was just a bit of a background hum, which Emily could imagine, in time, becoming soothing. Occasionally there was a deep metallic rattle, which she presumed must be a tram.

Late in the afternoon, Jake dropped them off at Simone's and made arrangements for her to take them to the airport in the morning before she went to work. It would be an early start; they'd have to leave Simone's no later than seven.

Emily was disappointed they wouldn't be spending the evening together, but he told her he had to sort out some emails and work matters before he went away so he could relax for a few days when he got to the farm. She consoled herself that she'd soon have him all to herself anyway.

\*

The following morning, Simone dropped Jake and Emily at the airport. Emily cursed the threatening tears. *Why do I get like this with every goodbye? I'm dying to get home, for goodness sake.*

'Look after him, you hear?' Simone said, hugging her tightly.

'I will. I promise. Thank you so much for having me to stay – and for everything. Anytime you want to get away, there's a place for you at my house. Consider it an open invitation.'

They hugged again quickly and then watched Simone walk away.

Jake grabbed her hand. 'Come on, I need a coffee,' he said, and dragged her towards a coffee stand.

Emily's heart pounded a little with excitement. They were finally alone together. She was taking him home.

# Chapter Forty-nine

'It's weird, but I feel a bit like I'm going home,' Jake said out of the blue as the flat saltbush plains gave way to greener trees and scrub.

Emily smiled warmly at him before returning her attention to the road ahead. She liked that they were comfortable enough with each other not to feel the need to fill the silence with meaningless chatter.

She remembered how, just before she'd married John, she'd asked Gran if she was doing the right thing. Gran had set her unusual blue-grey eyes on her and said, 'Dear, you just know. Your heart will tell you'. Emily had frowned. That was no help.

By the time she realised she hadn't listened to her heart it was too late.

Now, sitting here in the car next to Jake, she totally understood Gran's words. Jake was the one for her; no doubt about it. It didn't matter that they didn't know each other all that well, or that they hadn't slept together yet. It just felt right inside.

They didn't need to speak aloud because their hearts were so well fused they were communicating anyway.

'It's your home as long as you want it, Jake,' she said. *And I hope that's forever.*


Finally they arrived at the house, climbed out of the car and pulled their bags from the boot. Jake was already looking a bit better, she thought; ever so slightly more colour in his face.

'Welcome,' she said, unlocking the heavy glass sliding door and throwing it open. She led the way inside.

'This is a great space,' Jake said, taking in the enclosed verandah. The huge area was softly lit from the overcast weather outside.

'Oh, sorry, I forgot you haven't been here before,' Emily said, putting down her bag. 'Better give you the grand tour.'

'Great.'

'Bathroom and toilet down that end,' she said, pointing to their right. 'Kitchen is just through there. This way,' she said, turning left and striding forward. At the far end of the addition, she opened the door into the original part of the house and the first of the two spare rooms. 'That leads outside,' she said, pointing to the door at the end and to her left. 'I'll put you in here,' she said, opening the door into what had been John's office. She coloured slightly and got flustered. 'Not because I don't want there to be anything between us, but, um, er...'

Jake put a hand on her arm. 'It's okay, Em. It's a good idea. There's no need to rush things. Who knows, we might have the rest of our lives.'

*I hope so.*

'Great-sized room,' he said, erasing any lingering awkwardness.

Emily went through the room and opened another door that led into the next room. She had always thought it a bit of an odd space, with a door or window on every wall. There was the door into the other guest room, one onto the outside verandah against the road, and one into the lounge room, which was where they headed next.

'That door leads out to the front verandah,' Emily said, pointing, 'but I've never opened it.'

'They quickly passed through the lounge, poking their heads into the dining room that went off both the lounge room and the kitchen as they went. 'I never open the front door either,' Emily said, as they crossed the wide but short hall into the master bedroom.

'The house is certainly well-endowed with doors and windows,' Jake said, looking around her bedroom with its two double-hung sash windows occupying a wall each.

'Yeah, weird huh?' she said as she pulled back the curtains.

'Golly, the half-built hayshed really does spoil the view, doesn't it?'

One day she'd tell him about getting stuck up on it and having to be rescued. But for now it was still too new and far too embarrassing.

'I've been thinking about that. I'm going to get someone to pull it down and rebuild it over near the other sheds. It was a stupid place for it anyway. Come on, you haven't seen the best part of this house yet,' she said, grabbing his hand and dragging him back down the hall.

'Wow, a proper country kitchen,' Jake said, gazing around him in awe. 'It's huge.'

'It needs a facelift, but it does the trick. I'd love a dishwasher one day.'

'Well, it's not like you couldn't sacrifice a cupboard or two.'

'Check this out,' she said, opening the door into the pantry.

'God, this is nearly as big as my whole kitchen,' Jake said. On one wall was a large pine cupboard and on another a side-by-side fridge and freezer. Between them was a huge empty space.

'It's got lots of potential. You know, you could cut it in half and turn this side into an ensuite to your bedroom, and then have French doors out there to a barbeque area. I see an old Hills hoist clothesline,' he said, going to the large timber window, 'but where's your laundry? Have I missed it?'

'Yes and no. It's in that separate building just off the path outside. We walked past it. I'll show you properly later.'

'What a great spot, Em. I like it.'

'It doesn't have quite the same character as the other house – well, not to me anyway.'

'It will, just give it time,' he said, laying a hand gently on her shoulder. 'It feels very comfortable to me,' he said, drawing her into a hug. 'And anyway,' he added, 'it's where you are – that's all I care about.'

Emily sighed deeply. 'It feels so good to have you here,' she said into his chest.

'It feels so good to be here,' he said, kissing her on the top of her head. 'I might never want to leave,' he added, releasing her.

*Fine with me*, she thought, smiling back at him, but kept the words to herself. He had too much of a life in Melbourne for it to be that simple. He loved the city, she'd hated it. She didn't want to get her hopes up and risk disappointment.

'Right,' she said, gathering herself back together. 'Coffee? Still only instant, I'm afraid.'

'That's okay. No idea why, but it somehow works in the country.'

'Don't let Elizabeth hear you say that,' Emily said. They both laughed heartily.

It was four-thirty when they finished their second cup of coffee. Emily was feeling considerably fortified.

'I'm just going to phone Barbara and arrange to get Grace back,' she said, getting up and retrieving the cordless phone handset from its charger on the bench. She was starting to dial when Jake got up and went to the window over the sink.

'Are you expecting visitors, because there's a white dual cab pulling up out the front. And if I'm not mistaken, that's Grace right there on the back,' he said, heading towards the door.

Emily put down the phone.

Barbara and David were getting out of the ute when Emily and Jake appeared at the gate. They all hugged, and there was a gabble of jumbled voices as everyone spoke at once. Finally they calmed down.

'So how's it all going?' Emily asked.

'Good,' David said. 'I've just brought the stubble rollers down.'

'Great timing,' Emily said.

They all looked at Grace, who was wriggling and writhing to get free. At having their attention, she began whining. Emily went over and unclipped her. The dog leapt about, overjoyed to see her mistress; trying to lick her all over.

'Ew,' Emily said, jumping back. 'You stink like a real farm dog. What's she been into?' she asked, setting pretend glares on Barbara and then David.

'Farm dog stuff,' Barbara said with a laugh. 'She's been sleeping in the shearing shed with Sasha.'

'Well, she'll have to stay outside tonight; it's too late for a bath today. But tomorrow, missy, your number's up,' Emily said, pointing her finger at the dog. Ignoring her, Grace hopped off the ute and went over and greeted Jake like a long-lost friend.

As he ruffled her ears and then darted back and forth in a game of chase, she saw further signs of the happy-go-lucky guy she'd first met a month ago. She smiled at them engrossed in their play.

'How is he?' Barbara asked in a whisper close to Emily.

'If you'd asked me two days ago, I'd have said terrible. But he seems to be coming out of it. Must be the country air.'

'Or your TLC, more like,' David said.

'Hey, what are you doing for dinner?' Barbara asked as Jake rejoined them.

'No idea – haven't given it any thought.'

'Fancy going down to the Hope Springs pub? Apparently they've got a new chef. You're welcome to join us, unless you're too weary.'

'Sounds like a plan. Jake?' Emily asked.

'Sounds good. I'm not too tired, but it's up to you – you're the one who did the driving.'

'Well, it won't be until a bit later – say seven in Hope Springs. We have to go home and have showers. And seriously, we won't mind if you pike out between now and then – just call us on one of the mobiles.'

'Actually, we'll come back via here and drop Grace's things off anyway.'

'It's a bit out of your way,' Emily said.

'Not *that* far. We'll see you in an hour and a half, give or take.'

'Okay, we'll see how we're feeling then.'

'Come on Barb, we'd better get cracking,' David said, moving back out the gate. 'Great to see you again, Jake,' he added.

'Are you sure you're not too tired?' Emily asked, after they'd gone.

'Well, I'm not too tired to help you bath this stinky dog,' he said, pretending to dart away from Grace again.

'Don't you think it's a bit too cold? They're forecasting thirty-five tomorrow; perhaps we should wait until then.'

'I don't think she'll like being shut outside. Do you fancy listening to her whining all night to come in?' Jake said, looking at her with a knowing expression. 'You've got a hairdryer, haven't you?'

'Yes, but I've never used it on her before.'

'I'm sure between the two of us we'll be fine. Come on, before we chicken out.'

Side by side they washed Grace in the bathroom at the end of the enclosed verandah. Emily had bathed her plenty of times on her own, and Grace generally relished the attention.

Today, however, sensing things were different, and perhaps showing off for Jake, she misbehaved. It was nothing major, just wriggling and pawing at the suds and splashing water everywhere.

Finally their mission was complete. But when they tried to lift the slippery dog out of the bath, both Jake and Emily found themselves on their backs on the wet floor with the border collie on top of them, pinning them down. They erupted into laughter as Grace licked one face and then the other, obviously enjoying the game. When they finally got her off them, Grace began to enthusiastically shake the excess water from her coat, spraying the entire bathroom and mirror.

'Quick, shut the door!'

Jake rolled over and just managed to close it before Grace could escape.

They got to their knees and regained their composure. Grace, sensing the game was over, sat down and submitted to being towelled off.

Twenty minutes later, having been finished off with the hair-dryer, Grace was clean-smelling and fluffy, her black sections sleek and shiny and her white bits like fresh snow.

Still sitting on the wet floor, Jake leaned over and opened the door to let her out. He and Emily sat side by side with their backs against the tiled wall and their hands clasped around their bent knees.

'I'm exhausted,' he said with a deep sigh. 'I had no idea how tiring it was to wash a dog.'

'It's not normally that difficult. I think she was showing off for you.'

'Playing up more like.'

'Probably. Little monster. Thanks for your help.'

'I'm sure she'll be grateful to spend the night inside.'

'Hmm.' Emily suddenly realised how weary she was. She wasn't sure she could even get up off the floor, let alone get showered and dressed and drive the half hour over to the pub to be sociable.

'Would you mind if we didn't go out for tea after all?' Jake asked. 'I'm plum tuckered out.'

*Mind reader.* 'Me too. I'm not sure I can even get up from here,' Emily said with a laugh.

'Come on, before we seize up.' Jake got up and Emily accepted his hand.

'Thanks,' she said, when back on her feet. 'How 'bout you have first shower while I look in the cupboard for something to rustle up for tea?'

'I should be the one to cook since I'm putting you to the trouble.'

'I was going to pike out too, you just said it first. And anyway, you're the guest. I insist. You go shower, I'll sort out some food. Though I warn you, it won't be anything fancy.'

'Simple fare would be great right about now,' Jake said, giving her a quick kiss on the lips. 'Back soon,' he said, and disappeared out into the enclosed verandah and then in the direction of his room.

'I'll leave a clean towel in the bathroom for you,' Emily called after him.

'Righto, thanks.'

In less than ten minutes, Jake was back in the kitchen with wet, mussed hair and dressed in track pants and t-shirt.

'How about a toasted cheese sandwich?'

'Ah, that would really hit the spot.'

'Are you sure it would be okay?'

'Absolutely — it's one of my favourites.'

'How about I add a mug of tomato soup from a can — one of *my* favourites.'

'Even better. You know, I think we're going to get along just fine,' Jake said, beaming and drawing her to him. He kissed Emily on the forehead and released her. 'Do you want me to phone David and Barbara?'

'No, I think they shouldn't be too far away,' she said, checking her watch. 'I'll have my shower and then get tea organised.'

'I can do it.'

'So we don't get into an argument, why don't we do it together when I get back?' Emily said with a laugh.

'A fine plan.'

Emily had just reappeared in the kitchen when she heard the unmistakable sound of a vehicle pulling up outside. They went out and met Barbara and David on the path just inside the gate.

'How much stuff does one small dog have,' Jake said with a laugh, relieving David of his armful of bedding.

'Exactly!' David said, rolling his eyes.

'I'm afraid we're piking after all,' Emily said, taking the pile of stacked bowls from Barbara. 'We're going to have soup and toasted sandwiches – you're welcome to join us,' she added, shooting Jake a questioning glance. He nodded back. 'Though we'd understand if you'd rather something more fancy.'

'If it's tomato soup out of a can, count me in,' David said, grinning cheekily.

'It is indeed,' Emily said.

'Okay, sounds perfect,' Barbara said. 'As long as we're not intruding. You're tired, remember.'

'Too tired to drive all the way to Hope Springs, but not too tired to catch up with you guys for an hour or so.'

'Well, we promise not to outstay our welcome,' Barbara said.

'I just have to take a couple of tools down to the tractor. Forgot them last trip. Fancy keeping me company Jake?' David said.

'Sounds good. I'm keen to see what stubble rollers are.'

'Okay, come on then. We'll be back in twenty minutes tops. Don't you girls get up to any mischief while we're gone,' David called, as they climbed into the ute.

Barbara and Emily waved them off before making their way up the path towards the house.

'He really is lovely, Em,' Barbara said, as she closed the glass door behind them. 'He's even looking brighter than an hour ago.'

'Hmm, he's great. I've put him in the spare room,' she suddenly blurted.

'Why are you telling me that?'

'Because I don't want you and David getting the wrong idea,' she said with a shrug.

'What are you — twelve?!' Barbara said, with a laugh.

Emily flushed with embarrassment. 'Well, I just don't want you to think...' And then she wasn't sure what she was about to say. She frowned.

'That you're taking advantage of him when he's fragile and vulnerable?'

Emily nodded. 'We want it, whatever *it* is, to evolve on its own terms.'

'Of course you do. But Emily, anyone can see you're both smitten. You're perfect together. As far as I can see, slow or fast isn't going to make one iota of difference. You're already friends; there is no threat of it being a whirlwind romance that will fizzle out.'

'You think so?'

'I know so. But you both have to do what feels right.'

'Thanks Barb. I was just worried you might think we were rushing into things.'

'What, after him visiting twice, you going to Melbourne, and *still* not getting it on yet? Darling, I'm not your mother! You just keep following your heart and you'll be fine, Emily Oliphant. And that's the end of my sermon for today,' Barbara added, making a show of wiping her hands together.

'I think we could make a good team, Jake and I,' Emily said, wistfully, more to herself. 'We seem to be in sync.'

'My point exactly. And stop sounding so surprised.'

# Chapter Fifty

Emily stood at the stove stirring the soup. Having constructed the sandwiches, Barbara was hovering beside her to make sure they didn't burn in the griller. Jake and David were sorting out drinks and cutlery.

*God it's nice to be home and surrounded by friends,* Emily thought with a sigh as she stole a quick look around the room. Grace was lying on her bed on the floor, contentedly watching the goings-on.

Finally they were sitting around the table with bowls of soup and plates piled with toasted sandwiches in front of them.

'Oh, that hits the spot,' Jake said, tucking into his soup.

'Indeed it does,' David agreed.

Emily beamed. There was nothing quite like the sound and sight of happy people eating. Soup wasn't quite right for the middle of summer, but she was enjoying the comfort food.

'So, you haven't told us anything about your trip. Come on, what did you get up to?' Barbara demanded.

'Not a whole lot. I spent most of the time with Jake's sister, Simone, who is just lovely. She lives in a gorgeous old house somewhere close to the city.'

'North Melbourne,' Jake added.

'Thank you. North Melbourne. She's artistic – very talented and far too modest. You should see her paintings. And Jake's apartment is gorgeous. He lives right in the middle of the city. It's quite amazing. Though a little noisy for me with all the cars and trams and people...' She stopped. 'I mean...'

'So you're not ready to pack up and move to Melbourne then?'

'Not quite,' Emily said, flushing red. 'I quite liked...'

'You don't have to like it, Em, just because I live there. I know the city is an acquired taste.'

'Well I did find it a bit overwhelming, to be honest,' Emily admitted. Then she remembered. 'But I finally got to see some of Jake's amazing photos.'

They all noticed Jake dip his head and blush slightly.

'You know, one day we are going to demand a slide show – well, PowerPoint,' David said.

'That's right, Jake. You can run, but you can't hide from us,' Barbara said with a laugh.

'So how was Donald and Trevor's funeral?' Emily asked, changing the subject for Jake's sake.

Both David and Barbara shrugged. 'Nothing out of the ordinary, except Tara Wickham – who clearly didn't know them from Adam – standing up and giving the eulogy was a bit of a surprise,' David said.

'So what sights did you see, what else did you do?' Barbara persisted.

'Hmm, not a lot. Simone took me on a walk past the Queen Victoria Markets. They're not far from her house.'

'Oh wow, what was that like? Huge? I hear it's a must-see.'

'It did look pretty big. We didn't go in. You wouldn't believe the activity for a Sunday. Quite amazing really.'

'Must have been an eye-opener,' David said. 'Speaking of which, have you told Jake about your run-in with the steel sculpture across the way?' He asked jovially.

Emily blushed beetroot.

'What run-in?' Jake asked, looking from Emily, who now had her head in her hands, to David and Barbara, who had big grins on their faces.

'Can I tell him?' David asked. 'Pleeeease.'

'Come on, you're amongst friends,' Barbara said gently. 'We will be laughing with you, not *at* you.' She was now starting to laugh.

'No, it's too embarrassing.' Emily groaned.

'Oh but so bloody funny,' Barbara said.

'Is someone going to share the joke?' Jake asked, looking around the table.

'No,' Emily said.

'Oh come on, even you've got to admit it was pretty funny,' David said.

'Maybe from your point of view – safely on the ground! Oh all right,' Emily said, throwing her hands up. She turned to Jake. 'You're going to hear about it sometime, with or without my say-so. Go ahead, David,' she said with a melodramatic sigh. *May as well get it over with.*

David rubbed his hands together and then began to speak. 'Right, so on Friday we turn up with the boom sprayer. Grace is in the yard going nuts, which was really out of character. So we start investigating and...'

Between them, David and Barbara told the story and after a few minutes Emily joined in and filled in the details they didn't know about – that her being up there was a waste anyway since she'd forgotten the tools. Looking at it from their point of view, she had to admit it must have been pretty funny. And no one was hurt; they could laugh about it now. And they did. Before long they were all laughing so hard that tears were streaming down their faces.

'Bloody hilarious,' they muttered, shaking their heads as they finally calmed down enough to wipe their tears away and blow their noses on the paper serviettes.

'You poor thing,' Jake said when they were again settled. 'Thank goodness you weren't hurt.'

By eight-thirty they were all yawning. David and Barbara bid their farewells soon after.

Back in the kitchen after seeing them off, Emily refused Jake's help with the few dishes; they would wait until the morning.

They cleaned their teeth together in the bathroom and then there was a slightly awkward moment when they said their goodnights before retreating to opposite ends of the house.

Lying in bed, Emily wished she had Jake beside her, or at least that she had shown him more affection. Installing him in the spare room had been a head decision, but her heart felt very differently. He'd said it was a good idea. But was he just being polite and not wanting to embarrass her? She rolled over, telling herself what would be, would be, and to stop overthinking it. She'd discuss it with him in the morning; tell him she'd changed her mind.

She was almost asleep when she heard the floorboards creak in the hall outside her bedroom door. Grace lifted her head, hopped off the bed, and trotted out, her feet barely audible on the thick carpet. Emily sat up a little, holding her breath.

A silhouette appeared in the doorway. *Jake.*

Her heart rate quickened and her breath caught as he made his way across to the bed. Without a word, he climbed in beside her. Moments later they were entwined and kissing, tenderly at first and then more and more passionately. Within minutes all clothing had been shed and their naked bodies fused.

★

Emily woke to Jake's gentle kisses upon her face and lips. She opened her eyes, smiling as the night before came back to her. She turned towards him and held out her arms for his embrace.

'Thank you for last night,' she said, burying her head in his smooth, warm chest.

'Thank *you* for last night, and for coming to Melbourne and rescuing me,' he said, lowering his face and gently raising her chin towards him.

'I love you,' she said quietly.

'And I love you too, Emily Oliphant. Now my darling, can I get you coffee in bed?'

'Hmm, after you give me more of what I had last night,' Emily said, easing herself closer.

'Your wish is my command.'

Later, Emily sat propped up in bed, staring at the button jar on the tallboy. She thought back over the past few weeks; all she had learned, everything she had lost and everything she had gained.

*You were right, Gran. Sometimes the very best can come out of the very worst of situations.*

She could hear Jake rattling around in the kitchen, and Grace's gentle snoring at the foot of the bed. Who knew what the coming days and months would bring?

*Time will tell, indeed!*

# Meant to Be

# Fiona McCallum

Book Three of *The Button Jar* series —

Emily Oliphant's life finally seems to be settling down. Her new boyfriend Jake has joined her on the farm, they are looking forward to starting their life together, and her financial security seems safe and sound.

They both love the peace and tranquillity of the setting of Emily's beloved old cottage which had been reduced to rubble by her deceased husband. Jake suggests they rebuild it — it will be a big job, but a good project for them: a potential business for Emily, and a good advertisement for his building company.

Their plans and the building progress well. But where Emily is involved, life doesn't tend to run smoothly for long. This time it is her two best friends who face a personal crisis and Emily finally gets the chance to repay them for the kindness and support they gave her when she needed it. But now she has a new dilemma. How will she and Jake announce their news to Barbara and David? And what will happen to their friendship when they do?

harlequinbooks.com.au

# talk about it

Let's talk about *Time Will Tell.*

Join the conversation:

on facebook.com/fionamccallum.author OR

/harlequinaustralia

on Twitter: @harlequinaus

#ButtonJarSeries

Fiona's website: www.fionamccallum.com

If there's something you really want to tell
Fiona, or have a question you want answered,
then let's talk about it.